THE PRESTIGE

THE PRESTIGE

Christopher Priest

Copyright © Christopher Priest 1995, 2004
All rights reserved

The right of Christopher Priest to be identified as the author
of this work has been asserted by him in accordance with
the Copyright, Designs and Patents Act 1988.

First published in Great Britain in 1995
by Simon & Schuster

This edition published in Great Britain in 2004 by
Gollancz
an imprint of The Orion Publishing Group
Orion House, 5 Upper St Martin's Lane,
London WC2H 9EA

1 3 5 7 9 10 8 6 4 2

A CIP catalogue record for this book
is available from the British Library

ISBN-13 9 780 57507 906 9
ISBN-10 0 57507 906 1

Typeset at The Spartan Press Ltd,
Lymington, Hants

Printed and bound in Great Britain by
Clays Ltd, St Ives plc

The Orion Publishing Group's policy is to use papers that
are natural, renewable and recyclable products and
made from wood grown in sustainable forests. The logging
and manufacturing processes are expected to conform to
the environmental regulations of the country of origin.

www.orionbooks.co.uk

For Elizabeth and Simon

Part One

Andrew Westley

I

It began on a train, heading north through England, although I was soon to discover that the story had really begun more than a hundred years earlier.

I had no sense of any of this at the time: I was on company time, following up a report of an incident at a religious sect. On my lap lay the bulky envelope I had received from my father that morning, still unopened, because when Dad phoned to tell me about it my mind had been elsewhere. A bedroom door slamming, my girlfriend in the middle of walking out on me. 'Yes, Dad,' I had said, as Zelda stormed past with a boxful of my compact discs. 'Drop it in the mail, and I'll have a look.'

After I read the morning's edition of the *Chronicle*, and bought a sandwich and a cup of instant coffee from the refreshment trolley, I opened Dad's envelope. A large-format paperback book slipped out, with a note loose inside and a used envelope folded in half.

The note said, 'Dear Andy, Here is the book I told you about. I think it was sent by the same woman who rang me. She asked me if I knew where you were. I'm enclosing the envelope the book arrived in. The postmark is a bit blurred, but maybe you can make it out. Your mother would love to know when you are coming to stay with us again. How about next weekend? With love, Dad.'

At last I remembered some of my father's phone call. He told me the book had arrived, and that the woman who had sent it appeared to be some kind of distant relative, because she had been talking about my family. I should have paid more attention to him.

Here, though, was the book. It was called *Secret Methods of Magic*, and the author was one Alfred Borden. To all appearances it was one of those instructional books of card

3

tricks, sleight of hand, illusions involving silk scarves, and so on. At first glance, most of what interested me about it was that although it was a recently published paperback, the text itself appeared to be a facsimile of a much older edition: the typography, the illustrations, the chapter headings and the laboured writing style all suggested this.

I couldn't see why I should be interested in such a book. Only the author's name was familiar: Borden was the name I had been born with, although when I was adopted my name was changed to that of my adoptive parents. My name now, my full and legal name, is Andrew Westley, and although I have always known that I was adopted I grew up thinking of Duncan and Jillian Westley as Dad and Mum, loved them as parents, and behaved as their son. All this is still true. I feel nothing for my natural parents. I'm not curious about them or why they put me up for adoption, and have no wish ever to trace them now that I am an adult. All that is in my distant past, and they have always felt irrelevant to me.

There is, though, one matter concerning my past that borders on the obsessive.

I am certain, or to be accurate almost certain, that I was born one of a pair of identical twins, and that my brother and I were separated at the time of adoption. I have no idea why this was done, nor where my brother might be now, but I have always assumed that he was adopted at the same time as me. I only started to suspect his existence when I was entering my teens. By chance I came across a passage in a book, an adventure story, that described the way in which many pairs of twins are linked by an inexplicable, apparently psychic contact. Even when separated by hundreds of miles or living in different countries, such twins will share feelings of pain, surprise, happiness, depression, one twin sending to the other, and vice versa. Reading this was one of those moments in life when suddenly a lot of things become clear.

All my life, as long as I can remember, I have had the feeling that *someone else* is sharing my life. As a child, I thought little of it and assumed everyone else had the same

4

feelings. As I grew older, and I realised none of my friends was going through the same thing, it became a mystery. Reading the book therefore came as a great relief as it seemed to explain everything. I had a twin somewhere.

The feeling of rapport is in some ways vague, a sense of being cared for, even watched over, but in others it is much more specific. The general feeling is of a constant background, while more direct 'messages' come only occasionally. These are acute and precise, even though the actual communication is invariably non-verbal.

Once or twice when I have been drunk, for example, I have felt my brother's consternation growing in me, a fear that I might come to some harm. On one of these occasions, when I was leaving a party late at night and was about to drive myself home, the flash of concern that reached me was so powerful I felt myself sobering up! I tried describing this at the time to the friends I was with, but they joked it away. Even so I drove home inexplicably sober that night. It must be a psychic mechanism of some kind, which we use without understanding it. No one to my knowledge has ever satisfactorily explained it, even though it is common and well documented between twins.

There is in my case, however, an extra mystery.

Not only have I never been able to trace my brother, as far as official records are concerned I never had a brother of any kind, let alone a twin. I do have intermittent memories of my life before adoption, although I was only three when that happened, and I can't remember having a brother at all. Dad and Mum knew nothing about it; they have told me that when they adopted me there was no suggestion of my having a brother.

As an adoptee you have certain legal rights. The most important of these is protection from your natural parents: they cannot contact you by any legal means. Another right is that when you reach adulthood you are able to ask about some of the circumstances surrounding your adoption. You can find out the names of your natural parents, for instance, and the address of the court where the adoption was made, and therefore where relevant records can be examined.

I followed all this up soon after my eighteenth birthday, anxious to find out what I could about my background. The adoption agency referred me to Ealing County Court where the papers were kept, and here I discovered that I had been put up for adoption by my father, whose name was Clive Alexander Borden. My mother's name was Diana Ruth Borden (née Ellington), but she had died soon after I was born. I assumed that the adoption happened because of her death, but in fact I was not adopted for more than two years after she died, during which period my father brought me up by himself. My own original name was Nicholas Julius Borden. There was nothing about any other child, adopted or otherwise.

I later checked birth records at St Catherine's House in London, but these confirmed I was the Bordens' only child.

Even so, my psychic contacts with my twin remained through all this, and have continued ever since.

2

The book had been published in the USA by Dover Publications, and was a handsome, well-made paperback. The cover painting depicted a dinner-jacketed stage magician pointing his hands expressively towards a wooden cabinet, from which a young lady was emerging. She was wearing a dazzling smile and a costume which for the period was probably considered saucy.

Under the author's name was printed: 'Edited and annotated by Lord Colderdale.'

At the bottom of the cover, in bold white lettering, was the blurb: 'The Famous Oath-Protected Book of Secrets'.

There was a longer and more descriptive blurb on the back cover:

Originally printed in London in 1905, by the specialist publishers Goodwin & Andrewson, this book was sold only to professional magicians who were prepared to swear an oath of secrecy about its contents. First edition copies are now exceedingly rare, and virtually impossible for general readers to obtain.

Made publicly available for the first time, this new edition is completely unabridged and contains all the original illustrations, as well as the notes and supplementary text provided by Britain's Earl of Colderdale, a noted contemporary *amateur* of magic.

The author is Alfred Borden, inventor of the legendary illusion THE NEW TRANSPORTED MAN. Borden, whose stage name was 'Le Professeur de Magie', was in the first decade of this century the leading stage illusionist. Encouraged in his early years by John Henry Anderson, and as a protégé of Nevil Maskelyne's, Borden was a contemporary of Houdini, David Devant, Chung Ling Soo and Buatier de Kolta. He was based in London, England, but frequently toured the United States and Europe.

While not strictly speaking an instruction manual, this book with its broad understanding of magical methods will give both laymen and professionals startling insights into the mind of one of the greatest magicians who ever lived.

It was amusing to discover that one of my ancestors had been a magician, but I had no special interest in the subject. I happen to find some kinds of conjuring tedious; card tricks, especially, but many others too. The illusions you sometimes see on television are impressive, but I have never felt curious about how the effects are in fact achieved. I remember someone once saying that the trouble with magic was that the more a magician protects his secrets, the more banal they turn out to be.

Alfred Borden's book contained a long section on card tricks, and another described tricks with cigarettes and coins. Explanatory drawings and instructions accompanied each one. At the back of the book was a chapter about stage illusions, with many illustrations of cabinets with hidden compartments, boxes with false bottoms, tables with lifting devices concealed behind curtains, and other apparatus. I glanced through some of these pages.

The first half of the book was not illustrated, but consisted of a long account of the author's life and outlook on magic. It began with the following words:

'I write in the year 1901.

'My name, my real name, is Alfred Borden. The story of my life is the story of the secrets by which I have lived my life. They are described in this narrative for the first and last time; this is the only copy.

'I was born in 1856 on the eighth day of the month of May, in the seaside town of Hastings. I was a healthy, vigorous child. My father was a tradesman of that borough, a master wheelwright and cooper. Our house—'

I briefly imagined the writer of this book settling down to begin his memoir. For no exact reason I visualised him as a tall, dark-haired man, stern-faced and bearded, slightly hunched, wearing narrow reading glasses, working in a pool of light thrown by a solitary lamp placed next to his elbow. I imagined the rest of the household in a deferential silence, leaving the master in peace while he wrote. The reality was no doubt different, but stereotypes of our forebears are difficult to throw off.

I wondered what relation Alfred Borden was to me. If the line of descent was direct, in other words if he wasn't a cousin or an uncle, then he would be my great- or great-great-grandfather. If he was born in 1856, he would have been in his middle forties when he wrote the book; it seemed likely he was therefore not my father's father, but of an earlier generation.

The Introduction was written in much the same style as the main text, with several long explanations about how the book came into being. The book appeared to be based on Borden's private notebook, not intended for publication.

Colderdale had considerably expanded and clarified the narrative, and added the descriptions of most of the tricks. There was no extra biographical information about Borden, but presumably I would find some if I read the whole book.

I couldn't see how the book was going to tell me anything about my brother. He remained my only interest in my natural family.

At this point my mobile phone beeped. It was Sonja, the secretary of my editor, Len Wickham. I suspected at once that Len had got her to call me, to make sure I was on the train.

'Andy, there's been a change of plan about the car,' she said. 'Eric Lambert had to take it in for a repair to the brakes, so it's in a garage.'

She gave me the address. It was the availability of this car in Sheffield, a high-mileage Ford renowned for frequent breakdowns, that prevented me from driving up in my own car. Len wouldn't authorise the expenses if a company car was on hand.

'Did Uncle say anything else?' I said.

'Such as?'

'This story's still on?'

'Yes.'

'Has anything else come in from the agencies?'

'We've had a faxed confirmation from the State Penitentiary in California. Franklin is still a prisoner.'

'All right.'

We hung up. While I was still holding the phone I keyed in my parents' number, and spoke to my father. I told him I was on my way to Sheffield, would be driving from there into the Peak District and if it was OK with them (of course it would be) I could come and stay the night. My father sounded pleased. He and Jillian still lived in Wilmslow, Cheshire, and now I was working in London my trips to see them were infrequent.

I told him I had received the book.

'Have you any idea why it was sent to you?' he said.

'Not the faintest.'

'Are you going to read it?'

'It's not my sort of thing. I've already looked through it. Maybe I'll have another look later.'

'Andy, I noticed it was written by someone called Borden.'

'Yes. Did she say anything about that?'

'No. I don't think so.'

After we had hung up I put the book in my case and stared through the train window at the passing countryside. The sky was grey, and rain was streaking the glass. I tried to think about the incident I was being sent to investigate. I worked for the *Chronicle*, specifically as a general features writer, a label which was grander than the reality. The true state of affairs was that Dad was himself a newspaperman, and had formerly worked for the Manchester *Evening Post*, a sister paper to the *Chronicle*. It was a matter of pride to him that I had obtained the job, even though I have always suspected him of pulling strings for me. I am not a fluent journalist, and have not done well in the training programme I have been taking. One of my serious long-term worries is that one day I am going to have to explain to my father why I have quit what he considers to be a prestigious job on the greatest British newspaper.

In the meantime, I struggle unwillingly on. Covering the incident I was travelling to was partly the consequence of another story I had filed several months earlier, about a group of UFO enthusiasts. Since then Len Wickham, my supervising editor, had assigned me to any story that involved witches' covens, levitation, spontaneous combustion, crop circles, and other fringe subjects. I had already discovered that in most cases, once you went into these things properly, there was not much to say about them, and remarkably few of the stories I filed were ever printed. Even so, Wickham continued to send me to cover them.

There was an extra twist this time. With some relish, Wickham informed me that someone from the sect had phoned to ask if the *Chronicle* was planning to cover the story, and if so had asked for me in person. They had seen some of my earlier articles, thought I showed the right degree of honest scepticism, and could therefore be relied on for a forthright article. In spite of this, or perhaps because of it, it seemed likely to prove yet another dud.

A Californian religious sect called the Rapturous Church of Christ Jesus had established a community in a large country house in a Derbyshire village. One of the women members had died of natural causes a few days earlier. Her GP was present, as was her daughter. As she lay paralysed, on the point of death, a man had entered the room. He stood beside the bed and made soothing gestures with his hands. The woman died soon after, and the man immediately left the room without speaking to the other two. He was not seen afterwards. However, he had been recognised by the woman's daughter, and by two members of the sect who had come into the room while he was there, as the founder of the sect. This was Father Patrick Franklin, and the sect had grown up around him because of his claimed ability to bilocate.

The incident was newsworthy for two reasons. It was the first of Franklin's bilocations to have been witnessed by non-members of the sect, one of whom happened to be a professional woman with a local reputation. And the other reason was that Franklin's whereabouts on the day in question could be firmly established: he was known to be an inmate of the California State Penitentiary, and as Sonja had just confirmed to me on the phone he was still there.

3

The community was established on the outskirts of the Peak District village of Caldlow, once a centre of slate mining, now heavily dependent on day trippers. There was a National Trust shop in the centre of the village, a pony trekking club, several gift shops and an hotel. As I drove through, the chill rain was drizzling through the valley, obscuring the rocky heights on each side.

I stopped in the village for a cup of tea, thinking I might talk to some of the locals about the Rapturous Church, but apart from me the café was empty, and the woman who worked behind the counter said she drove in daily from Chesterfield.

While I was sitting there, wondering whether to take the opportunity to grab some lunch before going on, my brother unexpectedly made contact with me. The sensation was so distinct, so urgent, that I turned my head in surprise, thinking for a moment that someone in the room had addressed me. I closed my eyes, lowered my face, and listened for more.

No words. Nothing explicit. Nothing I could answer or write down or even put into words for myself. But it amounted to anticipation, happiness, excitement, pleasure, encouragement.

I tried to send back: what is this for? Why was I being welcomed? What are you encouraging me to do? Is it something about this religious community?

I waited, knowing that these experiences never took the form of a dialogue, so that raising questions would not receive any kind of answer, but I was hoping another signal would come from him. I tried to reach out mentally to him, thinking perhaps his contact with me was a way of getting me to communicate with him, but in this sense I could feel nothing of him there.

My expression must have revealed something of my churned-up inner feelings, because the woman behind the counter was staring at me curiously. I swallowed the rest of my tea, returned the cup and saucer to the counter, smiled politely, then hurried out to the car. As I sat down and slammed the door, a second message came from my brother. It was the same as the first, a direct urging of me to arrive, to be there with him. It was still impossible to put it into words.

4

The entrance to the Rapturous Church was a steep drive-way slanting off the main road, but barred by a pair of wrought iron gates and a gatehouse. There was a second gate to one side, also closed, marked Private. The two entrances formed an extra space, so I parked my car there and walked across to the gatehouse. Inside the wooden porch a modern bell push had been attached to the wall, and beneath this was a printed notice:

RAPTUROUS CHURCH OF CHRIST JESUS WELCOMES YOU
NO VISITORS WITHOUT APPOINTMENT
FOR APPOINTMENTS RING CALDLOW 393960
TRADESMEN AND OTHERS PRESS BELL TWICE
JESUS LOVES YOU

I pressed the bell twice, without audible effect.

Some leaflets were standing in a semi-enclosed holder, and beneath them was a padlocked metal box with a coin slot in the top, screwed firmly to the wall. I took one of the leaflets, slipped a fifty-pence piece into the box, then went back to the car and rested my backside against the nearside wing while I read it. The front page was a brief history of the sect, and carried a photograph of Father Franklin. The remaining three pages had a selection of Biblical quotes.

When I next looked towards the gates I discovered they were opening silently from some remote command, so I climbed back into the car and took it up the sloping, gravelled drive. This curved as it went up the hill, with a lawn rising in a shallow convex on one side. Ornamental trees and shrubs had been planted at intervals, drooping in the veils of misty rain. On the lower side were thick clumps of dark leafed rhododendron bushes. In the rear-view mirror I noticed the gates closing behind me as I drove out of sight of them. The main house soon came into view: it was a huge and unattractive building of four or five main storeys, with black slate roofs and solid-looking walls of sombre dark-brown brick and stone. The windows were tall and narrow, and blankly reflected the rain-laden sky. The place gave me a cold, grim feeling, yet even as I drove towards the part of the drive made over as a car park I felt my brother's presence in me once again, urging me on.

I saw a VISITORS THIS WAY sign, and followed it along a gravel path against the main wall of the house, dodging the drips from the thickly growing ivy. I pushed open a door and went into a narrow hallway, one that smelt of ancient wood and dust, reminding me of the Lower Corridor in the school I had been to. This building had the same institutional feeling, but unlike my school was steeped in silence.

I saw a door marked Reception, and knocked. When there was no answer I put my head around the door, but the room was empty. There were two old-looking metal desks, on one of which was perched a computer.

Hearing footsteps I returned to the hallway, and a few moments later a thin middle-aged woman appeared at the turn of the stairs. She was carrying several envelope wallet files. Her feet made a loud sound on the uncarpeted wooden steps, and she looked enquiringly at me when she saw me there.

'I'm looking for Mrs Holloway,' I said. 'Are you she?'

'Yes, I am. How may I help you?'

There was no trace of the American accent I had half-expected.

'My name is Andrew Westley, and I'm from the *Chronicle*.' I showed her my press card, but she hardly glanced at it. 'I was wondering if I could ask you a few questions about Father Franklin.'

'Father Franklin is in California at present.'

'So I believe, but there was the incident last week—'

'Which incident do you mean?' said Mrs Holloway.

'I understand Father Franklin was seen here. At this house.'

She shook her head slowly. She was standing with her back to the door which led into her office. 'I think you must be making a mistake, Mr Westley.'

'Did you see Father Franklin when he was here?' I said.

'I did not. Nor was he here.' She was starting to stonewall me, which was the last thing I had expected. 'Have you been in touch with our Press Office?'

'Are they here?'

'We have an office in London. All press interviews are arranged through them.'

'I was told to come here.'

'By our Press Officer?'

'No . . . I understood a request was sent to the *Chronicle*, after Father Franklin made an appearance. Are you denying that that happened?'

'Do you mean the sending of the request? No one here has been in contact with your newspaper. If you mean am I denying the appearance of Father Franklin, the answer is yes.'

We stared at each other. I was torn between irritation with her and frustration at myself. Whenever incidents like this did not go smoothly, I blamed my lack of experience and motivation. The other writers on the paper always seemed to know how to handle people like Mrs Holloway.

'Can I see whoever is in charge here?' I said.

'I am the head of administration. Everyone else is involved with the teaching.'

I was about to give up, but I said, 'Does my name mean anything at all to you?'

'Should it?'

'Someone requested me by name.'

'That would have come from the Press Office, not from here.'

'Hold on,' I said.

I walked back to the car to collect the notes I had been given by Wickham the day before. I stood for a moment by the door of the car, in the light rain, staring at the puddled ground. Mrs Holloway was still standing by the bottom of the stairs when I returned, but she had put down her bundle of files somewhere.

I stood beside her while I turned to the page Wickham

had been sent. It was a fax message. It said, 'To Mr L. Wickham, Features Editor, *Chronicle*. The necessary written details you requested are as follows: Rapturous Church of Christ Jesus, Caldlow, Derbyshire. Half a mile outside Caldlow village, to the north, on A623. Parking at main gate, or in the grounds. Mrs Holloway, administrator, will provide your reporter Mr Andrew Westley with information. K. Angier.'

'This is nothing to do with us,' Mrs Holloway said when she had read it. 'I'm sorry.'

'Who is K. Angier?' I said. 'Mr? Mrs?'

'*She* is the resident of the private wing on the east side of this building, and has no connection with the Church. Thank you.'

She had placed her hand on my elbow and was propelling me politely towards the door. She indicated that the continuation of the gravel path would take me to a gate, where the entrance to the private wing would be found.

I said, 'I'm sorry if there's been a misunderstanding. I don't know how it happened.'

'If you want any more information about the Church, I'd be grateful if you'd speak to the Press Office. That is its function, you know.'

'Yes, all right.' It was raining more heavily now, and I had brought no coat. I said, 'May I ask you just one thing? Is everybody away at present?'

'No, we have full attendance. There are more than two hundred people in training this week.'

'It feels as if the whole place is empty.'

'We are a group whose rapture is silent. I am the only person permitted to speak during the hours of daylight. Good day to you.'

She retreated into the building.

16

5

I decided to refer back to the office, since it was clear the story I had been sent to cover was no longer live. Standing under the dripping ivy, watching the heavy drizzle drifting across the valley, I rang Len Wickham's direct line, full of foreboding. He answered after a delay. I told him what had happened.

'Have you seen the informant yet?' he said. 'Someone called Angier.'

'I'm right outside their place now,' I said, and explained what I understood was the setup here. 'I don't think it's a story. I'm thinking it might just be a dispute between neighbours. You know, complaining about something or other.' But not about the noise, I thought as soon as I had spoken.

There was a long silence.

Then Len Wickham said, 'See the neighbour, and if there's anything in it, call me back. If not, get back to London for this evening.'

'It's Friday,' I said. 'I thought I'd visit my parents tonight.'

Wickham replied by cutting the line.

6

I was greeted at the main door of the wing by a woman in late middle age, whom I addressed as 'Mrs Angier', but she merely took my name, looked intently at my press card, then showed me into a side room and asked me to wait. The stately scale of the room, simply but attractively furnished with Indian carpets, antique chairs and a polished table, made me feel scruffy in my travel-creased and rain-dampened suit. After about five minutes the woman returned.

'Lady Katherine will see you now,' she said.

She led me upstairs to a large, pleasant living room that looked out across the valley floor towards a high rocky escarpment, at present only dimly visible.

A young-looking woman was standing by the open fireplace, where logs blazed and smoked, and she held out her hand to greet me as I went across to her. I had been thrown off guard by the unexpected news that I was calling on Lady Somebody, but her manner was cordial. I was struck, and favourably so, by the way she looked. She was tall, dark-haired and had a broad face with a strong jaw. Her hair was arranged so that it softened the sharper lines of her face. Her eyes were wide. She had a nervous intentness about her face, as if she were worried about what I might say or think.

She greeted me formally, but the moment the other woman had left the room her manner changed. She introduced herself as Kate, not Katherine, Angier, and told me to disregard the title as she rarely used it herself. She asked me to confirm if I was Andrew Westley. I said that I was.

'I assume you've just been to the main part of the house?'

'The Rapturous Church? I hardly got past the door.'

'I think that was my fault. I warned them you might be coming, but Mrs Holloway wasn't too pleased.'

'I suppose it was you who sent the message to my paper?'

'I wanted to meet you.'

'So I gathered. Why on earth should you know about me?'

'I plan to tell you. But I haven't had lunch yet. What about you?'

I followed her downstairs to the ground floor where the woman who had opened the door to me, addressed by Lady Katherine as Mrs Makin, was preparing a simple lunch of cold meats and cheeses, with salad. As we sat down, I asked Kate Angier why she had brought me all the way up here from London, on what now seemed a wild-goose-chase.

'I don't think it's that,' she said.

'I have to file a story this evening.'

'Well, maybe that might be difficult. Do you eat meat, Mr Westley?'

She passed me the plate of cold cuts. While we ate, a polite conversation went on, in which she asked me questions about the newspaper, my career, where I lived and so on. I was still conscious of her title, and felt inhibited by this, but the longer we spoke the easier it became. She had a tentative, almost nervous bearing, and she frequently looked away from me and back again while I was speaking. I noticed that her hands trembled whenever she reached out for something on the table. When I finally felt it was time to ask her about herself, she told me that the house we were in had been in her family for more than three hundred years. Most of the land in the valley belonged to the estate, and a number of farms were tenanted. Her father was the earl, but he lived abroad. Her mother was dead, and her only other close relative, an elder sister, was married and lived in Bristol with her husband and children.

The house had been a family home, with several servants, until the outbreak of the Second World War. The Ministry of Defence had then requisitioned most of the building, using it as regional headquarters for RAF Transport Command. At this point her family had moved into the east wing, which anyway had always been the part of the house they liked best. When the RAF left after the war the house was taken over by Derbyshire County Council as offices, and the present tenants (her phrase) arrived in 1980. She said her parents had been worried at first by the prospect of a religious sect moving in, but by this time the family needed the money and it had worked out well. The Church kept its teaching quiet, the members were polite and charming to meet, and these days neither she nor the villagers were concerned about what they might or might not be up to. There was a constant turnover of members, carried to and from the building in buses.

As by this point in the conversation we had finished our meal, and Mrs Makin had brought us some coffee, I said, 'So

I take it the story that brought me up here, about a bilocating priest, was false?'

'Yes and no. The cult makes no secret of the fact it bases its teaching on the words of its leader. Father Franklin is allegedly a stigmatic, and he's supposed to be able to bilocate, but he's never been seen doing it by independent witnesses, or at least not under controlled circumstances.'

'But was it true?'

'I'm really not sure. The local doctor was involved this time, and for some reason she said something to a tabloid newspaper, who ran a potted version of the story. I only heard about it when I was in the village the other day. I can't see how it can have been true: their leader's in prison in America, isn't he?'

'But if the incident really happened, that would make it more interesting.'

'It makes it more likely to be a fraud. How does Doctor Ellis know what this man looks like, for instance? There's only the word of one of the members to go on.'

'You made it out to be a genuine story.'

'I told you I wanted to meet you. And the fact that the man goes in for bilocation was too good to be true.'

She laughed in the way people do when they say something they expect others to find amusing. I hadn't the faintest idea what she was talking about.

'Couldn't you have just telephoned the newspaper?' I said. 'Or written a letter to me?'

'Yes I could . . . but I wasn't sure you were who I thought you were. I wanted to meet you first.'

'I don't see why you thought a bilocating religious fanatic had anything to do with me.'

'It was just a coincidence. You know, the controversy about the illusion, and all that.' Again, she looked at me expectantly.

'Who did you think I was?'

'The son of Clive Borden. Isn't that right? Great-grandson of Alfred.'

She tried to hold my gaze but her eyes, irresistibly, turned away again. Her nervous, evasive manner put tension between us, when nothing else was happening to create it. Remains of lunch lay on the table between us.

'A man called Clive Borden was my natural father,' I said. 'But I was adopted when I was three.'

'Well then. I was right about you. We met once before, many years ago, when we were both children. Your name was Nicky then.'

'I don't remember,' I said. 'I would have been only a toddler. Where did this happen?'

'Here, in this house. You came here with your father. You really don't remember it?'

'Not at all.'

'Do you have any other memories from when you were that age?' she said.

'Only fragments. But none about this place. It's the sort of house that would make an impression on a child, isn't it?'

'All right. You're not the first to say that. My sister . . . her name's Rosalie. She hates the house, and couldn't wait to move away.' She reached behind her, where a small bell rested on a counter, and dinged it twice. 'I usually take a drink after lunch. Would you care to join me?'

'Yes, thank you.'

Mrs Makin soon appeared, and Lady Katherine stood up.

'Mr Westley and I will be in the drawing room this afternoon, Mrs Makin.'

As we went up the broad staircase I felt an impulse to escape from her, to get away from this house. She knew more about me than I knew myself, but it was knowledge of a part of my life in which I had no interest. This was obviously a day when I had to become a Borden again, whether or not I wished to do so. First there was the book by him, now this. It was all connected, but I felt her intrigues were not mine. Why should I care about the man, the family, who had turned their back on me?

She led me into the room where I had first met her, and closed the door decisively behind us. It was almost as if she had sensed my wish to escape, and wanted to detain me as long as she could. A silver tray with a number of bottles, glasses and a bucket of ice had been placed on a low table set between a number of easy chairs and a long settee. One of the glasses already held a large drink, presumably prepared by Mrs Makin. Kate indicated I should take a seat, then said, 'What would you like?'

Actually I would have liked a glass of beer, but the tray bore only spirits. I said, 'I'll have whatever you're drinking.'

'It's American rye with soda. Would you like that too?'

I said I did, and watched as she mixed it. When she sat down on the settee she tucked her legs under her, then drank about half the glass of whiskey straight down.

'How long are you able to stay?' she said.

'Maybe just this drink.'

'There's a lot I want to ask you.'

'Why?'

'Because of what happened when we were children.'

'I don't think I'm going to be much help to you,' I said. She obviously liked drinking, and was used to the effect of it. That helped make me feel I was on familiar territory; I spent most weekends drinking with my friends. Her eyes continued to disconcert me, though, for she was always looking at me, then away, then back, making me feel someone was behind me, moving about the room where I could not see them.

'A one-word answer to a question might save a lot of time,' she said.

'All right.'

'Do you have an identical twin brother? Or did you have one who died when you were very young?'

I could not help my startled reaction. I put down my glass, before I spilled any more, and mopped at the liquid that had splashed on to my legs.

'Why do you ask that?' I said.

'Do you? Did you?'

'I don't know. I think I did, but I've never been able to find him. I mean . . . I'm not sure.'

'I think you've given me the answer I was expecting,' she said. 'But not the one I was hoping for.'

7

I said, 'If this is something to do with the Borden family, I might as well tell you that I know nothing about them.'

'Yes, but you *are* a Borden.'

'I was, but it doesn't mean anything to me.' I suddenly had a glimpse of this young woman's family, stretching back more than three hundred years in an unbroken sequence of generations: same name, same house, same everything. My own family roots went back to the age of three. 'I don't think you appreciate what being adopted means. I was just a little boy, a toddler, and my father dumped me out of his life. If I spent the rest of my own life grieving about that, I'd have time for nothing else. Long ago, I sealed it off because I had to. I've a new family now.'

'Your brother is still a Borden, though.'

Whenever she mentioned my brother I felt a pang of guilt, concern and curiosity. It was as if she used him as a way of getting under my defences. All my life the existence of my brother had been my secret certainty, a part of myself that I kept completely private. Yet here was this stranger speaking of him as if she knew him.

'Why are you interested in this?' I said.

'When you first heard of me, saw my name, did it mean anything to you?'

'No.'

'Have you ever heard of Rupert Angier?'

'No.'

'Or The Great Danton, the illusionist?'

'No. My only interest in my former family is that through them I might one day be able to trace my twin brother.'

She had been sipping quickly at her glass of whiskey while

23

we spoke, and now it was empty. She leant forward to mix another drink, and tried to pour more into my glass. Knowing I was going to have to drive later, I pulled my glass back before she could completely fill it.

She said, 'I believe the fate of your brother is connected with something that happened about a hundred years ago. One of my ancestors, Rupert Angier. You say you've never heard of him, and there's no reason why you should, but he was a stage magician at the end of the last century. He worked under the stage name The Great Danton. He was the victim of a series of vicious attacks by a man called Alfred Borden, your great-grandfather, who was also an illusionist. You say you know nothing about this?'

'Only the book. I assume you sent it.'

'They had this feud going, and it went on for years. They were constantly attacking each other, usually by interfering with the other one's stage show. The story of the feud is in Borden's book. At least, his side of it is. Have you read it yet?'

'It only arrived in the post this morning. I haven't had much of a chance—'

'I thought you would be fascinated to know what had happened.'

I was thinking, again: why go on about the Bordens? They are too far back, I know too little about them and they rejected me. She was talking about something that was of interest to her, not to me. I felt I should be polite to her, listen to what she was saying, but what she could never know was the resistance that lay deep inside me, the unconscious defence mechanism a kid builds up for himself when he has been abandoned by his family. To adapt to my new family I had had to throw off everything I knew of the old. How many times would I have to say that to her to convince her of it?

Saying she wanted to show me something, she put down her glass and crossed the room to a desk placed against the wall just behind where I was sitting As she stooped to reach into a lower drawer her dress sagged forward at the neck, and I stole a glimpse: a thin white strap, part of a lacy bra

24

cup, the upper curve of the breast nestling inside. She had to reach into the drawer, and this made her turn around so she could stretch her arm, and I saw the slender curves of her back, her straps again becoming discernible through the thin material of her dress, then her hair falling forward about her face. She was trying to involve me in something I knew nothing about, but instead I was crudely sizing her up, thinking idly about what it might be like to have sex with her. Sex with an honourable lady; it was the sort of semi-funny joke the journalists in the office would make. For better or worse that was my own life, more interesting and problematical to me than all this stuff about ancient magicians. She had asked me where in London I lived, not who in London I lived with, so I had said nothing to her of Zelda. Exquisite and maddening Zelda, with the cropped hair and nose-ring, the studded boots and dream body, who three nights before had told me she wanted an open relationship and walked out on me at half past eleven at night, taking a lot of my books and most of my records. I hadn't seen her since and was beginning to worry, even though she had done something like that before. I wanted to ask this honourable lady about Zelda, not because I was interested in what she might say, but because Zelda is real to me. How do you think I might get Zelda back? Or, how do I ease myself out of the newspaper job without appearing to reject my father? Or, where am I going to live if Zelda moves out on me, because it is Zelda's parents' flat? What am I going to survive on if I don't have a job? And if my brother's real, where is he and how do I find him?

Any one of these was more involving to me than the news of a feud between great-grandparents of whom I had never heard. One of them had written a book, though. Maybe that was interesting to be told about.

'I haven't had these out for ages,' Kate said, her voice slightly muffled by her exertions of reaching inside the drawer. She had removed some photo albums, and these were piled on the floor while she reached to the back of the deep drawer. 'Here we are.'

She was clutching an untidy pile of papers, apparently old and faded, all in different sizes. She spread them on the settee beside her, and picked up her glass before she began to leaf through them.

'My great-grandfather was one of those men who is obsessively neat,' she said. 'He not only kept everything, he put labels on them, compiled lists, had cupboards specifically in which to keep certain things. When I was growing up my parents had a saying: "Grandpa's stuff". We never touched it, weren't really allowed to look at it, even. But Rosalie and I couldn't resist searching some of it. When she left to get married, and I was alone here, I finally went through it all and sorted it out. I managed to sell some of the apparatus and costumes, and got good prices too. I found these playbills in the room that had been his study.'

All the time she had been talking she was sifting through the bills, and now she passed me a sheet of fragile, yellow-coloured paper. It had been folded and refolded numerous times, and the creases were furry with wear and almost separating. The bill was for the Empress Theatre in Evering Road, Stoke Newington. Over a list of performers it announced a limited number of performances, afternoons and evenings, commencing on 14th April until 21st April. ('See Newspaper Advertisements for Further Arrangements.') Top of the bill, and printed in red ink, was an Irish tenor called Dennis O'Canaghan ('Fill Your Heart With The Joy Of Ireland'). Other acts included the Sisters McKee ('A Trio of Lovely Chanteuses'), Sammy Renaldo ('Tickle Your Ribs, Your Highness?') and Robert and Roberta Franks ('Recitation Par Excellence'). Halfway down the bill, pointed out by Kate's prodding forefinger as she leaned over towards me, was The Great Danton ('The Greatest Illusionist in the World').

'This was before he actually was,' she said. 'He spent most of his life being hard up, and only really became famous a few years before he died. This bill comes from 1881, when he was first starting to do quite well.'

'What do all these mean?' I said, indicating a column of

neatly inked numbers inscribed in the margin of the playbill. More had been written on the back.

'That's what I call The Great Danton's Obsessive Filing System,' she said. She moved away from the settee, and knelt informally on the carpet beside my chair. Leaning towards me so she could look at the bill in my hand, she said, 'I haven't worked it all out, but the first number refers to the job. There's a ledger somewhere, with a complete list of every appearance he made. Underneath that, he puts down how many actual performances he carried out, and how many of those were matinées and how many in the evenings. The next numbers are a list of the actual tricks he did, and again he had about a dozen notebooks in his study with descriptions of all the tricks he could do. I have a few of the notebooks still here, and you could probably look up some of the tricks he did that week in Stoke Newington. But it's even more complicated than that, because most of the tricks have minor variations, and he's got all those cross-referenced as well. Look, this number here, "10g". I think that's what he was paid: ten guineas.'

'Was that good?'

'If it was for one night it was brilliant. But it was probably for the whole week, so it was just average. I don't think this was a big theatre.'

I picked up the stack of all the other playbills and as she had said each one was annotated with similar code numbers.

'All his apparatus was labelled as well,' she said. 'Sometimes, I wonder how he found time to get out into the world and make a living! But when I was clearing out the cellar, every single piece of equipment I came across had an identifying number, and each one had a place in a huge index, all cross-referenced to the other books.'

'Maybe he had someone else do it for him.'

'No, it's always in the same handwriting.'

'When did he die?' I said.

'There's actually some doubt about that, strangely enough. The newspapers say he died in 1903, and there was an obituary in *The Times*, but there are people in the village who say he was still living here the following year. What I find odd is that I came across the obituary in the scrapbook he kept, and it was stuck down and labelled and indexed, just like all the other stuff.'

'Can you explain how that happened?'

'No. Alfred Borden talks about it in his book. That's where I heard about it, and after that I tried to find out what had happened between them.'

'Have you got any more of his stuff?'

While she reached over for the scrapbooks, I poured myself another slug of the American whiskey, which I had not tried before and which I was finding I liked. I also liked having Kate down there on the floor beside my legs, turning her head to look up at me as she spoke, leaning towards me. It was all slightly bemusing to be there, not fully comprehending what was going on, talk of magicians, meetings in childhood, not at work when I should have been, not driving over to see my parents as I had planned.

In that part of my mind occupied by my brother, I felt a sense of contentment, unlike anything I had known from him before. He was urging me to stay.

Outside the window the cold afternoon sky was darkening and the Pennine rain continued to fall. An icy draught came persistently from the windows. Kate threw another log on the fire.

Part Two
Alfred Borden

I

I write in the year 1901.

My name, my real name, is Alfred Borden. The story of my life is the story of the secrets by which I have lived my life. They are described in this narrative for the first and last time; this is the only copy.

I was born in 1856 on the eighth day of the month of May, in the seaside town of Hastings. I was a healthy, vigorous child. My father was a tradesman of that borough, a master wheelwright and cooper. Our house at number 105 Manor Road was in a long, curving terrace built along the side of one of the several hills which Hastings comprises. Behind the house was a steep and secluded valley where sheep and cattle grazed during the summer months, but at the front the hill rose up, lined with many more houses, standing between us and the sea. It was from those houses, and from the farms and businesses around, that my father took his trade.

Our house was larger and taller than others in the road, because it was built over the gateway that led to the yard and sheds behind. My room was on the street side of the house, directly above the gateway, and because only the wooden floorboards and some thin lath-and-plaster lay between me and the open air the room was noisy through every day of the year, and viciously cold in the winter months. It was in that room that I slowly grew up and became the man that I am.

That man is Le Professeur de Magie, and I am a master of illusions.

It is time to pause, even so early, for this account is not intended to be about my life in the usual habit of auto-biographers, but is, as I have said, about my life's secrets. Secrecy is intrinsic to my work.

Let me then first consider and describe the method of writing this account. The very act of describing my secrets might indeed be construed as a betrayal of myself, except of course that as I am an illusionist I can make sure you only see what I wish you to see. A puzzle is implicitly involved.

It is therefore only fair that I should from the beginning try to elucidate those closely connected subjects – Secrecy, and the Appreciation Of Secrecy.

Here is an example.

There almost invariably comes a moment during the exercise of my profession when the illusionist will seem to pause. He will step forward to the footlights, and in the full glare of their light will face the audience directly. He will say, or if his act is silent he will seem to say, 'Look at my hands. There is nothing concealed within them.' He will then hold up his hands for the audience to see, raising his palms to expose them, splaying his fingers so as to prove nothing is gripped secretly between them. With his hands held thus he will rotate them, so that the backs are shown to the audi-ence, and it is established that his hands are, indeed, as empty as it is possible to be. To take the matter beyond any remaining suspicion, the magician will probably then tweak lightly at the cuffs of his jacket, pulling them back an inch or two to expose his wrists, showing that nothing is there concealed either. He then performs his trick, and during it, moments after this incontrovertible evidence of empty-handedness he produces something from his hands: a fan, a live dove or a rabbit, a bunch of paper flowers, sometimes even a burning wick. It is a paradox, an impossibility! The audience marvels at the mystery, and applause rings out.

How could any of this be?

The magician and the audience have entered into what I term the Pact of Acquiescent Sorcery. They do not articulate it as such, and indeed the audience is barely aware that such a Pact might exist, but that is what it is.

The performer is of course not a sorcerer at all, but an actor who plays the part of a sorcerer and who wishes the audience to believe, if only temporarily, that he is in contact with darker powers. The audience, meantime, knows that what they are seeing is not true sorcery, but they suppress the knowledge and acquiesce to the selfsame wish as the performer's. The greater the performer's skill at maintaining the illusion, the better at this deceptive sorcery he is judged to be.

The act of showing the hands to be empty, before revealing that despite appearances they could *not* have been, is itself a constituent of the Pact. The Pact implies special conditions are in force. In normal social intercourse, for instance, how often does it arise that someone has to prove that his hands are empty? And consider this: if the magician were suddenly to produce a vase of flowers without first suggesting to the audience that such a production was impossible, it would seem to be no trick at all. No one would applaud.

This then illustrates my method.

Let me set out the Pact of Acquiescence under which I write these words, so that those who read them will realise that what follows is not sorcery, but the appearance of it.

First let me in a manner of speaking show you my hands, palms forward, fingers splayed, and I will say to you (and mark this well): 'Every word in this notebook that describes my life and work is true, honestly meant and accurate in detail.'

Now I rotate my hands so that you may see their backs, and I say to you: 'Much of what is here may be checked against objective records. My career is noted in newspaper files, my name appears in books of biographical reference.'

Finally, I tweak at the cuffs of my jacket to reveal my

wrists, and I say to you: 'After all, what would I have to gain by writing a false account, when it is intended for no one's eyes but my own, perhaps those of my immediate family, and the members of a posterity I shall never meet?'

What gain indeed?

But because I have shown my hands to be empty you must now expect not only that an illusion will follow, but that you will acquiesce in it.

Already, without once writing a falsehood, I have started the deception that is my life. The lie is contained in these words, even in the very first of them. It is the fabric of everything that follows, yet nowhere will it be apparent.

I have misdirected you with the talk of truth, objective records and motives. Just as it is when I show my hands to be empty I have omitted the significant information, and now you are looking in the wrong place.

As every stage magician well knows there will be some who are baffled by this, some who will profess to a dislike of being duped, some who will claim to know the secret, and some, the happy majority, who will simply take the illusion for granted and enjoy the magic for the sake of entertainment.

But there are always one or two who will take the secret away with them and worry at it without ever coming near to solving it.

3

Before I resume the story of my life, here is another anecdote that illustrates my method.

When I was younger there was a fashion in the concert halls for Oriental Magic. Most of it was performed by European or American illusionists dressed and made up to look Chinese, but there were one or two genuine Chinese magicians who came to Europe to perform. One of these, and perhaps the greatest of them all, was a man from Shanghai called Chi Linqua, who worked under the stage name Ching Ling Foo.

I saw Ching perform only once, a few years ago at the Adelphi Theatre in Leicester Square. At the end of the show I went to the stage door and sent up my card, and without delay he graciously invited me to his dressing room. He would not speak of his magic, but my eye was taken by the presence there, on a stand beside him, of his most famous prop: the large glass bowl of goldfish, which, when apparently produced from thin air, gave his show its fantastic climax. He invited me to examine the bowl, and it was normal in every way. It contained at least a dozen ornamental fish, all of them alive, and was well filled with water. I tried lifting it, because I knew the secret of its manifestation, and marvelled at its weight.

Ching saw me struggling with it but said nothing. He was obviously unsure whether I knew his secret or not, and was unwilling to say anything that might expose it, even to a fellow professional. I did not know how to reveal that I *did* know the secret, and so I too kept my silence. I stayed with him for fifteen minutes, during which time he remained seated, nodding politely at the compliments I paid him. He had already changed out of his stage clothes by the time I arrived, and was wearing dark trousers and striped blue shirt, although he still had on his greasepaint. When I stood up to leave he rose from his chair by the mirror and conducted me to the door. He walked with his head bowed, his arms slack at his sides, and shuffling as if his legs gave him great pain.

Now, because years have passed and he is dead, I can reveal his most closely guarded secret, one whose obsessive extent I was privileged to glimpse that night.

His famous goldfish bowl was with him on stage throughout his act, ready for its sudden and mysterious appearance. Its presence was deftly concealed from the audience. *He carried it beneath the flowing mandarin gown he affected*, clutching it between his knees, kept ready for the sensational and apparently miraculous production at the end. No one in the audience could ever guess at how the trick was done, even though a moment's logical thought would have solved the mystery.

But logic was magically in conflict with itself! The only possible place where the heavy bowl could be concealed was beneath his gown, yet that was logically impossible. It was obvious to everyone that Ching Ling Foo was physically frail, shuffling painfully through his routine. When he took his bow at the end, he leaned for support on his assistant, and was led hobbling from the stage.

The reality was completely different. Ching was a fit man of great physical strength, and carrying the bowl in this way was well within his power. Be that as it may, the size and shape of the bowl caused him to shuffle like a mandarin as he walked. This threatened the secret, because it drew attention to the way he moved, so to protect the secret he shuffled for the whole of his life. Never, at any time, at home or in the street, day or night, did he walk with a normal gait lest his secret be exposed.

Such is the nature of a man who acts the role of sorcerer.

Audiences know well that a magician will practise his illusions for years, and will rehearse each performance carefully, but few people realise the *extent* of the prestidigitator's wish to deceive, the way in which the apparent defiance of normal laws becomes an obsession which governs every moment of his life.

Ching Ling Foo had his obsessive deception, and now that you have read my anecdote about him you may correctly assume that I have mine. My deception rules my life, informs every decision I make, regulates my every movement. Even now, as I embark on the writing of this memoir, it controls what I may write and what I may not. I have compared my method with the display of seemingly bared hands, but in reality everything in this account represents the shuffling walk of a fit man.

4

Because the yard was prospering my parents could afford to send me to the Pelham Scholastic Academy, a dame school run by the Misses Pelham in East Bourne Street, next to the remains of the mediaeval Town Wall and close to the harbour. There, amid the persistent stench from the rotten fish which littered the beach and all the environs of the harbour, and against the constant but eloquent braying of the herring gulls, I learnt the three Rs, as well as a modicum of History, Geography and the fearsome French language. All of these were to stand me in good stead in later life, but my fruitless struggles to learn French have an ironic outcome, because in adult life my stage persona is that of a French professor.

My way to and from school was across the ridge of West Hill, which was built up only in the immediate neighbourhood of our house. Most of the way led along steep narrow paths through the scented tamarisk bushes that had colonised so many of Hastings' open spaces. Hastings at the time was experiencing a period of development, as numerous new houses and hotels were being built to accommodate the summer visitors. I saw little of this, because the school was in the Old Town, while the resort area was being built beyond the White Rock, a former rocky spur that one day in my childhood was enthrallingly dynamited out of existence to make way for an extended seafront promenade. Despite all this, life in the ancient centre of Hastings continued much as it had done for hundreds of years.

I could say much about my father, good and bad, but for the sake of concentrating on my own story I shall confine myself to the best. I loved him, and learnt from him many of the cabinet-making techniques which, inadvertently by him, have made my name and fortune. I can attest that my father was hard-working, honest, sober, intelligent and, in his own way, generous. He was fair to his employees. Because he was not a God-fearing man, and no churchgoer, he brought up his family to act within a benign secularism, in which neither action nor inaction would occur to cause hurt or harm to others. He was a brilliant cabinet-maker and a good wheelwright. I realised, eventually, that whatever emotional outbursts our family had to endure (because there were several) his anger must have been caused by inner frustrations, although at what and of what sort I was never entirely sure. Although I was never myself a target for his worst moments, I grew up a little scared of my father but loved him profoundly.

My mother's name was Betsy May Borden (née Robertson), my father's name was Joseph Andrew Borden. I had a total of seven brothers and sisters, although because of infant deaths I knew only five of them. I was neither the oldest nor the youngest child, and was not particularly favoured by either parent. I grew up in reasonable harmony with most, if not all, of my siblings.

When I was twelve I was taken away from the school, and placed to work as a wheelwright's apprentice in my father's yard. Here my adult life began, both in the sense that from this time I spent more time with adults than with other children, and that my own real future started to become clear to me. Two factors were pivotal.

The first was, simply enough, the handling of wood. I had grown up with the sight and smell of it, so that both were familiar to me. I had little idea how wood *felt* when you picked it up, or cleaved it, or sawed it. From the first moment I handled wood with purposeful intent I began to respect it, and realise what could be done with it. Wood, when properly seasoned, and hewed to take advantage of the natural grain, is beautiful, strong, light and supple. It can be cut to almost any shape; it can be worked or adhered to almost any other material. You can paint it, stain it, bleach it, flex it. It is at once outstanding and commonplace, so that when something manufactured of wood is present it lends a quiet feeling of solid normality, and so is hardly ever noticed.

In short it is the ideal medium for the illusionist.

At the yard I was given no preferential treatment as the proprietor's son. On my first day, I was sent to begin learning the business by taking on the roughest, hardest job in the yard – I and another apprentice were put to work in a sawpit. The twelve-hour days of that (we started at 6.00 a.m. and finished at 8.00 p.m. every day, with only three short breaks for meals) hardened my body like no other work I can conceive of, and taught me to fear as well as respect the heavy cords of timber. After that initiation, which continued for several months, I was moved to the less physically demanding but more exacting work of learning to cut, turn and smooth the wood for the spokes and felloes of the wheels. Here I came into regular contact with the wheelwrights and other men who worked for my father, and saw less of my fellow apprentices.

One morning, about a year after I had left school, a contract worker named Robert Noonan came to the yard to carry out some long-needed repair and redecoration work to the rear wall of the yard, which had been damaged in a storm some years before. With Noonan's arrival came the second great influence on the direction of my future life.

I, busy about my labours, barely even noticed him, but at 1.00 p.m., when we broke for lunch, Noonan came and sat with me and the other men at the trestle table where we ate our food. He produced a pack of playing cards and asked if any of us would care to 'find the lady'. Some of the older men chaffed him and tried to warn off the others, but a few of us stayed to watch. Tiny sums of money began to change hands; not mine, for I had none to spare, but one or two of the workmen were willing to gamble a few pence.

What fascinated me was the smooth, natural way that Noonan manipulated the cards. He was so fast! So dexterous! He spoke softly and persuasively, showing us the faces of the three playing cards, placing them down on the small box in front of him with a quick but flowing motion, then moving them about with his long fingers before pausing to challenge us to indicate which of the cards was the Queen. The workmen had slower eyes than mine; they spotted the card rather less often than I did (although I was wrong more often than I was right).

Afterwards, I said to Noonan, 'How do you do that? Will you show me?'

At first he tried to fob me off with talk of idle hands, but I persisted. 'I want to know how you do it!' I cried. 'The Queen is placed in the middle of the three, but you move the cards only twice and she is not where I think she is! What's the secret?'

So one lunchtime, instead of trying to fleece the other men, he took me to a quiet corner of the shed and showed me how to manipulate the three cards so that the hand deceived the eye. The Queen and another card were gripped lightly between the thumb and middle finger of the left hand, one above the other; the third card was held in the right hand. When the cards were placed he moved his hands crosswise, brushing his fingertips on the surface and pausing briefly, so suggesting the Queen was being put down first. In fact, it was almost invariably one of the other cards that slipped quietly down before her. This is the classic trick whose correct name is THREE CARD MONTE.

When I had grasped the idea of that, Noonan showed me several other techniques. He taught me how to palm a card in the hand, how to shuffle the deck deceptively so that the order remained undisturbed, how to cut the pack to bring a certain chosen card to the top or bottom of the hand, how to offer a fan of cards to someone and force him to choose one card and not any of the others. He went through all this in a casual way, showing off rather than showing, probably not realizing the rapt attention with which I was taking it in. When he had finished his demonstration I tried the false dealing technique with the Queen, but the cards scattered all about. I tried again. Then again. And on and on, long after Noonan himself had lost interest and wandered away. By the evening of the first day, alone in my bedroom, I had mastered THREE CARD MONTE, and was setting to work on the other techniques I had briefly seen.

One day, his painting work completed, Noonan left the

yard and went out of my life. I never saw him again. He left behind him an impressionable adolescent boy with a compulsion. I intended to rest at nothing until I had mastered the art that I now knew (from a book I urgently borrowed from the lending library) was called Legerdemain.

Legerdemain, sleight of hand, prestidigitation, became the dominant interest of my life.

5

The next three years saw parallel developments in my life. For one thing I was an adolescent growing rapidly into a man. For another, my father was quick to realise that I had an appreciable skill as a woodworker, and that the comparatively coarse demands of the wheelwright's work were not making the best use of me. Finally, I was learning how to make magic with my hands.

These three parts of my life wove around each other like strands in a rope. Both my father and I needed to make a living, so much of the work I did in the yard continued to be with the barrels, axles and wheels that made up the main part of the business, but when he was able to, either he or one of his foremen would instruct me in the finer craft of cabinet-making. My father planned a future for me in his business. If I proved as adept as he thought, he would at the end of my apprenticeship set me up with a furniture workshop of my own, allowing me to develop it as I saw fit. He would eventually join me there when he retired from the yard. In this, some of his frustrations in life were laid plain before me. My carpentry skill reawakened memories of his own youthful ambitions.

Meanwhile, my other skill, the one I saw as my real one, was developing apace. Every possible moment of my spare time was devoted to practising the conjurer's art. In particular, I learnt and tried to master all the known tricks of playing-card manipulation. I saw sleight of hand as the foundation of all magic, just as the tonic scale lies at the foundation of the most complex symphony. It was difficult obtaining reference works on the subject, but books on magic do exist and the diligent researcher can find them. Night after night, in my chilly room above the arch, I stood before a full-length mirror and practised palming and forcing, shuffling cards and spreading them, passing and fanning them, discovering different ways of cutting and feinting. I learnt the art of misdirection, in which the magician trades on the audience's everyday experience to confound their senses – the metal birdcage that looks too rigid to collapse, the ball that seems too large to be concealed in a sleeve, the sword whose tempered steel blade could never, surely?, be pliant. I quickly amassed a repertoire of such legerdemain skills, applying myself to each one of them until I had it right, then re-applying myself until I had mastered it, then re-applying myself once again until I was perfect at it. I never ceased practising.

The strength and dexterity of my hands was the key to this.

Now, briefly, I break off from the writing of this to consider my hands. I lay down my pen to hold them before me again, turning them in the light from the mantle, trying to see them not in the so familiar way that I see them every day, but as I imagine a stranger might. Eight long and slender fingers, two sturdy thumbs, nails trimmed to an exact length; not an artist's hands, nor a labourer's, nor those of a surgeon, but the hands of a carpenter turned prestidigitator. When I turn them so that the palms face me, I see pale, almost transparent skin, with darker roughened patches between the joints of the fingers. The balls of the thumbs are rounded, but when I tense my muscles hard ridges form across the palms. Now I reverse them and see the fine skin again, with a dusting of blond hairs. Women are intrigued by my hands, and a few say they love them.

Every day, even now in my maturity, I exercise my hands. They are strong enough to burst a sealed rubber tennis ball.

I can bend steel nails between my fingers, and if I slam the heel of my hand against hardwood, the hardwood splinters. Yet the same hand can lightly suspend a farthing by its edge between my third and fourth fingertips, while the rest of the hand manipulates apparatus, or writes on a blackboard, or holds the arm of a volunteer from the audience, and it can retain the coin there through all this before sliding it dexterously to where it might seem magically to appear.

My left hand bears a small scar, a reminder of the time in my youth when I learnt the true value of my hands. I already knew, from every time that I practised with a pack of cards, or a coin, or a fine silk scarf, or with any one of the conjurer's props I was slowly amassing, that the human hand was a delicate instrument, fine and strong and sensitive. But carpentry was hard on my hands, an unpleasant fact I discovered one morning in the yard. A moment's lost attention while shaping a felloe, a careless movement with a chisel, and I cut a deep slash in my left hand. I remember standing there in disbelief, my fingers tensed like the talons of a claw, while dark-red blood welled out of the gash and ran thickly down my wrist and arm. The older men I was working with that day were used to dealing with such injuries, and knew what to do: a tourniquet was rapidly applied, and a cart readied for the dash to hospital. For two weeks afterwards my hand was bandaged. It was not the blood, not the pain, not the inconvenience; it was the dread that when the cut itself healed my hand would be found to have been *cut through* in some final, devastating way, immobilising it forever. As events turned out no permanent damage was done. After a discouraging period when the hand was stiff and awkward to use, the tendons and muscles gradually eased up, the gash healed and knitted properly, and within two months I was back to normal.

I took it as a warning, though. My legerdemain was then only a hobby. I had never performed for anyone, not even, like Robert Noonan, for the entertainment of the men I worked with. All my magic was practice magic, executed in dumb show before the tall mirror. But it was a consuming

43

hobby, a passion, even, yes, the beginning of an obsession. I could not allow an injury to put it in jeopardy!

That gashed hand was therefore another turning point, because it established the paramountcy of my life. Before it happened I was a trainee wheelwright with an engrossing pastime, but afterwards I was a young magician who would allow nothing to stand in his way. It was more important to me that I should be able to palm a hidden card, or deftly reach for a concealed billiard ball inside a felt-lined bag, or secretly slip a borrowed five-pound note into a prepared orange, trivial though these matters might seem, than that I might one day again hurt one of my hands while making a wheel for the cart of a publican.

6

I said nothing of this to me! What is it? How far is it to be taken? I must write no more until I know!

7

So, now we have spoken, it is agreed I may continue? Here it is again, on that understanding. I may write what I see fit, while I may add to it as I see fit. I planned nothing to which I would not agree, only to write a great deal more of it before I read it. I apologise if I think I was deceiving me, and meant no harm.

8

I have read it through several times, & I think I understand what I am driving at. It was only the surprise that made me react the way I did. Now I am calmer I find it acceptable so far.

But much is missing! I think I must write about the meeting with John Henry Anderson next, because it was through him I gained my introduction to the Maskelynes.

I assume there is no particular reason why I can't go straight to this?

Either I must do this now, or leave a note for me to find. Exchange me this more often!

I must not leave out on any account:

1. The way I discovered what Angier was doing, & what I did about him.
2. Olive Wenscombe (not my fault, NB).
3. What about Sarah? The children?

The Pact extends even to this, does it? That's how I interpret it. If so, either I have to leave a lot out, or I have to put in a great deal more.

I am surprised to discover how much I have already written.

9

When I was sixteen, in 1872, John Henry Anderson brought his Touring Magical Show to Hastings, and took up a week's residence at the Gaiety Theatre in Queens Road. I attended his show every night, taking seats as close to the front of the auditorium as I could afford. It would have been inconceivable to have missed a single performance of his. At that time not only was he the leading stage illusionist with a touring

show, not only was he credited with the invention of numerous baffling new effects, but he had a reputation for helping
and encouraging young magicians.

Every night Mr Anderson performed one particular trick
known in the world of magic as the MODERN CABINET ILLU-
SION. During this he would invite on stage a small committee
of volunteers from the audience. These men (they were
always men) would assist in pulling on to the stage a tall
wooden cabinet mounted on wheels, sufficiently raised from
the floor to show that no one could enter it via a trap in the
base. The committee would then be invited to inspect the
cabinet inside and out to satisfy themselves it was empty,
turn it around for the audience to see it from all sides, even
choose one of their number to step inside for a moment to
prove that no other person could be concealed within it.
They would then collaborate in locking the door and sec-
uring it with heavy padlocks. While the committee remained
on the stage Mr Anderson once again rotated the cabinet
for the audience to satisfy themselves that it was securely
sealed, then with quick motions he dashed away the restraining padlocks, threw open the door . . . and out would step a
beautiful young assistant, wearing a voluminous dress and
large hat.

Every night when Mr Anderson made his call for volunteers I would stand up eagerly to be selected, and every night
he would pass me by. I badly wanted to be chosen! I wanted
to find out what it was like to be on the stage under the
lights, in front of an audience. I wanted to be near to Mr
Anderson when he was performing the illusion. And I
positively craved a good close look at the way the cabinet
had been built. Of course I knew the secret of the MODERN
CABINET, because by this time I had learnt or worked out for
myself the mechanism of every illusion then current, but to
see a top magician's cabinet at close quarters would have
been a golden opportunity to examine it. The secret of that
particular illusion is all in the making of the cabinet. Alas,
such a chance was not to be.

After the last show of his short season I plucked up my

courage and went to the stage door, intending to waylay Mr Anderson when he left the theatre. Instead, I had been standing outside for no more than a minute when the doorman let himself out of his cubbyhole, and walked out to speak to me, his head slightly to one side, and looking at me curiously.

'Pardon me, sir,' he said. 'But Mr Anderson has left instructions that if you appear at this entrance I am to invite you to join him in his dressing room.'

Needless to say, I was astounded!

'Are you sure he meant me?' I said.

'Yes, sir. I'm positive.'

Still mystified, but extremely pleased and excited, I followed the doorman's directions along the narrow passages and stairways, and soon found the star's dressing room. Inside—

Inside, there followed a short, thrilling interview with Mr Anderson. I am loath to report it in detail here, partly because it was so long ago and I have inevitably forgotten details, but also partly because it was not so long ago that I have ceased to be embarrassed by my youthful effusions. My week in the front stalls of his performances had convinced me he was a brilliant performer, skilled in patter and presentation, and flawless in the execution of his illusions. I was rendered almost speechless by meeting him, but when I did unstop my mouth I found a torrent of praise and enthusiasm gushing out of me.

However, in spite of all this, two topics came up that are of some interest.

The first was his explanation of why he had never chosen me from the audience. He said he had almost picked me out at the opening performance because I had been the first to leap to my feet, but something had made him change his mind. Then he said that when he saw me at subsequent performances he realised that I must be a fellow magician (how my heart leapt with joy at such recognition!), and was therefore wary of inviting me to take part. He did not know, could have had no means of knowing, if I might

47

have ulterior motives. Many magicians, particularly rising young ones, are not above trying to steal ideas from their more established colleagues, and therefore I understood Mr Anderson's caution. Even so, he apologised for distrusting me.

The second matter followed on from this. He had realised I must be starting out in my career. With this in mind he penned me a short letter of introduction, to be presented at St George's Hall in London, where I would be able to meet Mr Nevil Maskelyne himself.

It was around this time that excitement took over and my youthful effusions become too painful to recall.

Some six months after the exciting meeting with Mr Anderson I did indeed approach Mr Maskelyne in London, and it was after this that my professional career as a magician properly began. That, in its barest outline, is the story of how I met Mr Anderson and, through him, Mr Maskelyne. I do not intend to dwell on all these or other steps I followed as I perfected my craft and developed a successful stage show, except where they have a bearing on the main point of this narrative. There was a long period when I was learning my trade by performing it, and to a large extent not performing it as well as I had planned. This time of my life is not of much interest to me.

There is though a relevant point in the particular matter of my meeting Mr Anderson. He and Mr Maskelyne were the only two major magicians I met before my Pact took its present shape, and therefore they are the only two fellow illusionists who know the secret of my act. Mr Anderson, I am sorry to say, is now dead, but the Maskelyne family, including Mr Nevil Maskelyne, is still active in the world of magic. I know I can trust them to remain silent; indeed, I *have* to trust them. That my secrets have sometimes been in jeopardy is not a charge I am prepared to lay at Mr Maskelyne's door. No, indeed, for the culprit is well known to me.

I shall now return to address the main thrust of this narrative, which is what I intended to do before I interrupted.

IO

Some years ago, a magician (I believe it was Mr David Devant) was reported as saying: 'Magicians protect their secrets not because the secrets are large and important, but because they are so small and trivial. The wonderful effects created on stage are often the result of a secret so absurd that the magician would be embarrassed to admit that that was how it was done.'

There, in a nutshell, is the paradox of the stage magician.

The fact that a trick is 'spoiled' if its secret is revealed is widely understood, not only by magicians but by the audiences they entertain. Most people enjoy the sense of mystery created by the performance, and do not want to ruin it, no matter how curious they feel about what they seem to have witnessed.

The magician naturally wishes to preserve his secrets, so that he may go on earning his living from them, and this is widely recognised. He becomes, though, a victim of his own secrecy. The longer a trick is part of his repertoire, and the more often it is successfully performed, and by definition the larger the number of people he has deceived with it, then the more it seems to him essential to preserve its secret.

The effect grows larger. It is seen by many audiences, other magicians copy or adapt it, the magician himself will let it evolve, so that his presentation changes over the years, making the trick seem more elaborate or more impossible to explain. Through all this the secret remains. It also remains small and trivial, and as the effect grows so the triviality seems more threatening to his reputation. Secrecy becomes obsessive.

So to the real subject of this.

I have spent my lifetime guarding my secret by appearing to hobble (I am alluding to Ching Ling Foo, not, of course, writing literally). I am now of an age, and, frankly, of an earned wealth, where performing on stage has lost its golden allure. Am I therefore to limp figuratively for the rest of my natural life so as to preserve a secret few know exists, and even fewer care about? I think not, and so I have set out at last to change the habit of a lifetime and write about THE NEW TRANSPORTED MAN. This is the name of the illusion that has made me famous, said by many to be the greatest piece of magic ever performed on the international stage.

I intend to write, firstly: a short description of what the audience sees.

And then, secondly: A Revelation of the Secret Behind It!

Such is the purpose of this account. Now I set aside my pen, as agreed.

I I

I have refrained from writing in this book for three weeks. I do not need to say why; I do not need to be told why. The secret of THE NEW TRANSPORTED MAN is not mine alone to reveal, & there's an end to it. What madness infects me?

The secret has served me well for many years, & has resisted numerous prying assaults. I have spent most of my lifetime protecting it. Is this not reason enough for the Pact?

Yet now I write that all such secrets are trivial. Trivial! Have I devoted my life to a *trivial* secret?

The first two of my three silent weeks slipped by while I reflected on this galling insight into my life's work.

This book, journal, narrative – what should I call it? – is itself a product of my Pact, as I have already recorded. Have I thought through all the ramifications of that?

Under the Pact, if I once make a statement, even something ill-advised or uttered in an unguarded moment, I always assume responsibility for it as if I had spoken the words myself. As do I when rôles are reversed, or so I have always assumed. This oneness of purpose, of action, of words, is essential to the Pact.

For this reason I do not insist that I go back & delete those lines above, where I promise a revelation of my secret. (For the same reason I may not later delete the very lines I am writing now.)

However, no revelation of my secret may be made, & is not even to be considered again. I must hobble a while longer.

I am ignoring the fact that Rupert Angier yet lives! I do indeed sometimes put him from my mind, wilfully drawing veils of forgetfulness across him & his deeds, but the wretch continues to draw breath. So long as he remains alive my secret is in peril.

I hear he still performs his version of THE NEW TRANSPORTED MAN, & during his execution of it continues to make that offensive remark across the footlights that what the audience is about to see 'has often been copied, but has never been improved upon'. I rankle at these reports, & more at other reports from insiders. Angier has hit on a new method of transportation, & it is said to look good when performed. His fatal flaw, though, is that his effect is slow. Whatever he might claim, he still cannot do the trick as quickly as me! How he must burn to know my truth!

The Pact must remain in place. No revelations!

12

Since Angier has been brought into the story I shall describe the problem he first presented to me, and give a detailed account of how our dispute began. It will soon become apparent that I started the feud, and I make no bones about this responsibility.

However, I was led astray by adhering to what I thought were the highest principles, and when I realised what I had done I did try to make amends. Here is how it started.

On the fringes of professional magic there are a few

individuals who see prestidigitation as an easy way of gulling the credulous and the rich. They use the same magical devices and apparatus as legitimate magicians, but they pretend their effects are 'real'.

It can be seen that this is only a shade away from the artifice of the stage magician, who acts the role of sorcerer. That shade of difference is crucial.

For example, I sometimes open my act with an illusion called CHINESE LINKING RINGS. I begin by taking up a position in the centre of a lighted stage, holding the rings casually. I make no claim for what I am about to do with them. The audience sees (or thinks it sees, or allows itself to think it sees) ten large separate rings made of shining metal. The rings are shown to a few members of the audience who are permitted to handle and inspect them, and discover on behalf of everyone present that the rings are solid, without joints, without openings. I then take the rings back and to everyone's amazement I immediately join them into one continuous chain, holding them up for all to see. I link and unlink rings at the touch of a spectator's hand on the exact spot where the joining or unjoining takes place. I link some of the rings into figures and shapes, then unlink them just as quickly, looping them casually over one of my arms or around my neck. At the end of the trick I am seen (or thought to be seen, et cetera) to be holding, once again, ten separate solid rings.

How is it done? The actual answer is that such a trick can only be performed after years of practice. There is a secret, of course, and because CHINESE LINKING RINGS is still a popular and widely performed trick, I cannot lightly reveal what it is. It is a trick, an illusion, one that is judged not for the apparently miraculous secret, but for the skill, the flair, the showmanship with which it is performed.

Now, take another magician. He performs the same illusion, using the identical secret, but he claims aloud that he is linking and unlinking the rings by sorcerous means. Would not his performance be judged differently? He would appear not skilled but mystical and powerful. He would be not a mere entertainer but a miracle worker who defied natural laws.

If I, or any other professional magician, were there, I should have to say to the audience: 'That is just a trick! The rings are not what they seem. You have not seen what you think you have seen.'

To which the miracle-worker would reply (falsely): 'What I have just shown the audience is a product of the supernatural. If you claim it is merely a conjuring trick, then pray explain to everyone how it is done.'

And here I would have no reply. I would not be able to reveal the workings of a trick, bound as I am by professional honour.

So the miracle would seem to remain a miracle.

When I first began performing there was a vogue for spirit effects, or 'spiritism'. Some of these manifestations were performed openly on the theatrical stage; others took place more covertly in studios or private homes. All had features in common. They allegedly gave hope to the recently bereaved or the elderly by making it seem that there was a life after death. Much money changed hands in pursuit of this reassurance.

From the viewpoint of the professional magician, spiritism had two significant features. First, standard magical techniques were being used. Second, the perpetrators invariably claimed that the effects were supernaturally produced. In other words, false claims were being made about miraculous 'powers'.

This was what aggravated me. Because the tricks were all easily reproducible by any stage illusionist worthy of the name, it was irritating, to say the least, to hear them claimed as paranormal phenomena, whose manifestation therefore 'proved' that there was an afterlife, that spirits could walk, that the dead could speak, and so on. It was a lie, but it was one that was difficult to prove.

I arrived in London in 1874. Under John Henry Anderson's tutelage, and Nevil Maskelyne's patronage, I began trying to obtain work in the theatres and music halls found all over the great capital. There was in those days a demand for stage magic, but London was full of clever magicians and an entry into the circuit was not easy. I managed to take a modest place in that world, finding what work I could, and although my magic was always well received my rise to prominence was a slow one. THE NEW TRANSPORTED MAN was then a long way from fruition, although to be entirely frank I had started to plan this great illusion even while I still hammered and fretted in my father's yard in Hastings.

At this time the spirit magicians were often seen advertising their services in newspapers and periodicals, and some of their doings were much discussed. Spiritism was presented to the populace as a more exciting, powerful and *effective* kind of magic than what they could see on the stage. If one is skilled enough to put a young woman into a trance and make her hover in mid-air, the argument seemed to go, why not direct that skill more usefully and communicate with the recently departed? Why not indeed?

13

Rupert Angier's name was already familiar to me. Writing from an address in North London he was an opinionated and long-winded correspondent to the letter columns of two or three of the private-circulation magic journals. His purpose was invariably to pour scorn on the people he described as the 'establishment' of older magicians, who with their secretive ways and courteous traditions were held up as tiresome relics of a former age. Although I worked within those traditions I did not allow myself to be drawn into Angier's various controversies, but some of the magicians I knew were greatly provoked by him.

One of his theories, to take a fairly typical example, was that if magicians were as skilful as they claimed to be, then they should be prepared to perform magic 'in the round'.

That is to say, the magician would be surrounded on all sides by the audience, and would therefore have to create illusions that did not depend on the framing, audience-excluding effect of the proscenium arch. One of my distinguished colleagues, by way of reply, gently pointed out the self-evident fact that no matter how well the magician prepared his act, there would always be a segment of the audience who could see the trick being worked. Angier's response was to deride the other correspondent. First, he said, the magical effect would be increased if the illusion could be viewed from all angles. Secondly, if it could not, and a small segment of the audience had to glimpse the secret, *it did not matter*! If five hundred people are baffled, he said, it was of no importance that five others should see the secret.

Such theories were almost heretical to the majority of professionals, not because they held secrets to be inviolable (which Angier seemed to imply), but because Angier's attitude to magic was radical and careless of the traditions which had held good for so long.

Rupert Angier was therefore making a name for himself, but perhaps not the one he had planned. One observation I often heard was the mock surprise that Angier rarely if ever performed on the public stage. His colleagues were therefore unable to admire his no doubt brilliant and innovative magic.

As I say, I did not get involved and he was not of great interest to me. However, destiny was soon to take a hand.

It happened that one of my father's sisters, living in London, had recently been bereaved and in her grief was intending to consult a spiritist. She had accordingly arranged a séance at her house. I heard about it in one of my mother's regular letters, passed to me as family chitchat, but at once my professional curiosity was aroused. I promptly made contact with my aunt, offered her belated condolences on the loss of her husband, and volunteered to be with her in her search for solace.

When the day came I was lucky that my aunt had invited me to lunch beforehand, because the spiritist arrived at the house at least an hour before he was expected. This threw the household into some confusion. I imagine it was part of his design, and enabled him to take certain preparations in the room where the séance was to be conducted. He and his two young assistants, one male and one female, darkened the room with black blinds, moved unwanted furniture to the side while importing some of their own which they had brought with them, rolled back the carpet to bare the floorboards, and erected a certain wooden cabinet whose size and appearance was enough to convince me that conventional stage magic was about to be performed. I stayed discreetly but attentively in the background while these preparations were put in place. I did not wish to make myself at all interesting to the spiritist, because if he was alert he might have recognised me. The previous week my stage act had drawn a favourable press notice or two.

The spiritist himself was a young man of about my own age, slight of build, dark of hair and narrow of forehead. He had a wary look to him, almost like that of a foraging animal going about its business. He made quick precise movements with his hands, a sure sign of a long-practising prestidigitator. The young woman who worked with him had a slender, agile body (because of her physique I assumed, wrongly as it turned out, that she would be employed in his illusions), and a strong, attractive face. She wore dark and modest clothes, and rarely spoke. The other assistant, a burly young man not long in his majority, had a broad thatch of fair hair and a churlish face, and he jibed and complained as he hauled in the heavy pieces of furniture.

By the time my aunt's other guests arrived (she had invited some eight or nine of her friends to be present, presumably to help spread the cost a little), the spiritist's preparations were complete and he and his assistants were sitting patiently in the prepared room, waiting for the time appointed. It was therefore impossible for me to examine their apparatus.

The presentation, which with all the preamble and atmospheric pauses lasted for well over an hour, broke down into three main illusions, carefully arranged so as to create feelings of apprehension, excitement and suggestibility.

First the spiritist performed a table-tipping illusion with a dramatic physical manifestation; the table spun around of its own accord, then reared up terrifyingly into the air, causing most of us to sprawl uncomfortably on the bare floor. After this the attendees were shaking with excited agitation, and ready for anything that might follow. What did follow was that with the aid of his female accomplice the spiritist appeared to fall into a Mesmeric trance. He was then blindfolded, gagged, and bound hand and foot by his assistants, and placed helpless within his cabinet, whence emanated, soon enough, numerous noisy, startling and inexplicable paranormal effects: strange lights flashed brilliantly, trumpets, cymbals and castanets sounded, and eerie 'ectoplasmic matter' rose of its own accord from the heart of the cabinet, and floated into the room illuminated by a mysterious light.

Released from the cabinet and his bonds (when the cabinet was opened he was found as efficiently tied up as when he went inside), and miraculously restored from his Mesmerised state, the spiritist then got down to his main business. After a short but colourful warning about the dangers of 'crossing over' to the spirit world, and a hint that the results justified the risk, the spiritist fell into another trance and soon was in touch with the other side. Before too long he was able to identify the spirit presence of certain departed relatives and close friends of the people gathered in the room, and comforting messages were conveyed from one group to the other.

14

How did the young spiritist achieve all this?

As I have already said, professional ethics constrain me. I could not then, and cannot now, reveal more than the barest outline of the secrets of what were without question straightforward magical effects.

The tipping table is actually not a conjuring trick at all (although it can be presented as one, as on this occasion). It is a little-known physical phenomenon that if ten or a dozen people cluster around a circular wooden table, press the palms of their hands on the surface, and are then told that soon the table will start to rotate, it is only a matter of a minute or two before that starts to happen! Once the motion is felt, the table almost invariably begins to tip to one side or the other. An adroitly placed foot suddenly lifting the appropriate table leg will dramatically unbalance the table, causing it to rear up and crash excitingly to the floor. With luck, it will take with it many of the participants, causing surprise and excitement but not physical harm.

I need not emphasise that the table being used at my aunt's was one of the spiritist's own props. It was constructed so that the four wooden legs connected to the central pillar in such a way that there was room for a foot to be slipped underneath.

The cabinet manifestations can only be adumbrated here; a skilled magician may easily escape from what appear to be irresistible bonds, especially if the ropes and knots have been tied by two assistants. Once inside the cabinet it would be the work of a few seconds to release himself sufficiently to make happen the otherwise perplexing display of paranormal effects.

As for the 'psychic' contacts which were the main purpose of the meeting, here too there are standard techniques of forcing and substitution which any good magician can readily perform.

15

I had gone to my aunt's house to satisfy professional curiosity, but instead, to my eventual shame and regret, I came away with a case of righteous indignation. Standard stage illusions had been used to gull a group of suggestible and vulnerable people. My aunt, believing that she had heard words of comfort from her beloved husband, was so overcome by grief that she retired immediately to her chamber. Several of the others were almost as deeply moved by messages they had heard. Yet I knew, I alone knew, that it was all a sham.

I felt an exhilarating sense that I could and should expose him as a charlatan, before he did any more harm. I was tempted to confront him then and there, but I was a little intimidated by the assured way he had performed his illusions. While he and his female assistant were putting away their apparatus I spoke briefly to the thatch-haired young man and was given the spiritist's business card.

Thus it was that I learned the name and style of the man who was to dog my professional career:

Rupert Angier
Clairvoyant, Spirit Medium, Séantist
Strictest Confidence Observed
45 Idmiston Villas, London N

I was young, inexperienced, heady with what I saw as high principles, and these, to my later chagrin, blinded me to the hypocrisy of my position. I set out to hound Mr Angier, intent on exposing his swindles. Soon enough, by methods I need not record here, I was able to establish where and when his next séance was to take place.

Once again it was a meeting in a private house in a suburb of London, although this time my connection with the family (bereaved by the sudden death of the mother) was contrived. I was able to attend only by presenting myself at the house the day before and claiming to be an associate of Angier's whose presence had been requested by the 'medium' himself. In their all-too-evident grief the remaining family seemed hardly to care.

The next day I made sure I was in the street outside the house well before the appointment, and thus was able to confirm that Angier's own early arrival at my aunt's house had been no accident, and indeed was a necessary part of the preparations. I watched covertly as he and his assistants unpacked their paraphernalia from a cart and carried it into the house. When I finally presented myself at the house an hour later, close to the appointed time, the room had been arranged and was in semi-darkness.

The séance began, as before, with the table-tipping trick, and as luck would have it I found myself standing unavoidably close beside Angier as he readied himself to begin.

'Don't I know you, sir?' he said softly and accusingly.

'I think not,' I replied, trying to make light of it.

'Make a habit of these occasions, do you?'

'No more than you, sir,' I said, as cuttingly as I could.

He responded with a disconcerting stare, but as everyone was waiting for him he had no alternative but to begin. I think he knew from that moment that I was there to expose him, but to do him credit he carried out his performance with the same flair I had seen before.

I was biding my time. It would have been pointless to uncover the secret of the table, but when he began the manifestations from within the cabinet it was tempting to dash across and throw open the door to reveal him inside. Without doubt we would then have seen that his hands were free of the ropes that were supposed to be restraining him, and the trumpet would be found held to his lips or the castanets clicking in his fingers. But I stayed my hand. I judged it best to wait until the emotional tension was at its greatest, when the supposed spirit messages were being sent to and fro. Angier performed this by using small scraps of paper, rolled up into little pellets. The family had earlier written names, objects, family secrets and the like on these scraps, and Angier pretended to read their 'spirit' messages by pressing the tiny pellets to his forehead.

When he had but barely begun I seized my chance. I stepped away from the table, breaking the chain of hands that was supposed to set up a psychic field, and snatched the blind down from the nearest window. Daylight flooded in.

Angier said, 'What the devil—?'

'Ladies and gentlemen!' I cried. 'This man is an impostor!'

'Sit down, sir!' The male assistant was moving quickly towards me.

'He is using legerdemain upon you!' I said emphatically. 'Look in the hand that hides beneath the table's surface! There is the secret of the messages he brings you!'

As the young man threw his arms around my shoulders I saw Angier moving quickly and guiltily to conceal the slip of paper he held, by which the trick was effected. The father of the family, his face contorted by rage and grief, rose from his seat and began to berate me loudly. First one of the children then the others began to wail with unhappiness.

As I struggled, the oldest boy said plaintively, 'Where is Mama? She was here! She was here!'

'This man is a charlatan, a liar and a cheat!' I shouted.

I was by this time almost at the door, being forced backwards out of the room. I saw the young woman assistant hastening to the window to replace the blind. With a tremendous thrashing of elbows I managed to break free temporarily from my assailant, and lunged across the room at her. I grabbed her by the shoulders and pushed her roughly to one side. She sprawled across the floorboards.

'He cannot talk to the dead!' I cried. 'Your mother is not here at all!'

The room was in an uproar.

'Hold him there!' Angier's voice was audible above the racket. The male assistant grabbed me a second time, and spun me around so that I was facing into the room. The young woman was still on the floor where she had fallen, and was staring up at me, her face contorted with spite. Angier, standing by the table, was erect and apparently calm. He was staring straight towards me.

'I know you, sir,' he said. 'I even know your damned name. I shall henceforward be following your career with the greatest attention.' Then to his assistant: 'Get him out of here!'

Moments later I was sprawling in the street. Mustering as much dignity as I could, and ignoring the gawping passers-by, I straightened my clothes and walked quickly away down the street.

For a few days afterwards I was sustained by the right-eousness of my cause, the knowledge that the family were being robbed of their money, that the skills of the stage magician were being put to warped uses. Then, inevitably, I began to be assailed by doubts.

The comfort that Angier's clients gained from the séances seemed genuine enough, no matter how derived. I remem-bered the faces of those children, who for a few minutes had been led to believe that their lost mother was sending con-soling messages from the other side. I had seen their inno-cent expressions, their smiles, their happy glances at each other.

Was any of this so different from the pleasurable mys-tification a magician gives to his music hall audience? Indeed, was it not rather more? Was expecting payment for this any more reprehensible than expecting payment for a performance at a music hall?

Full of regrets I brooded unhappily for nearly a month, until my conscience reached such depths of guilty feelings that I had to act. I penned an abject note to Angier, begging forgiveness, apologizing unconditionally.

His response was immediate. He returned my note in shreds, with a note of his own challenging me sarcastically to restore the torn paper with my own superior form of magic.

Two nights later, while I was performing at the Lewisham Empire, he stood up from the front row of the circle and shouted for all to hear, 'His female assistant is concealed behind the curtain at the left-hand side of the cabinet!'

It was of course true. Other than bringing down the main curtain and abandoning my act I had no alternative but to continue with the trick, produce my assistant with as much theatrical brio as possible, then wilt before the trickle of embarrassed applause. In the centre of the circle's front row an empty seat gaped like a missing tooth.

So was begun the feud that has continued over the years.

I can plead only youth and inexperience for starting the feud, a misguided professional zeal, an unfamiliarity with the ways of the world. Angier should shoulder some of the blame; my apology, although not swift enough, was sincerely meant and its rejection was mean-spirited. But then, Angier too was young. It is difficult to think back to that time, because the dispute between us has gone on so long, and has taken so many different forms.

If I committed both wrong and right at the outset, Angier must accept the blame for keeping the feud alive. Many times, sick of the whole thing, I have tried to get on with my life and career, only to find that some new attack was being mounted against me. Angier would often find a way of sabotaging my magical equipment, so that a production I was attempting on stage went subtly wrong. One night the water I was turning into red wine remained water; another time the string of flags I pulled flamboyantly from an opera hat appeared as string alone; at another performance the lady assistant who was supposed to levitate remained unmovably and mortifyingly on her bed.

On yet another occasion the placards announcing my act outside the theatre were defaced with 'The sword he uses is a fake', 'The card you will choose is the Queen of Spades', 'Watch his left hand during the mirror trick', and so on. All these graffiti were clearly visible to the audience as they trooped in.

I suppose these attacks might be dismissed as practical jokes, but they could damage my reputation as a magician, as Angier well knew.

How did I know he was behind them? Well, in some

cases he clearly declared his involvement. If one of my productions had been sabotaged, he would be there in the auditorium to heckle me, leaping to his feet at the very moment things started going wrong. But more significantly the perpetrator of these attacks revealed an approach to magic that I had learned was symptomatic of Angier. He was almost exclusively concerned with the magical secret, what magicians call the 'gimac' or 'gimmick'. If a trick depended on a concealed shelf behind the magician's table, that alone would be the focus of Angier's interest, not the imaginative use to which it might be put. No matter what else might cause strife between us, it was Angier's fundamentally flawed and limited understanding of magical technique that was at the heart of our dispute. The wonder of magic lies not in the technical secret, but in the skill with which it is performed.

And it was for this reason that THE NEW TRANSPORTED MAN was the one illusion of mine he never publicly attacked. It was beyond him. He simply could not work out how it was done, partly because I have kept the secret secure, but mostly because of the way in which I perform it.

16

An illusion has three stages.

First there is the setup, in which the nature of what might be attempted is hinted at, or suggested, or explained. The apparatus is seen. Volunteers from the audience sometimes participate in the preparation. As the trick is being set up, the magician will make every possible use of misdirection.

The performance is where the magician's lifetime of practice, and his innate skill as a performer, conjoin to produce the magical display.

The third stage is sometimes called the effect, or the prestige, and this is the product of magic. If a rabbit is pulled from a hat, the rabbit, which apparently did not exist before the trick was performed, can be said to be the prestige of that trick.

THE NEW TRANSPORTED MAN is fairly unusual among illusions in that the setup and performance are what most intrigue audiences, critics and my magical colleagues, while for me, the performer, the prestige is the main preoccupation.

Illusions fall into different categories or types, of which there are only six (setting aside the specialist field of mentalist illusion). Every trick that has ever been performed falls into one or more of the following categories:

1. *Production*: the magical creation of somebody or something out of nothing,
2. *Disappearance*: the magical vanishing of somebody or something into nothing,
3. *Transformation*: the apparent changing of one thing into another,
4. *Transposition*: the apparent changing of place of two or more objects,
5. *Defiance of Natural Laws*: for example, seeming to defeat gravity, making one solid object appear to pass through another, producing a large number of objects or people from a source apparently too small to have held them, and
6. *Secret Motive Power*: causing objects to appear to move of their own will, such as making a chosen playing card rise mysteriously out of the pack.

THE NEW TRANSPORTED MAN is not entirely typical, because it uses at least four of the above categories. Most stage illusions depend on only one or two. I once saw an elaborate effect on the Continent where five of the categories were employed.

Finally, there are the techniques of magic.

The methods available to magicians cannot be so neatly categorised as the other elements, because when it comes to technique a good magician will not disdain anything.

Magical technique can be as simple as the placing of one object behind another so that it may no longer be seen by the audience, and it can be so complex that it requires advance setting up in the theatre and the collusion of a team of assistants and stooges.

The magician can choose from an inventory of traditional techniques. The playing cards that have been 'gimmicked' so that one or more cards will be forced into use, the eye-dazzling backcloth that allows much necessary magical business to go on unnoticed, the black-painted table or prop that the audience cannot see properly, dummies and doubles and stooges and substitutes and blinds. And an inventive magician will embrace novelty. Any new device or toy or invention that comes into the world should provoke the thought: 'How could I make a new trick with that?' Thus, in the recent past we have seen new tricks that employ the reciprocating engine, the telephone, electricity, and one remarkable effect memorably created with Dr Warble's smoke-bomb toy.

Magic has no mystery to magicians. We work variations of standard methods. What will seem new or baffling to an audience is simply a technical challenge for other professionals. If an innovative new illusion is developed, it is only a matter of time before the effect is reproduced by others.

Every illusion can be explained, be it by the use of a concealed compartment, by an adroitly placed mirror, by an assistant planted in the audience to act as 'volunteer', or by simple misdirection of the audience's attention.

Now I hold my hands before you, fingers spread so that you can see nothing is concealed within them, and say: THE NEW TRANSPORTED MAN is an illusion like every other, and it can be explained. But by a combination of a simple secret that has been kept securely, many years of practice, a certain amount of audience misdirection, and the use of conventional magic techniques it has become the keystone of my act and my career.

It has also defied Angier's best efforts to penetrate its mystery, as I shall soon record.

66

17

Sarah and I have been with the children on a short holiday along the south coast, & I took my notebook with me.

We went first to Hastings, because it is years since I was there, but we did not stay long. The place has started a decline that I fear will prove irreversible. Father's yard, which was sold on his death, has been sold again. Now it is a bakery. A lot of houses have been built in the valley behind the house, & a railway line to Ashford is soon to run through.

After Hastings we went to Bexhill. Then to Eastbourne. Then to Brighton. Then to Bognor.

My first comment on the notebook is that it was I who tried to humiliate Angier, & I, in turn, who was humiliated by him. Other than this detail, which is after all not too important, I think my account of what happened is accurate, even in its other details.

I am putting in a lot of comments about the secret, & therefore making much of it. This strikes me as ironic, after I went to such pains to emphasise how trivial most magical secrets really are.

I do not think my secret is trivial. It is easily guessed, as Angier has apparently done, in spite of what I have written. Others have probably guessed too.

Anyone who reads this narrative will probably work it out for themselves.

What cannot be guessed is the *effect* the secret has had on my life. This is the real reason Angier will never solve the whole mystery, unless I myself give him the answer. He would never credit the extent to which my life has been shaped towards holding the secret intact. That is what matters.

So long as I can continue to monitor how it is being written, then I may proceed with my account of how the illusion looks to the audience.

18

THE NEW TRANSPORTED MAN is an illusion whose appearance has changed over the years, but whose method has always remained the same.

It has progressively involved two cabinets, or two boxes, or two tables, or two benches. One is situated in the downstage area, the other is upstage. The exact positioning is not crucial, and will vary from one theatre to the next, depending on the size and shape of the stage area. The only important feature of their positioning is that both pieces should be clearly and widely separated from each other. The apparatus is brightly lit and in full view of the audience from beginning to end.

I shall describe the oldest, and therefore the simplest, version of the trick, when I was using closed cabinets. At that time I called the illusion THE TRANSPORTED MAN.

Then, as now, my act was brought to its climax with this illusion, and only details have changed since. I shall therefore describe it as if the early version were still in my current act.

Both cabinets are brought on to the stage, either by scene-shifters, assistants or in some cases volunteer members of the audience and both are shown to be empty. Volunteers are allowed to step through them, open not only the doors but the hinged rear walls, and peer into the wheeled space below. The cabinets are rolled to their respective positions and closed.

After a short, humorous preamble (delivered in my French accent) about the desirability of being in two places at once, I go to the nearer of the two cabinets, the first, and open the door.

It is, of course, still empty. I take a large, brightly coloured inflatable ball from my props table, and bounce it a couple of times to show how vigorously it moves. I step into the first cabinet, leaving the door open for the time being.

Reaching out through the door I bounce the ball in the direction of the second cabinet.

From within, I *slam closed* the door of the first cabinet.

From within, I *push open* the door of the second cabinet, and step out. I catch the ball as it bounces towards me.

As the ball enters my hands the first cabinet collapses, the door and three walls folding out dramatically to show that it is completely empty.

Holding the ball I step forward to the footlights, and acknowledge my applause.

19

Let me briefly rehearse my life and career up to the last years of the century.

By the time I was 18 I had left home and was working the music halls as a full-time magician. However, even with help from Mr Maskelyne, jobs were hard to find, and I became neither famous nor rich and I did not earn my own place on the bill for several years. Much of the stage work I did was assisting other magicians with their performances, but for a long time I paid the rent by designing and building cabinets and other magical apparatus. My father's cabinet-making training stood me in good stead. I built a reputation as a reliable inventor and *ingénieur* of stage illusions.

In 1879 my mother died, followed a year later by my father.

By the end of the 1880s, when I was in my early thirties, I had developed my own solo act and adopted the stage name Le Professeur de Magie. I regularly performed THE TRANSPORTED MAN in its various early forms.

Although the working of the illusion was never a problem, I was for a long time dissatisfied with the stage effects. It always seemed to me that closed cabinets were not sufficiently mysterious to raise audience expectations of peril and impossibility. In the context of stage magic such cabinets are commonplace. I gradually found ways of elaborating the illusion; first to boxes that looked barely large enough to hold me, later to tables with concealing flaps, then finally, in a bravura move to 'open' magic, much applauded in magic circles at the time, I used flat benches on which my body could be seen by everyone in the audience up to the moment of transformation.

In 1892, though, came the idea I had been seeking. It happened indirectly, and the seed it sowed took a long time to germinate.

A Balkan inventor by the name of Nikola Tesla came to London in the February of that year to promote certain new effects he was then pioneering in the field of electricity. A Croatian of Serbian descent, with an allegedly impenetrable foreign accent, Tesla was to deliver several lectures about his speciality to the scientific community. Such events occur fairly frequently in London, and normally I would take little notice of them. However, in this case it turned out that Mr Tesla was a controversial figure in the USA, involved in scientific disputes about the nature and application of electricity, and it ensured him widespread reporting in the newspapers. It was from these articles that I was to glean my ideas.

What I had always needed was a spectacular stage effect, partly to highlight the effect of The Transported Man, and partly to mask its working. I gathered from the news reports that Mr Tesla was able to generate high voltages which could be made to flash and spark about, harmlessly and without incurring burns.

After Mr Tesla had left to return to the United States his influence remained behind him. It was not too long before London and other cities began supplying small amounts of electricity to those who could afford to buy it. Because of its revolutionary nature, electricity was often in the news, being applied to this task or solving that problem, and so on. Some time later, when I heard that Angier was mounting an imitation of The Transported Man, I began to think I should develop the illusion once again. I realised that without much difficulty I could probably include electricity in my act and I began a search through the obscure stocks of London scientific dealers. With the assistance of Tommy Elbourne, my *ingénieur*, I eventually managed to build stage equipment for THE NEW TRANSPORTED MAN. I was to go on adding to and improving it for years afterwards, but by 1896 the new effect had permanently entered my stage show. It caused a commotion of acclaim, ringing cash tills and fruitless speculation as to my secret. My illusion worked in a blinding flash of electrical light.

20

I will backtrack a little. In October 1891 I had married Sarah Henderson, whom I had met while I was taking part in a charity show performed in a Salvation Army hostel in Aldgate. She was one of the volunteer helpers, and during the interval in our performance she had sat informally with me while we both drank tea. My card tricks had amused her, and she teasingly challenged me to perform some more for her alone, so that she might see how I did them. Because she was young and pretty I did so, and greatly enjoyed the bafflement I saw in her eyes.

However, this was not only the first time I performed magic for her, it was also the last. My skill as a prestidigitator simply became irrelevant to our feelings about each other. We became walking-out companions soon after our meeting, and it was not long before we admitted to each other that we were in love. Sarah has no background in the theatre or the music halls, and in fact was a young woman of good birth. It is a testament to her devotion to me that even after her father threatened to disinherit her, which of course he eventually did, she remained true to me.

After our marriage we moved to rented rooms in the

Bayswater area of London, but we did not have long to wait before success smiled on me. In 1893 we bought the large house in St Johns Wood where we have lived ever since. In the same year our twin children, Graham and Helena, were born.

I have always kept my professional life separate from my family life. During the period I am describing I practised my profession from my office and workshop in Elgin Avenue, and when touring shows took me abroad or to remoter parts of Britain I did not take Sarah with me. When based in London, or when between shows, I lived quietly and contentedly at home with her.

I stress my contented domestic life because of what was soon to happen.

Shall I continue?

21

I think I must; yes. I suspect I know to what I am referring here.

22

I had been advertising in theatrical journals for a replacement lady assistant, because my existing young woman, Georgina Harris, was planning to marry. I always dreaded the upheaval caused by the arrival of a new member of my staff, especially one so important as the stage assistant. When Olive Wenscombe wrote and applied for an interview she did not seem immediately suitable, and her letter went unanswered for some time.

She was, she said in her letter, twenty-six. This was a little older than I should have preferred, and she went on to describe herself as a trained *danseuse* who had moved over to the work of magical assistant. Many illusionists do employ dance artistes because of their fit and supple bodies, but I have usually employed young women with specific magical experience, rather than those who took it up simply because a job had been offered to them. Nevertheless, Olive Wenscombe's letter came during one of those times when good assistants were hard to find, and so I finally made an appointment with her.

The work of magician's assistant is not one to which many people are suited. A young woman has to possess certain physical characteristics. She has to be young, of course, and if not naturally pretty then she has to have pleasing features that are capable of being made up to look pretty. In addition she has to have a slim, lithe and strong body. She has to be willing to stand, crouch, kneel or lie in confined places, often for several minutes at a time, and on release appear perfectly relaxed and unmarked by her period of enclosure. Above all, she has to be willing to endure the unusual demands and strange requests made to her by her employer, in pursuit of his illusions.

Olive Wenscombe's interview took place, as did all such, at my workshop in Elgin Avenue. Here, in opened cabinets and mirrored cubes and curtained alcoves, were laid bare many of the incidental secrets of my business. Although I never made a point of showing any of my staff exactly how a trick was worked, unless of course that knowledge was crucial to their part in it, I wanted them to understand that each trick had a rational explanation behind it and that I knew what I was doing. Some stage illusions, and some of those that I performed, used knives or swords or even firearms, and from the auditorium looked dangerous. THE NEW TRANSPORTED MAN, in particular, with its explosive electrical reactions and clouds of carbon discharge, regularly scares the wits out of the front six rows at any performance! But I wanted no one who worked for me to feel at risk. The only illusion whose secret I guarded fastidiously was THE NEW

73

TRANSPORTED MAN itself, and its working was concealed even from the young woman who shared the stage with me until the moment before the illusion began.

It should be clear from this that I do not work entirely alone, nor does any modern illusionist. In addition to my stage assistants, I had working for me Thomas Elbourne, my irreplaceable *ingénieur*, and two of his own young artisans, who helped him build and maintain the apparatus. Thomas had been in my employ almost from the start. Before he worked for me he had been at the Egyptian Hall, under Maskelyne.

(Thomas Elbourne knew my most guarded secret; he had to. But I trusted him; I had to. I say this as simply as possible, to convey the simplicity of my belief in him. Thomas had worked with magicians all his life, and nothing any more surprised him. There is little I know about magic today that I did not learn from him one way or the other. Yet never once, in all the years I worked with him – he retired several years ago – did he ever explicitly reveal the secret of another magician to me or to anyone else. To call his trust into question would be to question my very sanity. Thomas was a Londoner from Tottenham, a married man without children. He was many years older than me, but I never discovered exactly how many. At the time Olive Wenscombe began working for me I assume he must have been in his middle or late sixties.)

I decided to employ Olive Wenscombe almost as soon as she arrived. She was neither tall nor broad, but had an attractive and slim body. She held her head erect as she walked or stood, and her face had well-defined features. She was American-born, and had an accent she identified as East Coast, but had lived and worked in London for several years. I introduced her as informally as possible to Thomas Elbourne and Georgina Harris, then asked to see whatever references she might have brought with her. I generally gave references a great deal of weight when choosing an applicant, because a recommendation from a magician whose work I knew would almost certainly gain the applicant the job. Olive had brought two such references with her. One was from a magician working the resort towns of Sussex and Hampshire, whose name I did not recognise, but the other was from Joseph Buatier de Kolta, one of the greatest living performers. I was, I admit, impressed. I quietly passed de Kolta's letter to Thomas Elbourne, and watched his expression.

'How long did you work for Monsieur de Kolta?' I asked her.

'Only for five months,' she said. 'I was hired for a tour of Europe, and he let me go at the end of it.'

'So I see.'

After that, employing her was something of a formality, but even so I felt I had to subject her to the usual tests. It was for these that Georgina had come along to the audition, as it would not be right to ask any applicant, even one as experienced as Olive Wenscombe, to demonstrate her abilities without the presence of a chaperone.

'Did you bring a rehearsal costume with you?' I said.

'Yes, sir, I did.'

'Then if you would be so kind—'

A few minutes later, wearing a body-hugging costume, Olive Wenscombe was led by Thomas to a few of our cabinets, and asked to take up position inside one. The production of a living, healthy young woman from what appears to be an empty cabinet is one of the traditional stand-bys of magic. To bring off the effect, the assistant has to insinuate herself into a concealed compartment, and the smaller this compartment can be the more surprising the effect of the illusion. Careful choice of a voluminous costume, and one that is made of bright colours and has glittery ribbons sewn into the fabric, to catch and reflect the limelight, will enhance the mystery. It was obvious to us all that Olive was well versed in secret compartments and panels. Thomas took her first to our PALANQUIN (which even by that time we rarely used in the act, since the trick had become so well known), and she knew exactly where the hidden compartment was and promptly climbed into it.

Thomas and I next asked her to essay the illusion known as VANITY FAIR, in which a young woman is apparently made to pass through a solid mirror. This is not a difficult illusion to perform, but it does require agility and quickness of movement on the part of the girl. Although Olive said she had not taken part in it before, once we had explained the mechanism she showed she could wriggle through with commendable speed.

There remained only the need to test her for physical size, although by this time I think both Thomas and I would have rebuilt some of the apparatus for her had she proved too large. We need not have worried. Thomas placed her inside the cabinet used in the illusion called THE DECAPITATED PRINCESS (a notoriously tight fit for most assistants, and requiring several minutes of uncomfortable immobility), but she was able to climb in and out smoothly, and said she would not find it distressing to be kept inside during a performance.

Sufficient to say that Olive Wenscombe proved herself most suitable by all the usual tests, and as soon as these preliminaries were concluded I retained her at the customary wage. Within a week I had trained her to perform in all the illusions in my repertoire where she would be needed. In due course, Georgina left to marry her beau, and Olive took her place as my full-time assistant.

23

How neat it all seems when I write it down, how calm & professional! Now I have written the 'official' version of Olive, let me under our Pact add the ineradicable truth, the truth I have so far concealed from all those who matter most. Olive nearly made a fool of me, & the true account must be appended.

Georgina wasn't present at the audition, of course. Nor

was I. Tommy Elbourne was there, but as always he kept out of the way. She & I were effectively alone in my workshop.

I asked Olive about a costume, & she said she hadn't brought one. She looked me straight in the eye when she said this, & there was a long silence while I thought about what that meant & what *she* must think about what it meant. No young woman applying for the job would expect to be hired without being measured or fitted or tried out in some way. Applicants always brought a rehearsal costume.

Well, Olive apparently had not. Then she said, 'I don't need a costume, honey.'

'There is no chaperone present, my dear,' I said.

'I guess you can put up with that!' she said.

She promptly took off her outer clothes, & what she was wearing beneath was of the boudoir; she was left in garments that were immodest, loose-fitting & prone to accidents. I took her to the PALANQUIN, where although she obviously knew what it was & where she had to conceal herself, she asked me to help her climb inside. This required much intimate handling of her semi-clad body! The same happened when I showed her the mechanism of VANITY FAIR. Here she pretended to stumble as she came through the trap, & fell into my arms. The rest of the interview was conducted on the couch at the back of the workshop. Tommy Elbourne left quietly, without either of us noticing. He was not there afterwards, anyway.

The rest is substantially correct. I took her on as my assistant, & she learned how to operate all the illusions in which I needed her.

24

My performance always opens with the CHINESE LINKING RINGS. It is a routine which is a pleasure to work, and audiences love to watch it, no matter if they have seen it before. The rings gleam brightly in the limelight, they jingle metallically against each other, the rhythmic movements of the prestidigitator's hands and arms and the gentle linking and unlinking of the rings seem almost to Mesmerise the audience. It is a trick impossible to see through, unless you are standing a few inches away from the performer and are able to snatch the rings away from him. It always charms, always creates that electrifying sense of mystery and miracle.

With this accomplished I roll forward the MODERN CABINET, which has been standing upstage. A yard or so from the footlights I rotate the cabinet to show both sides and the back. I make sure that I am seen to pass behind it, to that the audience may glimpse my feet through the gap between the stage and the floor of the cabinet. They have seen that no one was clinging to the back of the cabinet, and now they can satisfy themselves that no one may be secreted beneath it. When I fling open the door to reveal the interior, then step inside to release the catch that holds the rear panel in place, the audience can see right through from front to back. They see me pass through, likewise from front to back, and close the back wall once more. The door hangs open, and while I am apparently busy behind the cabinet they take their chance to peer more intently at the interior. There is nothing for them to see: the cabinet is, must be, completely empty. Quickly, then, I slam the front door closed, rotate the cabinet on its castors, and throw open the door. Inside – beautiful, large, bulkily dressed, smiling and waving her arms, entirely filling the cramped interior of the cabinet – is a young woman. She steps down, takes her bow to thunderous applause and leaves the stage.

I roll the cabinet to the side of the stage, whence it is quietly retrieved by Thomas Elbourne.

So to the next. This is less spectacular, but involves two or three members of the audience. Every magic act includes a few moments with a pack of cards. The magician must show his skill with sleight of hand, otherwise he runs the risk of being thought by his professional colleagues merely to be an operator of self-working machinery. I walk to the footlights, and the curtains close behind me. This is partly to create a closed, intimate atmosphere for the card tricks, but mainly so that behind them Thomas may be setting up the apparatus for THE NEW TRANSPORTED MAN.

With the cards finished, I need to break the feeling of quiet concentration, and so I move swiftly into a series of colourful productions. Flags, streamers, fans, balloons and silk scarves stream out unstoppably from my hands, sleeves and pockets, creating a bright and chaotic display all around me. My female assistant walks on stage behind me, apparently to clear away some of the streamers, but in reality to slip me more of the compressed materials for release. By the end, the brightly coloured papers and silks are inches deep around my feet. I acknowledge the applause.

While the audience is still clapping the curtains open behind me, and in semi-darkness my apparatus for THE NEW TRANSPORTED MAN may be seen. My assistants move quickly on to the stage, and deftly clear away the coloured streamers.

I return to the footlights, face the audience and address them directly, in my fractured, French-accented English. I explain that what I am about to perform has become possible only since the discovery of electricity. The performance draws power from the bowels of the Earth. Unimaginable forces are at work, that even I do not fully comprehend. I explain that they are about to witness a veritable miracle, one in which life and death are chanced with, as in the game of dice my ancestors played to avoid the tumbril.

While I speak the stage lights brighten, and catch the polished metal supports, the golden coils of wire, the glistening globes of glass. The apparatus is a thing of beauty, but it is a menacing beauty because everyone by now has heard for themselves of some of the deadly power of the electrical current. Newspapers have carried accounts of horrible deaths and burns caused by the new force already available in many cities.

The apparatus of THE NEW TRANSPORTED MAN is designed to remind them of these appalling accounts. It carries numerous incandescent electric lamps, some of which come alight even as I speak. At one side is a large glass globe, inside which a brilliant arc of electricity fizzes and crackles excitingly. The main part of the apparatus appears, to the audience, to be a long wooden bench, three feet above the floor of the stage. They can see past it, around it, underneath it. At one end, by the arc-lit glass chamber, a small raised platform is bestrewn with dangling wires, their bare ends dangerously exposed. Above the platform is a canopy where many of the incandescent lamps are placed. At the further end is a metal cone, decorated with a spiral of smaller glowing lamps. This is mounted on a gimbals device that allows it to be swivelled in several directions. All around the main part are small concavities and shelves, where bare terminals lie in wait. The whole thing is emitting a loud humming noise, as of immense hidden energies within.

I explain to the audience that I would invite some of its members on to the stage to examine the device for themselves, but for the immense danger to them. I hint at earlier accidents. Instead, I say, I have devised a few simple demonstrations of the power inherent within the machine. I allow some magnesium powder to fall across two bared contacts, and a brilliant white flash momentarily blinds the members of the audience closest to the stage! While the smoke from it balloons upwards I take a sheet of paper and drop it across another semi-concealed part of the apparatus. It immediately bursts into flame and its smoke also rises dramatically to the rigging loft above. The humming sound increases in volume. The apparatus seems to be alive, only barely constraining the frightful energies that lie within.

At stage left my female assistant appears with a wheeled cabinet. This is strongly made of wood, but because it is built on wheels she is able to turn the thing around so it might be seen from all sides. Then she lets down the front and sides to show that it is empty.

I grimace sadly at the audience then signal to the girl, who brings to me two immense dark-brown gauntlets, made to seem as if they are of leathern material. When these are covering my hands she leads me to the apparatus, until I stand behind it. The audience can see most of my body still, and satisfy themselves that there are no concealed mirrors or shields. I lower my two gauntleted hands to the surface of the platform, and as I do so the sound of electrical tension increases, and there is another brilliant discharge of electrical energy. I reel back, as if in shock.

The girl moves away from the apparatus, cowering a little. I break off from my introduction to plead with her to leave the stage for her own safety. At first she resists, then gladly hurries into the wings.

I reach up to the directional cone, grip it gingerly with my heavily gauntleted hands, and move it with great care until its apex is pointed directly at the cabinet.

The illusion is approaching its climax. From the orchestra pit there comes a roll of drums. I place both hands on the platform once more, and magically all the remaining lamps shine out brightly. The sinister hum increases. I first sit on the platform, and swivel around so that I can stretch my legs out, then lower myself until I am lying full length, surrounded by the evidence of the terrible electrical forces.

I raise my arms, and pull off first one, then the other gauntlet. As I lower my arms I allow my hands to droop below the level of the platform. One of them, the one the audience can see, falls casually into the receptacle where, a few seconds earlier, a piece of paper had been ignited.

There is a brilliant, blinding flash of light, and all the lights on the apparatus fuse into darkness.

In the same instant . . . I vanish from the platform.

The cabinet bursts open, and I am seen hunched up inside.

I roll slowly out of the cabinet, and collapse on to the floor, bathed in stage lights. Gradually I come to my senses. I stand. I blink in the brightness of the lights. I face the audience. I turn towards the platform, indicate where I had been, turn back to the cabinet immediately behind me, and indicate where I had arrived.

I take my bow.

The audience has seen me transmogrified. Before their eyes I was catapulted by the power of electricity from one part of the stage to another. Ten feet of empty space. Twenty feet, thirty feet, depending on the size of the stage.

A human body transmitted in an instant. A miracle, an impossibility, an illusion.

My assistant returns to the stage. Clasping her hand I am smiling and bowing as the applause rings out and the curtains close before me.

25

If I say no more of this, it will be acceptable. I shall not intervene again. I may continue to the conclusion.

26

Life in my flat in Hornsey, an area of north London several miles from my house in St Johns Wood, left much to be desired. I had chosen the flat, one of ten in an apartment house in a quiet side-street, simply because its anonymity seemed to fulfil my needs. It was on the second floor at the rear of a modest, mid-century building, occupying one of the corners, so that although it had several windows looking out into the surrounding small garden, entry to it was by a single plain door leading off the stairwell.

Not long after I had taken up occupancy, I began to regret the choice. Most of the other tenants were lower-middle-class families, running modest households; all the other flats on my floor had children living in them, for instance, and there was much coming and going of domestic servants of one kind or another. My single state, especially in a flat of

such a size, obviously aroused the curiosity of my neighbours. Although I gave out every sign of wishing not to be
drawn into conversations, some were nevertheless inevitable
and soon I felt exposed to their speculations about me. I
knew I should move to another address, but at the time I first
took the flat I craved to have a steady place in which I could
stay between performances, and even if I were to move I
knew there would be no guarantee I would not attract
curiosity elsewhere. I decided to adopt a pretence of polite
neutrality, and came and went discreetly, neither mixing too
much with my neighbours nor appearing secretive in my
movements. Eventually I believe I became dull to them. The
English have a traditional tolerance of eccentrics, and my
late-night arrivals, my solitary presence without servants, my
unexplained method of making my living, came eventually
to seem harmless and familiar.

All this aside, I found life in the flat disagreeable for a
long time after I first moved in. I had rented it unfurnished,
and because I was necessarily sinking most of my earnings
into the family house in St Johns Wood, I could at first only
afford cheap and uncomfortable furniture. The main source
of heating was a stove, for which logs had to be brought up
from the yard below, and which provided fierce heat in the
immediate vicinity and none at all discernible in any other
part of the flat. There were no carpets to speak of.

Because the flat was a refuge for me, it was essential that I
should make it a comfortable place to live in, and convenient
for living quietly, sometimes for long periods at a time.

The physical discomforts aside, which of course began to
ease as I was able to acquire the various practical things I
wanted, the worst of it was the loneliness and the feeling
of being cut off from my family. There has never been any
cure for this, then or now. At first, when it was just Sarah
from whom I was separated, it was intolerable enough, but
during her difficult confinement with the twins I was often in
agonies of worry about her. It became even more difficult,
after Graham and Helena were born, especially when one
of them fell ill. I knew my family was being cared for and

looked after with love, and that our servants were dedicated and trustworthy, and that should the worst illnesses occur we had sufficient funds to be able to afford the best treatment, but none of this was ever quite enough, even though such thoughts did provide a measure of consolation and reassurance.

In the years when I had been planning THE TRANSPORTED MAN and its modern sequel, and my overall magical career, it had never occurred to me that having a family might one day threaten to make it unworkable.

Many times I have been tempted to give up the stage, never perform the illusion again, abandon, in effect, the performance of magic altogether, and always because I have felt calls of affection and duty to my lovely wife, and of fervent love for my children.

In those long days in the Hornsey flat, and sometimes in the weeks when the theatrical season gave no openings for my act, I had more than abundant time to reflect.

The significant point is, of course, that I did not give up.

I kept going through the difficult early years. I kept going when my reputation and earnings began to soar. And I keep going now when, to all intents and purposes, most of what remains of my famous illusion is the mystery that surrounds it.

However, things have been a lot easier recently. During the first two weeks that Olive Wenscombe was working for me I happened to discover that she was staying in a commercial hotel near Euston Station, a most dubious address. Explaining why, she told me that the Hampshire magician had provided lodgings with his job, but she had of course given these up when she left his employ. By this time, Olive and I were making regular intimate use of the couch at the rear of my workshop. It did not take me long to realise I too might be able to offer her permanent lodgings.

The Pact controlled all decisions of such a nature, but in this case it was just a formality. A few days later, Olive moved into my flat in Hornsey. There she stayed, and has stayed, ever since.

Her revelation, that was to change everything, came a few weeks after she arrived.

27

Towards the end of 1898 a theatre cancellation meant that I had to spend more than a week between performances of THE NEW TRANSPORTED MAN. I passed the time in the Hornsey flat, and although I went across to the workshop once, for most of the week I was ensconced happily with Olive. We began redecorating the flat, and with some of the recent proceeds of a successful run at the Illyria Theatre in the West End we bought several attractive items of furniture.

The night before the idyll was to end – I was due to take my show to the Hippodrome in Brighton – she sprung her surprise. It was late at night, and we were resting companionably together before falling asleep.

'Listen, hon,' she said. 'I've been thinking you might want to start looking around for a new assistant.'

I was so thunderstruck that at first I did not know how to answer. Until that moment it had seemed to me I had reached the kind of stability I had been seeking all my working life. I had my family, I had my mistress. I lived in my house with my wife, and I stayed in my flat with my lover. I worshipped my children, adored my wife, loved my mistress. My life was in two distinct halves, kept emphatically apart, neither side suspecting the other even existed. In addition, my lover worked as my beautiful and bewitching stage assistant. She was not only brilliant at her job but her lovely appearance, I was certain, had doubtless helped me obtain the much larger audiences I had been playing to since she joined me. In popular parlance, I had my cake and was greedily eating it. Now, with those words, Olive seemed to be unbalancing everything, and I was thrown into dismay.

Seeing my reaction, Olive said, 'I got a lot I want to get off my chest. It isn't so bad as maybe you think.'

'I can't imagine how it could be much worse.'

'Well, if you hear half of what I say, it'll be worse than you ever imagined, but if you stick around to hear it all, I guess you'll end up feeling good.'

I took a careful look at her and noticed, as I should have done from the start, that she seemed tense and keyed up. Clearly, something was afoot.

The story came out in a flood of words, quickly confirming her warning. What she said filled me with horror.

She began by saying that she wanted to stop working for me for two reasons. The first was that she had been treading the boards for several years, and simply wanted a change. She said she wished to live at home, be my lover, follow my career from that standpoint. She said she would continue to work as my assistant as long as I asked her to, or until I could find a replacement. So far so good. But, she said, I hadn't yet heard the second reason. This was that she had been sent to work for me by someone who wanted her to find out my professional secrets and pass them on to him. This man, she said—

'It's Angier!' I exclaimed. 'You were sent to spy on me by Rupert Angier?'

To this she readily confessed and on seeing my anger she moved back and away from me, then began to weep. My mind was racing as I tried to remember everything I had said to her in the preceding weeks, and to recall what apparatus she had seen or used, what secrets she might have learned or discovered for herself, and what she might have been able to communicate back to my enemy.

For a time I became unable to listen to her, unable to think calmly or logically. For much of the same time she was weeping, imploring me to listen to her.

Two or three hours passed in this distressing and unproductive way, then at last we reached a point of emotional numbness. Our impasse had lasted into the small hours of the morning, and the need for sleep loomed heavily over us both. We turned out the light, and lay down together, our habits not yet broken by the terrible revelation.

I lay awake in the darkness, trying to think how to cope with this, but my mind was still circling distractedly. Then out of the dark beside me I heard her say quietly, insistently, 'Don't you realise that if I was still Rupert Angier's spy I would not have told you? Yes, I was with him but I was *bored* with him. And he'd been messing around with some other lady, and it kind of annoyed me. All the time he was obsessed with attacking you, and I needed a change and so I cooked up this idea myself. But when I met you . . . well, I felt differently. You're so unlike Rupert in everything. You know what happened, and all that was real between us, right? Rupert thinks I'm spying for him, but I guess by now he's realised he isn't going to hear anything back from me. I want to stop being your assistant because so long as I'm up there doing the act with you, Rupert's waiting for me to do what he wants. I just want to get out of it all, live here in this apartment, be with you, Alfred. You know, I think I love you . . .'

And so on, long into the night.

In the morning, in the grey and dispiriting light of a rainy dawn, I said to her, 'I have decided what to do. Why don't you take a message back to Angier? I will tell you what to say, and you will deliver it, telling him it's the secret for which he has been searching. You may say whatever you wish to make him believe that you stole the secret from me, and that it is the prime information he has been seeking. After that, if you return, and if you then swear that you will never again have anything to do with Angier, and if, *and only if*, you can make me believe you, then we will start our lives together again. Do you agree?'

'I will do it today,' she swore. 'I want to put him out of my life forever!'

'First I have to go to my workshop. I have to decide what I can safely tell Angier.'

Without further explanation I left her in the flat and took the omnibus to Elgin Avenue. Sitting quietly on the

87

top deck, smoking my pipe, I wondered if I was indeed a fool in love, and that I was just about to throw away everything.

The problem was discussed in full when I arrived at the workshop. Although potentially serious, it was just one of several crises the Pact has had to confront over the years, and I felt no great or novel problem was being presented this time. It was not easy, but at the end of it the Pact emerged as strong as ever. Indeed, as a recordable testament of my continued faith in the Pact, I can say that it was I who remained in the workshop while I returned to the flat.

Here I dictated to Olive what she should inscribe on the sheet of paper, in her own handwriting. She wrote it down, tense but determined to do what she saw as necessary. The message was intended to send Angier searching in the wrong direction, so it needed to be not only plausible but something he would not have thought of on his own.

She left Hornsey with the message at 2.25 p.m., and did not return to the flat until after 11.00 p.m.

'It is done!' she cried. 'He has the information I gave him. I shall likely never see him again, and I certainly shall never again, in this lifetime, speak a friendly word of, about or to him.'

28

I never enquired what had taken place during those eight and a half hours she was absent, and why it had taken her so long to deliver a written message. The explanation she gave is probably the true one for being the simplest, that with the time taken to travel about London on public transport, and with not finding Angier immediately, and with discovering that he was in performance in another part of the city, the time was innocently used up. But as that long evening went by I harboured many grim fantasies that the double agent I had turned against her first master might have doubled back once more, and either I should never see her again or that she would return with a renewed subversive mission on his behalf.

However, all this occurred at the end of 1898, and I write these words at the end of the momentous month of January 1901. (The events in the outside world resound in my ears. The day before I penned these words Her Majesty the Queen was finally laid to rest, and the country is at last emerging from a period of mourning.) Olive returned to me more than two years ago, true as her word, and she remains with me, true to my wishes. My career continues smoothly, my position in the world of illusions is unassailable, my family is growing, my wealth is assured. Once again I run two peaceful households. Rupert Angier has not attacked me since Olive passed him the false information. All is quiet around me, and after the turbulent years I am at last settled in my life.

29

I write once more, this time unwillingly, in the year 1903. I had planned to leave my notebook closed forever, but events have conspired against me.

Rupert Angier has died suddenly. He was forty-six, only a year younger than myself. His death, according to a notice in *The Times*, was caused by complications following injuries incurred while performing a stage illusion at a theatre in Suffolk.

I scoured this notice, and a shorter one that appeared in the *Morning Post*, for what information I might at last discover about him, but there was little that was new to me.

I had already suspected he was ill. The last time I saw him in the flesh he had a frail look about him, and I guessed he was the victim of some debilitating chronic ailment.

I can summarise the published obituaries, which I have

before me as I write. He was born in Derbyshire in 1857, but moved to London at a young age, where he had subsequently worked for many years as an illusionist and prestidigitator, achieving a considerable measure of success. He had performed his act throughout the British Isles and Europe, and had toured the New World three times, the last occasion being earlier this year. He was credited with inventing several notable stage illusions, in particular one called BRIGHT MORNING (it involved releasing an assistant from what appeared to be a sealed flask held in full view of the audience), and this had been widely imitated. More recently, he had successfully devised an illusion called IN A FLASH, which he was performing at the time of the fatal accident. A master of legerdemain, Angier had been a popular performer at small or private gatherings. He was married, had fathered a son and two daughters, and until the end had lived with his family in the Highgate area of London. He had been performing regularly until the accident which led to his death.

30

It gives me no pleasure to write of Angier's death. It has come as a tragic climax to a sequence of events which had been building up for more than two years. I disdained to record any of them because, I regret to say, they had threatened to renew the unpleasantness that existed between us.

As I noted earlier, I had reached a state of pleasant equilibrium and stability in my life and career. I felt and sincerely believed that should Angier make any kind of attack or reprisal against me I could merely shrug it off. Indeed, I had every reason to believe that the trail of false clues offered in Olive's note to him was a concluding action between us. It was intended to put him off course, to send him searching for a secret that did not exist.

The fact that he vanished from my awareness for more than two years suggested my ruse had worked.

However, soon after I had completed the first part of this narrative I happened to notice a magazine review of a show taking place at the Finsbury Park Empire. Rupert Angier was one of the acts, and by all accounts was low on the bill. The notice mentioned him only in passing, observing 'it is good to acknowledge that his talent remains undimmed'. This in itself suggested that his career had been going through a hiatus.

Two or three months later, all had changed. One of the magic journals featured an interview with him, even publishing a photographic picture of him alongside. One of the daily newspapers referred in an editorial to the 'revival of the prestidigitator's art', pointing out that numerous magical acts were once again topping the bill in our music halls. Rupert Angier was mentioned by name, although so were several others.

Later still, because of the necessary delays in producing such things, one of the subscription magic journals published a detailed article about Angier. It described his present act as a triumphant departure in the art of open magic. His new illusion, called IN A FLASH, was singled out for special mention, and for expert critical acclaim. It was said to set new standards of technical brilliance, being such that unless Mr Angier himself chose to reveal the secrets of its workings, it was unlikely that any other illusionist would be able to reproduce its effect, at least in the foreseeable future. The same article mentioned that IN A FLASH was a significant development from 'previous efforts' in the field of transference illusions, and there was a slighting reference not only to THE NEW TRANSPORTED MAN but also to myself.

I tried, I honestly tried, to disregard such aggravation, but these mentions in the press were only the first of many to come. Unquestionably, Rupert Angier was at the top of our profession.

Naturally, I felt I should do something about it. Much of my work in recent months had involved touring, concentrating on smaller clubs and theatres in the provinces. I decided that to re-establish myself I needed a season at a prominent London theatre as a showcase for my skills. Such was the interest in stage illusions at this time that my booking agent had little difficulty arranging what promised to be a major show. The venue was the Lyric Theatre in the Strand, and I was placed top of the bill at a variety show scheduled to run for a week in September 1902.

We opened to a house that was half empty, and the next day our press notices were few and far between. Only three newspapers even mentioned me by name, and the least unfavourable comment referred to me as 'a proponent of a style of magic remarkable more for its nostalgic value than its innovative flair'. The houses for the next two nights were almost empty, and the show closed halfway through the week.

31

I decided I had to see Angier's new illusion for myself, and when I heard at the end of October that he was starting a two-week residence at the Hackney Empire I quietly bought myself a ticket in the stalls. The Empire is a deep, narrow theatre, with long constricted aisles and an auditorium kept fairly well in the dark throughout the performance, so it exactly suited my purposes. My seat had a good view of the stage, but I was not so close that Angier was likely to spot me there.

I took no exception to the main part of his perform-ance, in which he competently performed illusions from the standard magical repertoire. His style was good, his patter amusing, his assistant beautiful, and his showmanship above average. He was dressed in a well-made evening suit, and his hair was smartly brilliantined to a high gloss. It was during this part of his act, though, that I first observed the wasting that was affecting his face, and saw other clues that suggested an unwell state. He moved stiffly, and several times favoured his left arm as if it were weaker than the other.

Finally, after an admittedly amusing routine that involved a message written by a member of the audience appearing inside a sealed envelope, Angier came to the closing illusion. He began with a serious speech, which I scribbled down quickly into my notebook. Here is what he said:

Ladies and Gentlemen! As the new century moves apace we see around us on every side the miracles of science. These wonders multiply almost every day. By the end of the new century, which few here tonight shall live to see, what marvels will prevail? Men might fly, men might speak across oceans, men might travel across the firmament. Yet no miracle which science may produce can compare with the greatest wonders of all . . . the human mind and the human body.

Tonight, ladies and gentlemen, I shall attempt a magical feat that brings together the wonders of science and the wonders of the human mind. No other stage performer in the world can reproduce what you are about to witness for yourself!

With this he raised his good arm theatrically, and the curtains were swept apart. There, waiting in the limelight, was the apparatus I had come to see.

It was substantially larger than I had expected. Magicians normally prefer to work with compactly built apparatus so as to heighten the mystery of the uses to which they are put. Angier's equipment practically filled the stage area.

In the centre of the stage was an arrangement of three long metal legs, joined tripodally at the apex and supporting a shining metal globe about a foot and a half in diameter. There was just room beneath the apex of the tripod for a man to stand. Immediately above the apex, and below the globe, was a cylindrical wooden and metal contraption firmly attached to the joint. This cylinder was made of wooden slats with distinct gaps between them, and wound around hundreds of times with thin filaments of wires. From where I was sitting, I judged the cylinder to be at least four feet in height, and perhaps as many in diameter. It was slowly rotating, and catching and reflecting the stage lights into our eyes. Shards of light prowled the walls of the auditorium.

Surrounding the contraption, at a radial distance of about ten feet was a second circle of eight metal slats, again much wound around with wires. These were standing on the surface of the stage and concentric to the tripod. The slats were widely and evenly spaced, with a large gap between each one. The audience could see clearly into the main part of the apparatus.

I was totally unprepared for this, as I had been expecting some kind of magical cabinet of the same general size as the ones I used. Angier's apparatus was so immense that there was no room anywhere on the stage for a second concealing cabinet.

My magician's brain started racing, trying to anticipate what the illusion was to be, how it might differ from my own, and where the secret might lie. First impression – surprise at the sheer size of it. Second impression – the remarkable workaday quality of the apparatus. With the exception of the rotating cylinder just above the apex, there was no use of bright colours, distracting lights or areas of deliberate black. Most of the contraption appeared to be made of unvarnished wood or unbrightened metal. There were cords and wires running off in several directions. Third impression – no hint of what was to come. I have no idea what the apparatus was *intended* to look like. Magical apparatus often assumes commonplace shapes, to misdirect the audience. It will look like an ordinary table, for example, or a flight of steps, or a cabin trunk, but Angier's equipment made no concessions to familiarity.

Angier began his performance of the trick.

There appeared to be no mirrors on stage. Every part of the apparatus could be seen directly, and as Angier went through his preparations he roamed about the stage, walking through each of the gaps, passing momentarily behind the slats, always visible, always moving. I watched his legs, often the part of an illusionist's anatomy to observe closely when he moves around and particularly behind his apparatus (an inexplicable movement can indicate the presence of a mirror or some other device), but Angier's walk was relaxed and normal. There appeared to be no trapdoors that he could use. The stage was covered in a single large rubber sheet, making access to the mezzanine floor beneath the stage difficult.

Most curious of all, there was no apparent rationale to the illusion. Magical apparatus normally serves to set up or misdirect audience expectations. It consists of the box that is obviously too small to contain a human being (yet will turn out to do so), or the sheet of steel that apparently cannot be penetrated, or the locked trunk from which it would be impossible to escape. In every case, the illusionist confounds the exact assumptions that his audience has made from their own assessment of what they see before them. Angier's equipment looked like nothing ever seen before, and it was impossible to guess what it might be from simply looking at it.

Meanwhile, Angier strode around his stage set, still invoking the mysteries of science and life.

He resumed centre stage, and faced his audience.

'Good sirs, mesdames, I request of one of you, a volunteer. You need not fear for what might happen. I require you for a simple act of verification only.'

He stood in the glare of the footlights, leaning invitingly towards the members of the audience in the first rows of the *fauteuils*. I suppressed a sudden mad urge to rush forward and volunteer myself, so that I might have a closer look at his machinery, but I knew that if I should do so Angier would instantly recognise me, and probably bring his performance to a premature close.

After the usual nervous hesitation a man stepped forward and mounted the stage by the side ramp. As he did so, one of Angier's assistants walked on to the stage, carrying a tray laden with several articles, the purpose of which soon became apparent, as each one offered a means of marking or identifying. There were two or three wells filled with different coloured inks; there was a bowl of flour; there were some chalks; there were sticks of charcoal. Angier invited the volunteer to choose one, and when the man selected the bowl of flour, Angier turned his back on him and invited him to tip it across the back of his jacket. This the man did, with a cloud of white that drifted spectacularly in the stage lights.

Angier turned again to face the audience, and asked the volunteer to select one of the inks. The man chose the red. Angier held out his floury hands so that red ink might be poured across them.

Now distinctively marked, Angier requested the man to return to his seat. The stage lights dimmed, but for one brilliant shaft of light from a spot.

There was an unearthly crackling noise, as if the air itself were being split asunder, and to my amazement a bolt of blue-white electrical discharge abruptly curled out and away from the shining globe. The arc moved with a horrid suddenness and arbitrariness, dashing about inside the arena enclosed by the outer slats, into which Angier himself now walked. The crackling and snapping of the bolt seemed blessed with a vicious life of its own.

The electrical discharge abruptly doubled, then tripled, with the extra bolts snaking around, as if searching the enclosed space. One inevitably found Angier and instantly wrapped itself around him, seeming to illumine him with cyanic light that glowed not only around his body but also from within. He welcomed the shot of electricity, raising his good arm, turning about, allowing the snaking, hissing fire to encircle him and surround him.

More bolts of electricity appeared, fizzing malignantly around him. He disregarded these as he had disregarded the others. Each seemed to attack him in turn; one would snap back away from him like a raised whip, allowing another, or two others, to blaze across him and lash his body with ever-contorting fire.

The smell of this discharge was soon assaulting the audience. I breathed it with the others, mentally reeling from thoughts of what it might contain. It had an unearthly, atomic quality, as if it represented the liberation of a force hitherto forbidden to man, and now, released, exhaled the stench of sheer energy rampant.

As more streaming arcs of electricity swooped about him, Angier moved to the tripod at the heart of the inferno, directly beneath the source. Once here he seemed safe. Apparently unable or unwilling to double back on themselves, the brilliant arcs of light snapped away from him, and with ferocious bangs impacted on the larger, outer slats. In moments, each of these had one arc reaching across to it, fizzing and spitting with restless animation, but contained in its place.

So these eight dazzling streamers formed a kind of canopy above the arena in which Angier stood, alone. The spotlight was suddenly extinguished, and all other stage lights had been dimmed. He was illuminated only by the light that fell on him from the incandescent discharge. He stood immobile, his good arm raised, his head barely an inch or so below the metal cylinder whence all the electricity emanated. He was saying something, a declaration to the audience, but one that was lost to me in the noisy commotion that scorched the air above him.

He lowered his arms, and for two or three seconds stood in silence, submitting to the awful spectacle he had made.

Then he vanished.

One moment Angier was there; the next he was not. His apparatus made a shrieking, tearing sound, and appeared to shake, but with his going the bright shards of energy instantly died. The tendrils fizzed and popped like small fireworks, and then were gone. The stage fell into darkness.

I was standing; without fully realizing it I had been standing for some time. I, and the rest of the audience, stood there aghast. The man had disappeared in front of our eyes, leaving no trace.

I heard a commotion in the aisle behind me, and with everyone else I turned to see what was happening. There were too many heads and bodies, I could not see clearly, some kind of motion in the darkened auditorium! Thankfully, the house lights came on, and one of the manned spotlights turned from its position high above the boxes, and its shaft of light picked out what was going on.

Angier was there!

Members of the theatre's staff were hurrying down the aisle towards him, and some of the audience were trying to get to him, but he was on his feet and pushing them away from him.

He was staggering down the aisle, heading back towards the stage.

I tried to recover from the surprise, and quickly made estimates. No more than a second or two could have elapsed between his disappearance from the stage, and his reappearance in the aisle. I glanced to and from the stage, trying to work out the distance involved. My seat was at least sixty feet away from the front of the stage, and Angier had appeared well to the back of the aisle, close to one of the audience exits. He was a long way behind me, at least another forty feet.

Could he have dashed one hundred feet in a single second, while the darkness from the stage masked his movement?

It was then, and is now, a rhetorical question. Clearly he could not, without the use of magical techniques.

But which ones?

His progress along the aisle towards the stage briefly brought him level with me, where he stumbled on one of the steps before continuing onwards. I was certain he had not seen me, because self-evidently he had no eyes for anyone at all in the audience. His comportment was entirely that of a man wrapped in his own anguish; his face was tormented, his whole body moved as if racked with pain. He shambled like a drunk or an invalid, or a man finally exhausted with life. I saw the left arm he favoured hanging limply by his side, and the hand was smudged with flour, the red ink smeared into a dark mess. On the back of his jacket the burst of flour was still visible, still in the haphazard shape the volunteer had created when he slapped the bag against him, just a few seconds ago, and a hundred feet away.

We were all applauding, with many people cheering and whistling their approval, and as he neared the stage a second spotlight picked him out and tracked him up the ramp to the stage. He walked wearily to the centre of the stage, where at last he seemed to recover. Once more in the full glare of the stage lights he took his ovation, bowing to the audience, acknowledging them, blowing kisses, smiling and triumphant. I stood with the rest, marvelling at what I had seen.

Behind him, unobtrusively, the curtains were closing to conceal the apparatus.

32

I did not know how the trick was done! I had seen it with my own eyes, and I had watched in the knowledge of how to watch a magician at work, and I had looked in all the places from which a magician traditionally misdirects his audience. I left the Hackney Empire in a boiling rage. I was angry that my best illusion had been copied; I was even angrier that it had been bettered. Worst of all, though, was the fact that I could not work out how it was done.

He was one man. He was in one place. He appeared in another. He could not have a double, or a stooge; equally he could not have travelled so quickly from one position to the other.

Jealousy made my rage worse. In a Flash, Angier's catchpenny title for his version of, his damnable *improvement* on, The New Transported Man, was unmistakably a major illusion, one which introduced a new standard into our often derided and usually misunderstood performing art. For this I had to admire him, no matter what my other feelings about him might be. Along with, I suspect, most of my fellow members of the audience, I felt that I had been privileged to be present when the illusion was performed. As I walked away from the front of the theatre I passed the narrow alley that led down to the stage door, and I even momentarily wished it were possible for me to send up my card to Angier's dressing room, so that I might visit him there and congratulate him in person.

I suppressed these instincts. After so many years of bitter rivalry I could not allow one polished presentation of a stage illusion to make me humiliate myself before him.

I returned to my flat in Hornsey, where at that time I happened to be staying, and underwent a sleepless night, tossing restlessly beside Olive.

The next day I settled down to some hard and practical thinking about his version of my trick, to see what I could make of it.

I confess yet again: I do not know how he did it. I could not work out the secret when I saw the performance, and afterwards, no matter what principles of magic I applied, I still could not think of the solution.

At the heart of the mystery were three, possibly four, of the six fundamental categories of illusion. He had made himself *Disappear*, he had then *Produced* himself elsewhere, somehow there seemed to be an element of *Transposition*, and all had been achieved in apparent *Defiance of Natural Laws*.

A disappearance on stage is relatively easy to arrange. The placement of mirrors or half-mirrors, use of lighting, use of magician's 'black art' or blinds, use of distraction, use of stage trapdoors, and so on. Production elsewhere is usually a question of planting in advance the object, or a close copy of it . . . or if it is a person, planting a convincing double of the person. Working these two effects together then produces a third. In their bafflement the audience believes it has seen natural laws defied.

Laws that I felt I had seen defied that evening in Hackney.

All my attempts to solve the mystery on conventional magical principles were unsuccessful, and although I thought and worked obsessively I did not come even close to a solution that satisfied me.

I was constantly distracted by the knowledge that this magnificent illusion would have at its heart a secret of infuriating simplicity. The central rule of magic always holds good – what is *seen* is not what is *actually being done*.

This secret continued to elude me. I had only two minor compensations.

The first was that no matter how brilliant his effect, my own secret was still intact from Angier. He did not carry out the illusion my way, as indeed he could never have done.

The second was that of speed. No matter what his secret, Angier's performance effect was still not as quick as mine. My body is made to transport from one cabinet to the other in an instant. Not, I emphasise, that it happens quickly. The illusion is worked in an *instant*. There is no delay of any kind. Angier's effect was measurably slower. On the evening I witnessed the illusion I estimated one or at most two seconds had elapsed, which meant to me that he was one or at most two seconds slower than me.

In one approach towards a solution I tried checking the times and distances involved. On the night, because I had had no idea what was about to happen, and I had no scientific means of measurement, all my estimates were subjective.

This is part of the illusionist's method. By not preparing his audience, the performer can use surprise to cover his tracks. Most people, having seen a trick performed, and asked how quickly it was carried out, will be unable to give an accurate estimate. Many tricks are based on the principle that the illusionist will do something so quickly that an unprepared audience will afterwards swear that it could not have happened because there was insufficient time.

Knowing this, I made myself think back carefully over what I had seen, re-running the illusion in my mind, and trying to estimate how much time had actually elapsed between Angier's apparent disappearance and his materialization elsewhere. In the end I came to the conclusion that certainly it had been no less than my first estimate of one or two seconds, and maybe as many as five seconds had passed. In five seconds of complete and unexpected darkness a skilled magician can carry out a great deal of invisible trickery!

This short period of time was the obvious clue to the mystery, but it still did not seem enough for Angier to have dashed almost to the back of the stalls.

Two weeks after the incident, by arrangement with the front-of-house manager, I went round to the Hackney Empire on the pretext of wishing to take measurements in advance of one of my own performances. This is a fairly regular feature of magical acts, as the illusionist will often adapt his performance to suit the physical limitations of the theatre. In the event, my request was treated as a normal one, and the manager's assistant greeted me with civility and assisted me with my researches.

I found the seat where I had been, and established that it was just over fifty feet from the stage. Trying to discover the precise point in the aisle where Angier had rematerialised was more difficult, and really all I had to go on was my own memory of the event. I stood beside the seat I had been using, and tried to triangulate his position by recalling the angle at which I had turned my head to see him. In the end the best I could do was to place him somewhere in a long stretch of the stepped aisle: its closest point to the stage was more than seventy-five feet, and its furthest extremity was greatly in excess of one hundred feet.

I stood for a while in the centre of the stage, approximately in the place where the tripod's apex had been, and stared along the central aisle, wondering how I myself would contrive to get from one position to the other, in a crowded auditorium, in darkness, in under five seconds.

33

I travelled down to discuss the problem with Tommy Elbourne, who by this time was living in retirement in Woking. After I had described the illusion to him I asked him how he thought it might be explained.

'I should have to see it myself, sir,' he said after much thought and cross-questioning of me.

I tried a different approach. I put it to him that it might be an illusion I wished to design for myself. He and I had often worked like this in the past – I would describe an effect I wanted to achieve, and we would, so to speak, design the workings in reverse.

'But that would be no problem for you, would it, Mr Borden?' he said, referring to my secret method.

'Yes, but I am different! How would we design it for another illusionist? Think of it that way.'

'I would not know how,' he said. 'The best way would be to use a double, someone already planted in the audience, but you say—'

'That is not how Angier worked it. He was alone.'

'Then I have no idea, sir.'

34

I laid new plans. I would attend Angier's next season of performances, visiting his show every night if necessary, until I had solved the mystery. Tommy Elbourne would be with me. I would cling to my pride so long as I could, and if I were able to wrest his secret from him, without arousing his suspicions, then that would be the ideal result. But if, by the end of the season, we had not come to a workable theory we would abandon all the rivalry and jealousies of the past, and

I would approach him direct, pleading with him if necessary for an insight into the explanation. Such was the maddening effect on me of his mystery.

I write without shame. Mysteries are the common currency of magicians, and I saw it as my professional duty to find out how the trick was being worked. If it meant that I had to humble myself, had to acknowledge that Angier was the superior magician, then so be it.

None of this was to be, however. After an extended Christmas break Angier departed for a tour of the USA at the end of January, leaving me fretting with frustration in his wake.

A week after his return in April (announced in *The Times*) I called at his house, determined to make my peace with him, but he was not there. The house, a large but modest building in a terrace not far from Highgate Fields, was closed and shuttered. I spoke to neighbours, but I was repeatedly told that they knew nothing of the people who lived there. Angier obviously kept his life as secure from the outside world as I did.

I contacted Hesketh Unwin, the man I knew to be his booking agent, but was brushed off. I left a second message with Unwin, pleading with Angier to contact me urgently. Although the agent promised the message would reach Angier in person it was never answered.

I wrote to Angier directly, personally, proposing an end to all the rivalry, all bitterness, offering any apology or amends he would care to name in the cause of conciliation between us.

He did not answer, and at last I felt I had been taken to a point that was beyond reason.

My response to his silence, I fear, was insensible.

35

During the third week of May I caught a train from London to the seaside town and fishing port of Lowestoft, in Suffolk. Here, Angier was booked for a week of performances. I went with only one intent, and that was to infiltrate myself backstage and discover the secret for myself.

Normally, access to the backstage area of a theatre is controlled by the staff who are employed to ensure just that restriction, but if you are familiar either with theatrical life or with a particular building there are generally ways of getting inside. Angier was playing at the Pavilion, a substantial and well-equipped theatre on the seafront, one in which I myself had performed in the past. I expected no difficulties.

I was rebuffed. It was hopeless to try at the stage door, because a prominent handwritten notice outside announced that all intending visitors had to obtain authorization in advance before being allowed even so far as the door manager's stall. As I did not want to draw attention to myself, I retreated without pressing my case.

I found similar difficulties in the scenery bay. Again, there are ways and means of getting inside if you know how to go about it, but Angier was taking many precautions, as I soon discovered.

I came across a young carpenter at the back of the bay, preparing a scenery flat. I showed him my card, and he greeted me in a friendly enough way. After a short conversation with him on general matters, I said, 'I wouldn't mind being able to watch the show from behind the scenes.'

'Wouldn't we all!'

'Do you think you could get me in one evening?'

'No hope, sir, and no point neither. The main act this week's gone and put a box up. Can't see nothing!'

'How do you feel about that?'

'Not too bad, since he slipped me a wad . . .'

Again I retreated. Boxing a stage is an extreme measure

employed by a minority of magicians nervous of having their secrets discovered by scene-shifters and other backstage workers. It's usually an unpopular move, and unless substantial tips are handed out brings a noticeable lack of cooperation from the people with whom the artiste has to work. The mere fact that Angier had gone to so much trouble was further evidence that his secret required elaborate defences.

There remained only three possible ways to infiltrate the theatre, all of them fraught with difficulties.

The first was to enter the front of house, and use one of the access doors to reach the back. (Doors to the Pavilion auditorium from the foyer were locked, and staff were watching all visitors vigilantly.)

The second was to try to obtain a temporary backstage job. (No one was being hired that week.)

The third was to go to a show as a member of the audience, and try to get up on the stage from there. As there was no longer any alternative I went to the box office and bought myself a stalls seat for every available performance of Angier's run. (It was additionally galling to discover that Angier's show was such a success that most performances were completely sold out, with waiting lists for cancellations, and those that were left had only the most expensive seats available.)

36

My seat, at the second of Angier's shows I attended, was in the front row of the stalls. Angier looked briefly at me soon after he walked on the stage, but I had disguised myself expertly and was confident he had not recognised me. I knew from my own experience that you can sometimes sense in advance which members of the audience will volunteer to assist, and taking an unobtrusive glance at the people in the front two or three rows is something most magicians do.

When Angier began his playing-card routine and called for volunteers I stood up with a show of hesitation, and sure enough was invited on to the stage. As soon as I was close to Angier I realised how nervous he was. He barely looked at me as we went through the amusing process of choosing and concealing cards. I played all this straight, because wrecking his show was not what I wished to do.

When the routine was complete, his female assistant came swiftly up behind me, took my arm in a polite but firm grip, and led me towards the wings. At the earlier performance, the volunteer had then walked down the ramp on his own while the assistant went quickly back to the centre of the stage, where she was needed for the next illusion.

Knowing this, I grasped my opportunity. Under the noise of the applause, I said to her in the rustic accent I was using as part of my disguise, 'It's all right, m'dear. I can find my seat.'

She smiled gratefully, patted me on the arm, then turned away towards Angier. He was pulling forward his props table while the applause died. Neither of them was looking at me. Most of the audience was watching Angier.

I stepped back, and slipped into the wings. I had to push my way through a narrow flap in the heavy canvas screen of the box.

Immediately, a stagehand stepped out to block my way.

'Sorry, sir,' he said loudly. 'You aren't allowed backstage.'

Angier was just a few feet away from us, starting his next routine. If I argued with the man Angier would doubtless hear us and realise something was up. With a flash of inspiration I reached up and pulled off the hat and wig I had been wearing

'It's part of the act, you damned fool!' I said urgently but quietly, using my normal voice. 'Out of the way!'

The stagehand looked disconcerted, but he muttered an apology and stepped back again. I brushed past him. I had spent much time planning where the best place to search for clues would be. With the stage boxed it was more likely that I would find what I was seeking on the mezzanine floor. I went along a short corridor until I reached the steps leading down to the sub-stage area.

With the rigging loft and flies, the mezzanine is one of the main technical areas of the theatre. There were several trap and bridge mechanisms here, as well as the windlasses used for powering the scenery sliders. Several large flats were stored in their cuts, presumably for a forthcoming production. I stepped briskly between the various pieces of machinery. If the show had been a major theatrical production, with numerous scene and scenery changes, the mezzanine floor would be occupied by technicians operating the machinery, but because a magic show largely depends on the props the illusionist himself provides, technical requirements are mainly confined to curtains and lighting. I was therefore glad, but not surprised, to find the area deserted.

Towards the back of the mezzanine floor I found what I was seeking, almost without at first realising what it was. I came across two large and strongly built crates, equipped with many lifting and handling points, and clearly stamped: PRIVATE – THE GREAT DANTON. Next to them was a bulky voltage converter of a type unfamiliar to me. My own act used a similar device for powering the electrical bench, but it was a small affair of no great complication. This one of Angier's bespoke raw power. It was radiating heat as I approached it, and a low, powerful humming noise was issuing from somewhere deep within.

I leaned over the converter, trying to fathom its workings. Overhead, I could hear Angier's footsteps on the stage, and the sound of his voice raised to be heard across the auditorium. I could imagine him striding to and fro as he made his speech about the wonders of science.

Suddenly, the converter made a loud knocking noise, and to my alarm a thin but toxic blue smoke began emerging from a grille in its upper panel. The humming noise intensified. At first I moved back, but a growing sense of alarm made me go forward again.

I could hear Angier's measured tread continuing a few feet above my head, clearly unaware of what might be happening down here.

Again, the knocking noise sounded within the device, this time accompanied by a most sinister screeching noise, as of thin metal being sawn. The smoke was pouring out more quickly than before, and when I moved round to the other side of the object I discovered that several thick metal coils were glowing red hot.

All around me was the clutter of the mezzanine area. There were tons of dry timber, windlasses grimed with lubricant, miles of ropes, numerous scraps and heaps of discarded paper, huge scenery flats painted with oils. The whole place was a tinderbox, and in the centre of it was something that seemed about to explode into flames. I stood there in terrible indecision – could Angier or his assistants know what was happening down here?

The converter made more noises, and once again the smoke belched from the grille. It was getting into my lungs, and I was beginning to choke. In desperation I looked around for some kind of fire extinguisher.

Then I saw that the converter was taking its power from a thick insulated cable that ran from a large electrical junction box attached to the rear wall. I dashed over to it. There was an EMERGENCY ON/OFF handle built into it, and without another thought I grabbed hold of it and pulled it down.

The infernal activity of the converter instantly died. Only the acrid blue smoke continued to belch out of its grille, but this was thinning by the second.

Overhead there was a heavy thud, followed by silence.

A second or two passed, while I stared contritely up at the stage floor above me.

I heard footsteps dashing around and Angier's voice shouting angrily. I could hear the audience too, a more indistinct noise, neither cheering nor applauding. The racket of hurrying feet and raised voices from up there was increasing. Whatever I had done had wreaked havoc on Angier's illusion.

I had come to this theatre to solve a mystery, not to interrupt the show, but I had failed in the former and inadvertently succeeded in the latter. For the sake of this, what I had learned was that he used a more powerful voltage converter than mine, and that his was a fire risk.

I realised that I would be discovered if I remained where I was, so I stepped away from the rapidly cooling converter and returned the way I had come. My lungs were starting to ache from the smoke I had inhaled and my head was spinning. Overhead, on the stage and in the general backstage area, I could hear many people moving quickly and noisily around, a fact that might work in my favour. Somewhere in the building, not too far away, I heard someone screaming. I should be able to slip away in the confusion.

As I ran up the steps, taking them two at a time, and intending to stop for no one, I saw an amazing sight!

My mind was unhinged by the smoke, or by the excitement of what I had just done, or by the fear of being caught. I could not have been thinking clearly.

Angier himself was standing at the top of the steps, waiting for me, his arms raised in anger. But it seemed to me he had assumed the form of an apparition! I glimpsed lights beyond him, and by some trick they also seemed to glint through him. Immediately, several thoughts flashed through me – this must be a special garment he wears to help him do that trick!

A treated fabric! Something that becomes transparent! Makes him invisible! Is *this* his secret?

But in the selfsame instant my upward momentum propelled me into him, and we both sprawled on the floor. He tried to grab me, but whatever he had smeared on himself prevented him from getting a good grip on me. I was able to release myself and slither away from him.

'Borden!' His voice was hoarse with anger, no more than a terrible whisper. 'Stop!'

'It was an accident!' I shouted. 'Keep away from me!'

Having gained my feet I ran from him, leaving him lying there on the hard floor. I sprinted down a short corridor, the noise of my shoes echoing from the shinily painted bare bricks, rounded a corner, ran down a short flight of steps, went along another bare corridor, then came across the doorkeeper's cubicle. He looked up in surprise as I dashed past, but he had no hope of challenging or stopping me.

Moments later I was outside the stage door, and hurrying along the dimly lit alley to the seafront.

Here I paused for a moment, facing out to sea, leaning forward and resting my hands on my knees. I coughed a few times, painfully, trying to clear the remains of the smoke from my lungs. It was a fine dry evening in early summer. The sun had just set, and the coloured lights were coming on along the promenade. The tide was high and the waves were breaking softly against the sea wall.

The audience was straggling out of the Pavilion Theatre, and dispersing into the town. Many of the people wore be-mused expressions, presumably because of the sudden way the show had ended. I walked along the promenade with the crowd, then when I reached the main shopping street I turned inland and headed towards the railway station.

Much later, long after midnight, I was back in my London house. My children were asleep in their rooms, Sarah was warm beside me, and I lay there in the darkness wondering what the night had achieved.

37

Then, seven weeks later, Rupert Angier died.

To say I was consumed by feelings of guilt would be an understatement, especially as both of the newspapers which recorded his passing referred to the 'injuries' he had sustained while performing his illusion. They did not say that the accident had happened on the date I was in Lowestoft, but I knew that must be the one.

I had already established that Angier cancelled the rest of

the week's performances at the Pavilion, and as far as I knew he had not appeared anywhere else in public afterwards. I had no idea why.

Now it transpired that he had been fatally injured that night.

What was inexplicable to me was that I had run into Angier less than a minute after my accidental intervention. He did not seem fatally injured then, or even hurt to a minor extent. On the contrary he was in strenuous health and determined to confront me. We had scrapped briefly on the floor before I managed to get away from him. The only unusual thing about him was the greasy compound he had smeared on himself or his costume, presumably to perform the illusion, or to help in some way with making himself vanish. That was a genuine puzzle, because after I had recovered from the effects of the smoke inhalation, my memory of those few seconds was exact. It had quite definitely been the case that for a split second I had 'seen through' him, as if parts of him were transparent, or if all of him were partly so.

Another minor mystery was that none of the compound had rubbed off on me during our brawl. His hands had definitely gripped my wrists, and I had distinctly felt the slimy sensation, but no trace was left. I even recall sitting on the train returning to London, holding my arm up to the light to discover if I could 'see through' myself!

There was enough doubt, though, for feelings of contrition to dominate my reaction to the news. In fact, confronted with the awfulness of what had happened I felt I had to try to make some kind of amends.

Unfortunately, the newspaper obituaries had not been published until several days after Angier had died, when the funeral had already been held. This event would have been an ideal place for me to start the process of belated reconciliation with his family and associates. A wreath, a simple note of condolence, would have paved the way for me, but it was not to be.

After much thought I decided to approach his widow directly, and wrote her a sincere and sympathetic letter.

In it I explained who I was, and how I, when much younger, had to my eternal regret fallen out with her husband. I said that the news of his premature death had shocked and saddened me and that I knew the whole magical community would feel the loss. I paid tribute to his skills as a performer, and as an *ingénieur* of marvellous illusions.

I then moved on to what was for me the main thrust of the letter, but which I hoped would seem to the widow to be an afterthought. I said that when a magician died it was customary in the world of magic for his colleagues to offer to purchase whatever pieces of apparatus remained, for which the family might no longer have a use. I added that in view of my long and troubled relationship with Rupert during his lifetime I saw it as a duty and a pleasure to make such an offer now that he had died, and that I had considerable means at my disposal.

With the letter sent, and presciently supposing that I could not necessarily count on the widow's cooperation, I made enquiries through my contacts in the business. This was an approach I also had to judge sensitively, because I had no idea how many other magicians were as interested in getting their hands on Angier's equipment as I was. I assumed many of them would be. I could not have been the only professional magician to have seen the stunning performance. I therefore let it be known that if any of Angier's pieces were to come on to the market I would be interested in buying them.

Two weeks after I wrote to Angier's widow I received a reply, in the form of a letter from a firm of solicitors in Chancery Lane. It said, and I transcribe it exactly:

My Dear Sir,
    Estate of Rupert David Angier Esquire, Dec'd
    Pursuant to your recent enquiry to our client, I am instructed to advise you that all necessary arrangements for the disposal of the late Rupert David Angier's major chattels and appurtenances have been made, and that you need not embark on further enquiries as to their destination or enjoyment.

We anticipate instruction from our former client's estate
as to the disposal of various minor pieces of property, and
these shall be made available through public auction,
whose date and place shall be announced in the usual
gazettes.

In this we remain, Sir, yr. obedient servants,
Kendal, Kendal & Owen
(Solicitors & Commissioners for Oaths)

38

I step forward to the footlights, and in the full glare of their
light face you directly.

I say, 'Look at my hands. There is nothing concealed
within them.'

I hold them up, raising my palms for you to see, spreading
my fingers so as to prove nothing is gripped secretly between
them. I now perform my last trick, and produce a bunch
of faded paper flowers from the hands you know to be
empty.

39

It is 1st September 1903, and I say that to all intents and
purposes my own career ended with Angier's death.

Although I was reasonably wealthy, I was a married man
with children and had an expensive and complicated way of
life to sustain. I could not walk away from my responsibilities, and so I was obliged to accept bookings so long as
they were offered to me. In this way I did not fully retire, but
the ambition that had driven me in the early years, the wish
to amaze or baffle, the sheer delight of dreaming up the

impossible, all these left me. I still had the technical ability to perform magic, my hands remained dexterous, and with Angier gone I was once again the only performer of THE NEW TRANSPORTED MAN, but none of this was enough.

A great loneliness had descended on me, one the Pact yet prevents me from describing in full, except to say that I was the only friend I craved for myself. Yet I, of course, was the only friend I could not meet.

I touch on this as delicately as I can.

My life is full of secrets and contradictions I can never explain.

Whom did Sarah marry? Was it me, or was it *me*? I have two children, whom I adore. But are they mine to adore, really mine alone . . . or are they actually *mine*? How will I ever know, except by the cravings of instinct? Come to that, with which of me did Olive fall in love, and with whom did she move into the flat in Hornsey? It was not I who first made love to her, nor was it I who invited her to the flat, yet *I* took advantage of her presence, knowing that I too was doing the same.

Which of me was it who tried to expose Angier? Which of me first devised THE NEW TRANSPORTED MAN, and which of me was the first to be transported?

I seem, even to myself, to be rambling, but every word here is coherent and precise. It is the essential dilemma of my existence.

Yesterday I was playing at a theatre in Balham, in southwest London. I performed the matinée, then had two hours to wait before the evening show. As I often did at such times I went to my dressing room, pulled the curtains to and dimmed the lights, closed and locked the door, and went to sleep on the couch.

I awoke.

Did I wake at all? Was it a vision? A dream?

I awoke to find the spectral figure of Rupert Angier standing in my dressing room, and he was holding a long-bladed knife in both hands.

Before I could move or call out he leapt at me, landing on

the side of the couch and crawling quickly on top of me so that he was astride my chest and stomach. He raised the knife, and held it with the point of the blade resting above my heart.

'Prepare to die, Borden!' he said in his harsh and horrid whisper.

In this hellish vision it seemed to me that he barely weighed anything at all, that I could easily flip him away from me, but fear was weakening me. I brought my hands up and gripped his forearms, to try to stop him thrusting the knife fatally into me, but to my amazement I found that he was still wearing the greasy compound that prevented my getting a strong hold on him. The harder I tried, the more quickly my fingers slipped around his disgusting flesh. I was breathing his foul stink, the rank smell of the grave, of the boneyard.

I gasped in horror, because I felt the pointed blade pressing painfully against my breast.

'Now! Tell me, Borden! Which one of them are you? Which one?'

I could scarcely breathe, such was my fear, such was the terror that at any second the blade would thrust through my ribcage and puncture my heart.

'Tell me and I spare you!' The pressure of the knife increased.

'I don't know, Angier! I no longer know myself!'

And somehow that ended it, almost as soon as it had begun. His face was inches away from mine, and I saw him snarl with rage. His rancid breath flowed over me. The knife was starting to pierce my skin! Fear galvanised me into valour. I swung at him once, twice, fists across his face, battering him back from me. The deadly pressure on my heart softened. I sensed an advantage, and swung both my arms at his body, clenching my fists together. He yelled, swaying back from me. The knife lifted away. He was still on me, so I hit him again, then thrust up the side of my body to unseat him. To my immense relief he toppled away, releasing the knife as he fell to the floor. The deadly blade clattered against the wall and landed on the floor, as the spectral figure rolled across the floorboards.

He was quickly on his feet, looking chastened and wary, watching me in case I attacked again. I sat up on the couch, braced against another assault. He was the phantasm of ultimate terror: the spectre in death of my worst enemy in life.

I could see the lamp glinting through his semi-transparent body.

'Leave me alone,' I croaked. 'You are dead! You have no business with me!'

'Nor I with you, Borden. Killing you is no revenge. It should never have happened. Never!'

The ghost of Rupert Angier turned away from me, walked to the locked door, then passed bodily through it. Nothing of him remained, except a persistent trace of his hideous carrion stench.

The haunting had paralysed me with fear, and I was still sitting immobile on the couch when I heard beginners called. A few minutes later my dresser came to the door, and it was his insistent knocking that at last roused me from the couch.

I found Angier's knife on the floor of the dressing room, and I have it with me now. It is real. It was carried by a ghost.

Nothing makes sense. It hurts to breathe, to move; I still feel that pressing point of the knife against my heart. I am in the Hornsey flat, and I do not know what to do or who I really am.

Every word I have written here is true, and each one describes the reality of my life. My hands are empty, and I fix you with an honest look. This is how I have lived, and yet it reveals nothing.

I will go alone to the end.

PART THREE
Kate Angier

I

I was only five at the time, but there's no doubt in my mind that it really happened. I know that memory can play tricks, especially at night on a shocked and terrified child, and I know that people patch together memories from what they think happened, or what they wish had happened, or what other people later tell them had happened. All of these went on, and it has taken many years for me to piece together the reality.

It was cruel, violent, unexplained and almost certainly illegal. It wrecked the lives of most of the people involved. It has blighted my own life.

Now I can tell the story as I saw it take place, but tell it as an adult.

2

My father is Lord Colderdale, the sixteenth of that name. Our family name is Angier, and my father's given names were Victor Edmund; my father is the son of Rupert Angier's only son Edward. Rupert Angier, the magician known as 'The Great Danton', was therefore my great-grandfather, and the 14th Earl of Colderdale.

My mother's name was Jennifer, though at home my father always called her Jenny. They met when my father was working for the Foreign Office, where he had been throughout the Second World War. He was not a career diplomat, but for health reasons he had not been able to enter the military, so he volunteered instead for a civil post. He had read German Literature at university, spent some time in Leipzig during the 1930s, and was seen as possessing a skill useful to the British Government in wartime. Translation of messages intercepted from the German High Command apparently came into it. He and my mother met in 1946 on a train journey from Berlin to London. She was a nurse who had been working with the Occupying Powers in the German capital, and was returning to England at the end of her tour of duty.

They married in 1947, at about the same time my father was released from his post at the Foreign Office. They came to live here in Caldlow, where my sister and I were born. I don't know much about the years that passed before we came into the world, or why my parents left it so long before having a family. They travelled a great deal, but I believe the driving force behind it was an avoidance of boredom, rather than a positive wish to see different places. Their marriage was never entirely smooth. I know that my mother briefly walked out during the late 1950s, because one day many years later I overheard a conversation between her and her sister, my Auntie Caroline. My sister Rosalie was born in 1962, and I followed in 1965. My father was then nearly fifty, and my mother was in her late thirties.

Like most people, I can't recall much about my first years of life. I remember that the house always seemed cold, and that no matter how many blankets my mother piled on top of my bed, or how hot was my hot-water bottle, I always felt chilled through to the bone. Probably I am remembering just one winter, or one month or one week in one winter, but even now it seems like always. The house is impossible to heat properly in winter. The wind curls through the valley from October to the middle of April. We have snow coverage for about three months of the year. We always burnt wood from the trees on the estate, and still do, but it isn't an efficient fuel, like coal or electricity. We lived in the smallest wing of the house, and so as I grew up I really had little idea of the extent of the place.

When I was eight I was sent away to a girls' boarding school near Congleton, but while I was little I spent most of my life at home with my mother. When I was four she sent me to a nursery school in Caldlow village, and later to the primary school in Baldon, the next village along the road towards Chapel. I was taken to and from the school in my father's black Standard, driven carefully by Mr Stimpson, who with his wife represented our entire domestic staff. Before the Second World War there had been a full household of servants, but all that changed during the war. From 1939 to 1940 the house was used partly to accommodate evacuees from Manchester, Sheffield and Leeds, and partly as a school for the children. It was taken over by the RAF in 1941, and the family has not lived in the main part of the house since. The part of it in which I live is the wing where I grew up.

3

If there had been any preparations for the visit, Rosalie and I were not told what they were. The first we knew about it was when a car arrived at the main gate and Stimpson went down to let it in. This was in the days when Derbyshire County Council was using the house, and they always wanted the gates locked at weekends.

The car that drove up to the house was a Mini. The paint had lost its shine, the front bumper was bent from a collision, and there was rust around the windows. It was not at all the sort of car that we were used to seeing come to the house. Most of my parents' other friends were apparently well-off or important, even during this period when our family had fallen on hard times.

The man who had been driving reached into the back seat of the Mini, and pulled out a little boy, just now waking up. He cradled the boy against his shoulder. Stimpson conducted them politely to the house. Rosalie and I watched from an upstairs window as Stimpson returned to the Mini to unload the luggage they had brought with them, but we were told to come down from the nursery and meet the visitors. Everyone was in our main sitting room. Both my parents were dressed up as if it was an important occasion, but the visitors looked more casual.

We were introduced. The man's name was Mr Clive Borden, and the boy, his son, was called Nicholas, or Nicky. Nicky was about two, which was three years younger than me and five years younger than my sister. There did not appear to be a Mrs Borden, but this was not explained to us.

I've subsequently found out a little more about this family. I know for instance that Clive Borden's wife died shortly after the birth of her baby. Her maiden name was Diana Ruth Ellington, and she came from Hatfield in Hertfordshire. Nicholas was her only son. Clive Borden himself was the son of Graham Borden, the son of Alfred Borden, the magician. Clive Borden was therefore the grandson of Rupert Angier's greatest enemy, and Nicky was his great-grandson, my contemporary.

Obviously, Rosalie and I knew nothing of this at the time, and after a few minutes Mama suggested that we might like to take Nicky up to our nursery and show him some of our toys. We meekly obeyed, as we had been brought up to do, with the familiar figure of Mrs Stimpson on hand to look after us all.

What then passed between the three adults I can only guess at, but it went on all afternoon. Clive Borden and his boy had arrived soon after lunchtime, and we three children played together until it was almost dark. Mrs Stimpson kept us occupied, leaving us to play together when we were happy to do so, but reading to us or encouraging us to try new games when we showed signs of flagging. She supervised toilet visits, and brought us snacks and drinks. Rosalie and I grew up surrounded by expensive toys, and to us, even as children, it was clear that Nicky was not used to such excess. With adult hindsight I imagine the toys of two girls were not all that interesting to a two-year-old boy. We got through the long afternoon, however, and I can't remember any squabbles.

What were they talking about downstairs?

I realise that this meeting must have started as one of the occasional attempts our two families have made to patch up the row between our ancestors. Why they, we, could not leave the past to fester and die I do not know, but it seems deep in the psychological make-up of both sides to need to keep fretting over the subject. What could it possibly matter now, or then, that two stage magicians were constantly at each other's throats? Whatever spite, hatred or envy that rankled between those two old men surely could not concern distant descendants who had their own lives and affairs? Well, so it might seem in all common sense, but passions of blood are irrational.

In the case of Clive Borden, irrationality seems part of him, no matter what might have happened to his ancestor. His life has been difficult to research, but I know he was born in west London. He led an average childhood and had a fair talent for sports. He went to Loughborough College after he left school but dropped out after the first year. In the decade afterwards he was frequently homeless, and seems to have stayed in the houses of a number of friends and relatives. He was arrested several times for drunk and disorderly behaviour, but somehow managed to avoid a criminal record. He described himself as an actor and made a precarious living in the film industry, doing extra and stand-in work whenever he could find it, with periods on the dole between.

The one short period of emotional and physical stability in his life was when he met and married Diana Ellington. They set up home together in Twickenham, Middlesex, but the marriage turned out to be tragically short-lived. After Diana died Clive Borden stayed on in the flat they had been renting and managed to persuade a married sister, who lived in the same area, to help bring up the baby boy. He kept working in films, and although he was again drifting socially, he appears to have been able to provide for the child. This was his general situation at the time he came to visit my parents.

After this visit he left the flat in Twickenham, apparently moved back to the centre of London, and in the winter of 1971 went abroad. He went first to the USA, but after that travelled on to either Canada or Australia. According to his sister he changed his name, and deliberately broke all contacts with his past. I have done what searches I can, but I can't even be sure whether he is still alive or not.

4

But now I return to that afternoon and evening of Clive Borden's visit to Caldlow House, and try to reconstruct what took place while we children played upstairs.

My father would have been making a great show of hospitality, offering drinks and opening a good wine to celebrate the occasion. The evening meal would be lavish. He would enquire genially about Mr Borden's car journey, or about his views on something that was in the news, or even about his general well-being. This is the way my father invariably behaved when thrust into a social situation whose outcome he could not predict or control. It was the bluff, agreeable façade put up by a decent English gentleman, lacking in sinister connotation but completely inappropriate for the occasion. I can imagine that it would have made more difficult any reconciliation that they were trying to achieve.

My mother, meanwhile, would be playing a more subtle part. She would be much better attuned to the tensions that existed between the two men, but would feel constrained by being, in this matter, a relative outsider. I believe she would not have said much, at least for the first hour or so, but would be conscious of the need to focus on the one subject that concerned them all. She would have kept trying, subtly and unobtrusively, to steer the conversation in that direction.

I find it harder to talk about Clive Borden, because I hardly knew him, but he had probably suggested the meeting. I feel certain neither of my parents would have done so. There must have been a recent exchange of letters, which led to the invitation. Now I know his financial situation at the time, maybe he was hoping something might come his way as a result of patching things up with our family. Or perhaps at last he had traced a family memoir that might explain or excuse Alfred Borden's behaviour. (Borden's book then existed, of course, but few people outside the world of magic knew about it.) On the other hand, he might have found out about the existence of Rupert Angier's personal diary. It's almost certain he kept one, because of his obsession with dates and details.

I'm sure that an attempt to patch up the feud was behind the meeting, no matter who suggested it. What I saw at the time and can remember now was cordial enough, at least at first. It was after all a face-to-face meeting, which was more than their own parents' generation had ever managed.

The old feud was behind it, no matter what. No other subject joined our families so securely, nor divided them so inevitably. My father's blandness, and Borden's nervousness, would eventually have run out. One of them would have said: well, can you tell us anything new about what happened?

The idiocy of the impasse looms around me as I think back. Any vestige of professional secrecy that once constrained our great-grandfathers would have died with them. No one who came after them in either family was a magician, or showed any interest in magic. If anyone has the remotest interest in the subject it's me, and that's only because of trying to carry out my research. I've read several books on stage magic, and biographies of a few of the great magicians. Most of them were modern works, while the oldest one I read was Alfred Borden's. I know that the art of magic has progressed since the end of the last century, and that what were then popular tricks have long since gone out of fashion, replaced by more modern illusions. In our great-grandfathers' time, for instance, no one had heard of the trick in which a woman appears to be sawn in half. That familiar illusion was not invented until the 1920s, long after both Danton and the Professeur were dead. It's in the nature of magic that illusionists have to keep thinking up more baffling ways of working their tricks. The magic of Le Professeur would now seem quaint, unfunny, slow and above all unmysterious. The trick that made him famous and rich would look like a museum piece, and any self-respecting rival illusionist would be able to reproduce it without trouble, and make it seem more baffling.

In spite of this the feud has continued for nearly a century.

On the day of Clive Borden's visit we children were eventually brought down from the nursery, and taken to the dining room to eat with the grown-ups. We liked Nicky, and the three of us were pleased to be seated together along one side of the table. I remember the meal clearly, but only because Nicky was there with us. My sister and I thought he was acting up to amuse us, but I realise now that he could never have sat at a formally laid table before, nor have been served by other people. He simply did not know how to behave. His father sometimes spoke to him harshly, trying to correct him or to calm him down, but Rosalie and I were egging the little boy on. Our parents said nothing to us, because they almost never said anything to us. Parental discipline was not something my kind of parents went in for, and they would never dream of berating us in front of a stranger.

Without our knowing it, our rowdy behaviour must have contributed to the tension between the adults. Clive Borden's raised voice became a hectoring, grating sound, one I started to dislike. Both my parents were responding badly to him, and any pretence of courtesy was abandoned. They began arguing and my father addressed him in the voice we usually heard him use in restaurants where the service was slow. By the end of the meal my father was half-drunk, half-enraged;

my mother was pale and silent, and Clive Borden (presumably also more than a little drunk) was talking endlessly about his misfortunes. Mrs Stimpson ushered the three of us out into the room next door, our sitting room.

Nicky, for some reason, began to cry. He said he wanted to go home, and when Rosalie and I tried to calm him down he struck out at us, kicking and punching.

We'd seen my father in this sort of mood before.

'I'm frightened,' I said to Rosalie.

'I am too,' she said.

We listened at the double door connecting the two rooms. We heard raised voices, then long silences. My father was pacing about, clicking his shoes impatiently on the polished parquet floor.

5

There was one part of the house into which we children were never allowed. Access to it was by way of an unprepossessing brown-painted door, set into the triangular section of wall beneath the back staircase. This door was always locked, and until the day of Clive Borden's visit I never saw anyone in the household, family or servants, go through it.

Rosalie had told me there was a haunted place behind it. She made up horrifying images, some of them described, some of them left vague for me to imagine for myself. She told me of the mutilated victims imprisoned below, of tragic lost souls in search of peace, of clutching hands and claws that lay in wait for our arms and ankles in the darkness a few inches beyond the door, of shifting and rattling and scratching attempts to escape, of muttered plans for horrid vengeance on those of us who lived in the daylight above. Rosalie had three years' advantage, and she knew what would scare me.

I was constantly frightened as a child. Our house was no place for the nervous. In winter, on still nights, its isolation set a silence around the walls. You heard small, unexplained noises. Animals, birds, frozen in their hidden places, moved suddenly for warmth; trees and leafless shrubs brushed against each other in the wind; noises on the far side of the valley were amplified and distorted by the funnel shape of the valley floor; people from the village walked along the road that runs by the edge of our grounds. At other times, the wind came down the valley from the north, blustering after its passage across the moors, howling because of the rocks and broken pastures all over the valley floor, whistling through the ornate woodwork around the eaves and shingles of the house. And the whole place was old, filled with memories of other people's lives, scarred with the remains of their deaths. It was no place for an imaginative child.

Indoors, the gloomy corridors and stairwells, the hidden alcoves and recesses, the dark wall-hangings and sombre ancient portraits, all gave a sense of oppressive threat. The rooms in which we lived were brightly lit and filled with modern furniture, but much of our immediate domestic hinterland was a lowering reminder of dead forefathers, ancient tragedies, silent evenings. I learned to hurry through some parts of the house, fixing my stare dead ahead so as not to be delayed by anything from this macabre past. The downstairs corridor beside the rear stairs, where the brown-painted door was found, was one such area of the house. Sometimes I would inadvertently see the door moving slightly to and fro in its frame, as if pressure were being applied from behind. It must have been caused by draughts, but if ever I saw that door in motion I invariably imagined some large and silent being, standing behind it, trying it quietly to see if it could at last be opened.

All through my childhood, both before and after the day that Clive Borden came to visit, I passed the door on the far side of the corridor, never looked at it unless I did so by mistake. I never paused to listen for movement behind it. I always hastened past, trying to ignore it out of my life.

The three of us, Rosalie, myself and the Borden boy Nicky, had been made to wait in the sitting room, next to the dining room where the adults still conducted their inexplicable conflict. Both of these rooms led out into the corridor with the brown door.

Voices were raised again. Someone passed the connecting door. I heard my mother's voice and she sounded upset.

Then Stimpson walked briskly across the sitting room and slipped through the connecting door into the dining room. He opened and closed it deftly, but we had a glimpse of the three adults beyond. They were still in their positions at the table, but were standing. I briefly saw my mother's face, and it seemed distorted by grief and anger. The door closed quickly before we could follow Stimpson into the room. He must have taken up position on the other side, to prevent us pushing through.

We heard my father speaking, issuing an order. That tone of voice always meant trouble would follow. Clive Borden said something and my father replied angrily, in a sufficiently loud voice for us to hear every word.

'You will, Mr Borden!' he said, and in his agitation his voice broke briefly into falsetto. 'Now you will! You damned well will!'

We heard the dining-room door to the corridor being opened. Borden said something again, still indistinctly.

Then Rosalie whispered against my ear, 'I think Daddy is going to *open the brown door!*'

We both sucked in our breath, and I clung to Rosalie in panic. Nicky, infected with our fear, let out a wail. I too started making a yowling noise so that I could not hear what the adults were doing.

Rosalie hissed at me, '*Hush!*'

'I don't want the door opened!' I cried.

Then, tall and sudden, Clive Borden burst into the sitting room from the corridor and found the three of us cowering there. How our little scene must have seemed to him I cannot imagine, but somehow he too had become tainted with the terror that the door symbolised. He stepped forward and down, bracing himself on a bended knee, then scooped Nicky into his arms.

I heard him mutter something to the boy, but it was not a reassuring sound. I was too wrapped up in my own fears to pay attention. It could have been anything. Behind him, across the corridor, beneath the stairs, I saw the open rectangle where the brown door had been. A light was on in the area behind and I could see two steps leading down, then a half-turn with more steps below.

I watched Nicky as he was carried out of the room. His father was holding him high, so that he could wrap his arms around his father's neck, facing back. His father reached up and placed a protective hand on the boy's head as he ducked through the doorway and went down the steps.

6

Rosalie and I had been left behind and we were faced with a choice of terrors. One was to remain alone in the familiar surroundings of our living room, the other was to follow the adults down the steps. I was holding on to my older sister, both of my arms wrapped around her leg. There was no sign of Mrs Stimpson.

'Are you going with them?' Rosalie said.

'No! You go! You look and tell me what they're doing!'

'I'm going up to the nursery,' she said.

'Don't leave me!' I cried. 'I don't want to be here on my own. Don't go!'

'You can come with me.'

'No. What are they going to do to Nicky?'

But Rosalie was extricating herself from me, slapping her hand roughly against my shoulder and pushing me away from her. Her face had gone white, and her eyes were half-closed. She was shaking.

'You can do what you like!' she said, and although I tried

to grab hold of her again she eluded me and ran out of the room. She went along the dreaded corridor, past the open doorway, then turned on the stone flags at the bottom of the staircase and rushed upstairs. At the time I thought she was being contemptuous of my fear, but from an adult perspective I suspect she had frightened herself more than me.

Whatever the reason I found myself truly alone, but because Rosalie had forced it on me the next decision was easier. A sense of calm swept over me, paralysing my imagination. It was only another form of fear, but it enabled me to move. I knew I could not stay alone where I was, and I knew I did not have the strength to follow Rosalie up those distant stairs. There remained only one place to go. I crossed the short distance to the open brown door and looked down the steps.

There were two light-bulbs in the ceiling illuminating the way down, but at the bottom, where there was another doorway leading to the side, much brighter light was spilling across the steps. The staircase looked bare and ordinary, surprisingly clean, with no hint of any danger, supernatural or otherwise. I could hear voices rising up from below.

I went down the steps quietly, not wishing to be noticed, but when I reached the bottom and looked into the main cellar I realised there was no need to hide myself. The adults were busy with what they were doing.

I was old enough to understand much of what was happening, but not to be able to recall now what the adults were saying. When I first reached the bottom of the steps my father and Clive Borden were arguing again, this time with Borden doing most of the talking. My mother stood to one side, as did the servant, Stimpson. Nicky was still being held to his father's chest.

The cellar was of a size, extent and cleanliness that came as a complete surprise to me. I had no idea that our part of the house had so much space beneath it. From my childish perspective the cellar seemed to have a high ceiling, stretching away on all sides to the white-painted walls, and that these walls were at the limits of my vision. (Although most adults can move around in the cellar without lowering their heads the ceiling is not nearly as high as in the main rooms upstairs, and of course the extent of the cellar is no greater than the area of the house itself.)

Much of the cellar was filled with stuff brought down from the main house for storage: a lot of the furniture moved out during the war was still there, draped with white dust-sheets. Along the length of one wall was a stack of framed canvases, their painted sides facing in so that they could not be seen. An area close to the steps, partitioned off by a brick wall, was made over as a wine cellar. On the far side of the main cellar, difficult to see from where I was standing, was another large stack of crates and chests, tidily arranged.

The overall impression of the cellar was spacious, cool, clean. It was a place that was in use but it was also kept tidy. However, none of this really impressed itself on me at the time. Everything that I've described so far is modified memory, based on what I know.

On the day, what grabbed my attention from the moment I reached the bottom of the steps was the apparatus built in the centre of the cellar.

My first thought was that it was a kind of shallow cage, because it was a circle of eight sturdy wooden slats. Next I realised that it had been built in a pit in the floor. To enter it one had to step down, so that it was in fact larger than it looked at first. My father, who had stepped into the centre of the circle, was only visible from about his waist up. There was also an arrangement of wiring overhead, and something whose shape I could not clearly make out rotating on a central axis, glittering and flashing in the cellar lights. My father was working hard; there was obviously some kind of control arrangement below my line of sight, and he was bending over, pumping his arm at something.

My mother stood back, watching intently, with Stimpson at her side. These two were silent.

Clive Borden stood close to one of the wooden bars, watching my father as he worked. His son Nicky was upright in his arms, and had turned around to look down too. Borden was saying something, and my father, while continuing to pump, answered loudly, and with a gesticulating arm. I knew my father was in a dangerous mood, the sort Rosalie and I suffered when we had enraged him to the point where he felt he had to prove something to us, no matter how ridiculous.

I realised Borden was provoking him into this kind of rage, perhaps deliberately.

I stepped forward, not to any of the adults, but towards Nicky. This small boy was caught up in something he could not possibly understand, and my instinct was to rush across to him, take hold of his hand and perhaps lead him away from the dangerous adult game.

I had walked half the distance to the group, entirely unnoticed by any of them, when my father shouted, 'Stand back, everyone!'

My mother and Stimpson, who presumably knew what was going to happen, immediately moved back a few paces. My mother said something in what was for her a loud voice, but her words were drowned by a rising din from the device. It hummed and fizzed, restlessly, dangerously. Clive Borden had not moved, and stood only a foot or two away from the edge of the pit. Still no one looked at me.

A series of loud bangs suddenly burst forth from the top of the device, and with each one appeared a long, snaking tendril of white electrical discharge. As each shot out it prowled like the reaching tentacle of some terrible deep-sea creature, groping for its prey. The noise was tremendous: every flash, every waving feeler of naked energy, was accompanied by a screeching, hissing sound, loud enough to hurt my ears. My father looked up towards Borden, and I could see a familiar expression of triumph on his face.

'Now you know!' he yelled at him.

'Turn it off, Victor!' my mother cried.

'But Mr Borden has insisted! Well, here it is, Mr Borden! Does this satisfy your insistence?'

Borden was still standing as if transfixed, just a short

distance from the snaking electrical discharge. He was holding his little boy in his arms. I could see the expression on Nicky's face, and I knew he was as scared as I was.

'This proves nothing!' Borden shouted.

My father's response was to close a large metal handle attached to one of the pillars inside the contraption. The zigzagging beams of energy immediately doubled in size, and snaked with more agility than ever around the wooden bars of the cage. The noise was deafening.

'Get in, Borden,' my father shouted. 'Get in and see for yourself!'

To my amazement my father then climbed out of the pit, stepping up to the main floor of the cellar between two of the wooden bars. Instantly, a number of the electrical rays flashed across to him, hissing horribly about his body. For a moment he was surrounded by them, consumed by fire. He seemed to fuse with the electricity, illuminated from within, a figure of gruesome menace. Then he took another step and he was out of it.

'Not *scared*, are you, Borden?' he shouted harshly.

I was close enough to see that the hair on my father's head was standing up from his scalp, and the hairs that stuck out from his sleeves were on end. His clothes hung oddly on his body, as if ballooning away from him, and his skin seemed to my mortified eyes to be glowing permanently blue as a result of his few seconds bathed in the electricity.

'Damn you, damn you!' cried Borden.

He turned on my father, and thrust the horror-struck child at him. Nicky tried to hang on to his father, but Borden forced him away. My father accepted the boy reluctantly, taking him in an awkward hold. Nicky was yelling with terror, and struggling to be released.

'Jump in now!' my father yelled at Borden. 'It will go in the next few seconds!'

Borden took a step forward until he was at the edge of the zone of electricity. My father was beside him, while Nicky was reaching out with his arms, screaming and screaming for his daddy. Waving blue snakes of discharge moved crazily a fraction of an inch in front of Borden. His hair rose from his scalp, and I could see him clenching and unclenching his fists. His head drooped briefly forward, and as it did so one of the tendrils instantly found him, snaking down his neck, around his shoulders and back, splattering noisily on the floor between his shoes.

He leapt back in terror, and I felt sorry for him.

'I can't do it!' he gasped. 'Turn the bloody thing off!'

'This is what you wanted, isn't it?'

My father was filled with madness. He stepped forward, away from Clive Borden, and into the deadly barrage of electricity. Half a dozen tentacles instantly wound themselves around him and the boy, imbuing them both with the lethal cyanic glow. All the hairs on his head were standing on end, making him more terrible than ever I had seen him.

He threw Nicky into the pit.

My father stepped back, away from the deadly barrage.

As Nicky fell, his arms and legs scrabbling wildly at the air, he screamed again, one despairing yell. It was a single sustained outburst of sheer terror, loneliness and fear of abandonment.

Before he hit the ground the device exploded with light. Flames leapt from the overhead wires, and a crash rang out violently. The wooden struts seemed to swell outwards with the pressure from within, and as the tentacles of light withdrew into themselves they did so with a screech as of sharp steel sliding against steel.

Horribly, it had ended. Thick blue smoke hung heavily in the air, spreading torpidly outwards across the ceiling of the cellar. The device was at last silent, and doing nothing. Nicky lay motionless on the hard floor beneath the structure.

Somewhere in the distance, it seemed, I could hear his terrible scream echoing still.

My eyes were half blind from the brilliant dazzle of the electric flares; my ears were singing from the assault of the noise; my mind ran deliriously with the shock of what I had witnessed.

I walked forward, drawn by the sight of that smoking pit. Now still and apparently in repose, it was full of threat, yet even so I felt myself drawn inexorably to it. Soon I was standing at the edge, beside my mother. My hand went up, as so often before, and folded itself into her fingers. She too was staring down in revulsion and disbelief.

Nicky was dead. His face had frozen in death as he screamed, and his arms and legs were twisted, a snapshot of his flailing as he was thrown into the pit by my father. He lay on his back. His hair had horripilated as he went through the electric field, and it stood up around his petrified face.

Clive Borden emitted a dreadful howl of misery, anger and despair, and leapt down into the pit. He threw himself on the ground, wrapped his arms around the body of his son, tried tenderly to pull the boy's limbs back to their normal position, cradled the boy's head with a hand, pressed his face against the boy's cheek, all the while shaking with terrible sobs coming from deep within him.

And my mother, as if realising for the first time that I was there beside her, suddenly swept her arms around me, pressed my face into her skirt, then lifted me up. She walked quickly across the cellar, bearing me away from the scene of the disaster.

I was facing back over her shoulder, and as we went quickly out to the staircase my last sight was of my father. He was staring down into the pit, and his face bore such an expression of harsh satisfaction that more than two decades later I can still remember it only with a shudder of repulsion.

My father had known what would happen, he had allowed it to happen, he had made it happen. Everything about his stance and his expression said: *I've proved my point.*

I noticed also that Stimpson, the servant, was crouching on the floor, balancing himself with his hands. His head was bowed.

8

I've lost, or suppressed, all memories of what happened in the immediate aftermath. I only recall being at school during the following year, and then changing schools, making new friends, gradually growing up through childhood. There was a rush of normality around me, like a flood of embarrassed compensation for the appalling scene I had witnessed.

Nor can I remember when my father walked out of his marriage, leaving us behind. I know the date it happened, because I found it in the diary my mother kept in the last years of her life, but my own memory of that time is lost. Because of her diary I also know most of her feelings about the split-up, and a little of what caused it. For my part I remember a general sense of his being there when I was small, an unnerving and unpredictable figure, thankfully at a remove from our day-to-day lives. I also remember life afterwards without him, a strong sense of his absence, a tranquillity that Rosalie and I made the most of and which has continued ever since.

I was glad at first that he went. It was only when I was older that I began to miss him, as I do now. I believe he must be alive still, because otherwise we would have heard. Our estate is complicated to run, and my father is still responsible for that. There is a family trust, administered by solicitors in Derby, and they are apparently in touch with him. The house and land and title are still in his name. Many of the direct charges, such as taxation, are dealt with and paid by the trust, and money is still made available to Rosalie and me.

Our last direct contact with him was about five years ago, when he wrote a letter from South Africa. Passing through, he said, although he didn't say where from or where to. He is in his seventies now, probably hanging out somewhere with other British exiles, not letting on about his background. Harmless, a bit dotty, vague on details, an old Foreign Office hand. I can't forget him. No matter how much time passes, I always remember him as the cruel-faced man who threw a small boy into a machine he must have known would certainly kill him.

9

Clive Borden left the house the same night. I've no idea what happened to Nicky's body, although I believe Borden must have taken it with him.

Because I was so young I accepted my parents' authority as final and when they told me the police would not be interested in the boy's death, I believed them. In the event, they seemed to be right.

Years later, when I was old enough to realise how wrong it was, I tried to ask my mother what had happened. This was after my father had left home, and about two years before she died.

It felt to me then as if the time had come to clear up the mysteries of the past, to put some of the darkness behind us. I also saw it as a sign of my own growing up. I wanted her to be frank with me and treat me like an adult. I knew she had received a letter from my father earlier that week, and it gave me an excuse to bring up the subject.

'Why did the police never come round to ask questions?' I said, when I had made it plain that I wanted to talk about that night.

She said, 'We do never talk about that, Katherine.'

'You mean that you never do,' I said. 'But why did Daddy leave home?'

'You would have to ask him that.'

'You know I can't,' I said. 'You're the only one who knows. He did something wrong that night, but I'm not sure why and I'm not even sure how. Are the police looking for him?'

'The police aren't involved in our lives.'

'Why not?' I said. 'Didn't Daddy kill that boy? Wasn't that murder?'

'It was all dealt with at the time. There is nothing to hide, nothing to feel guilty about. We paid the price for what happened that night. Mr Borden suffered most, of course, but look what it has done to all our lives. I can tell you nothing you want to know. You saw for yourself what happened.'

'I can't believe that's the end of it,' I said.

'Katherine, you should know better than to ask these questions. You were there too. You're as guilty as the rest of us.'

'I was only five years old!' I said. 'How could that possibly make me guilty of something?'

'If you're in any doubt you could establish that by going to the police yourself.'

My courage failed me in the face of her cold and unyielding demeanour. Mr and Mrs Stimpson still worked for us then, and later I asked Stimpson the same questions. Politely, stiffly, tersely, he denied all knowledge of anything that might have taken place.

10

My mother died when I was eighteen. Rosalie and I half-expected news of it to bring our father out of exile, but it did not. We stayed on in the house, and slowly it dawned on us that the place was ours. We reacted differently. Rosalie gradually freed herself psychologically of the place, and in the end she moved away. I began to be trapped by it, and I'm still here. A large part of what held me was the feeling of guilt I could not throw off, about what had happened down there in the cellar. Everything centred on those events, and in the end I realised I would have to do something about purging myself of what happened.

I finally plucked up my courage and went down to the cellar to discover if anything of what I had seen was still there.

I chose to do it on a day in summer, when friends were visiting from Sheffield and the house was full of the sounds of rock music and the talk and laughter of young people. I told no one what I was planning, but simply slipped away from a conversation in the garden and walked into the house. I was braced with three glasses of wine.

The lock on the door had been changed soon after the Borden visit, and when my mother died I had it changed again, although I had never actually ventured inside. Mr Stimpson and his wife were long gone, but they and the housekeepers who came after them used the cellar for storage. I had always been too nervous even to go to the top of the steps.

On that day, though, I wasn't going to let anything stop me. I had been preparing myself for some time. Once through the door I locked it from the inside (one of the changes I had ordered), switched on the electric lights and walked down to the cellar.

I looked immediately for the apparatus that had killed Nicky Borden but, not too surprisingly, it was no longer there. However, the circular pit was still in the centre of the cellar floor, and I went over and inspected that. It appeared to have been constructed more recently than the rest of the screed floor. It had clearly been excavated with a plan in mind, because several steel ties were drilled into the concrete sides at regular intervals, presumably to act as stays for the wooden bars of the apparatus. In the ceiling overhead, directly above the centre of the pit, there was a large electrical junction box. A thick cable led away to a voltage converter at the side of the cellar, but the box itself had become dirty and rusty.

I noticed that there were numerous scorch marks on the ceiling radiating out from the box, and although someone had put a coat of white emulsion paint over them they still showed through.

Apart from all this there was no sign that the apparatus had ever been in place.

I found the thing itself a few moments later, when I went to investigate the collection of crates, cases and large mysterious objects stored neatly along most of the length of one wall. I soon realised that this was where my great-grandfather's magic paraphernalia had been stored, presumably after his death. Near the front, but otherwise stacked unobtrusively, were two stoutly made wooden crates, each of them so heavy I was unable to budge them, let alone get them out of the cellar on my own. Stencilled in black on one of them, but greatly faded with age, were routing names: 'Denver, Chicago, Boston, Liverpool (England)'. A Customs manifest was stapled to the side, although it was so frayed that it came off in my hand when I touched it. Holding it under the nearest light I saw that someone had written in copperplate, 'Contents – Scientific Instruments'. Metal hoops had been attached on all four sides of both crates, to facilitate hoisting, and there were obvious handholds all over the crates.

I tried to open the nearer of the two, fumbling along the edge of the lid to find some way to force it open, when to my surprise the top swivelled upwards lightly, balanced within in some way. I knew at once I had found the workings of the electrical apparatus I had seen that night, but because it had been dismantled all menace was gone.

Attached to the inside of the lid were several large sheets of cartridge paper, still uncurled and unyellowed, even in great age, and instructions had been written in a clear but tiny and fastidious hand. I glanced over the first few:

Locate, check, and test local ground connection. If insufficient, do not proceed. See (27) below for details of how to install, check, and test a ground connection. Always check wiring colors; see chart attached.

[If not used in USA or Great Britain.] Locate, check, and test local electricity supply. Use instrument located in Wallet 4.5.1 to determine nature, voltage, and cycle of current. Refer to (15) below for settings to main transforming unit.

Test reliability of local electricity supply while assembling the apparatus. If there is divergence of ± 25V do not attempt to operate the apparatus.

When handling components, always wear the protective gloves located in Wallet 3.19.1 (spares in 3.19.2).

And so on, an exhaustive checklist of assembly instructions, many of them using technical or scientific words and phrases. (I have since arranged for a copy to be made, which I keep in the house.) The list was signed with the initials 'F.K.A.'.

Inside the lid of the second crate was a similar list of instructions, these dealing with safely disconnecting the apparatus, dismantling it and stowing the components inside the crates in their correct places.

It was at this moment that it began to dawn on me who my great-grandfather had actually been. What I mean by this is the sense of what he had done, what he had been capable of, what he had achieved in his life. Until then he was just an ancestor, Grandpa who had his stuff about the house. It was my first glimpse of the person he might have been. These crates, with their meticulous instructions, had been his and the instructions had been written by or more likely for him. I stood there for a long time, imagining him unpacking the apparatus with his assistants, racing against the clock to get the thing set up in time for the first performance. I still knew almost nothing about him, but at last I had an insight into what he did, and a little of how he did it.

Later in the year I sorted through the rest of his stuff and this too helped me sense what he was like. The room that had been his study was full of neatly filed papers: bills, magazines, correspondence, booking forms, travel documents, playbills, theatre programmes. A large part of his life was filed away there, and there was more in the cellar, costumes and paraphernalia from his shows. Most of the costumes had fallen to bits with old age, and I threw them out, but the cabinet illusions were in working or repairable condition, and because I needed the money I sold the best examples to magic collectors. I also disposed of Rupert Angier's collection of magic books. From the people who came to buy, I learnt that much of his material was valuable, but only in cash terms. Little of it had more than curiosity value to modern magicians. Most of the illusions The Great Danton performed were of an everyday variety, and to the expert or collector they contained no surprises. I did not sell the electrical apparatus, and it is still down in the cellar in its crates.

By some means I had not expected, the act of going down into the cellar put my childish fears behind me. Perhaps it was as simple as that in the intervening years I had become an adult, or in the absence of the rest of the family was now in effect the head of the household. Whatever the reason, when I emerged from the old brown door, locking it behind me, I believed I had thrown off something unwelcome that had dogged my life until then.

I I

It was not enough, though. Nothing could excuse the fact that I had seen a small boy cruelly murdered that night, and by my own father.

This secret has wormed itself into my life, indirectly influencing everything I do, inhibiting me emotionally and immobilising me socially. I am isolated here. I rarely make friends, I want no lovers, a career does not interest me. Since Rosalie moved out to get married I have lived here alone, as much a victim as my parents were.

I want to distance myself from the madness that the feud has brought to my family over the years, but as I grow older I believe more strongly that the only way out is to face up to it. I cannot get on with my life until I understand how and why Nicky Borden died.

His death nags at me. The obsession would end if I knew more about the boy, and what really happened to him that night. But as I have learned about my family's past, I have learned inevitably about the Bordens.

I traced you, Andrew, because you and I are the key to the whole thing – you are the sole surviving Borden, while I am to all intents the last living Angier.

Against all logic, I know Nicky Borden was *you*, Andrew, and that somehow you survived that ordeal.

12

The rain had turned to snow during the evening, and it was still falling as Andrew Westley and Kate Angier sat together over the remains of the dinner. Her story appeared at first to produce no response from him, because he merely looked quietly at his empty coffee cup, fingering the spoon in the saucer. Then he said he needed to walk around for a bit. He crossed the room to the window to stare out at the garden and cradled his hands behind his neck, waggling his head from side to side. It was pitch black out there in the grounds. She knew there was nothing for him to see. The main road was behind the house and at a lower level. On this side of the house there was just the lawn, the wood, the rising hill, and beyond all that the rocky crag of Curbar Edge. He did not change position for some time. Without being able to see his face Kate felt that either his eyes must be closed or he was staring blankly into the dark.

In the end he said, 'I'll tell you all I know. I lost contact with my twin brother when I was about the same age as you're describing. Maybe what you've told me would explain that. But his birth wasn't registered, so I can't prove he exists. I know he's real. You've heard how twins have a kind of rapport? That's how I'm sure. The other thing I know is that he is connected in some way with this house. Ever since I arrived today I've been sensing him here. I don't know how, and I can't explain.'

'I've looked at the records too,' she said. 'You were a sole child. There was never any hint of a twin, brother or sister.'

'Could someone have tampered with the records? Is that possible?'

'Of course I've wondered that. If the boy was killed, wouldn't that give someone enough motive to find a way of falsifying the records?'

'Maybe so. All I can say for sure is that I don't remember anything about it. It's all blank. I don't even remember my father. All I know is his name, Clive Borden. That child who died obviously couldn't have been me, and it's absurd even to think it was. It must have been someone else.'

'But it was your father . . . and Nicky was his only child.'

He turned from the window, and went back to his chair.

'There are only two or three possibilities,' he said. 'The boy was me and I was killed and now I'm alive again. That's just illogical. Or the boy who died was my twin brother, and the person who killed him, presumably that's your father, later managed to get official records changed. I don't believe that either, frankly. Or you were mistaken, the child survived, and it might or might not have been me. Or . . . I suppose you could have imagined the whole thing.'

'No. I didn't imagine it. I know what I saw. Anyway my mother as good as admitted it.' She picked up her copy of the Borden book, and opened it at a page she had previously marked with a slip of paper. 'There's another explanation, but it's as irrational as the others. If you weren't actually killed that night, then it might have been some kind of trick. The thing I saw being used that night was magical apparatus, built for a stage illusion.'

She turned the book around, and held it out to him, but he waved it away.

'The whole thing is ridiculous,' he said.

'I saw it happen.'

'I think you were either mistaken in what you saw, or it happened to someone else.' He glanced again towards the windows with their undrawn curtains, then looked at his watch in a distracted way. 'Do you mind if I use my mobile? I must tell my parents I'm going to be late. And I'd like to ring my flat in London.'

'I think you should stay the night.' He grinned briefly then, and Kate knew she had said it the wrong way. She found him fairly attractive, in a harmlessly coarse sort of way, but he was apparently the kind of man who never gave up about sex. 'I meant that Mrs Makin will prepare the spare room for you.'

'If she has to.'

There had been that moment before they came in here for dinner. She must have given him too much rye whiskey, or had said too often that there were irreconcilable differences between her family and his. Or perhaps it was a combination of the two. Until then she had been rather liking the way he had leered in an open and unembarrassed way at her, off and on all afternoon, but an hour and a half ago, just before they came in here for dinner, he'd made it plain that he would like to try another rapprochement between the families. Just the two of them, the last generation. A part of her remained flattered, but what he had in mind was not what she had had in mind. She'd brushed him off, as gently as she knew how.

'Are you fit to drive in snow, with drink inside you?' she said now.

'Yes.'

But he did not move from the chair. She laid the Borden

book on the table between them, face-down at the open pages.

'What do you want from me, Kate?' he said.

'I don't know any more. Perhaps I never did. I think this is what happened when Clive Borden came to see my father. They both felt they should try to sort something out, went through the motions of trying, but the ancient differences still mattered.'

'There's only one thing that interests me. My twin brother is somewhere here. In this house. Ever since you showed me your grandfather's stuff this afternoon I've been aware of him. He tells me not to leave, to come, to find him. I've never known his presence as strong in me. Whatever you say, whatever the birth register shows, I think it was my brother who came here to the house in 1970, and I think he's somehow still here.'

'In spite of the fact that no twin exists. We both know that.'

'Yes, in spite of that.'

She felt herself at an impasse. It was the same one she had always known. The certain death of a little boy, whom she later discovered had somehow survived. Meeting the man who had been the boy had changed nothing. It was him, it had not been him.

She poured herself another drop of brandy, and Andrew said, 'Is there somewhere I can make those calls?'

'Stay in here. This is the warmest place in the house in winter. I've got something I want to check.'

As she left the room she heard him clicking the keys of his mobile. She went down to the main hall and looked through the front door. There was already a solid covering of snow, three or four inches. It always settled smoothly here, on the pathway in the lee of the house, but she knew that further down the valley, where the main road was, the snow would already be drifting against the hedges and roadside banks. There were no sounds of traffic, which could usually be heard from here. She went around to the back of the house and saw that a drift was building up against the woodshed.

The wind was sending streamers of flakes into the dark, moulding the drifts into mounds. Mrs Makin was in the kitchen, so she spoke to her and asked her to get the spare room ready.

She and Andrew remained in the dining room after Mrs Makin had cleared away the meal, sitting on opposite sides of the open fireplace, talking about various everyday things. She told him about the local council, who wanted some of her land for building purposes. Later he told her he was having trouble over the girl he lived with, who had walked out on him leaving him unsure if he wanted her back or not.

But Kate was tired and had no real appetite for this.

At eleven she took him upstairs and showed him the spare room, and the bathroom he could use. Rather to her surprise a second proposition was not made. He thanked her politely for her hospitality, said goodnight, and that was that.

Kate returned to the dining room, where she had left some of her great-grandfather's papers. They were already stacked neatly; some hereditary trait, perhaps, that prevented her from scattering paper everywhere. There had always been a part of her that wanted to be untidy, casual, free, but it was in her nature not to be.

She sat down in the chair closest to the fire, and felt the glow against her legs. She threw on another log.

Now Andrew had gone to bed she felt less sleepy. It hadn't been him that had worn her out, but talking to him, dredging up all those memories from childhood. To talk them out was a kind of purging, a release of pent-up poisons, and she felt better.

She sat by the fire, thinking about that old incident, trying as she had done for a quarter of a century to confront what it meant. It still struck fright to the core of her. And the boy that Andrew called his brother was at the heart of it all, a hostage to the past.

Mrs Makin came in just then, and Kate asked if she would make her a cup of decaffeinated coffee before she went to bed. She listened to the midnight news on Radio 4 as she sipped the coffee, and later the BBC World Service came on.

She continued to be wide awake. The spare room Andrew was in was immediately overhead, and she could hear him turning frequently in the ancient bed. She knew how cold that room could be. It had been her bedroom as a child.

PART FOUR
Rupert Angier

THE STORY OF MY LIFE   21st September 1866

My History, my name is ROBBIE (Rupert) DAVID
ANGIER and I am 9 nine years old today. I am to write in
this book every day until I am old.

My Ancestors, I have many but Papa and Mama are the
first. I have one brother: HENRY RICHARD ANGUS
ST JOHN ANGIER, and he is 15 he goes to school and is a
border.

I live in Caldlow House Caldlow Derbyshire. I have had
something wrong with my throte this week.

The Staff, I have a Nan and there is Grierson and a maid
who changes with the other maid in the afternoons, but I
don't know her name.

I have to show this to Papa when I have written it.

The cnd. Signed Rupert David Angier.

THE STORY OF MY LIFE   22nd September 1866

Today the doctor came to see me again and I am all right.
Got a letter today from Henry my brother who says I must
call him Sir from now on because he is a prefect.

Papa has gone to London to sit in the House. He said that
I am the head of the house until he gets back. This means
Henry would call me sir but he is not here.

Told this to Henry when I wrote to him.

Went for walk, talked to Nan, was read to by Grierson
who fell asleep as usual.

I do not have to show this to Papa any more, provided I
keep it up.

                              23rd September 1866

Throte much better. Went for drive today with Grierson,
who did not say much but he told me that Henry says that

155

when he takes over the house he will be going. Grierson will be going when Henry takes over the house, I mean. Grierson said he thought it had all been decided but it would not happen for many years god willing.

I am waiting for Mama to come and see me she is late tonight.

22nd December 1867

Yesterday evening there was a party for me and several boys and girls from the village, it being Christmas they are allowed here. Henry was here too but he would not come to the party because of the others. He missed a great treat because we had a conjuror at the party!

This man, who was called Mr A. Presto, did the most wonderful tricks I have ever seen. He started by making all sorts of banners and flags and umbrellas appear from no-where, with lots of balloons and ribbons. Then he did some tricks with playing cards, making us choose cards which he was able to guess. He was very clever. He made billiard balls come out of one of the boy's nose, and a whole lot of coins fell out of a little girl's ear when he grabbed hold of it. There was a piece of string which he cut in half then joined up again, and at the end of it all he produced a white bird out of a small glass box that we could *see* was empty before he began!

I pleaded and pleaded to be told how these tricks were done, but Mr Presto would not tell me. Even afterwards when the others had gone, but nothing I could say would make him change his mind.

This morning I had an idea, and I got Grierson to drive into Sheffield for me and buy all the magic tricks he could find, and to see if there were any books that told you how to do it. Grierson was gone nearly all day, but in the end he came back with most of what I wanted. It includes a special glass box for hiding a bird in so I can produce it by magic. (Special floor to the box, which I hadn't thought of.) The other tricks are a bit harder, because I have to practice. But already I have learnt a trick where I can guess which card someone else has chosen and I have tried it out several times on Grierson.

17th February 1871

I managed to see Papa alone this afternoon for the first time in many months, and found that the situation was much as Henry has already described it. There is nothing apparently to be done about it, except to make the best of a bad job.

I could gladly kill Henry.

31st March 1873

Today I removed and destroyed all entries from the last two years. It was the first act I performed on returning from school.

1st April 1873

Home from school. I now have sufficient privacy to write in this book.

My father, the 12th Earl of Colderdale, died three days ago, 29th March 1873. My brother Henry assumes his title, lands and property. The future of myself, my mother, and every other member of the household, be they ever so mighty or humble, is now uncertain. Even the future of the house itself cannot be counted upon, as Henry has openly spoken in the past of making drastic changes. We can only wait, but for the time being the house is preoccupied with funereal preparations.

Papa will be buried tomorrow in the vault.

This morning I am feeling more sanguine about my prospects. I have been here in my room this morning, practising my magic. My progress with this field was one of the victims of my recent purge of this diary's pages, because from the start I kept a detailed record of what it took to become proficient in sleight of hand . . . but all this had to go when I decided to remove the rest. Suffice to say that I believe I have now attained performance standard, and although I have not yet put it to test, I have often practised new tricks on the fellows at school. They feign a lack of

157

interest in magic, and indeed some of them declare that they know my secrets, but I have had one or two moments when, gratifyingly, I have seen genuine bafflement in their expressions.

There is no need for haste. All the magic books I have read advise the novitiate not to rush, but instead to prepare thoroughly so that one's performance has surprise as well as skill. If they know not who you are, it adds to the mystique of what you are, and what you are about to do.

So it is said.

I wish, and this is my only wish in this saddest of weeks, that I could use my magic to bring Papa back to his life. A selfish wish, because it would undoubtedly help restore my own life to where it was three days ago, but also a fervently loving wish, because I loved my Papa and already I miss him, and regret his passing. He was forty-nine years old, and I believe that is too young by far to be a victim of failure of the heart.

2nd April 1873

The funeral has taken place, and my father has been laid to rest. After the ceremony in the chapel, his body was taken to the family vault, situated beneath the East Rise. The mourners all walked in a line to the entrance to the vault, and then Henry and I, together with the undertaker and his staff, bore the coffin underground.

Nothing had prepared me for what followed. I had never been inside the vault. From outside, where a door has been built between a couple of columns, it looks at most as if it might be a small cave or passage dug into the hill. When you go inside it turns out to be a huge natural cavern stretching back into the hill, widened and enlarged for use as the family tomb. It is in complete darkness, the ground underfoot is uneven and rocky, the air is foetid, we saw several rats, and the numerous jagged shelves and ledges protrude into the passageway causing painful collisions in the dark. We were each carrying a lantern, but once we were at the bottom of the steps and away from the daylight they proved of little use. The undertakers accepted all this in a professional manner, even though carrying the casket must have been extremely difficult under the circumstances, but for my brother and I it was a short but significant ordeal. Once we had found a suitable ledge and deposited the coffin, the senior undertaker intoned a few scriptural words and we returned without delay to the surface. We emerged into the bright spring morning we had left a few minutes earlier, where the East Lawn was festooned with daffodils and the buds were bursting from the trees around us, but for me at least the sojourn in that dark tunnel cast a shadow across the rest of the day. I shuddered as the stout wooden portal closed, and I could not throw off the memory of those ancient broken caskets, the dust, the smell, the lifeless despair of the place.

Evening

An hour or so ago came the ceremony, and I use the word with the sense that it is exactly the one I want, the *ceremony* around which the day has been built. For this, the reading of my father's will, the interment was a mere preliminary.

We were all there, assembled in the hall beneath the main staircase. Sir Geoffrey Fusel-Hunt, my father's solicitor, called us to silence, and with steady, deliberate hands he opened the stout brown envelope that contained the dread document, and slipped out the folded sheets of vellum. I looked around at the others. My father's brothers and sisters were there, with their spouses and, in some cases, their children. The men who managed the estate and who guarded the game, patrolled the moor, protected the farms and the fishery, stood in a group to one side. Next to them, also clustering, the tenant farmers, eyes wide with hope. In the centre of this huge group, directly facing Sir Geoffrey across his desk, myself and Mama, with the servants behind us. In front of us all, standing, arms folded across his chest, central to the moment, Henry dominated the occasion.

There were no surprises. Henry's main inheritance is of course not subject to my father's will, nor are the hereditary rights of property. But there are freeholds to be disposed of, portfolios of shares, amounts of cash and stocks of valuables, and, most important of all, rights of possession, of occupation.

Mama is given the choice, for the remainder of her life, of occupying a principal wing of the main house or total occupation of the dower house by the gate. I am allowed to remain in the rooms I presently occupy until I finish my education or gain my majority, after which my fate will be decided by Henry. The destiny of our personal servants is linked to our own. The rest of the household is to stay or be disposed of as Henry sees fit.

Our life is to be unravelled.

A few cash legacies have gone to favoured retainers, but the bulk of the fortune is now Henry's. He made no move, showed no sign, when this was announced. I kissed Mama, then shook hands with several of the estate managers and farmers.

Tomorrow I shall try to decide how I am to live my life, and to make this decision before Henry can make it for me.

3rd April 1873

What am I to do? There is more than another week before I return to school, for what will be my last term.

3rd April 1874

It seems appropriate to return to this diary after the space of a year. I remain at Caldlow House, partly because until I am twenty-one I am in the charge of Henry, my legal guardian, but mainly because Mama wishes me to.

I am minded by Grierson. Henry has taken a residence in London, from where it is reported that he daily attends the House. Mama is in good health, and I walk to the dower house every morning, which is her best time, and we speculate unprofitably about what I might be able to do once I gain my majority.

Following Papa's death I allowed my practice of legerdemain to fall into neglect, but about nine months ago I returned to it. Since then I have been practising intently, and taking every opportunity to watch the performance of stage magic. For this purpose I travel to the music halls of Sheffield or Manchester, where although the standards are variable I do see a sufficient variety of turns to stimulate my interest. Many of the illusions are already known to me, but at least once in every performance I see something that excites or baffles me. After this the hunt for the secret is on. Grierson and I now have a well-trodden path around the various magic dealers and suppliers, where, with persistence, we eventually gain access to what I require.

Grierson, alone in our diminished household, knows of my magical interest and ambition. When Mama speaks pessimistically of what is to become of me, I dare not tell her what I plan, but deep inside me I feel a knot of confidence that when I am eventually cast adrift from this half-life in Derbyshire I shall have a career to follow. The magic journals to which I subscribe write of the immense fees a top illusionist may now command for a single performance, not to mention the social kudos that attaches to a brilliant career on the stage.

Already I am playing a part. I am the disinherited younger brother of a peer, down on his luck, reduced to hand-outs from a guardian, and I trudge through my dispiriting life in these rainy hills of Derbyshire.

I am waiting in the wings, however, because once I am of age my real life will begin!

Idmiston Villas, London N   31st December 1876

I have finally been able to get my boxes and cases from storage, and I spent a dismal Christmas going through my old belongings, sorting out those that I no longer want, and those I am glad to find again. This diary was one of the latter, and I have been reading through it for the last few minutes.

I remember that once before I decided to set down the minutiae of my magical career, and as I write this now I have the same thought. Too many gaps already exist, though. I tore out all those pages where I described my rows with Henry, and with them went the records I kept of my progress. I cannot be bothered to go back in memory and summarise all the various tricks, forces, moves I learnt and practised in those days.

Also I see from my last entry, more than two and a half years ago, that I was then waiting in dejected stupor to reach the age of twenty-one, so that Henry could throw me out of the house. In fact, I did not wait that long, and took matters into my own hands.

So here I am, at the age of nineteen, living in rented lodgings in a respectable street in a London suburb, a man free of his past, and, for the next two years at least (because irrespective of where I am living Henry has to continue my allowance), free of financial worries. I have already performed my magic once in public, but was not paid for it. (The less said about that humiliating occasion the better.)

I have become, and shall remain, plain Mister Rupert Angier. I have turned my back on my past. No one in this new life of mine will ever find out the truth of my birthright.

Tomorrow, being the first day of the new year, I shall summarise my magical aspirations and perhaps set down my resolutions.

1st January 1877

The morning post has brought with it a small parcel of books from New York for which I have been waiting for many weeks, and I have been looking through them for ideas.

I love to perform. I study the craft of using a stage, of presenting a show, of entertaining an audience with a stream of witty or droll remarks . . . and I dream of laughter, gasps of surprise, and tumults of applause. I know I can reach the top of my profession simply by the excellence of presentation.

My weakness is that I never understand the working of an illusion until it is explained to me. When I see a trick for the first time I am as baffled by it as any other member of the audience. I have a poor magical imagination, and find it difficult to apply known general principles to produce a desired effect. When I see a superb performance I am dazzled by the shown and confounded by the unseen.

Once, in a stage performance at the Manchester Hippodrome, a magician presented a glass carafe for all to see. He held it before his face, so that we could glimpse his features through it. He struck it lightly with a metal rod, so that by its gentle ringing noise we could tell it was symmetrically and perfectly made. Finally, he held it upside down for a moment so that we could see for ourselves it was empty. He then turned to his table of props where a metal jug was in place. He poured from this, into the carafe, about half a pint of clear water. Then, without further ado, he went to a tray of wineglasses set up on one side of the stage and poured into each of them a quantity of red wine!

The point of this is that I already had in my possession the device that enabled me to appear to pour water into a folded newspaper, then pour *back* from it a glass of milk (the sheet of paper remaining unaccountably dry).

The principle was much the same, the presentation was different, and in admiring the latter I lost all sight of the former.

I spend a large amount of my monthly allowance in magic shops, where I have purchased the secret or the device that has allowed me to add one trick or another to my steadily expanding repertoire. It is devilish hard to discover secrets when they cannot be purchased for cash! And even when I can, it is not always the answer, because as competition increases so illusionists are forced to invent their own tricks. I find it simultaneously a torment and a challenge to see such illusions performed.

Here the magic profession closes ranks on the newcomer. One day, I dare say, I shall join those ranks myself and try to exclude newcomers, but for the present I find it vexing that the older magicians protect their secrets so jealously. This afternoon I penned a letter to *Prestidigitators' Panel*, a monthly journal sold by subscription only, setting out my thoughts on the widespread and absurd obsession with secrecy.

Every weekday morning, from 9.00 a.m. to midday, I patrol what has become a well-worn path between the offices of the four main theatrical agencies who specialise in magic or novelty acts. Outside the door of each one I brace myself against the inevitability of rejection, then enter with as brave a face as I can feign, make my presence known to the attendant who sits in the reception area, and enquire politely if any commissions might be available to me.

Invariably, so far, the answer has been in the negative. The mood of these attendants seems to vary, but most of the time they are courteous to me while brusquely saying no.

I know they are pestered endlessly by the likes of myself, because a veritable procession of unemployed performers trudges the same daily path as me. Naturally I see these others as I go about my applications, and naturally I have befriended some of them. Unlike most I am not short of a bob or two (or at least not at the moment), so when we make tracks at lunchtime to one or another tavern in Holborn or Soho I am able to stand a few drinks for them. I am popular for this, of course, but I do not fool myself that it is for any other reason. I am glad of the company, and also for the more subtle hope that through any of these hail-fellows I will one day make a contact who might find or offer me some work.

It is a congenial enough life, and in the afternoons and evenings I have abundant time left to myself in which to continue to practise.

And I have time enough to write letters. I have become a persistent and, I fancy, a controversial correspondent on the subject of magic. I make a point of writing to every issue of the magic journals I see, and try always to be acute, provocative, disputatious. I am partly motivated by the sincere belief that there is much about the tawdry world of magic which needs putting to rights, but also by a sense that my name will not become known unless I spread it about in a way that makes it remembered.

Some letters I sign with my own name; others with the name I have chosen for my professional career: Danton. The use of two names allows me a little flexibility in what I say.

These are early days and few of my letters have so far been published. I imagine that as they start to appear my name will soon be on the lips of many people.

16th April 1877

My financial sentence of death has been pronounced, made official! Henry has informed me, through his solicitors, that my allowance will end as expected on my twenty-first birthday. I have the continuing right to reside in Caldlow House, but only in the rooms already allocated to me.

I am glad in a way that he has at last uttered the words. Uncertainty no longer dogs me. I have until September next year. Seventeen months in which to break this vicious circle of failure to get work, leading to failure to become known, leading to failure to build an audience for my skills, leading to failure to find work.

I have continued to trail my coat around the theatrical agencies, and now, from tomorrow, I must do so with renewed resolve.

13th June 1877

Summer weather is here, but springtime has belatedly arrived for me. At last I have been offered some work!

It is not much, some card tricks to perform at a conference of Brummagem businessmen in a London hotel, and the fee is only half a guinea, but this is a red-letter day.

Ten shillings and sixpence! More than a week's rent for these lodgings. Riches indeed!

19th June 1877

One of the books I have studied is by a Hindoo magician called Gupta Hilel. In this he gives advice to the illusionist whose trick goes wrong. There are several resorts Hilel offers, and most of them are concerned with methods of distracting the audience. But he also offers the counsel of fatalism. A magic career is full of disappointment and failure, which must be expected and dealt with stoically.

So it is with stoicism that I record the launch of Danton's professional magical career. I merely report that the first trick I attempted (a simple card shift) went wrong, immobilizing me with sheer terror and ruining the rest of my act.

I was paid off with a half-fee of five shillings and threepence, and the promoter advised me that I should practise more before trying again. Mr Hilel also advises this.

20th June 1877

Despairing, I have decided to abandon my magical career.

14th July 1877

I have been back to Derbyshire to see Mama, and have now returned in a darker mood of melancholy than the one that was blighting me before I left. Also there is news that my rent is to increase to ten shillings a week from next month.

I still have just over a year before I must be able to support myself.

10th October 1877

I am in love! Her name is Drusilla MacAvoy.

15th October 1877

Too hasty by far! The MacAvoy woman was not for me. I am planning to kill myself, and if the remainder of these pages are blank anyone who comes across this diary will know I succeeded.

22nd December 1877

Now at last I have found the real woman in my life! I have never been so happy. Her name is Julia Fensell, she is but two months younger than I, her hair is a glowing reddish brown and it cascades about her face. She has blue eyes, a long straight nose, a chin with a tiny dimple, a mouth that seems always about to smile, and ankles whose slender shape drives me wild with love and passion. She is easily the most beautiful young woman I have ever seen, and she says she loves me as much as I love her.

It is impossible to believe, impossible to credit my good fortune. She drives from my mind all worries, all fears, all anger and despair and ambitions. She fills my life entirely. I almost cannot bear to write of her, in case I again curse myself with ill-fortune!

31st December 1877

I still cannot write of Julia, or of my life in general, without trembling. The year is ending, and tonight, at 11.00 p.m., I am joining Julia so that we might be together as the new year begins.

Total Income for 1877: 5s 3d.

3rd January 1878

I have been seeing Julia every day since the middle of last month. She has become my dearest, closest friend. I must write of her as objectively as possible, for my knowing her has already set fair to change my fortune.

First let me record that since my abysmal performance at the Langham Street Hotel several months ago I have not secured any other bookings. My confidence was low, and for a day or two I could not summon even false optimism to get me round the agency offices. However, I had to resume, for it is the only way to find work. It was during one of these melancholy tours that I first met Julia. I had seen her before, as I saw everybody on that circuit, but her sheer beauty had made her forbidden to me. We finally spoke to each other while being made to wait together in the outer office of one of the agents in Great Portland Street. It was unheated, bare-boarded, drably painted, furnished with the hardest of wooden seats. Alone with her I could not pretend not to notice her so I plucked up my courage and spoke to her. She said she was an actress; I said I was an illusionist. From the few bookings I soon learned she had been getting recently, her description of herself was as theoretical as my own. We found our duplicity amusing and became friends.

Julia is the first person, apart from Grierson, to whom I have shown my tricks in private. Unlike Grierson, who always applauded anything I did, no matter how clumsy or ill performed, Julia was critical and appreciative in more or less equal measure. She encouraged me, but also she devastated and withered me if she found me failing. From anyone else I should have taken this poorly, but whenever her criticism was most merciless, words of love, or support, or constructive suggestion soon followed.

I began with simple sleight of hand involving coins, some of the first tricks I had learned. Card tricks followed, then handkerchief tricks, hat tricks, billiard ball tricks. Her interest spurred me on. I gradually worked my way through most of my repertoire, even the illusions I had not yet fully mastered.

Sometimes, in her turn, Julia would recite for me: lines from the great poets, the great playwrights, work that was always new to me. It amazed me that she could remember so much, but she said there were techniques that were easily learned. This was Julia – half artiste, half craftsman. Art and technique.

Soon Julia began talking to me about presentation, a subject close to my heart. Our affair began to deepen.

Over the Christmas holiday, while the rest of London celebrated, Julia and I were alone, chastely, in my rented lodgings, teaching each other the disciplines to which we each had become attached. She came to me in the mornings, stayed with me through the short hours of daylight, then soon after nightfall I would walk her back to her own lodgings in Kilburn. I spent the evenings and nights alone, thinking of her, of the excitement she was bringing me, of the matters of the stage to which she was introducing me.

Julia is gradually, inexorably, drawing out of me the true talent I think I have always possessed.

'Why should we not, between us, devise a magical act of a kind no one before us has ever performed?'

This is what Julia said, the day after I wrote the entry above.

Such simple words! Such havoc on my life, one that had become settled into a cycle of despair and depression, because we are building a mentalist act. Julia has been teaching me her techniques of memory. I am learning the science of mnemonics, the use of memory aids.

Julia's memory has always seemed to me extraordinary. When I first knew her, and had been showing her some of my hard-learned card tricks, she challenged me to call out any two-digit numbers I cared to think of, in any order at all, and to write them down so she could not see. When I had filled a whole page of my notebook, she calmly recited the numbers to me, without pause or error . . . and while I was still marvelling, she recited them again, this time in reverse order!

I assumed it was magic, that she had somehow forced me into nominating numbers she had previously memorised, or that she somehow had access to the notes that I thought I was keeping privy. Neither of these was true, she assured me. It was no trick, and there was no subterfuge. In opposition to the methods of a magician, the secret of her performance was exactly as it seemed – she was memorizing the numbers!

Now she has revealed to me the secret of mnemonics. I am not yet as adept as her, but already I am capable of apparent feats of memory that once I should always have doubted.

26th January 1878

We are ready. Imagine that I am seated on a stage, my eyes blindfolded. Volunteers from the audience have supervised the placing of the blindfold, and have satisfied themselves that I cannot see out. Julia moves amongst the audience, taking items of their personal property and holding them aloft for everyone, bar myself, to see.

'What do I hold?' she cries.

'It is a gentleman's wallet,' I answer.

The audience gasps.

'Now I have taken——?' says Julia.

'It is a wedding ring made of gold.'

'And it belongs to——?'

'A lady,' I declare.

(Were she to say, '*Which* belongs to——?' I should reply, with equal conviction, 'A gentleman.')

'Here I am holding?'

'A gentleman's watch.'

And so it goes. A litany of pre-arranged questions and answers, but one which presented with sufficient aplomb to an audience unready for the spectacle, will clearly imply mentalist contact between the two performers.

The principle is easy, but the learning is hard. I am still new to mnemonics, and, as in all magic, practice has to make perfect.

While the practice goes on we are able to avoid thinking about the most difficult part – obtaining an engagement.

1st February 1878

Tomorrow night we begin. We have wasted two weeks trying to obtain a firm booking from a theatre or hall, but this afternoon, while we walked disconsolately on Hampstead Heath, Julia suggested we should take matters into our own hands.

Now it is midnight, and I have just returned from an evening of preliminary reconnoitre. Julia and I visited a total of six taverns within a reasonable walking distance, and selected the one which seemed the most likely. It is the Lamb and Child, in Kilburn High Road, on the corner with Mill Lane. The main bar is a large, well-lit room, with a small raised platform at one end (presently bearing a piano, which was not being played while we were there). The tables are set out with sufficient room for Julia to move between them while speaking to members of the audience. We did not make our intentions known to the landlord or his staff.

Julia has returned to her lodgings, and soon I will be abed. We rehearse all day tomorrow, then venture forth in the evening.

3rd February 1878

Between us Julia and I have counted £2 4s 9d, tossed to us in single coins by an appreciative crowd in the Lamb and Child. There was more, but I fear some of it was stolen, and some might have been lost when the landlord's patience with us ran out and we were removed to the street.

But we did not fail. And we have learnt a dozen lessons about how to prepare, how to announce ourselves, how to claim attention, and even, we think, how to ingratiate ourselves with the landlord.

Tonight we are planning to visit the Mariner's Arms in Islington, a good distance from Kilburn, where we shall try again. Already we have made changes to our act, based on Saturday night's experience.

4th February 1878

Only 15s 9d between us, but again what we lack in financial reward we have gained in experience.

28th February 1878

As the month ends I can record that Julia and I have so far earned a total of £11 18s 3d from our mentalist act, that we are exhausted by our efforts, that we are elated by our success, that we have now made enough mistakes that we believe we know how to proceed in future, and that already (sure sign of success!) we have heard of a rival pair performing in the inns of south London.

Furthermore, on the 3rd of next month, I shall be performing a legitimate magical act at Hasker's Music Hall in Ponders End. Danton is to appear seventh on the bill after a singing trio. Julia and I have temporarily retired from our mentalist act so as to rehearse me for this great occasion. Already it seems a rather staid booking after the uncertain thrills of busking our act through the gin palaces of London, but it is a real job in a real theatre, and it is what I have worked for over all these years.

4th March 1878

Received: £3 3s od from Mr Hasker, who has said he would like to book me again in April. My trick with the coloured streamers was especially popular.

12th July 1878

A departure. My wife (I have not written in this diary for some time, but Julia and I were wed on 11th May, and now live together contentedly at my lodgings in Idmiston Villas) is feeling that we should once again branch out. I agree. Our mentalist act, although impressive to those who have not seen it before, is repetitive and tiring to perform, and the behaviour of the audiences is unpredictable. I am blind-folded for much of the act so that Julia is, to a great extent, alone in an often drunken and rowdy crowd. Once, while I sat in blindfolds, my pocket was picked.

We both feel it is time for a change, even though we have been earning money regularly. I cannot yet make a living from the stage, and in just over two months I will receive the last of my monthly allowances.

Theatrical bookings have in fact shown a recent improvement, and I have six of them between now and Christmas. In readiness, and while I am still relatively solvent, I have been investing in some large-scale illusions. My workshop (this I acquired last month) is stocked with magical devices, from which I may at fairly short notice put together a fresh and stimulating performance.

The real problem with theatrical bookings is that while they pay well they provide no continuity. Each is at the end of a blind alley. I do my act, I take my applause, I collect my fee, but none of these ensures another booking. Even the reviews in the press are small and grudging. For instance, after a performance at the Clapham Empire, one of my best so far, the *Evening Star* remarked, '. . . and a conjuror named Dartford followed the *soubrette*.' With such pebbles of formal encouragement I am supposed to lay the path of my career!

The idea for a new departure came to me (or I should more properly say, it came to Julia) while I was glancing through a daily newspaper.

I saw a report that evidence had emerged recently that life, or a form of it, continued after death. Certain psychic adepts were able to make contact with newly deceased people, and communicate back from the after-world to their bereaved relatives. I read out a part of the report to Julia. She stared at me for a moment, and I could see her mind was working.

'You don't *believe* that, do you?' she said at last.

'I take it seriously,' I confirmed. 'After all, there are an increasing number of people who have made contact. I treat evidence as it arises. You must not ignore what people say.'

'Rupert, you cannot be serious!' she cried.

I continued oafishly, 'But these séances have been investigated by scientists with the highest academic qualifications.'

'Am I hearing you properly? You, whose very profession is deception!'

At this I began to see the argument she was making, but still I could not forget the testimony from (for instance) Sir Angus Johns, whose endorsement of the existence of the spirit world I had just read in the newspaper. 'You are always saying,' my beloved Julia continued, 'that the easiest people to deceive are those who are the best educated. Their intelligence blinds them to the simplicity of magic secrets!'

At last I had it.

'So you are saying these séances are . . . ordinary illusions?'

'What else could they be?' she said triumphantly. 'This is a new enterprise, my dear. We must be part of it.'

And so, I think, our departure is to be into the world of spiritism. In recording this exchange with Julia, I know it must make me seem stupid. I have always had difficulty understanding magic until the secret is pointed out to me.

15th July 1878

It has happened that two of the letters I wrote to magic journals at the end of last year have appeared this week. I am a little disconcerted to see them! A lot has changed in my life since then. I remember drafting one of the letters, for example, the day after I discovered the truth about Drusilla MacAvoy. As I read my own words I remember that dreary October day in my poorly heated lodgings, sitting at my desk and venting my feelings on some hapless magician who had been whimsically reported, in the journal, as wishing to set up some kind of bank in which magical secrets would be stored and protected. I realise now that it was one of those comments made half in jest, but there is my letter, in full flood of tedious seriousness, castigating the poor fellow for it.

And the other letter, just as embarrassing now to behold, and one for which I cannot even recall mitigating circumstances in which I might have written it.

All this has reminded me of the state of emotional bitterness in which I had lived until I met dear Julia.

31st August 1878

We have attended a total of four séances, and know what is involved. The trickery is generally of a low standard. Perhaps the recipients are in such a state of distress that they would be receptive to almost anything. Indeed, on one of these unfortunate occasions the effects were so patently unconvincing that self-willed credulousness could be the only explanation.

Julia and I have spent much time discussing how we might go about this, and we have decided that the best and only way is to think of our efforts as professional magic, performed to the highest standards. There are already too many charlatans doing the rounds in spiritism, and I have no wish to become one more of them.

This endeavour is for me a means to an end, a way of making and perhaps accumulating a little money until I can support myself in a theatrical career.

The illusions involved in a séance are simple, but already we have seen ways of elaborating them a little to make them seem more supernatural in effect. As we found with our mentalist act, we will learn by experience, and so we have already drafted and paid for our first advertisement in one of the London gazettes. We shall charge modestly at first, partly because we can afford to do so while we learn, and partly so as to ensure as many commissions as possible.

I am already in receipt of, and therefore spending, my last month's allowance. Three weeks from now I shall be entirely self-sufficient, whether I like it or not.

9th September 1878

Our advertisement has elicited fourteen enquiries! As we offered our services at two guineas a time, and the advertisement cost me 3s 6d, we are already making a profit!

As I write this, Julia is drafting letters of response, trying to arrange a schedule of steady appointments for us.

All this morning I have been practising an illusion known as the JACOBY ROPE TIE. This is a technique in which a magician is tied to a plain wooden chair with an ordinary rope, yet which still allows an escape. With a minimum of supervision from the illusionist's assistant (Julia, in my case), any number of volunteers may tie, knot and even seal the rope, yet still permit escape. The performer, once hidden inside a cabinet, can not only release himself enough to perform apparent miracles within the cabinet, but can afterwards return to his bonds, to be found, checked and released by the same volunteers who restrained him.

This morning I was twice unable to free one of my arms. Because nothing must be left to chance, I shall devote the rest of this afternoon and evening to further rehearsal.

We have our two guineas, the client was literally sobbing with gratitude, and contact, I modestly say, was briefly made with the dead.

However, tomorrow, which also happens to be my twenty-first birthday, and the day in which my adult life commences in every way, we have to conduct a séance in Deptford, and we have much to prepare!

Our first mistake yesterday was to be punctual. Our client and her friends were *waiting* for us, and as we entered the house and tried to set up our equipment they were *watching* us. None of this must be allowed to happen again.

We need physical assistance. Yesterday we rented a cart to convey us to the address, but the carter was totally un-willing to help us carry our apparatus into the house (which meant that Julia and I had to do it alone, and some of it is heavy and most of it bulky). When we left the client's house the damned carter had not waited for us as instructed, and I was obliged to stand with all our magical apparatus in the street outside the house we had just left, while Julia went to find a replacement.

And we must never again depend on being able to find *in situ* the domestic furniture we need for some of our effects. Today we were lucky: there was a table we could use, but we cannot chance that next time.

Many of these improvements have already been arranged. I have today purchased a horse and cart. (The horse will have to be kept temporarily in the small yard behind my workshop until a proper stable can be rented.) And I have hired a man to drive the cart and to help us in and out with all our stuff. Mr Appleby might not be suitable in the long term (I was hoping to find a man closer to my own age, who would be physically strong) but for the time being he is a great improvement over that whey-faced churl of a carter who let us down yesterday.

Our expenses are increasing. For a mentalist act we required only ourselves, two good memories and a blindfold;

to become spiritists requires us to make outlays that threaten to overwhelm our potential earnings. Last night I lay awake a long time, thinking of this, wondering how much more expense will follow.

Now we must travel to Deptford for our next! Deptford is one of the more inaccessible parts of London from here, being not only beyond the East End but on the far side of the river too. To get there in good time means we must leave at dawn. Julia and I have agreed that in future we shall only accept commissions from people who live within reasonable distance of us, otherwise the work is altogether too hard, the day is too long, the financial rewards too small for what we have to do.

2nd November 1878

Julia is with child! The baby is expected next June. With all the excitement this has caused we have cancelled a few of our appointments, and tomorrow we are departing to Southampton, so as to take the news to Julia's mother.

15th November 1878

Yesterday and the day before were given over to séances; no problems at either, and the clients were satisfied. I am growing concerned, however, at the possible effects of strain on Julia, and I am thinking that I must quickly find and hire a female assistant to work with me.

Mr Appleby, as suspected, handed in his notice after a few days. I have replaced him with one Ernest Nugent, a strongly built man in his late twenties who until last year was a corporal volunteer in Her Majesty's Army. I find him a bit of a rough diamond but he is not stupid, he works all day without complaint, and already he has shown himself loyal. At the séance two days ago (the first since our return from Southampton), I belatedly discovered that one of the people I thought was a relative of the deceased was in fact a reporter from a newspaper. This man was on some kind of mission to expose me as a charlatan, but once we had realised his purpose, Nugent and I removed him quickly (but politely) from the house.

So another precaution has to be added to this work – I must be on my guard against active sceptics.

For indeed I *am* the sort of charlatan they seek to discredit. I am not what I say I am, but my deceptions are harmless and, I do believe, helpful at a time of personal loss. As for the money that changes hands the amounts are modest, and so far not a single client has complained to me of short measure.

The rest of this month is filled with appointments, but there is a quiet patch before Christmas. Already we have learned that these occasions are often the result of a sudden tormented decision, and are not booked a long way ahead. So we advertise, and will have to keep advertising.

20th November 1878

Today Julia and I have interviewed five young women, all hopeful to replace Julia as my assistant.

None was suitable.

Julia has been feeling continually sick for two weeks, but says now that this is starting to improve. The thought of a baby son or daughter coming into our lives illumines our days.

23rd November 1878

A peculiarly unpleasant incident has occurred, and I am so engulfed in rage that I have had to wait until now (11.25 p.m., when Julia is at last asleep), before I can trust myself to record it with any equanimity.

We had gone to an address near the Angel, in Islington. The client was a youngish man, recently bereaved by the death of his wife, and now having to cope with a family of three young children, one of them barely more than a babe. This gentleman, whose name I shall render as Mr L____, was the very first of our spiritist clients who had come to us on the recommendation of another. For this reason, we had approached the appointment with particular care and tact, because by now we appreciate that if we are to prosper as spiritists then it must be by a spiral of gradually rising fees, sustained by the grateful recommendation of satisfied clients.

We were just about to begin when a latecomer arrived. I was immediately suspicious of him, and I say this without hindsight. None of the family seemed to know him, and his arrival caused a feeling of nervousness in the room. I have already grown sensitive to such impressions at the start of one of these performances.

I signalled to Julia, in our private unspoken code, that I suspected a newspaper reporter was present, and I saw by her expression that she had come to a similar conclusion. Nugent was standing before one of the screened-off windows, not privy to our silent language. I had to make a quick decision about what to do. If I were to insist on the man's removal before the séance began, it would likely create an unpleasant ruckus of the sort of which I already have some experience. On the other hand, if I were to do nothing I would doubtless be exposed as a charlatan at the end of the performance, thus probably denying me of my fee and my client of the solace he sought.

I was still trying to decide what to do when I realised that I had seen the man before. He had been present at an earlier séance, and I remembered him because of the way he had stared at me throughout. Was his presence here a coincidence? If so, what were the chances of his being bereaved twice in a short period, and what extra chances were there that I should be called to officiate in a séance twice in his company?

If not a coincidence, which I suspected, what was his game? Presumably he was there to make some move against me, but he had had his chance before and had not taken it. Why not?

So went my thoughts in the extremity of the moment. I could barely concentrate on them, such was the need to maintain the appearance of calm preparation for communion with the departed. But my quick assessment was that on balance of probabilities I should go ahead with the séance, and so I did. Writing this now I realise I made the wrong decision.

For one thing, without raising a hand against me he almost ruined my performance. I was so nervous that I could hardly concentrate on the matter in hand, to the extent that when Julia and one of the other men present put me in the JACOBY TIE, I allowed one of my hands to be restrained more tightly than I wanted. Inside the cabinet, thankfully away from the baleful staring of my silent adversary's eyes, I had a protracted struggle before I was able to free my hands.

Once the cabinet illusion was done with, my enemy sprang his trap. He left the table, shouldered poor Nugent aside, and snatched down one of the window blinds. A great deal of shouting ensued, causing intense and uncontrollable grief for my client and his children. Nugent was struggling with the man, and Julia was trying to comfort Mr L____'s children, when disaster struck.

The man, in his madness, grabbed hold of Julia by her shoulders, dragged her back, swung her around, and pushed her to the floor! She fell heavily on the uncarpeted boards, while I, in the greatest distress, stood up from the table where I had been performing and tried to reach her. The assailant was between us.

Again Nugent grabbed him, this time restraining from behind, clasping his arms at the back.

'What shall I do with him, sir?' Nugent cried valorously.

'Into the street with him!' I yelled. 'No, wait!'

The light from the window was falling directly on his face. Behind him I saw the sight I then most wanted to see: dearest Julia was rising once more to her feet. She signalled quickly to me that she was not hurt, and so I turned my attention on the man.

'Who are you, sir?' I questioned him. 'What interest do you have in my affairs?'

'Get your ruffian to release me!' he muttered, breathing stertorously. 'Then I will depart.'

'You will depart when I decide!' I said. I stepped closer to him, for now I recognised him. 'You are Borden, are you not? Borden!'

'That is not correct!'

'Alfred Borden, indeed! I have seen your work! What are you doing here?'

'Let me go!'

'What's your business with me, Borden?'

He made no answer, but instead struggled violently against Nugent's hold.

'Get rid of him!' I ordered. 'Throw him where he belongs, into the gutter!'

Then it was done, and with commendable despatch Nugent dragged the wretch out of the room, and returned alone a few moments later.

By this time I had taken Julia into my arms and was holding her close, trying to reassure myself that she was indeed unharmed, even after being thrown so roughly to the floor.

'If he has hurt you or the baby—' I whispered to her.

'I am not injured,' Julia replied. 'Who was he?'

'Later, my dear,' I said softly, because I was all too aware that we were still in the shambles of the ruined séance, with an angry or humiliated client, his miserable children, his four adult relatives and friends now visibly shocked.

I said to them all with as much gravity and dignity as I could muster, 'You understand I cannot continue?'

They showed their assent.

The children were led away, and Mr L____ and I went into private conference. He was indeed a sympathetic, intelligent man, proposing at once that we should leave all matters as they presently stood, and that we should meet again in a day or two to decide our next move. I assented gratefully, and after Nugent and I had transported our apparatus back to the cart we set off for home. While Nugent drove, Julia and I huddled together behind him in a state of distress and introspection.

I voiced my suspicions as we trundled along in the gathering twilight.

'That was Alfred Borden,' I explained. 'I know little of him other than that he is a magician, barely distinguished in the business. Since his interruption I have been trying to recall how I know him. I think I must have seen him perform on the stage. But he is hardly a major figure in our field. Perhaps he was deputing for another when I saw him.'

I was speaking as much to myself as to Julia, trying to make the assailant comprehensible. I could only explain his attack on me in terms of professional jealousy. What other motive could there be? We were virtual strangers to each other, and unless there was a lapse in my memory our paths had never crossed before. Yet his whole demeanour was that of a man bent on a mission of revenge.

Julia was hunched beside me in the foggy evening air. I questioned her about her health many times, trying to reassure myself she had not been harmed by the fall, but she said only that she was anxious to return home.

Soon enough we were here in Idmiston Villas, and I made her go straight to bed. She looked exhausted and strained, but she continued to assert that all she required was rest. I sat with her until she fell asleep, and after a hastily prepared bowl of soup, and a quick and energetic walk through local side-streets to try to clear my mind, I returned to write this account of the day.

I have twice broken off to see Julia, and she is sleeping peacefully.

24th November 1878

The worst day of my life.

27th November 1878

Julia is home from hospital, once more she is sleeping, and once again I come to this diary, such barely adequate source of temporary distraction and comfort as it is.

Briefly, Julia wakened in the small hours of the 24th. She was bleeding heavily and racked with pain. This seemed to course through her like a series of waves, making her scream and contort in agony before giving her temporary surcease, then beginning again.

I dressed at once, roused my neighbours, and begged Mrs

Janson to leave her own bed and sit with Julia while I sought help. She agreed without complaint, allowing me to rush off into the night. Luck, if that is the word, was briefly with me. I came across a hackney cabman, apparently returning to his home at the end of a night of work, and I pleaded with him to help me. This he did. Within an hour Julia was in St Mary's Hospital in Paddington, and the surgeons did their necessary work.

Our baby was lost. I almost lost Julia too.

She remained in the public ward for the rest of the day, and for the two days following until this morning, when I was allowed at last to collect her.

There is a single name that has now unexpectedly entered my life, and it is one I shall never forget. It is Alfred Borden's.

3rd December 1878

Julia is still weak, but she says she hopes to be able to help me with my séances from next week. I have not yet told her, but I have already decided that never again shall she be put at risk. I have advertised once more for a female assistant. Meanwhile, this evening I have a stage performance to carry out, and have had to search through my repertoire to put together an act that does not require assistance.

11th December 1878

I came across Borden's name today. He is advertised as a guest magician in a variety show in Brentford. I checked with Hesketh Unwin, the man whom I have recently appointed as my agent, and learned to my satisfaction that Borden was a replacement for another illusionist who had been suddenly taken ill, and in the process caused the magical act to be moved from second on the bill to the graveyard of all magicians: the first act after the interval! I showed this to Julia.

31st December 1878

Total Income From Magic for 1878: £326 19s 3d. From this must be deducted expenses, including the hiring of Appleby and

Nugent, the purchase and stabling of the horse, purchase of costumes, and much apparatus.

12th January 1879

My first séance of the new year, and the first in which I was assisted by Letitia Swinton. Letitia was formerly in the chorus at the Alexandria and has much to learn about the magic profession, but I am hopeful she will improve. At the end of the séance I asked Nugent to hurry me back to Idmiston Villas, where I have been with Julia, telling her of my day.

A letter was waiting for me here. Mr L____ has decided, in the event, that he no longer requires a séance in his home, but that in careful consideration of what happened he has decided I should be paid the full fee, as agreed. His payment was enclosed.

13th January 1879

Today Julia locked herself in the bedroom, ignored all my knocking and pleading and admitted only the maid, who took her tea and some bread. I was not working today and had been planning to be at the workshop, but in view of Julia's strange mood felt I should remain at home. Julia emerged after 8.00 p.m., and said nothing of what she had done or why she had done it. I am perplexed by all this. She says she is no longer in pain, but other than this refuses to discuss what happened.

15th January 1879

Nugent, Letitia Swinton and I conducted a séance this afternoon. Already it has become a routine event for me, the only novelties being, firstly, the unavoidable need to work with an assistant new to magic, secondly, the particular circumstances of whatever bereavement I am attending, and, thirdly, the physical layout of the room in which the séance takes place. These last two do not in general present problems to me, and even Letitia is showing herself to be a quick learner.

Returning afterwards I asked Nugent to let me off in the West End. I walked to the Empress Theatre in High Holborn, bought a ticket, and sat in the deep recesses of the rear stalls.

Borden's act was in the first half of the programme and I watched intently what he did. He performed a total of seven tricks and, of these, three were ones whose explanation I do not know. (By tomorrow evening I shall have them!) He is a fairly plausible performer, and carried out his tricks smoothly, but for some reason he addresses the audience in an unconvincing French accent. It made me wish to taunt him as an impostor!

However, I must bide my time. I wish my revenge to be sweet.

On my return Julia was uncommunicative with me, and even after I told her what I had been doing she remained cold towards me.

O Julia! You were not like this before that day!

19th January 1879

We both mourn the loss of the child we never knew. Julia's grief is so deep, so inner-directed, that she sometimes seems unaware that I am even in the same room with her. I am just as miserable, but I have my work to distract me. This is the only difference between us.

For the last week I have been applying myself to perfecting my magic, trying by intensive application to relaunch myself into my intended profession. To this end:

I have tidied up my workshop, thrown away a lot of junk, repaired and repainted several of the illusions, and generally made the workshop into a businesslike place where I might prepare and rehearse properly.

I have started discreet enquiries through Hesketh Unwin's office, and through other magic contacts, for an *ingénieur* to work with me. I need expert assistance. Of this there is no question.

I have set myself a practice schedule, to which I adhere absolutely: two hours every morning, two hours every afternoon, one hour (if time with Julia permits) in every evening. The only breaks I allow myself are when I am actually working.

I have ordered myself and Letitia new costumes, to give the act professional polish.

Finally, I have promised myself to quit the séances as soon as I can afford to do so. Meanwhile, I am taking on as many of them for which the time can be found, because they are my only secure means of making a living. My financial responsibilities are immense. I have the lodgings to pay for, rent to find of the workshop and stable, wages to pay for Nugent and Letitia, and soon for my new *ingénieur* too . . . as well as running the household and feeding Julia and myself.

All this to be paid for by the credulous bereaved!

(Tonight, though, another theatrical performance.)

31st December 1879

Total Income From Magic for 1879: £637 12s 6d.
Before expenses.

31st December 1880

Total Income From Magic for 1880: £1,142 7s 9d.
Before expenses.

31st December 1881

Total Income From Magic for 1881: £4,777 10s 0d.
Before expenses.

1881 is the last year in which I shall record my earnings here. This twelvemonth has been sufficiently successful for me to purchase the house in which, hitherto, we have merely rented our lodgings. Now we occupy the whole building, and we have a domestic staff of three. The restlessness that beset me when I was younger is directed fruitfully into the energy of performance, and I may record that I am probably the most sought-after stage illusionist in Britain. My bookings diary for next year is already full.

186

Ten years ago I put aside my diary, intending never to reopen it, but the humiliating events earlier this evening at the Sefton Theatre of Varieties in Liverpool (whence I am returning to London *en train* as I write this) cannot go unrecorded. As it has been so long since I wrote in my diary these loose sheets will tonight have to suffice while I am without my notebook and file system.

I was in the second part of my act, heading towards what is currently the climax of my performance. This is the UNDERWATER ESCAPE, an effect which combines physical strength, a certain amount of controlled risk, and a little magic.

The illusion begins with my being tied, apparently inescapably, to a stout metal chair. To effect this I invite on to the stage a committee of six volunteers: these are all genuine members of the audience, none planted, but Ernest Nugent and my *ingénieur* Harry Cutter do keep an eye on things.

With the committee on stage I engage them in humourous banter, partly to relax them, partly to misdirect the audience while Ellen Tremayne (my present assistant; it is a long time since I wrote in here) begins the JACOBY ROPE TIE.

Tonight, though, I had just taken my seat in the chair when I realised that Alfred Borden was one of the committee! He was the Sixth Man! (Harry Cutter and I use codes to identify and place the on-stage volunteers. The Sixth Man is positioned furthest from me during these preparatory stages, and is given the task of holding one end of the rope.) Tonight Borden was the Sixth Man, only a few feet away from me. The audience was watching us all! The trick had already begun!

Borden played his part well, moving clumsily and with well-faked embarrassment about his small part of the stage. No one in the audience would have guessed that he is almost as practised a performer as me. Cutter, apparently not realising who he was, propelled Borden into his place. Ellen

Tremayne was meanwhile roping my hands together, and tying my wrists to the arms of the chair. It is here that my preparations went awry, because my attention was on Borden. By the time two other volunteers had been given the ends of the rope and instructed to tie me as tightly as possible to the chair, it was too late. In the full glare of the limes I was trussed helplessly.

Amid a roll of drums I was hoisted by the pulley into the air space above the glass tank, and I dangled and rotated on the end of the chain as if a helpless victim of torture. In truth tonight I was, but during a normal performance I would by this stage have freed my wrists, and moved my hands to a position from which I could release them instantly. (My rotating on the chain is an effective cover for the necessarily quick arm movements as I release myself.) Tonight, with my arms tied immovably to the chair, I could only stare down in horror at the cold, waiting water.

Moments later, according to plan, I was plunged into it in a gouting spray of overflow. As the water closed over my head I tried by facial expressions to signal my predicament to Cutter, but he was already engaged in lowering the concealing curtain around the tank.

In semi-darkness, half inverted in the chair, tied hand and foot, and entirely submerged in cold water, I began to drown—

My only hope was that the water would cause the rope to loosen a little (part of my secret preparations, in case the volunteers have tied the secondary knots too tightly for a timely escape), even though I knew that the little extra movement this would allow would not be enough to save me tonight.

I tugged urgently at the ropes, already feeling the pressure of air in my lungs, desperate to burst out of me and allow the deadly water to flood in and take me—

Yet here I am writing this. Obviously I escaped.

I would not be alive to write were it not, by an irony, for Borden's own intervention. He overplayed his hand, could not resist gloating at me.

Here is a reconstruction of what must have happened on the remainder of the stage, hidden from me by the curtain.

In a normal performance, all that can be seen on the stage is the committee of six standing self-consciously around the curtain that encloses the tank. They no more than the audience can see what I am doing. The orchestra plays a lively medley, partly to fill the time, partly to mask any noises I cannot avoid making while I escape. But time goes by, and soon both the committee and the audience start to feel disquiet at how much time has elapsed.

The orchestra too becomes distracted, and the music peters out. An anti-climactic silence falls. Harry Cutter and Ellen Tremayne run anxiously on to the stage, as if in response to the emergency, and the audience makes a hubbub of concern. With the help of the committee Cutter and Ellen snatch away the concealing curtain, to reveal—

—The chair is still in the water! The ropes are still tied around it! But I am not there!

While the audience gasps in amazement I dramatically appear. It is usually from the wings, but if I have time I prefer to announce myself in the middle of the auditorium. I run to centre-stage, take my bow, and make sure that everyone notices that my clothes and hair are perfectly dry—

Tonight Borden was there to ruin it all, and, inadvertently perhaps, to save me from a watery end. Long before the illusion was due to finish, thankfully long before, and while the orchestra yet played, he left the position on the stage where Cutter had placed him, strode across to the curtains and snatched them aside!

My first awareness of this was that a shaft of bright light burst upon me. I looked up in vast and sudden hope, as the last air from my lungs bubbled up around my eyes! I felt then my prayers had been answered, that Cutter had interrupted the performance to save my life. Nothing else mattered in that second of bursting hope. What I saw, through the horrid distortions of swirling water and strengthened glass, was the jeering visage of my deadliest enemy! He leaned forward, pressing his face triumphantly against the tank.

I felt unconsciousness rising in me, believed myself to be on the point of death.

Then there is a gap. My next awareness was that I was lying on a hard wooden floor, in semi-darkness, freezing cold, with faces staring down at me. Music was playing close at hand, deafening me as the water drained in gulps from my ear passages. I could feel the floor moving up and down rhythmically. I was in the wings, on the floor of one of the rope alcoves next to the stage. When I raised my head I saw, unfocused and wandering in my sight, the brightly lit stage just a few feet away from me, where the chorus was treading the boards, while the *coryphée* strutted to the bawdy tune from the orchestra pit. I groaned with relief, closed my eyes, and allowed my head to fall back to the floor. Cutter had dragged me to safety, somehow restored my breathing, brought the humiliating spectacle to an end.

Not long after I was carried to the green room, where my recovery properly began. For half an hour I felt as wretched as ever I have felt in my life, but I am in general strong and as soon as I was able to breathe without choking on the water in my lungs I began to recover quickly. It was still reasonably early in the evening, and I believed fervently (and still believe, as I write) that I had plenty of time to return to the stage and attempt my illusion again, before the show ended. I was not allowed to do this.

Instead, in a sad postmortem of the ruined performance, I convened with Ellen, Cutter and Nugent in my dressing room. We arranged to meet in two days' time at my workshop in London to improve the method of the escape, so that never again would my life be put in peril. At last my three stalwarts conducted me to the station, satisfied themselves of my mental and physical well-being, then returned to the hotel where we had all been planning to stay.

For myself, I seek only a swift return to London to see Julia and the children, as the incident, the brush with what felt like certain death, has made me hungry to be with them. This train will not arrive in Euston Station until just before dawn, but it makes it possible to see them sooner than would otherwise be possible.

By an irony, my failure to keep this diary has been caused by the domestic contentment to which I now hurry to return, and of which I could have written volumes or (as happened) nothing. For most of the past decade I have been not only successful in my career but unprecedentedly happy at home.

At the beginning of 1884, Julia at long last found herself with child again, and in due course safely delivered our son Edward. Two years later came the first of my daughters, Lydia, and last year, belatedly but to our delight, our baby Florence was born.

Against this background, the feud with Borden has taken on trivial proportions. True, we have played pranks on each other over the years. True, the spirit behind them has often been malicious. True, I have shown as much malice as he, and of this I am not in the least proud. It is no coincidence that none of these exploits made reopening the diary seem worthwhile.

Until tonight, though, Borden and I have not directly threatened each other's lives.

Once, years ago, Borden was directly responsible for the miscarriage of my first child. Although my instinct then was one of revenge, as the months went by my anger slowly died, and I satisfied myself instead with a number of retaliations on him designed only to embarrass him or to confound his illusion-making at just the moment he least enjoyed it.

In his turn, he has exacted a few moments of unexpected revenge on me, though none, I declare, as cleverly designed as my own have been on him.

What happened tonight has forced our feud to a new level. He tried to kill me. It is as plain as that. He is a magician. He knows how ropes must be tied to ensure a rapid and safe release.

Now I want revenge again. I hope and pray that time will quickly pass, soothe my feelings, bring sense and sanity and calmness to me, that I do not act as tonight I feel!

Last night I saw an extraordinary thing. There is a scientist called Nikola Tesla visiting London, and the extravagant claims he makes were last week the talk of the town. Veritable miracles were being spoken of and several informed newspapers reported that in Tesla's hands lay the future of our world. The interviews he gave, and the articles that were written about his work, did not manage to explain why it should be so. It was widely said that his work must be seen demonstrated before its importance might be grasped.

So, swept along by curiosity, yesterday I and several hundred others clamoured at the doors of the Institution of Electrical Engineers to see the great man in action.

What I witnessed was a thrilling, alarming and mostly incomprehensible display of the powers of electricity. Mr Tesla (who spoke excellent American English, almost without hint of his European roots) is an associate of the inventor Thomas Edison. To modern-minded Londoners the use of electrical power for lighting is becoming a commonplace, but Tesla was able to show that it has many other uses.

I watched his sensational experiments uncritically, dazzled and impressed. Many of his effects are astonishing, and many more are deeply mysterious to a layman. When Tesla spoke, it was in the tones of an evangelist. More than his sparking, fizzing outbursts of lightning, his visionary words thrilled me beyond anything I had hitherto known. He is indeed a prophet of what the next century will hold for us. A worldwide net of electrical generating stations, power given over to the humble as well as the mighty, instantaneous transmission of energies and matter from one part of the world to the other, the air itself vibrating with the essence of the aether!

I grasped an important truth from Mr Tesla's presentation. His show (for it was nothing less than this) bore an odd resemblance to any good illusionist's. The audience did not need to understand the means to enjoy the effects. In short, Mr Tesla described many scientific theories. While few in that audience understood more than the most basic concepts, every one of us was afforded a compelling glimpse into the future.

I have written off to the address Tesla supplied, and requested copies of his explanatory notes.

14th April 1892

I have been busy preparing for my European Tour, which starts in the latter half of this summer, and have had little time for anything else. To complete the above entry from February, though, I eventually received Mr Tesla's explanatory notes, but could not make head nor tail of them.

In Paris   15th September 1892

They have hailed me in Vienna, Rome, Paris, Istanbul, Marseilles, Madrid, Monte Carlo . . . yet now that all this is behind me I crave only to see my beloved Julia once more, and Edward and Lydia, and of course my little Florence. Since we spent our weekend together here in Paris two months ago, I have had only letters to buoy me up with news of my precious family. Two days from now, should the sailing be on time, and the trains reliable, I shall be at home and able to rest at last.

We are all exhausted, though mainly through the endless round of travelling and staying in hotels, than because of the exigencies of life on the European stage. But it has over-all been a famous success. We planned to be home by the middle of July, but such was our popular reception that a dozen theatres clamoured for us to make an additional visit, and to bless them with our magic. This we were only too glad to do when we realised the scale of the interest, and concomitantly the fees we could command for these extra performances. It would be unwise to record the extent of my earnings until all expenses have been calculated, and the agreed bonuses paid to my assistants, but I may safely say that for the first time in my life I feel I am a wealthy man.

I had expected to be basking in the afterglow of the tour, but instead I find that while I was away Borden has been gaining lavish attention. It seems that one of the illusions he has been performing for years has finally caught the public's fancy, and he is in terrific demand.

Although I have watched his act several times, I have never seen him attempt anything unusual. This could of course be that for various reasons I have rarely stayed to the end of his act!

Cutter knows as little about this applauded trick as I do, for the obvious reason that he has been in Europe with me. I was about to shrug it off as an irrelevance until I read through some of the correspondence that was waiting for me here. Dominic Brawton, one of my magic scouts, had sent a terse note.

Performer: Alfred Borden (Le Professeur de Magie). *Illusion*: The New Transported Man. *Effect*: brilliant, not to be missed. *Adaptability*: difficult, but Borden manages it somehow, so I imagine you could too.

I showed this to Julia.

Later I showed her another letter. I have been invited to take my magic show to the New World. If I agree we would begin touring in February with a week-long residency in Chicago. And then a tour to the dozen or so largest American cities.

The thought of it simultaneously thrills and exhausts me.

Julia said to me, 'Forget Borden. You must take your show to the USA.'

And I too think I must.

14th October 1892

I have seen Borden's new illusion, and it is good. It is devilishly good. It is the better for being simple. It galls me to say it, but I must be fair.

He begins by wheeling on to the stage a wooden cabinet, of the sort familiar to all magicians. This is tall enough to contain a man or a woman, has three solid walls (back and two sides), and a door at the front that opens wide enough to reveal the whole of the interior. It is mounted on castors, and these raise the entire thing high enough to show that no escape or entry would be possible through the base, without being noticed by the audience.

With the usual demonstrations of present vacancy completed, Borden closes the cabinet door, then moves the apparatus up to stage left.

Standing at the footlights he then delivers, in his wonderfully unconvincing French accent, a short lecture on the great dangers involved in what he is about to do.

Behind him, a remarkably pretty young woman wheels on to the stage a second cabinet, identical to the first. She opens the door, so that the audience can see that it too is empty. With a swirl of his black cape, Borden then turns and steps briskly into the cabinet.

On cue, the drummer starts a roll.

What happens next takes place in an instant. Indeed, it takes longer to write down than it does to see it performed.

As the drum rolls louder, Borden removes his top hat, steps back into the recesses of his cabinet, then tosses his hat high into the air. His assistant slams closed the door of the cabinet. *In the same instant*, the door of the first cabin bursts open, and Borden is now impossibly inside! The cabinet he entered only moments before collapses, and folds emptily on to the floor of the stage. Borden looks up to the rigging loft, sees his top hat plummeting towards him, catches it, puts it on his head, taps it down into place . . . then beaming and smiling steps forward to the footlights to take his bow!

The applause was raucous, and I admit I joined in myself. I am damned if I know how he did that!

Last night I took Cutter to the Watford Regal, where Borden was performing. The illusion with the two cabinets was not part of his act.

During the long journey back to London, I described to Cutter again what I had seen. His verdict was the same as when I first told him about it, two days ago. Borden, he says, is using a double. He tells me about a similar act he saw performed twenty years ago, involving a young woman.

I'm not sure. It didn't look like a double to me. The man who went into one cabinet and the man who emerged from the other was one and the same. I was there, and that is what I saw.

25th October 1892

Because of my own commitments it has been impossible to see Borden's act every night, but Cutter and I have been to his performances twice this week. He has still not repeated the illusion with the two cabinets. Cutter refuses to speculate until he has seen it himself, but declares I am wasting his time and my own. It is becoming a source of friction between us.

13th November 1892

At last I have seen Borden perform his two-cabinets illusion again, and this time Cutter was with me. It happened at the Lewisham World Theatre, on an otherwise straightforward variety bill.

As Borden produced the first of his two cabinets, and went through his routine of revealing it to be empty, I felt a thrill of anticipation. Cutter, beside me, raised his opera glasses in a businesslike way. I glanced at him to try to see where he was looking, and was interested to note that he was not watching the magician at all. With quick movements of the glasses he appeared to be inspecting the rest of the stage area: the wings, the flies, the backcloth. I cursed myself for not thinking of this, and left him to get on with it.

I continued to watch Borden. As far as I could tell the trick was conducted exactly as I had observed it before, even to an almost word-for-word repetition of the French-accented speech about danger. When he went into the second cabinet, though, I noticed a couple of tiny deviations from the earlier occasion. The more trivial of these was that he had left the first cabinet closer to the rear of the stage, so that it was not at all well lit. I again glanced quickly at Cutter, and found that he was paying no attention to the magician, but had his glasses turned steadfastly on the upstage cabinet.

The other deviation interested me, and in fact rather amused me. When Borden removed his top hat and flung it into the air, I was leaning forward, ready to see the next and most amazing step. Instead, the hat rose quickly into the flies, and did not reappear! (Clearly, there was a stagehand up there, slipped a ten-bob note to catch it.) Borden turned to the audience with a wry smile, and got his laugh. While the laughter was still ringing out, he extended his left hand calmly . . . and the top hat skittered down from the flies, for him to catch with a natural and unforced movement. It was excellent stagecraft, and he deserved the second laugh for that.

Then, without waiting for the laughter to die, and with dashing speed:

Up went the hat again! The cabinet door was slammed! The upstage cabinet door burst open! Borden leapt out, hatless! The second cabinet collapsed! Borden skipped nimbly across the stage, caught the top hat, rammed it down on his head!

Beaming, bowing, waving, he took his well-deserved applause. Cutter and I joined in.

In the taxicab rattling back to north London I demanded of Cutter, 'Well, what do you think of that!'

'Brilliant, Mr Angier!' he stated. 'Quite brilliant! It is not often that one has the chance to see a completely new illusion.'

I found this acclaim none too pleasing, I must say.

'Do you know how he did it?' I insisted.

'Yes, sir, I do,' he replied. 'And so I fancy do you.'

'I'm as baffled as ever I was. How the devil could he be in two places at once? I cannot see that it is possible!'

'Sometimes you do surprise me, Mr Angier,' Cutter said trenchantly. 'It is a logical puzzle, solved only by the application of our own logic. What did we see before us?'

'A man who transported himself instantly from one part of the stage to the other.'

'That is what we thought we saw, what we were intended to see. What was the reality?'

'You still maintain he uses a double?' I queried him.

'How else could it be effected?'

'But you saw it as I did. That was no double! We saw him clearly before and after. He was the same man! The very same!'

Cutter winked at me, then turned away and gazed out at the dimly lit houses of Waterloo past which we were presently driving.

'Well?' I clamoured of him. 'What do you say?'

'I say what I have said, Mr Angier.'

'I pay you to explain the unexplainable, Cutter. Do not trifle with me about this! It is a matter of high professional importance!'

At this he realised the seriousness of my mood, and not a moment before time, because the piqued admiration induced in me by Borden's performance was being transmuted to frustration and anger.

'Sir,' he said steadily. 'You must know of identical twins. There is your answer!'

'No!' I exclaimed.

'How else might it be done?'

'But the first cabinet was empty—'

'So it did appear,' said Cutter.

'And the second cabinet collapsed the moment he left it—'

'Very effectively too, I thought.'

I knew what he was saying. These were standard stage

198

effects for making apparatus that is concealing someone seem empty. Several of my own illusions turn on similar deceptions. My difficulty was the same I have always suffered. When I see another's illusion from the auditorium, I am as easily misdirected as anyone else. But identical twins! I had not thought of that!

Cutter had given me much food for thought, and after I had dropped him off at his lodgings, and I had returned here, I did some thinking. Now I have written down this account of the evening, I think I have to agree with him. The mystery is solved.

Damn Borden! Not one man but two! Damn his eyes!

14th November 1892

I have told Julia what Cutter suggested last night, and to my surprise she laughed delightedly.

'Brilliant!' she cried. 'We hadn't thought of that, had we?'

'Then you too think it's possible?'

'It is not merely possible, my dear . . . it is the *only* way it could be performed on an open stage.'

'I suppose you are right.'

Now, irrationally, I feel angry at my Julia. She has not seen the illusion herself.

30th November 1892

Yesterday I obtained an extremely interesting view on Borden, and, into the bargain, some remarkable facts about him.

I should mention that all this week I have been unable to add to this diary because I have been appearing top of the bill at the London Hippodrome. This is an immense honour, one that has been signified not only by full houses at every performance (bar one matinée), but also by the audiences' reactions. One other consequence is that the gentlemen of the Press are paying me some attention, and yesterday a young reporter from the *Evening Star* came to interview me. His name was Mr Arthur Koenig. This young man turned out to be an informant as well as an interviewer.

During the course of a question-and-answer session he asked me if I had any opinions I would wish to record about my magical contemporaries. I duly launched into an appreciative summary of the best of my colleagues.

'You have not mentioned Le Professeur,' said my interlocutor, when I eventually paused. 'Do you not hold an opinion on Mr Borden's work?'

'I regret I have not been present at any of his performances,' I demurred. 'Not recently, in any case.'

'Then you must go to see his work!' ejaculated Mr Koenig. 'His is the best show in London!'

'Indeed.'

'I have seen his act several times,' the reporter went on. 'There is one trick he does, not every night for he says it exhausts him too much, but there is this one trick—'

'I have heard of it,' I said, affecting disdain. 'Something to do with two cabinets.'

'That's the one, Mr Danton. He vanishes and reappears in a trice. No one knows how he does it.'

'No one, that is, except his fellow magicians,' I corrected him. 'He is using standard magical procedures.'

'Then you know how it is done?'

'Of course I know,' I said. 'But naturally you will not expect me to divulge the exact method—'

Here I confess I was torn. Over the last two weeks I have been thinking hard about Cutter's theory that 'Borden' must in fact be played by two identical twins, and I had convinced myself that he must be right. Here was my chance to reveal Borden's secret. I had an eager listener, a journalist with access to one of the great newspapers of our city, a man whose curiosity was already roused by the mystery of magic performance. I felt the lust for revenge that I normally suppressed, that I had told myself a score of times was a weakness to which I must never again succumb. Naturally, Koenig knew nothing of the bitterness between Borden and myself.

But no magician gives away the secret of another.

At length I said, 'There are ways and means. An illusion is not what it seems. A great deal of practice and rehearsal—'

Whereat the young reporter practically leapt out of his seat.

'Sir, you believe he has an identical twin, and uses him as a double! Every magician in London thinks the same! I thought so too when I saw it the first time.'

'Yes, that is his method.' I was relieved to discover that I need give nothing away. I tried to sound uninterested by this commonplace revelation. 'Identical twins are often used in illusions.'

'Then you are wrong like all the others, sir!' cried the young man. 'Le Professeur *does not use a double*. This is what is so amazing!'

'He has a twin brother,' I said. 'There is no other way.'

'With respect, that's not true. He has neither twin brother nor a double who can pass for him. I have personally investigated his life, and I know the truth. He works alone but for the female assistant seen on the stage with him, and a technical manager who builds his apparatus with him. In this he is no different from any other in your profession. You too—'

'I do have an *ingénieur*,' I confirmed readily. 'But tell me more. You interest me greatly. You are certain of this information?'

'I am.'

'Can you prove it to me?'

'As you know, sir,' Mr Koenig replied, 'it is not possible to prove that which does not exist. All I can say is that for the last few weeks I have been bringing journalistic methods to the investigation, and have not found a single jot of evidence to confirm what you assume.'

At this point he produced a thin sheaf of papers and showed them to me. They contained certain information about Mr Borden that I found instantly intriguing, and I begged the reporter to let me have them.

There followed something of a wrangle between our two professions. He maintained that as a journalist he could not impart the fruit of his researches to a third party. I countered that even if he were to discover the final, absolute truth about Borden, he would never be able to publish it while the subject remained alive.

On the other hand, I said, if *I* were to start my own investigations, then I might be able at some future time to guide him to a truly uncommon story.

The upshot of it was that Koenig agreed to let me take handwritten extracts from several of his notes, and these I scribbled down on the spot at his dictation. His conclusions were not conveyed to me, and to be candid I was not greatly interested in them. At the end I passed him five sovereigns.

As I finished, Mr Koenig said to me, 'May I ask what you are hoping to learn from this, sir?'

'I seek only to improve my own magical art,' I affirmed.

'I understand.' He stood up to leave, and took hold of his hat and stick. 'And when you have so *improved*, do you suppose you too will be able to perform Le Professeur's illusion?'

'I assure you, Mr Koenig,' I said with cold disdain, as I showed him to the door. 'I assure you that should the occasion arise I could take his bauble of a trick and make it mine this very night!'

Then he was gone.

Today I have not been working, and so I have written up this account of the meeting. All through it that final taunt of Koenig's has been in my thoughts. It is imperative that I learn the secret of Borden's illusion. I can think of no sweeter revenge than to outshine him with his own trick, outperform him, outdo him in every way.

And, courtesy of Mr Koenig, the facts I possess about Mr Borden will prove to be of immense value. First, though, I must check them.

9th December 1892

I have in fact so far done nothing about Borden. The American tour has been confirmed as definite, and Cutter and I are in the thick of preparations. I am to be travelling for more than two whole months, and to be separated from Julia and the children for such a length of time is almost unthinkable.

However, I cannot miss the tour. Setting aside the matter of the generous fees, I am probably the youngest magician from Britain or Europe to have been invited to follow in the steps of some of magic's greatest performers. The New World is the source and location of some of the finest magicians currently in performance, and it is a magnificent compliment to be invited to undertake this tour.

And Borden has not so far visited the USA!

10th December 1892

I had been looking forward to a quiet Christmas at home. No magic, no rehearsals, no travelling. I wanted to sub-merge myself in my family and set everything else aside. But following a cancellation I have been offered a lucrative and irresistible two-week residency in Eastbourne, and it is such that I might take my entire household with me. My family shall spend Christmas at the Grand Hotel, overlooking the sea!

11th December 1892

A propitious discovery. Looking at a gazetteer this afternoon I could not help but notice that Eastbourne is just a few miles away from Hastings, and that the two towns are linked by a direct railway line. I think I shall spend a day or two in Hastings. I hear it is a pleasant place to visit.

17th January 1893

All of a sudden my life is overshadowed by the immensity of the journey before me. In two days' time I leave for South-ampton, and embark for New York City, thence to Boston and beyond, into the American heartland. The last week has been a nightmare of packing and preparations, and arrang-ing for the apparatus I need with me to be dismantled, crated, then despatched ahead of me. Nothing can be left to chance, for without my equipment I have no stage show. A lot depends on this transatlantic adventure.

But now I have a day or two of leisure in which to prepare myself mentally and relax at home for a while. Today I have visited London Zoo with Julia and the children, already feeling a sense of loss because I know I shall be away from them for so long. The children are asleep, Julia is reading in her sitting room, and in the calm of this dark January evening, quietly in my study, I may at last record, thanks to the industrious Mr Koenig, the fruits of my enquiries about Mr Alfred Borden.

The following are facts I have personally verified.

He was born on 8th May 1856, in the Royal Sussex Infirmary in Bohemia Road, Hastings. Three days after his birth he and his mother, Betsy Mary Borden, returned to their house at 105 Manor Road, where the father worked as a carpenter. The child's full name was Frederick Andrew Borden, and according to the almoner's records his was a single birth. Frederick Andrew Borden was not one of two identical twins at birth, so therefore neither can he be one today.

Next I looked into the possibility of Frederick Borden having brothers of a close age to him, and bearing a strong family resemblance. Frederick was the sixth-born child. He had three older sisters and two older brothers, but of these one brother was eight years his senior, and the other had died at the age of two weeks.

Using the files of the *Hastings & Bexhill Announcer*, I obtained a description of Frederick's older brother Julius (who according to the newspaper had won a prize at school). At the age of fifteen Julius was said to have straight blond hair. Frederick Borden is dark-haired, but there was a possibility that Julius was the stage double, having coloured his hair. This line of enquiry came to nothing, when I later discovered that Julius had died of consumption in 1870, when Frederick was fourteen.

There was a younger brother too. This was Albert Joseph Borden, seventh-born into the family, on 18th May 1858. (Albert + Frederick = Alfred? Is this how Frederick chose his first *nom de théâtre?*)

Again, the existence of a brother whose age was reasonably close to Frederick's raised the possibility of a double. I dug out and examined Albert's birth records at the hospital, but I found it difficult to discover much more about him. However, the enterprising Mr Koenig had suggested a visit to a photogenic portrait artiste called Charles Simpkins, who has his studio in Hastings High Street.

Mr Simpkins greeted me cordially and was pleased to show me a selection of his daguerreotypes. Amongst these, as Mr Koenig had hinted to me, was a studio portrait of Frederick Borden and his younger brother. It had been taken in 1874, when Frederick was eighteen and his brother was sixteen.

The two are clearly unalike in appearance. Frederick is tall, he has the sort of features often referred to as 'noble', and his bearing is arrogant (all of these I have frequently observed for myself), while Albert is much less prepossessing. He has a slack-jawed expression; his features are puffy, and his cheeks are round. His hair is wavier than his brother's and apparently paler in colour; and from his stance I would say he was at least four or five inches shorter than his brother.

This portrait convinced me that Koenig was correct. Frederick Borden does not have a close relation he can use as a double.

It remains possible that he has scoured the streets of London to find a man sufficiently like him to pass as a double, with the aid of stage make-up, but no matter what Cutter says I have myself *seen* Borden's performance. Most illusionists' doubles are only briefly glimpsed, or they mis-direct the perceptions of the audience by wearing identical costumes, so that in the few seconds in which the double is visible he seems to be the original.

Borden, after the transformation, allows himself to be seen, and to be seen clearly. He steps forward to the foot-lights, he bows, he smiles, he takes the hand of his female assistant, he bows again, he walks to and fro. There is no question but that the man who emerges from the second cabinet is the man who entered the first.

I still do not know how Borden works that damnable illusion, but I do at least know that he works it *alone*.

So it is with a certain frustrated equanimity that I am able to prepare myself for my long journey to the New World.

I am going to what is fast becoming the centre of the world of magic, and for two months I shall be meeting, and perhaps working with, some of the finest illusionists in the United States of America. There will be many there who can work out how it is done. I go to America to build my reputation, and to amass what must certainly be reckoned as a small fortune in fees, but I now have an extra quest.

I swear that when I return in two months I shall have Borden's secret with me. I also swear that within a month of returning I shall be performing a superior version of the same trick on the London stage.

On board SS Saturnia   21st January 1893

One day out from Southampton, a vile day in the English Channel behind us, and a short stay in Cherbourg, and now we are in the Western Approaches ploughing steadily towards America. The ship is a magnificent vessel, coal-fired, triple-stacked, equipped to house and entertain the finest of Europe and America. My cabin is on the second deck, and I share it with an architect from Chichester. I have not told him my own profession, in spite of well-mannered and tentative enquiries. Already I am in pain – the pain of being away from my family.

I see them still in my mind's eye on the rain-swept quay, waving and waving. At times like this I yearn for the magic reality my profession seems to conjure from nowhere: O! that I could wave my wand, utter some mumbo jumbo, and manifest them here with me!

Still on board SS Saturnia   24th January 1893

I have been suffering *mal de mer*, but not nearly as badly as my friend from Chichester, who last night spewed disgustingly across our cabin floor. The poor fellow was overcome with contrition and apology, but the deed was done. Partly as a consequence of this unenjoyable experience I have not eaten for two days.

27th January 1893

As I write, the city of New York is visible on the horizon ahead. I have arranged a meeting with Cutter in half an hour, to make sure he has right all the arrangements for disembarkation. No more time for diary writing!

Now the adventure begins.

13th September 1893

I am not surprised to discover that nearly eight months have elapsed since last I came to this diary to record my life. In returning to it I am tempted, as before I have sometimes been tempted, simply to destroy it in its entirety.

Such an act would stand as a summary of my own actions, as I have destroyed, removed or abandoned every aspect of my life that existed when I last wrote here.

One tiny shred remains, however. When I began the diary it was with a childish earnest to write of my entire life, no matter how it might turn out. I can no longer remember what I thought I might actually become, by my thirty-sixth year of life, but I certainly did not imagine this.

Julia and the children are gone. Cutter is gone. Much of my wealth is gone. My career has withered away and gone, through apathy.

I have lost everything.

But I have gained Olivia Svenson.

I shall write little of Olivia here, as in glancing back over the pages I see I depict my love for Julia with such enthusiasm that now I can only recoil in shame. I am old enough, and have travelled far enough in matters of the heart, no longer to trust my emotions in such things. It is enough to say that I have left Julia so that I might be with Olivia, after I fell in love with her during my American tour.

I met Olivia at a reception given in my honour in the fine city of Boston, Massachusetts, where she approached me and made her admiration known, in the way many women have approached me in the past. (I record this without vanity.) Perhaps it was because I was so far from home, and ironically so lonely without my family, that for once a woman's forthright intention was one I could not resist. Olivia, then working as a *danseuse*, joined my party. When I left Boston she remained with us, and thereafter we travelled together. More than this, within a week or two she was working on stage with me as my assistant, and has returned with me to London.

Cutter did not care for this, and although he saw out the tour we parted immediately on our return.

As, inevitably, did Julia and I. Sometimes, even now, I lie awake at night to marvel at the madness of my sacrifice. Once Julia meant the very world to me, and indeed she helped build the world I inhabit today. My children, my three helpless and innocent children, are nothing less than victims of the same sacrifice. All I can say is that my madness is the madness of love. Olivia blinds me to every other feeling that is not passion for her.

So I cannot bring myself to write down, even in the privacy of this journal, what was said, done and suffered at that time. Much of the saying and doing was mine, while all the suffering was Julia's.

I now support Julia in a household of her own, where to maintain appearances she lives the life of a widow. She has the children with her, she has her material needs taken care of, and she has never to see me again if that should be what she wants. Indeed, were I to be seen at her house the appearances would be betrayed, so I have perforce become a dead man. I can never meet my children in their own house again, and have to make do with the occasional excursion with them. Naturally, I blame only myself for this predicament.

Julia and I meet briefly on such occasions, and her sweetness of nature wrenches at my heart. But there is no going back. I have made my bed and now I lie in it. When I manage to close my mind to the family I have lost I am a happy man. I expect no favourable judgement of myself. I know I have wronged my wife.

I have always tried never to hurt the people around me.

Even in my dealings with Borden I have shrunk from causing him pain or danger, preferring to take revenge by irritating or embarrassing him. But now I find I have caused the
greatest hurt of all, to the four people who meant the most to
me. At the risk of humbug, I can only aver that I shall never
do anything like this again.

14th September 1893

My career struggles towards a new version of stability. In the
upheavals of the weeks following my return from the United
States, I let go most of the bookings Unwin had taken while
I was away. I had, after all, returned from the tour with a
tidy sum in hand, so I felt that I could survive for some time
without having to work.

This diary entry is to record, though, that I feel at last I
can emerge from the hole of misery and lethargy into which
I declined, and I am ready to return to the stage. I have
instructed Unwin to find me bookings, and my career may
resume.

To celebrate the decision, Olivia and I went this afternoon to the premises of a theatrical costumier, where she
chose, and was measured for, her new stage outfit.

1st December 1893

In my appointments book I have a thirty-minute Christmas
show that I am to perform for a school of orphans. Other
than that, my book is empty. 1894 looms up, bereft of work.
Since the end of September I have earned only £18. 18s. od.

Hesketh Unwin speaks of a whispering campaign against
me. He warns me to disregard it, because the success of
my tour of America is well known and it is easy to cause
jealousy.

I am disturbed by this news. Is Borden behind it?

Olivia and I have been discussing a return to spiritism, to
keep body and soul together, but so far I am thinking of it
only as a last-ditch resort.

Meanwhile, I occupy my days with practice and rehearsal. A magician can never practise enough, because every

moment spent will improve his performance. So I toil in my workshop, usually alone, but sometimes with Olivia, and rehearse until I feel sick with preparation. Although my skill with prestidigitation increases, sometimes, in my darker moments, I do wonder why I am continuing to rehearse at all.

At least the orphans will see a marvellous entertainment!

14th December 1893

Bookings have been made for January and February. Not major appearances, but our spirits have nevertheless risen.

20th December 1893

More bookings for January, one of them, I do declare, left vacant by a certain Professeur de Magie! I am pleased to take his guineas.

23rd December 1893

A Happy Christmas! I have been visited with an amusing idea, one I hasten to record before I change my mind. (Once committed to pen and paper, my actions will be set!) Unwin has sent me the contract for my appearance on 19th January at the Princess Royal Theatre in Streatham. This happens to be the booking left free by Borden. I was glancing through the contract (contracts have lately been so few and far between that I should likely have signed anything) when my gaze fell on one of the clauses toward the end. It contained a common enough provision found when one act is booked in place of another; that my performance should be to the same general standard of excellence as the act that was being replaced.

My first reaction was a sardonic snort. The idea that I should live up to Borden's standards was ironic indeed. Then I thought again. If I was to replace Borden, why should I not produce a replica of the act they were no longer going to see? In short, why shall I not at last perform Borden's illusion for him?

I am so taken with the idea that I have been dashing around London all day, trying to find someone who will act

210

as my double. This is the wrong time of year to be looking: all the unemployed actors one can generally count on finding in any public bar in the West End are working in the numerous pantomimes and Christmas shows around the town.

I have just over three weeks in which to prepare. Tomorrow I shall start to build the cabinets!

4th January 1894

Two weeks to go, and at last I have my man! His name is Gerald William Root, an actor, reciter of declamatory verse, monologist . . . and, by all accounts, regular drunkard and brawler. Mr Root is however desperate for cash and I have drawn from him a pledge that so long as he works for me he shall only taste liquor after each performance. He is anxious to please, and the cash that even I am able to offer him is so generous, by his usual standards, that I believe I can purchase his reliability.

He is the same height as me, and his general stance and figure are roughly mine. He is a little stouter than I am, but either he will lose those extra folds of flesh, or I shall wear padding. It is of no concern. His colouring is fairer than mine, but again this is a small matter that can be solved with greasepaint. Although his eyes are an impure blue, while mine are the colour generally described as hazel, the difference is not noticeable, and again we can use theatrical make-up to misdirect attention.

None of the details matters. More potentially serious is the problem of his gait, which is noticeably looser than mine, with longer strides, and his feet turn slightly outwards as he walks. Olivia has taken charge of the problem and believes she can coach him in time. As any actor knows, you convey more about a character with a walk or a bearing than any number of facial characteristics, accents or gestures. If my double walks differently from me while on the stage he will not be mistaken for me. It is as simple as that.

Root, fully briefed in the deception to which he is privy, says that he understands the problem. He tries to dismiss

my worries on this score by regaling me with his professional reputation, but I care for none of it. Provided that
on the night he is mistaken for me, he will have earned his
money.

A fortnight remains in which to rehearse.

6th January 1894

Root goes through the movements in which I rehearse him,
but I cannot help feeling that he does not relish the *illusion*.
Actors play a part, but the audience is in on the deception
throughout. They know that behind the appearance of
Prince Hamlet is a man who merely speaks the lines. My
audiences must leave the theatre foxed by what they have
seen. They must both believe and disbelieve the evidence of
their eyes!

10th January 1894

I have given Mr Root tomorrow as a day off, so that I might
consider. He is not right, not right at all! Olivia too thinks it
is all a mistake, and urges me to drop the Borden illusion
from my act.

But Root is a disaster.

12th January 1894

Root is a marvel! We both needed the time to think it
through. He told me he passed the day with friends, but I
suspect from the smell about him that he spent the time with
a bottle to his lips.

No matter. His moves are right, his timing is nearly
right, and as soon as we have been fitted out in our identical costumes, the deception will be good enough to pass
muster.

Tomorrow, I go with Root and Olivia to Streatham,
where we will inspect the stage, and make final preparations.

18th January 1894

I am unaccountably nervous about tomorrow's performance, even though Root and I have rehearsed it until we

are sick of it. In perfection lies a risk: if tomorrow I perform Borden's illusion, and improve on it, and I shall, word that I have done so will reach him within days.

In these quiet hours around midnight, with Olivia abed, the house silent and my thoughts welling around me, I know there is yet a terrible truth that I have not faced up to. It is that Borden will instantly know the means by which I have brought off the illusion, but I still do not know his.

20th January 1894

It was a triumph! Applause rang out to the very rafters! Today, in its final edition, the *Morning Post* describes me as 'probably Britain's greatest living illusionist'. There are two small qualifications there that I could gladly live without, but it will be enough to rattle Mr Borden's complacency.

It is sweet. But it also has a sour side I had not anticipated. How could I not have thought of this? At the conclusion of the illusion, at the climax of my act, I am perforce huddled ignominiously in the artfully collapsed panels of my cabinet. While the applause fills the hall, it is the drunkard Root who strides out in the spotlight. It is he who takes the ovation, who holds Olivia's hand in his, who bows and waves and blows kisses, who acknowledges the bandmaster, who salutes the gentry in the loges, who doffs his hat and bows again and again—

And I can only wait for the darkness of the stage when the curtain descends, before I make my escape.

This will have to change. We must arrange it that *I* am the one who emerges from the unexpected cabinet, so the switch with Root must be made before the illusion begins. I shall have to think of a way.

21st January 1894

Yesterday's notice in the *Post* has made its impact, and already today my agent has taken several enquiries about and three firm bookings for my act. My miraculous illusory switch is demanded each time.

I have rewarded Root with a small cash bonus.

Already the events of two years ago seem like a fading nightmare. I return to this journal at the half-year merely to record that I am once again on an even keel. Olivia and I co-exist harmoniously, and although she can never be the driving stimulus that Julia once was, her quiet support has become the bulwark on which I build my life and career.

I intend another discussion with Root, since the last one had little effect. In spite of the excellence of his performance he is a trouble to me, and another reason for returning to this diary is to record the fact that he and I will at last be having words.

There is a cardinal rule in the world of magic (and if there is not one, let me formulate it) that you do not antagonise your assistants. This is because they know many of your secrets, and they therefore have a particular power over you.

If I fire Root I shall be at his mercy.

The problem he presents is partly his alcoholic addiction, and partly his arrogance.

He has often been inebriated during my performance, a fact he does not deny. He claims he can control it. The trouble is that there is no predicting the behaviour of a heavy drinker and I am terrified that one evening he will be too drunk to take part. A magician should never leave any aspect of his act to chance, yet here am I, dicing with it every time I perform the switch with him.

His arrogance is, if anything, a worse problem. He is convinced that I am unable to function effectively without him, and whenever he is around me, be it in rehearsal, backstage at the theatres, or even in my own workshop, I have to suffer a constant stream of advice based on his years of experience as a thespian.

Last night we had our long-planned 'discussion', although in the event he did most of the talking. I have to report that much of what he said was nasty and threatening indeed. He said the words I most feared to hear: that he could expose my secrets and ruin my career.

And worse. He has somehow found out about my relationship with Sheila Macpherson, a matter which I had thought was strictly under the wraps. I am being blackmailed, of course. I need him, and he knows it. He has power over me, and I know it.

I was forced even to offer him a raise in his performance fees, and this, of course, he promptly accepted.

19th August 1895

This evening I returned early from my workshop because there was something (I forget what) I had left at home. Calling in first on Olivia, I was surprised, to say the least, to discover Root with her in her parlour.

I should explain that after I bought my house at 45 Idmiston Villas I left it in its former configuration of two self-contained flats. During our marriage Julia and I moved freely between the two, but since Olivia has been with me we have lived apart under the same roof. This is partly to preserve the proprieties, but it also reflects the more casual nature of our association. While maintaining separate households, Olivia and I call without ceremony on each other whenever it pleases us.

I heard laughter while I climbed the stair. When I opened the door to her flat, which opens directly into her parlour, Olivia and Root were still merrily laughing away. The sound quickly died when they saw me standing there. Olivia looked angry. Root attempted to stand up, but swayed unsteadily and sat down again. I noticed, to my intense aggravation, that a half-empty bottle of gin stood on the table to the side, and that another, completely empty, was beside it. Both Olivia and Root were holding glasses containing the liquor.

'What is the meaning of this?' I demanded of them.

'I was calling in to see you, Mr Angier,' replied Root.

'You knew I was rehearsing in my workshop this evening,' I riposted. 'Why did you not seek me there?'

'Honey, Gerry just called round for a drink,' said Olivia.

'Then it is time he left!'

I held the door open with my arm, indicating he should depart, and this he did, promptly in spite of his inebriation, but staggeringly because of it. His gin-soaked breath curled briefly around me as he passed.

A tense conversation ensued between Olivia and I, which I shall not record in detail. We left it at that, and I retired to pen this account. I have many feelings I have not described here.

24th August 1895

I learnt today that Borden is taking his magical show on a tour of Europe and the Levant, and that he will be out of England until the end of the year. Curiously, he will not be performing his own version of the two-cabinets illusion.

Hesketh Unwin informed me of this when I saw him earlier today. I made the pleasantry that I hoped that by the time he reached Paris Borden's spoken French would be better than when I last heard him at it.

25th August 1895

It took me twenty-four hours to work it out, but Borden has just done me a favour. I finally realised that with Borden out of the country I have no need to keep performing the switch illusion, and so without delay or scruple I have given Root the sack.

By the time Borden returns from his tour abroad, either I shall have replaced Mr Root or I shall no longer be performing the illusion at all.

14th November 1895

Olivia and I worked on the stage together for the last time tonight, at a performance at the Phoenix Theatre in Charing Cross Road. Afterwards, we drove home together, holding hands contentedly in the back of the cab. Since Mr Root departed, we have been perceptibly more contented. (I have been seeing less and less of Miss Macpherson.)

Next week, when I open for a short season at the Royal County Theatre in Reading, my assistant will be a young lady I have been training for the last two weeks. Her name is Gertrude, she is blessed with a supple and beautiful body, she has both the prettiness and the mental ability of a china ornament, and is the fiancée of my other new employee, a carpenter and apparatus technician named Adam Wilson. I am paying them both well, and am satisfied with their contributions so far to my act.

Adam, I must record, is an almost exact double for me in terms of physique, and although I have not yet broached it to him I shall keep him in mind as Root's replacement.

12th February 1896

I have tonight learned the meaning of the phrase one's blood runs cold.

I was engaged in one of my customary tricks with playing cards in the first half of my show. In this, I ask a member of the audience to select a card and then to write his name upon it in full view of the audience. When this is done I take the card from him and tear it up before his eyes, tossing aside the pieces. Moments later, I show a live canary in a metal cage. When my volunteer takes the cage from me it unaccountably collapses in his hand (the bird vanishes from sight), and leaves him holding what appears to be the remains of the cage in which can be seen a single playing card. When he removes it, he discovers that it is the very one on which his name is inscribed. The trick ends, and the volunteer returns to his seat.

Tonight, at the conclusion of the trick, as I beamed towards the audience in anticipation of the applause, I heard the fellow say, 'Here, this isn't my card!'

I turned towards him. The fool was standing there with the remains of the cage dangling from one hand, and the playing card in the other. He was trying to read it.

'Let me take it, sir!' I boomed theatrically, sensing that my forcing of the card might have gone wrong, and preparing to cover the mistake with a sudden production of a multitude of coloured streamers which I keep on hand for just such an eventuality.

I tried to snatch the card from him, but calamity piled on disaster.

He swung away from me, shouting in a triumphant voice, 'Look, it's got summat else written on it!'

The man was playing to the audience, making the most of the fact that he had somehow beaten the magician at his own game. To save the moment I had to take possession of the card, and I did, wrenching it out of his hand. I showered him with coloured streamers, cued the bandmaster, and waved the audience to applaud, to waft the appalling fellow back towards his seat.

In the swelling music and the paltry applause I stood transfixed, reading the words that had been written there.

They said: '*I know the address you go to with Sheila Macpherson – Abracadabra! – Alfred Borden.*'

The card was the trey of clubs, the one I had forced on the volunteer for the trick.

I simply do not know how I managed to get through the rest of the performance, but somehow I must have done so.

18th February 1896

Last night I travelled alone to the Empire Theatre in Cambridge where Borden was performing. As he went through the rigmarole of setting up a conventional illusion with a cabinet, I stood up in my seat in the auditorium and denounced him. As loudly as I could I informed the audience that an assistant was already concealed inside the cabinet. I immediately left the theatre, glancing back only as I exited the auditorium, to be rewarded by the sight of the tabs coming down prematurely.

Then, unexpectedly, I found I had to pay a price for what I had done. Conscience struck me as I took my long, cold and solitary train journey back to London. In that dark night I had abundant opportunity to reflect on my actions. I bitterly regretted what I had done. The ease with which I destroyed his magic appalled me. Magic is illusion, a temporary suspension of reality for the benefit and amusement of an audience. What right had I (or he, when he took his turn) to destroy that illusion?

Once, long ago, after Julia lost our first baby, Borden wrote to me and apologised for what he had done. Foolishly, O how foolishly!, I spurned him. Now the time has come when I anxiously desire a surcease of the feud between us. How much longer do two grown men have to keep sniping at each other in public, to settle some score that no one but they even know about, and one that even they barely comprehend? Yes, once, when Julia was hurt by the buffoon's intervention I had a valid case against him, but so much has happened since.

All through that cold journey back to Liverpool Street Station, I wondered how it might be achieved. Now, twenty-four hours later, I still think about it. I shall brace myself, write to him, call an end to it, and suggest a private meeting to thrash out any remaining scores that he feels have to be settled.

20th February 1896

Today, after she had opened her letters, Olivia came to me and said, 'So what Gerry Root told me about is true!'

I asked what she could possibly mean.

'You're still seeing Sheila Macpherson, right?'

Later, she showed me the note she had received, in an envelope addressed to 'Occupant, Flat B, 45 Idmiston Villas'. It was from Borden!

27th February 1896

I have made peace with myself, with Olivia, even with Borden!

Let me simply record that I have promised Olivia I shall never see Miss Macpherson again (nor shall I), and that my love for her is undying.

And I have decided that never again shall I conduct a feud with Alfred Borden, no matter how provoked I feel. I still expect a public reprisal from him for my ill-advised outburst in Cambridge, but I shall ignore him.

5th March 1896

Sooner even than I had expected, Borden tried successfully to humiliate me while I was performing a well-known but popular illusion called TRILBY. (It is the one where the assistant lies on a board balanced between two chair backs, then is seen to hover apparently unaided in the air when the chairs are removed.) Borden had somehow secreted himself backstage.

As I removed the second chair from beneath Gertrude's board, the concealing backdrop lifted quickly to reveal Adam Wilson crouched behind, operating the mechanism.

I brought down the main curtains, and discontinued my act.

I shall not retaliate.

31st March 1896

Another Borden incident. So soon after the last!

17th May 1896

Another Borden incident.

This one puzzles me, for I had already established he was also performing this same evening, but somehow he got across London to the Great Western Hotel to sabotage my performance.

Again, I shall not retaliate.

16th July 1896

I shall not even record any more Borden incidents here, such is my disdain for him. (Another one this evening, yes, but I plan no retaliation.)

4th August 1896

Last night I was performing an illusion comparatively new to my act, which involves a revolving blackboard on which I chalk simple messages called out to me by members of the audience. When a certain number have been written for all to see, I suddenly spin the blackboard over . . . to reveal that by some apparent miracle the same messages are already written there too!

Tonight when I rotated the blackboard I found that my prepared messages had been erased. In their place was the message:

I SEE YOU HAVE GIVEN UP TRYING TO TRANSPORT
YOURSELF.
DOES THIS MEAN YOU STILL DON'T KNOW THE SECRET?
COME AND WATCH AN EXPERT!

Still I shall not retaliate. Olivia, who perforce knows every fact relating to our feud, agrees that a dignified disdain is the only response I should make.

3rd February 1897

Another Borden incident. How tiresome it is to open this journal only to report this!

He is becoming more daring. Although Adam and I carefully check our apparatus before and after every performance, and scour through the backstage parts of the theatre immediately before going on, somehow tonight Borden gained access to the mezzanine floor, beneath the stage.

I was performing a trick known simply as THE DISAP-PEARING LADY. This is an attractive illusion both to perform and see, as the apparatus is straightforward. My assistant sits on a plain wooden chair in the centre of the stage, and I throw over her a large cotton sheet. I spread it out smoothly around her. Her figure can be plainly seen still sitting on the chair, thinly veiled by the sheet. Her head and shoulders, in particular, may easily be made out as proof of her pres-ence.

Suddenly, I whip away the sheet in a continuous move-ment . . . and the chair is empty! All that remains on the bare stage is the chair, the sheet and myself.

Tonight, when I pulled away the sheet, I discovered to my

amazement that Gertrude was still in the chair, her face a torment of confusion and terror. I stood there, aghast.

Then, compounding the moment, one of the stage trap-doors snapped open, and a man came rising into view from below. He was wearing full evening dress, with silk hat, scarf and cape. As calmly as the devil, Borden (for it was he) doffed his hat to the audience, then strode in a leisurely way towards the wings, a drift of tobacco smoke swirling in his wake. I dashed after him, determined at last to confront him, when my attention was drawn by an immense discharge of brilliant light, from over my head!

An electrified sign was being lowered from the flies! In bright blue lettering, picked out in some electrical device, it said:

LE PROFESSEUR DE MAGIE
AT THIS THEATRE — ALL NEXT WEEK!

A ghastly cyanic pallor imbued the stage. I signalled to the stage manager in the wings and at last the curtain came down, concealing my despair, my humiliation, my rage.

When I arrived home and told her what had happened, Olivia said, 'You got to take revenge, Robbie. And you better make it good!'

At last I agree with her.

18th April 1897

Tonight, for the first time in public, Adam and I performed the switch illusion. We have been rehearsing it for more than a week, and technically the performance was faultless.

Yet the applause at the end was polite rather than enthusiastic.

13th May 1897

After many long hours of work and rehearsal, Adam and I have developed our cabinet switching routine to a standard which I know cannot be bettered. Adam, after eighteen months working closely with me, can imitate my movements and mannerisms with uncanny accuracy. Given an identical suit of clothes, a few touches of greasepaint and a (most expensive) hairpiece, he is my double to the last detail.

Yet each time we perform it we bring the show to what we imagine will be a devastating climax, and our audiences declare themselves, by their lukewarm ripples of applause, to be unimpressed.

I do not know what I have to do to better the illusion. Two years ago the mere suggestion that I might be prevailed upon to include it in my act was enough to double my fee. These days, it is almost an irrelevance. I am brooding long.

1st June 1897

I have been hearing rumours for some time that Borden has 'improved' his switch illusion, but without further information I have taken no notice. It is years since I saw him performing it, and so yesterday evening I betook myself and Adam Wilson to a theatre in Nottingham, where Borden has been in residence for the last week. (I have a show tonight in Sheffield, but I left London a day early so that I might visit Borden at work *en route*.)

I disguised myself with greyed hair, cheek pads, untidy clothes, a pair of unnecessary eye-glasses, and took a seat only two rows from the front. I was just a few feet away from Borden as he performed all his tricks.

Everything is suddenly explained! Borden has substantially advanced his version of the illusion. He no longer conceals himself inside cabinets. There is no more stuff-and-nonsense with some object tossed across the stage (which I have been continuing to work with until this week). And he does not use a double.

I say with certainty: *Borden does not use a double*. I know everything there is to know about doubles. I can spot one as easily as I can spot a cloud in the sky. I am as sure as I can be that Borden works alone.

The first part of his act was performed before a half-drop, which only allowed the full stage set to be seen when he came to the climactic illusion. At this, the half-drop was raised and the audience saw an array of jars fuming with chemicals, cabinets adorned with coiling cables, glass tubes and pipettes, and above all a host of gleaming electrical wires. It was a glimpse into the laboratory of a scientific fiend.

Borden, in his embarrassing persona of a French academic, strolled around the equipment, lecturing the audience on the perils of working with electrical power. At certain moments he touched one wire against another, or to a flask of gas, and there came an alarming flash of light, or a loud bang. Sparks flew around him and a mist of blue smoke began to hover about his head.

When he was ready to perform, he indicated that a roll of drums be played from the orchestra pit. He seized two heavy wires, brought them dramatically together and made an electrical connection.

In the brilliant flash that followed, the switch took place. Before our very eyes, Borden vanished from where he was standing (the two thick wires fell snaking to the stage floor, emitting a trail of dangerous fizzing sparks), and he instantly reappeared on the other side of the stage – at least twenty feet away from where he had been!

It was impossible for him to have moved across that distance by normal means. The switch was too quick, too perfect. He arrived with his hands still flexed as if gripping the wires, the ones that even at that moment were zigzagging spectacularly across the stage.

Borden stepped forward in tumultuous applause to take his bow. Behind him the scientific apparatus still frothed and fumed, a deadly backdrop that seemed, perversely, to heighten his ordinariness.

As the applause continued to thunder, he reached into his breast pocket as if to produce something. He smiled modestly, inviting the audience to urge him to one final magical production. The applause accordingly lifted, and with his smile broadening into a full beam Borden thrust his hand into the pocket and produced . . . a paper rose, brilliant pink in colour.

This production was a reference back to an earlier trick.

In this he had allowed a lady from the audience to select one flower from a whole bunch, before wonderfully making it vanish. To see the rose reappear utterly charmed his audience. He held the little flower aloft – it was most definitely the one the lady had chosen. When he had displayed it long enough he turned it in his fingers, to reveal that part of it had been charred black, as if by some infernal force. With a significant glance towards his apparatus behind him, Borden made one more sweeping bow, then departed the stage.

The applause continued for long afterwards, and I report that my hands were clapping as loudly as anyone's.

Why should this fellow-magician, so gifted, so endowed with skill and professionalism, pursue a sordid feud against me?

5th March 1898

I have been working hard, with little time for the diary. Once more, several months have passed between my last entry and this. Today (a weekend) I have no bookings, so I may make a brief entry.

To record that Adam and I have not included our switch illusion in my act since that night in Nottingham.

Even without this mild provocation, the *soi-disant* greatest living magician has meanwhile dignified me with two more unprovoked attacks while I was performing. Both involved potentially risky interruptions to my act. One of them I was able to joke away, but the other was for a few minutes an unsustainable disaster.

I have as a result abandoned my façade of disdain.

I am left with two apparently unachievable ambitions. The first is to try to forge some kind of reconciliation with Julia and the children. I know I have lost her forever, but the distance she puts between us is terrible to endure. The second is minor in comparison. It is that now my unilateral truce with Borden has ended, I of course wish to discover the secret of his illusion so that I might again outperform him.

Olivia has proposed an idea!

Before describing it I should say that in recent months the ardour between Olivia and myself has noticeably cooled. There is neither rancour nor jealousy between us, but a vast indifference has been hanging like a pall over the house. We continue to cohabit peacefully, she in her apartment, I in mine, and at times we behave as man and wife, but overall we no longer act as if we love or care for each other. Yet we cling together.

The first clue I had came after dinner. We had eaten together in my apartment, but at the end she absented herself with some haste, taking with her a bottle of gin. I have grown used to her solitary drinking, and no longer remark on it.

A few minutes later, though, her maid, Lucy, came up and asked me if I would step downstairs for a few minutes.

I found Olivia seated at her green-baize card table, with two or three bottles and two glasses standing on it, and an empty chair opposite her. She waved me to sit down, and then poured me a drink. I added some orange syrup to the gin, to take away the taste.

'Robbie,' she said with her familiar directness. 'I'm going to leave you.'

I mumbled something in reply. I have been expecting some such development for months, although I had no idea how I would cope with it if, as at this moment, it happened.

'I'm going to leave you,' she said again, 'and then I'm going to come back. Do you want to know why?'

I said that I did.

'Because there's something you want more than you want me. I figure that if I get out there and find it for you, then I have a chance to make you want me all over again.'

I assured her I wanted her as much as ever, but she cut me short.

'I know what's going on,' she declared. 'You and this Alfred Borden are like two lovers who can't get along together. Am I right?'

226

I tried to prevaricate, but when I saw the determination in her eyes I quickly agreed.

'Look at this!' she said, and brandished this week's copy of *The Stage*. 'See here.'

She folded the paper in half and passed it across to me. She had circled one of the classified advertisements on the front page.

'That's your friend Borden,' she said. 'See what he says?'

An attractive young female stage assistant is required for full-time employment. She must be terpsichorally adept, strong and fit, and willing to travel and to work long hours, both on and off stage. Pleasing appearance is essential, and so is a willingness to participate in exciting and demanding routines before large audiences. Please apply, with suitable references, to . . .

The address of Alfred Borden's rehearsal room followed.

'He's been advertising for an assistant for a couple of weeks, so he must be finding it difficult to hire the right one. I guess I could help him out.'

'You mean you—'

'You always said I was the best assistant you ever had.'

'But you . . . ? Going to work for *him*?' I shook my head sadly. 'How could you do this to me, Olivia?'

'You want to find out how he does that trick, don't you?' she said.

As it dawned on me what she was saying I sat silently before her, staring at her and marvelling. If she could gain his confidence, work with him in rehearsal and on stage, move freely in his workshop, it would not be long before Borden's secret was mine.

We soon got down to details.

I was worried in case he recognised her, but Olivia was not.

'You think I'd dream up this idea if I thought he knew my name?' she drawled. She reminded me that he had once had to address her as 'Occupant'. The need to supply references seemed for a time to be an insurmountable problem, because Olivia had worked for no one but me, but she pointed out that I was entirely capable of forging letters.

And I had doubts, I don't mind admitting here. The thought of this beautiful young woman, who had wreaked such exciting emotional havoc on me, and who had given up her own life to be with me, and who had shared almost everything with me for five years, the thought of her preparing to enter the camp of my blackest enemy was almost too much to countenance.

Two hours or more went quickly by while we discussed her idea, and began to lay our plans. We emptied the bottle of gin, while Olivia kept saying, 'I'll get the secret for you, Robbie. That's what you want me to do, isn't it?' And I said yes, but that I did not want to lose her.

The spectre of Borden's ruthlessness loomed over us. I was torn between the euphoria of making a definitive strike against him, and the prospect of him taking some even greater revenge should he realise Olivia was mine. I voiced these fears. She replied, 'I'll come back to you Robbie, and I'll bring you Borden's secret—' We were soon both of us inebriated, both of us frolicsome and affectionate, and I did not return to my own apartment until after breakfast this morning.

At the moment she is in her own apartment, drafting a letter of application to Alfred Borden. I must go to forge one or two testimonials for her. We are using the address of her maid for *poste restante*; as a further subterfuge she is taking her mother's maiden name.

7th August 1898

It is a week since Olivia applied to Borden for a job, and there has been no reply. In some ways this is almost an irrelevance, as since the idea came into being Olivia and I have been as tender and loving to each other as we were during those heady weeks of my American tour. She looks more comely than she has for many months, and she has entirely given up her gin.

Borden has replied (at least, an assistant called T. Elbourne replied on his behalf), proposing an interview early next week.

I am suddenly dead against it, having in the last few days found a renewal of happiness with Olivia, and more unwilling than ever to see her fall into Borden's clutches, even if it should be for something we dreamed up together.

Olivia still wants to go through with it. I argue against her. I minimise the importance of his trick, shrug off the earnestness of the feud, try to laugh the whole thing off.

I fear that in the past I gave Olivia too many months and years to think alone, however.

18th August 1898

Olivia has been to the interview and returned from it, and she says the job is hers.

While she was gone I was in a torment of fears and regrets. Such is my suspicion of Borden that the moment she had left me I imagined that he had placed the advertisement in an attempt to snare her, and I had to restrain myself from dashing after her. I went around to my workshop and tried to distract myself with mirror practice, but at last I came home and paced around my room again.

Olivia was gone far longer than either of us had expected, and I was seriously wondering what I should do when suddenly she arrived back. She was safe and sound, elated and excited.

Yes, the job is hers. Yes, Borden read the references I had written, and he accepted them as genuine. No, there was no apparent suspicion of me, and no, he appeared not to suspect there was any link between us.

She told me about some of the apparatus she had seen in his workshop, but it was all disappointingly ordinary.

'Did he say anything at all about the switch illusion?' I queried her.

'Not a word. But he told me there were several tricks

he did alone, and for which he did not need a stage assistant.'

Later, saying she was tired, she went to her flat to sleep, and here I am, once more alone. I must try to understand. It is tiring going through an audition, no matter what the circumstances.

19th August 1898

It transpires that Olivia has started work with Borden immediately. When I went to the door of her flat this morning the maid told me Olivia had risen early, and would not be home until this afternoon.

20th August 1898

Olivia came in at 5.00 p.m. yesterday, and although she went straight to her flat she did admit me when I went to her door. She looked tired again. I was eager for news, but all she would say was that Borden had spent the day showing her the illusions in which she would be needed, and she had been rehearsing them intensively.

Later we had dinner together, but she was plainly exhausted and went again to sleep alone in her flat. This morning she departed at an early hour.

21st August 1898

A Sunday, and even Borden does not work. At home with me all day Olivia is being tight-lipped about what she is seeing and doing in his workshop, and it puzzles me. I asked her if she felt constrained by professional ethics, that she perhaps felt she must not reveal to me the workings of his magic, but she denied it. For a few seconds I glimpsed Olivia in the mood of two weeks ago. She laughed and said that of course she realised where her loyalties lay.

I know I can trust her, however difficult it is proving, and so I have let the subject rest all day. As a consequence, we have together enjoyed an innocent, ordinary day today, while we went for a long walk in the warm sunshine on Hampstead Heath.

27th August 1898

The end of another week, and still Olivia has no information for me. She seems unwilling to talk to me about it.

Tonight she gave me a free pass to Borden's next series of performances. Billed as an 'extravaganza', his show will occupy the Leicester Square Theatre for a two-week run. Olivia will be on stage with him at every performance.

3rd September 1898

Olivia has not returned home at all this evening. I am mystified, alarmed, and full of forebodings.

4th September 1898

I sent a boy to Borden's workshop with a message for her, but he returned to say the place was bolted up with no one apparently inside.

6th September 1898

Abandoning subterfuge I went in search of Olivia. First to Borden's workshop, which was empty as described, then to his house in St Johns Wood, and propitiously discovered a coffee shop from where I could observe the front of the building. I sat there as long as I was able, but without being rewarded with a single glimpse of any significant matter. I did however see Borden himself, leaving his house with a woman I took to be his wife. A carriage drew up outside the house at 2.00 p.m., and after a short pause Borden and the woman appeared, then climbed into the carriage. Shortly afterwards it drove off in the direction of the West End.

Having waited for a full ten minutes to be certain he was away from the house, I walked nervously across to the door and rang the bell. A male servant answered.

I said directly, 'Is Miss Olivia Svenson here?'

The man looked surprised.

'I think you must be calling in error, sir,' he said. 'We have no one here of that name.'

'I'm sorry,' I said, remembering just in time that we had

231

used her mother's maiden name. 'I meant to ask for Miss Wenscombe. Would she be here?'

Again the man shook his head, politely and correctly.

'There is no Miss Wenscombe here, sir. Maybe you should enquire at the Post Office in the High Street.'

'Yes, indeed I shall,' I replied, and, no longer wanting to draw attention to myself, I beat a retreat.

I went back to my vigil in the coffee shop and waited there for another hour, by the end of which Borden and his wife returned to the house.

12th September 1898

With no further sign of Olivia coming home, I took the pass she had given me and went to the box office of the Leicester Square Theatre. Here I claimed a ticket for Borden's show. I deliberately selected a seat near the rear of the stalls, so that my presence might not be noticed from the stage.

After his customary opening with CHINESE LINKING RINGS, Borden quickly and efficiently produced his assistant from a cabinet. It was of course my Olivia, resplendent in a sequined gown that glittered and flashed in the electrically powered lights. She strode elegantly into the wings, whence she emerged a few moments later, now clad in a fetching costume of the leotard type. The blatant voluptuousness of her appearance quickened my pulse, even in spite of my intense and despairing feelings of loss.

Borden climaxed his show with the electrical switch illusion, performing it with a flair that plunged me further into depression. When Olivia returned to the stage to take the final bow with him my gloom was complete. She looked beautiful, happy and excited, and it seemed to my troubled gaze that as Borden held her hand for the applause he did so with unnecessary affection.

Determined to see the thing through, I raced from the auditorium and hurried around to the Stage Door. Although I waited while the other artistes filed out into the night, and until the doorman had locked the door and turned off the lights, I saw neither Borden nor Olivia departing the building.

Today Olivia's maid, whom I have retained in the household for the time being lest Olivia should return, brought me a letter she had received from her erstwhile mistress.

I read it anxiously, clinging to the hope that it might contain a clue as to what had happened, but it merely said:

Lucy—
    Would you kindly make up packages and cases of all my belongings, and have them delivered as soon as possible to the Stage Door of the Strand Theatre.
    Please be sure that everything is clearly labelled as being for myself, and I will arrange collection.
    I enclose an amount to cover the costs, and that which is left over you must keep for yourself. If you require a reference for your next employment Mr Angier will of course write it for you.
    Thank you, &c
    Olivia Svenson

I had to read this letter aloud to the poor girl, and to explain what she had to do with the five-pound note Olivia had enclosed.

4th December 1898

I am currently engaged for a season of shows at the Plaza Theatre in Richmond, by the side of the River Thames. This evening, I was relaxing in my dressing room between first and second performances, just prior to going out to find a sandwich meal with Adam and Gertrude. Someone knocked on the door.

It was Olivia. I let her into the room almost without thinking what I was doing. She looked beautiful but tired, and told me she had been trying to locate me all day.

'Robbie, I have gotten you the information you want,' she

233

said, and she held up a sealed envelope for me to see. 'I brought you this, even though you must understand that I'm not going to be coming back to you. You have to promise me that your feud with Alfred will end immediately. If you do, I'll let you have the envelope.'

I told her that as far as I was concerned the feud was already at an end.

'Then why do you still need his secret?'

'You surely know why,' I said.

'Only to continue the feud!'

I knew she was touching the truth, but I said, 'I'm curious.'

She was in a hurry to depart, saying that already Borden would be suspicious of her long absence. I did not remind her of the similar wait I had endured when this endeavour began.

I asked her why she had written down the message, when she could as easily have told me in words. She said it was too complicated, too intricately devised, and that she had copied the information from Borden's own notes. Finally, she handed over the envelope.

Holding it, I said, 'Is it really the end of the mystery for me?'

'I believe it is, yes.'

She turned to go and opened the door.

'Can I ask you something else, Olivia?'

'What is it?'

'Is Borden one man, or two?'

She smiled, and maddeningly I glimpsed the smile of a woman thinking of her lover. 'He is just one man, I do assure you.'

I followed her out into the corridor, where technical staff were loitering within earshot.

'Are you happy now?' I asked her.

'Yes, I am. I'm sorry if I've hurt you, Robbie.'

She left me then, without an embrace or even a smile or a touch of hands. I have hardened myself against her in the last few weeks, but even so it was painful to be with her like that.

I returned to the dressing room, closed the door and leant my weight upon it. I slit the envelope at once. It contained one sheet of paper, and on it Olivia had written a single word.

Tesla.

Somewhere in Illinois   3rd July 1900

We departed promptly from Chicago Union Street Station at 9.00 a.m., and after a slow journey through the industrial wasteland that surrounds that most vibrant and thrilling of cities we have since been moving at a fair speed across the agricultural plains to the west.

I have a splendid sleeping berth and a seat permanently reserved for me in the first-class saloon. American trains are sumptuously fitted and magnificently comfortable. The meals, prepared in one of the carriages entirely set aside as a galley, are large, nutritious and attractively served. I have been travelling for five weeks on American railroads, and I have rarely been happier or better fed. I dare not weigh myself! I feel I am ensconced securely in the great American world of convenience, plenty and courtesy, while the terrific American realm slips by beyond the windows.

My fellow travellers are all Americans, a mixed bunch in appearance, friendly towards me and curious about me in equal measure. About a third of them, I hazard, are commercial travellers of the superior kind, and several more appear to be employed in business in one way or another. In addition, there are two professional gamblers, a presbyterian minister, four young men returning to Denver from college in Chicago, several well-to-do farmers and landowners, and one or two others I have not yet been able to pin down exactly. In the American way we have all been on first-name terms from the moment of meeting. I long ago learned that the name Rupert attracts amused inquisitiveness, so while I am in the United States I am always Rob or Robbie.

The train stopped last night in Galesburg, Illinois. Because today is American Independence Day the railroad company gave all first-class passengers the choice of staying aboard the train in our cabins or of spending the night in the town's largest hotel. Since I have been sleeping in many trains in the last few weeks I opted for the hotel.

I was able to take a brief tour of the town before turning in. It is an attractive place, and possesses a large theatre. A play happens to be on this week, but I was told that variety shows ('vaudeville') are frequent and popular. Magic acts often appear. I left my card with the manager, hoping for an engagement one day.

I must record that the theatre, the hotel and the streets of Galesburg are lit by electricity. At the hotel I learned that most American towns and cities of any significance are so equipping themselves. Alone in my hotel room I had the experience of personally switching on and off the electric incandescent lamp in the centre of the ceiling. I dare say as a novelty this would quickly pall and become commonplace, but the light cast by electricity is bright, steady and cheerful. In addition to lighting I have seen many different appliances on sale: ventilating fans, clothes irons, room heaters, even an electrically driven hairbrush! As soon as I return to London I shall make enquiries about having electrical current installed in my home.

Crossing Iowa   5th July 1900

I stare for long periods through the window of the carriage, hoping for a break in the monotony, but the agricultural land stretches flat and wide in all directions. The sky is a bright pale blue, and it hurts the eyes to look at it for more than a few seconds. Clouds pile somewhere to the south of us, but they seem never to shift their position or shape, no matter how far we travel.

A Mr Bob Tannhouse, a fellow passenger on the train, is by small coincidence the vice-president of sales in a company that manufactures the sort of electrical appliances that have caught my eye. He confirms that as we move towards the 20th century there is no limit, no bound, to what we might expect electricity to do for our lives. He predicts that men will sail the seas in electric ships, sleep in electric beds, fly in electric heavier-than-air machines, eat electrically cooked food . . . even shave our beards with electric razor blades! Bob is a fantasist and a salesman, but he fires me with a tremendous hope. I believe that in this enthralling country, as a new century dawns, anything really is possible, or it can be made possible. My present quest into the unknown heart of this land will give me the secrets for which I hunger.

Denver, Colorado   7th July 1900

In spite of the luxuries of railroad travel, it is undoubtedly a blessing not to be travelling. I plan to rest in this city for a day or two before continuing my journey. This is the longest continuous break I have ever made from magic: no performances, no practising, no conferences with my *ingénieur*, no auditions or rehearsals.

Denver, Colorado   8th July 1900

To the east of Denver lies the great plain, across part of which I came while travelling from Chicago. I have seen enough of Nebraska to last me the rest of my lifetime. Memories of its dull scenery daunt me even yet. All day yesterday a wind blew from the southeast, hot and dry and apparently laden with grit. The staff at the hotel complain that it is from the arid neighbouring states, like Oklahoma, but no matter what its source it meant that my explorations of the town were hot and unpleasant. I curtailed them and returned to the hotel. However, before I did so, and when the haze finally cleared, I saw for myself what lies immediately to the west of Denver: the great jagged wall of the Rocky Mountains. Later in the day, when it was cooler, I went out to the balcony of my room and watched the sun setting behind these stunning peaks. I estimate that twilight must last half an hour longer here than elsewhere, because of the vast shadow thrown by the Rockies.

Colorado Springs, Colorado   10th July 1900

This town is about seventy miles to the south of Denver, but the journey has taken all day in a horse-drawn omnibus. It made frequent stops to take on and put down passengers, to change horses, to change drivers. I felt uncomfortable, prominent and travel-weary. My appearance was probably ridiculous, to judge by the expressions on the faces of the farming people who rode with me. However, I have arrived safe and sound, and am immediately charmed by the place in which I find myself. It is not anywhere near as large as Denver, but abundantly reveals the care and affection that Americans lavish on their small towns.

I have found a modest but attractive hotel, suitable for my needs, and because I liked my room on sight I have registered for a week's stay with an option to extend it if necessary.

From the window of my room I can see two of the three features of Colorado Springs that have brought me here.

The whole town dances with electric lights after the sun has set: the streets have tall lamps, every house has brightly illuminated windows, and in the 'downtown' area, which I can see from my room, many of the shops, businesses and restaurants have dazzling advertising signs that glisten and flash in the warm night.

Beyond them, bulking against the night sky, is the black mass of the famous mountain that stands beside the town: Pike's Peak, nearly 15,000 feet in height.

Tomorrow, I shall make my first ascent of the lower slopes of Pike's Peak, and seek out the third singular feature that has brought me to this town.

12th July 1900

I was too weary to write in my diary yesterday evening, and I have perforce to spend today alone here in the town, so I have plenty of opportunity to recount at leisure what transpired.

I was awake at an early hour, took my breakfast in the hotel, and walked quickly to the central square of the town where my carriage was supposed to be waiting for me. This was something I had arranged by letter before leaving London, and although everything had been confirmed at that time I had no way of knowing for sure that my man would be there for me. To my astonishment, he was.

In the casual American manner we quickly became great friends. His name is Randall D. Gilpin, a Colorado man born and bred. I call him Randy, and he calls me Robbie. He is short and round, with a great circling of grey whiskers about his cheerful face. His eyes are blue, his face is burned red ochre by the sun, and his hair, like the whiskers, is steel-grey. He wears a hat made of leather, and the filthiest trousers I have ever seen in my life. He has a finger missing from his left hand. He carries a rifle under the seat from which he drives the horses, and he told me he keeps it loaded.

Though polite, and effusively friendly, Randy displayed a reserve about me that I was only able to detect by having spent so many weeks in the USA. It took me most of the ride up the Pike's Peak ascent for me to work out the probable cause.

It seemed to be a combination of things. From my letters he had assumed that I, like many people who come to this region, was a prospector (from this I discovered that the mountain has many rich seams of gold). As he became more talkative, though, he told me that when he saw me crossing the square he guessed from my clothes and general demeanour that I was a minister of the church. Gold he could understand, one of God's ministers he could also accord a place in the scheme of things, but not a combination of the two. That this weird Briton should then direct him to drive to the notorious laboratory on the mountain only compounded the mystery.

Thus arose Randy's caution about me. There was little I could do to mollify him, as my real identity and purpose would probably have seemed just as incomprehensible!

The route to Nikola Tesla's laboratory is a steady climb of mixed gradients across the eastern face of the great mountain, the land densely wooded for the first mile or so as the lane wends its way out of the town, but soon thinning into rocky ground supporting immensely tall and well-spaced firs. The views to the east were vast, but the landscape in this region is so flat and uniformly used that there was virtually nothing scenic at which to marvel.

After an hour and a half we came to an area of level ground, on the northeast face of the mountain, and here no trees grew at all. I noticed many fresh stumps, indicating that what few trees had actually once grown here had been recently felled.

In the centre of this small plateau, not nearly as large as I had been led to believe, was Tesla's laboratory.

'You got business here, Robbie?' said Randy. 'You watch how you go. It can get darn dangerous up here, from what folks say.'

'I know the risks,' I averred. I negotiated with him briefly, unsure of what arrangements, if any, Tesla himself had for descending to the town, and wanting to be sure that I could later get back to my hotel without difficulty. Randy told me that he had business of his own to attend to, but would return to the laboratory in the afternoon and wait for me until I appeared.

I noticed that he would not take the carriage too close to the building, and I had to walk the last four or five hundred yards by myself.

The laboratory was a square construction with sloping roofs, built with unstained or unpainted wood, showing many signs of impromptu decisions about its design. It appeared that various small extensions had been added after the main structure went up, because the roofs were not all at the same pitch, and in places met at odd angles. A large wooden derrick had been built on (or through) the main roof, and another, smaller rig had been built on one of the side sloping roofs.

In the centre of the building, rising vertically, was a tall metal pole that tapered gradually to what would have been a point, although there was no visible apex because at the top there was a large metal sphere. This was glinting in the bright morning sunshine, and waving gently to and fro in the fresh breeze that was blowing along the mountainside.

On each side of the path a number of technical instruments of obscure purpose had been set on the ground. There were many metal poles driven into the stony soil, and most of these were connected to each other with insulated wires. Close by the side of the main building was a wooden frame with a glass wall, inside which I saw several measuring dials or registers.

I heard a sudden and violent crackling sound, and from within the building there came a series of brilliant and horrific flashes: white, blue-white, pink-white, repeated erratically but rapidly. So fierce were these explosions of light that they glared not only at the one or two windows in my sight, but revealed the tiny cracks and apertures in the fabric of the walls.

I confess that at this moment my resolve briefly failed, and I even glanced back to see if Randy and his carriage were still within hailing distance. (No sign of him!) My faint heart became even fainter when, within two or three more steps, I came upon a hand-painted sign mounted on the wall beside the main door. It said:

GREAT DANGER
KEEP OUT!

As I read this the electric discharges from within died away as abruptly as they had started, and it seemed a positive omen. I banged my fist on the door.

After a wait of a few moments, Nikola Tesla himself opened the door. His expression was the abstracted one of a busy man who has been irritatingly interrupted. It was not a good start, but I made the best of it.

'Mr Tesla?' I said. 'My name is Rupert Angier. I wonder if you recall our correspondence? I have been writing to you from England.'

'I know nobody in England!' He was staring behind me, as if wondering how many more Englishmen I had brought with me. 'Say your name again, good sir?'

'My name is Rupert Angier. I was present at your demonstration in London, and was greatly interested—'

'You are the magician! The one Mr Alley knows all about?'

'I am the magician,' I confirmed, although the meaning of his second query was for the moment lost on me.

'You may enter!'

So many impressions about him at once, of course reinforced by my having spent several hours with him after our first exchange. At the time I noticed his face first. It was gaunt, intelligent and handsome, with strong Slavic cheekbones. He wore a thin moustache, and his lanky hair was parted in the middle. His appearance was in general untended, that of a man who worked long hours and slept only when there was no alternative to exhaustion.

Tesla is equipped with an extraordinary mind. Once I had made my identity clear to him he remembered not only what we had corresponded briefly about, but that I had written to him earlier, some eight years ago, asking for a copy of his notes.

Inside the laboratory he introduced me to his assistant, a Mr Alley. This interesting man appears to fulfil many rôles in Tesla's life, from scientific assistant and collaborator, to domestic servant and companion. Unexpectedly, Mr Alley declared himself to be an admirer of my work. He had been in the audience during my show in Kansas City in 1893, and spoke briefly but knowledgeably about magic.

By all appearances the two men work in the laboratory alone, with only the astonishing research equipment for company. I ascribe this near-human quality to the apparatus because Tesla himself has a habit of referring to his equipment as if it had thoughts and instincts. Once, yesterday, I heard him say to Alley, 'It knows there's a storm coming'; at another moment he said, 'I think it's waiting for us to start again.'

Tesla seemed relaxed in my company, and the brief hostility I had experienced at the door was nowhere evident during the rest of my time with him. He declared that he and Alley had been soon to break for luncheon, and the three of us sat down to simple but nourishing food that Alley quickly produced from one of the side rooms. Tesla sat apart from us, and I noticed he was a finicky eater, holding up each morsel for close inspection before putting it in his mouth, and discarding as many of them as he consumed. He wiped his hands and dabbed his lips on a small cloth after each mouthful. Before he rejoined us, he swept away his un-eaten food into a bin outside the building, then scrupulously washed and wiped dry his utensils before placing them inside a drawer, which he locked.

Rejoining Alley and myself, Tesla interrogated me about the use of electricity in Britain, how widespread it was becoming, what was the British government's commitment to long-term generation and transmission of power, the kinds of transmission being envisioned and the uses to which it was being put. Fortunately, because I had planned to have this meeting with Tesla, I had done my homework on the subject before leaving England, and was able to converse with him on a reasonably informed level. He seemed appreciative of this. He was especially gratified to learn that many British installations appeared to favour his polyphase system, which was not the case here in the USA.

'Most cities still prefer the Edison system,' he growled, and went into a technical exposition of the failings of his rival's methods.

I sensed that he had rehearsed these sentiments many times in the past, and to listeners better equipped to take them in than I was. The upshot of his complaint was that in the end people would come around to his alternating current system, but that they were wasting a lot of time and opportunities while they did so. On this subject, and on several others related to his work, he sounded humourless and forbidding, but at other times I found him delightful and amusing company.

Eventually, the focus of his questions turned to myself, my career, my interest in electricity, and to what uses I might wish to put it.

I had resolved, before leaving England, that were Tesla to enquire into the secrets of my illusions he would be one person to whom I would make an exception and reveal anything in which he might show interest. It seemed only right. When I had seen his lecture in London he had had all the appearance of a member of my own profession, taking the same delight in surprising and mystifying the audience, yet, unlike a magician, being more than willing, anxious even, to reveal and share his secrets.

He turned out to be incurious, though. I sensed that nothing would be gained by my harking on the subject. Instead, I let him direct our conversation, and for an hour or two he rambled entertainingly over his conflicts with Edison, his struggles against bureaucracy and the scientific establishment, and most of all his successes. His present laboratory had been funded, in effect, by the work of the last few years. He had installed the first water-powered city-sized electricity generator in the world: the generating station was at Niagara Falls, and the beneficiary city was Buffalo. It is true to say that Tesla had made his fortune at Niagara, but like many men of sudden wealth he wondered how long he could make last what he had.

As gently as I could I kept the conversation centred on money, because this is one of the few subjects where our interests genuinely meet. Of course he would not impart details of his finances to me, a virtual stranger, but funding is clearly a preoccupation. He mentioned J. Pierpoint Morgan, his present sponsor, several times.

Nothing was discussed between us that touched directly on the reason for my visit here, but there will be plenty of time for that in the days ahead. Yesterday, we were just getting to know one another, and learning of each other's interests.

I have said little of the dominant feature of his laboratory. All through the meal, and during the long conversation that followed, we were overshadowed by the bulk of his Experimental Coil. Indeed, the entire laboratory can be said to *be* the Coil, for there is little else there apart from recording and calibrating apparatus.

The Coil is immense. Tesla said that it had a diameter in excess of fifty feet, which I can well believe. Because the interior of the laboratory is not brightly lit the Coil has a gloomy, mysterious presence, at least while it is not being used. Constructed around a central core (the base of the tall metal pole that I had seen protruding through the roof), the Coil is wound around numerous wooden and metal battens, in a complexity that increases the closer in to the core you explore. With my layman's eyes I could make no sense of its design. The effect was to a large extent that of a bizarre cage. Everything about it and around it seemed haphazard. For instance, there were several ordinary wooden chairs in the laboratory, and several of these were in the immediate vicinity of the Coil. As indeed were many other bits and pieces: papers, tools, scraps of dropped and forgotten food, even a grubby-looking kerchief. I duly marvelled at the Coil when Tesla conducted me around it, but it was impossible for me then to understand any of it. All I grasped was that it was capable of using or transforming huge amounts of electricity. The power for it is sent up the mountain from Colorado Springs below. Tesla has paid for this by installing the town generators himself.

'I have all the electricity I want!' he said at one juncture. 'As you will probably find during the evenings.'

I asked him what he meant.

'You will notice that from time to time the town lights momentarily dim. Sometimes they even go off altogether for a few seconds. It means we are at work up here! Let me show you.'

He led me out of the ramshackle building and across the uneven ground outside. After a short distance we came to a place where the side of the mountain dropped steeply away, and there, a long way below, was the whole extent of Colorado Springs, shimmering in the summer heat.

'If you come up here one night I'll demonstrate,' he promised. 'With a pull on one lever I can plunge that whole city into the dark.'

As we headed back, he said, 'You must indeed visit me one night. Night-time is the finest time in the mountains. As you have no doubt observed for yourself, the scenery here is on a grand scale but intrinsically lacking in interest. To one side, nothing but rocky peaks; to the other, land as flat as the top of a table. It is a mistake to look down or around. The real interest is above us!' He gestured towards the sky. 'I have never known such clarity of air, such moonlight. Nor have I ever seen such storms as occur here! I chose this site because of the frequency of storms. There is one coming at this moment, as it happens.'

I glanced around me, looking for the familiar sight of the piling anvil-topped cloud in the distance, or, if closer, the black mass of rain-bearing cloud that darkens the sky in the minutes before a storm actually breaks, but the sky was an untrammelled blue in every direction. The air, too, remained crisp and lively, with no hint of the ominous sultriness that always presages a downpour.

'The storm will arrive after seven this evening. In fact, let us examine my coherer, from which we can ascertain the exact time.'

We walked back to the laboratory. As we did so I noticed that Randy Gilpin and his carriage had arrived, and were parked well away from where we were. Randy waved to me, and I waved back.

Tesla indicated one of the instruments I had noted earlier. 'This shows that a storm is currently in the region of Central City, about eighty miles to the north of us. Watch!'

He indicated a part of the device that could be seen through a magnifying lens, and jabbed a finger at it at odd moments. After peering at it for a while I saw what he was trying to show me – a tiny electrical spark was bridging the visible gap between two metal studs.

'Each time it sparks it is registering a flash of lightning,' Tesla explained. 'Sometimes I will note the discharge here, and more than an hour later I will hear the thunder rumbling in from far away.'

I was about to express my disbelief when I remembered the intense seriousness of the man. He had moved to another instrument, next to the coherer, and noted down two or three readings from it. I followed him to it.

'Yes,' he said. 'Mr Angier, would you be good enough to look at your timepiece this evening, and note the moment it happens to be when you see the first flash of lightning. By my calculation it should be between 7.15 p.m. and 7.20 p.m.'

'You can predict the exact moment?' I said.

'Within about five minutes.'

'Then you could make your fortune with this alone!' I exclaimed.

He looked uninterested.

'It is peripheral,' he said. 'My work is purely experimental, and my main concern is to know when a storm is going to break so that I might make the best use of it.' He glanced over to where Gilpin was waiting. 'I see your carriage has returned, Mr Angier. You plan to make another visit to see me?'

'I came to Colorado Springs for one reason only,' I said. 'That is so that I might put a business proposition to you.'

'The best kind of proposition, in my experience,' Tesla said gravely. 'I shall expect you the day after tomorrow.'

He explained that today was going to be taken up by a trip to the railhead to collect some more equipment.

With this I departed, and in due course returned with Gilpin to the town.

I must record that at exactly 7.19 p.m. there was a flash of lightning visible in the town, followed soon after by a crack of thunder. There then began one of the more spectacular storms it has been my lot to experience. During the course of it I ventured on to the balcony of my hotel room, and looked up at the heights of Pike's Peak for some glimpse of Tesla's laboratory. All was darkness.

Today Tesla gave me a demonstration of his Coil in operation.

At the start he asked me if I was of a nervous disposition, and I said I was not. Tesla then gave me an iron bar to hold, one that was connected to the floor by a long chain. He brought to me a large glass dome, apparently filled with smoke or gas, and put it on the table before me. While I continued to hold the iron rod in my left hand, I placed, at his direction, the palm of my right hand against the glass chamber. Instantly, a brilliant light burst out inside the dome and every hair on my arm rose proud from my skin. I pulled back in alarm and the light went out. Noticing Tesla's amused smile, I returned my hand to the glass and held it there steadily as the uncanny radiance burst forth once more.

There followed several more such experiments, some of which I had seen Tesla himself demonstrating in London. Determined not to reveal my nervous feelings, I endured the electrical discharging of each piece of apparatus stoically. Finally, Tesla asked me if I should care to sit within the main field of his Experimental Coil while he raised its power to twenty million volts!

'Is it entirely safe?' I enquired, but jutting my jaw a little, as if I were accustomed to taking risks.

'You have my word, sir. Is this not why you have come to see me?'

'Indeed it is,' I confirmed.

Tesla indicated I should sit on one of the wooden chairs, and I did so. Mr Alley also came forward. He was dragging one of the other chairs and he placed it beside me and sat down. He handed me a sheet of newspaper.

'See if you can read by unearthly light!' he said, and both he and Tesla chuckled.

I was smiling with them as Tesla brought down a metal handle and with an ear-shattering crashing noise there was a sudden discharge of electrical power. It burst out from the coils of wire above my head, folding out like the petals of some vast and deadly chrysanthemum. I watched in stupefaction as these jerking, spitting electrical bolts curved first up and around the head of the coil, then began moving down towards Alley and myself, as if seeking us as prey. Alley remained still beside me, so I forced myself not to move. Suddenly, one of the bolts touched me, and ran up and down the length of my body as if tracing my outline. Again, my skin horripilated and my eyes were scorched by the light, but otherwise there was no pain, no burning sensation, no feeling of electrical shock.

Alley indicated the newspaper I was still clutching, so I held it before me and discovered, sure enough, that the radiance from the electricity was more than bright enough to read by. As I held the page before me, two sparks ran across its surface, almost as if an attempt was being made to ignite the paper. Marvellously, miraculously, the page did not burn.

Afterwards, Tesla suggested I might like to take another short walk with him, and as soon as we were outside in the open air he said, 'Sir, let me congratulate you. You are brave.'

'I was determined not to show how I really felt,' I demurred.

Tesla told me many visitors to his laboratory were offered the same demonstrations I had just seen, but that few of them seemed ready to submit themselves to the imagined ravages of electrical discharge.

'Maybe they have not seen your demonstrations,' I suggested. 'I know you would not risk your own life, nor indeed that of someone who has travelled all the way from Great Britain to make you a business offer.'

'Indeed not,' said Tesla. 'Perhaps now is the time when we should quietly discuss business. May I beg details of what you have in mind?'

'This is what I am not entirely sure about—' I began, and paused, trying to formulate the words.

'Do you propose to invest in my researches?'

'No, sir, I do not,' I was able to say. 'I know that you have had many experiences with investors.'

'That indeed I have. I am thought by some to be a difficult man to work with, and little I have in mind is likely to turn a short-term profit for an investor. It is something that has in the past caused vexed relationships.'

'And in the present too, may I dare to venture? Mr Morgan was clearly on your mind when we spoke the other day.'

'Mr J. P. Morgan is indeed a current preoccupation.'

'Then let me say candidly that I am a wealthy man, Mr Tesla. I hope I might be able to assist you.'

'But not by investment, you say.'

'By purchase,' I replied. 'I wish you to build me an electrical apparatus, and if we can agree a price I shall gladly pay for it.'

We had been strolling around the circumference of the cleared plateau on which the laboratory stands, but now Tesla came to a sudden halt. He struck a pose, staring thoughtfully towards the trees that covered the rising side of the mountain ahead of us.

'Which piece of apparatus do you require?' he said. 'As you have seen my work is theoretical, experimental. None of it is for sale, and everything I am using at present is invaluable to me.'

'Before I left England,' I said, 'I read an article about your work in *The Times*. In the article it was said that you had established theoretically that electricity might be transmitted through the air, and that you planned to demonstrate the principle in the near future.' Tesla was watching me fiercely while I spoke, but having declared my interest to such an extent I had to go on. 'Many of your scientific colleagues have apparently said it is impossible, but you are confident of what you are doing. Would this be true?'

I stared directly into Tesla's eyes as I asked this final question, and saw that another great change had come across his features. Now his expression and gestures became animated and expressive.

'Yes, it is entirely true!' he cried, and at once launched into a wild and (to me) not entirely comprehensible account of what he planned.

Once thus begun he was unstoppable! He strode off in the direction we had been heading, speaking quickly and excitedly, making me trot to keep up with him. We were circling the laboratory at a distance, with the great balled spire constantly in view. Tesla gesticulated towards it several times while he spoke.

If I understand him correctly, the essence of what he said was this. He had long ago established that the most efficient way of transmitting his polyphase electrical current was to boost it to high voltages and direct it along high-tension cables. Now he was able to show that if the current was boosted to an even greater voltage then it became of extremely high frequency, and no cables at all would be required. The current would be *sent out*, radiated, cast broadly into the aether, whereupon by a series of detectors or receivers the electricity could be captured once more and turned to use.

'Imagine the possibilities, Mr Angier!' Tesla declared. 'Every appliance, every utility, every convenience known to man or imaginable by him will be propelled by electricity that emanates from the air!'

Then, in a way I found curiously reminiscent of my erstwhile fellow train-passenger Bob Tannhouse, Tesla launched into a litany of possibilities: light, heat, hot-water baths, food, houses, amusements, automobiles . . . all would be electrically powered in some mysterious and undescribed way.

'You have this working?' I asked.

'Without question! On an experimental basis, you understand, but the experiments are repeatable by others, should they bother to try, and they can be controlled. This is no phantasm! Within a few years I shall be generating power for the whole world in the way that at present I power the cities of Buffalo and Colorado Springs.'

We had circled the large area of ground twice while this

251

exposition poured out of him, and I kept my pace beside him, determined to let his scientific rapture run its course. I knew that with his great intelligence he would return eventually to what I had first told him.

Finally he did. 'Do I understand you to say you wish to buy this apparatus from me, Mr Angier?' he said.

'No, sir,' I replied. 'I am here to ask for another purchase.'

'I am fully engaged in the work I am describing.'

'I appreciate that, Mr Tesla. I am seeking something new. Tell me this: if electrical energy may be transmitted, could physical matter also be sent from one place to another?'

The steadiness of his answer surprised me. He said, 'Energy and matter are but two manifestations of the same force. Surely you realise that?'

'Yes, sir,' I said.

'Then you already know the answer. Though I must add that I cannot see why anyone should wish to transmit matter.'

'But could you make me the apparatus that would achieve this?'

'How much mass would be involved? What weight would there be? What size object?'

'Never more than two hundred pounds,' I said. 'And the size . . . let us say two yards in height, at most.'

He waved a hand dismissively. 'What sum are you offering me?'

'What sum do you require?'

'I desperately need eight thousand dollars, Mr Angier.'

I could not prevent myself laughing aloud. It was more than I had planned, but still it was within my means. Tesla looked apprehensive, apparently thinking me mad, and backed away from me a little . . . but only a few moments later we were embracing on that windy plateau, clapping our hands against each other's shoulders, two needs meeting, two needs met.

As we drew apart, and clasped hands in contract together, a loud peal of thunder rang out somewhere in the mountains behind us, and rolled around us, rumbling and echoing in the narrow passes.

14th July 1900

Tesla drives a harder bargain than I had reckoned. I am to pay him not eight but *ten* thousand dollars, a small fortune by any standards. It seems he sleeps on important matters just like ordinary men, and awoke this morning with the realisation that the eight thousand dollars would cover only the shortfall he was bearing before I arrived. My apparatus will cost more. Beside this, he has demanded that I pay him a goodly percentage in cash, and in advance. I have three thousand dollars I can produce in cash, and can raise another three with the bearer bonds I have brought with me, but the remainder will have to be sent from England.

Tesla agreed promptly to the arrangement.

Today he has quizzed me more closely about what I require of him. He is incurious about the magical effect I plan to achieve, but is concerned instead with practicalities. The size of the apparatus, the source of power for it, the weight it will need to be, the degree of portability required.

I find myself admiring his analytical mind. Portability was one aspect I had not thought about at all, but of course this is a critical factor for a touring magician.

He has already drawn up rough plans, and has banished me to Colorado Springs for two days, while he visits Denver to acquire the constituent parts.

Tesla's reaction to my project has finally convinced me of something that until now I have only suspected. Borden has not been to Tesla!

I am learning about my old adversary. Through Olivia he was trying to misdirect me. His illusion uses the sort of flashy effects that ordinary people think are the power of electricity, but are in fact nothing more than flashy effects. He thought I would go on a wild-goose chase, while Tesla and I are actually confronting the heart of the hidden energy itself.

But Tesla works slowly! I am anxious about the passage of

time. Naïvely I had thought that once I commissioned Tesla it would be a matter of hours before he produced the mechanism I required. I see, by the abstracted expression he bears as he mutters to himself, that I have started a process of invention that might know no practical end. (In an aside, Mr Alley confirmed that Tesla sometimes worries at a problem for months.)

I have firm bookings in England in October and November, and must be home well before the first of them.

I have two idle days until Tesla returns, and so I suppose I might use the time to research train and ship timetables. I find that America, a country great in many things, is not good at providing such information.

21st July 1900

Tesla's work apparently proceeds well. I am allowed to visit his laboratory every two days, and although I have seen something of the apparatus there has been no question yet of a demonstration. Today I found him tinkering with his research experiments. He seemed abstracted by them and was partly irritated and partly puzzled to see me.

4th August 1900

Violent thunderstorms have been playing around Pike's Peak for three days, casting me into gloom and frustration. I know that Tesla will be involved with his own experiments, not with mine.

The days are slipping by. I must be aboard the train out of Denver before the end of this month!

8th August 1900

Tesla told me on my arrival at the laboratory this morning that my apparatus was ready for demonstration, and in a state of great excitement I readied myself to see it. When it came to it, though, the thing refused to function, and after I had watched Tesla fiddling with some of the wiring for more than three hours I returned here to the hotel.

I am told by the First Colorado Bank that more of my

money should be available in a day or two. Perhaps that will spur Tesla to greater efforts.

12th August 1900

Another abortive demonstration today. I was disappointed by the outcome. Tesla seemed puzzled, claiming that his calculations could not be in error.

The failure is briefly recorded. The prototype apparatus is a smaller version of his Coil, with the wiring arranged in a different fashion. After a prolonged lecture about the principles (none of which I understood, and which I soon came to realise was delivered by Tesla mainly for his own sake, a form of thinking aloud), Tesla produced a metal rod which he or Mr Alley had painted in a distinctive orange colour. He placed it on a platform, immediately beneath a kind of inverted cone of wiring. The apex of the cone was focused directly on the rod.

When at Tesla's instruction Mr Alley worked a large lever situated close by the original Coil, there was the noisy but now familiar outburst of arcing electrical discharge. Almost at once the orange rod was surrounded by blue-white fire, which snaked around it in a most intimidating way. (I, thinking of the illusion I wished to work on the stage, was quietly satisfied by the appearance of this.) The noise and incandescence built up quickly, and soon it seemed as if molten particles of the rod itself were splashing to the floor; that they were not was evidenced by the unchanged, unharmed appearance of the rod.

After a few seconds Tesla waved his hands dramatically, Mr Alley threw back the control lever, the electricity instantly died away, and the rod was still in place.

Tesla immediately became absorbed in the mystery, and, as has happened before, my presence was thereafter ignored. Mr Alley has recommended me to stay away from the laboratory for a few days, but I am acutely conscious of time running out. I wonder if I have sufficiently impressed this upon Mr Tesla?

Today is notable less for a second failed demonstration than for the fact that Tesla and I have argued with some bitterness. This quarrel happened in the immediate aftermath of his machine's failure to work, and so we were both keyed up, I with disappointment, Tesla with frustration.

After the orange-painted rod had failed to move again, Tesla picked it up and offered it to me to hold. A few seconds before it had been bathed in radiant light, with sparks flying in every direction. I took it from him gingerly, expecting my fingers to be singed by it. Instead, it was cold. This is the odd thing: it was not just cool, in the sense that it had not been heated, but actively cold, as if it had been surrounded by ice. I hefted the rod in my hand.

'Any more failures like this, Mr Angier,' Tesla said, in a friendly enough voice, 'and I might be obliged to give you that as a souvenir.'

'I shall take it,' I replied. 'Although I should prefer to take with me what I came here to buy.'

'Given enough time I shall move the Earth.'

'Time is what I do not have much of,' I riposted, tossing the rod to the floor. 'And it is not the Earth I wish to move. Nor is it this metal stick.'

'Then pray name your preferred object,' Tesla said, with sarcasm. 'I shall concentrate on that instead.'

At that moment I felt impelled to release some of the feelings I have been holding back for several days.

'Mr Tesla,' I said. 'I have stood by while you have been using a chunk of metal, assuming that you needed to do so for experimental purposes. Is it my understanding, at this belated moment, that you could be using something else instead?'

'Within reason, yes.'

'Then why do you not build the thing to do what I require?'

'Because, sir, you have not expressly described your requirements!'

'They do not involve the sending of short iron sticks,' I said hotly. 'Even if the contraption were to work in the way I thought I had specified, it would be of little use to me. I wish it to transmit a living body! A man!'

'So you wish me to demonstrate my failures not on a hapless iron rod, but on a human being? Whom do you nominate for this dangerous experiment?'

'Why should it be dangerous?' I said.

'All experiment is risky.'

'I am the one who will be using this.'

'You wish to submit *yourself*?' Tesla laughed with brittle menace. 'Sir, I shall require the remainder of your money before I start experimenting on you!'

'It is time for me to leave,' I said, and turned away, feeling angry and chastened. I pushed past him and Alley, and made it to the outside. There was no sign of Randy Gilpin but I strode off anyway, determined if necessary to walk the whole way down to the town.

'Mr Angier, sir!' Tesla was standing at the door to his laboratory. 'Let us not exchange hasty words. I should have explained properly to you. Had I but known that you wished to transmit living organisms, you would not have presented me with such a challenge. It is difficult to deal with massy, inorganic compounds. Living tissue is not of the same order of problem.'

'What are you saying, Professor?' I asked.

'If you wish me to transmit an organism, please return here tomorrow. It shall be done.'

I nodded my confirmation then continued on my way, stepping on the loose gravel of the path that descended the mountainside. I expected to meet Gilpin on the way down, but even should he not appear I was anyway determined to make the most of the exercise. The road snaked down the mountain in a series of sharp bends doubling back on each other, often with a precipitous drop to the side.

When I had walked about half a mile my attention was caught by a flash of colour in the long grass beside the track, and I stopped to investigate. It was a short iron rod, painted orange, apparently identical to the one Tesla had been using. Thinking I might after all keep a souvenir of this extraordinary meeting with Tesla, I picked it up, brought it down the mountain, and I have it with me now.

19th August 1900

I found Tesla in a mood of despond when Gilpin deposited me at the laboratory this morning.

'I fear I am about to let you down,' he said to me when he came to the door. 'Much work remains, and I know how pressing is your return to Britain.'

'What has occurred?' I inquired, glad to discover that the anger that had flared between us yesterday was a thing of the past.

'I believed it would be a simple matter with life organisms. The structure is so much simpler than that of the elements. Life already contains minute amounts of electricity. I was working on the assumption that all I had to do was boost that energy. I am at a loss as to why this has not worked. The computations worked out exactly. Come and see the evidence for yourself.'

Inside the laboratory I noticed Mr Alley was adopting a stance I had never associated with him before. He stood in bellicose fashion, arms folded protectively, jaw jutting pugnaciously, a man angry and defensive if ever I saw one. Beside him on the bench was a small wooden cage, containing a diminutive black cat with white whiskers and paws, presently asleep.

As his eyes were fixed on me as I walked in, I said, 'Good morning, Mr Alley.'

'I hope you will not be a party to this, Mr Angier!' Alley cried. 'I brought my children's cat on the firm promise that it would not be harmed. Mr Tesla gave me an exact assurance last night. Now he insists that we submit the wretched creature to an experiment that will undoubtedly kill it.'

'I don't care for the sound of this,' I said to Tesla.

'Nor I. Do you think I am inhumane, capable of torturing

258

one of God's more beautiful creatures? Come and see what you think.'

He led me to the apparatus, which I immediately saw had been entirely rebuilt overnight. When I was a foot or two away from it, I recoiled in horror! About half a dozen enormous cockroaches, with shiny black carapaces and long antennae, were scattered all around. They were the most repulsive creatures I had ever seen.

'They are dead, Angier,' said Tesla, noticing my reaction. 'They cannot harm you.'

'Yes, dead!' said Alley. 'And that's the rub! He intends me to place the cat in the same jeopardy.'

I looked down at the huge and disgusting insects, wary of any sign from them of a return to life. I stepped back again when Tesla nudged at one with the toe of his boot, and turned it over for me to see.

'It seems I have built a machine that murders roaches,' Tesla murmured gently. 'They are God's creatures too, and I am made despondent by it all. I did not intend that this device should take life.'

'What's going wrong?' I said to Tesla. 'Yesterday you sounded so sure.'

'I have calculated and recalculated a dozen times. Alley has checked the mathematics too. It is the nightmare of every experimental scientist: an inexplicable dichotomy between theoretical and actual results. I confess I am confounded. Such a thing has never happened to me before.'

'May I see the calculations?' I said.

'Of course you may, but if you are not a mathematician I fear they will not convey much to you.'

He and Alley produced a great loose-leaf ledger in which his computations had been carried out, and together we pored over them for a long time. Tesla showed me, as best I was able to understand, the principle behind them, and the calculated results. I nodded as intelligently as I could, but only at the end, when I could take the calculations for granted and concentrate on the results, did an unexpected glimmering of sense shine through.

259

'You say that this determines the distance?' I said.

'That is a variable. For purposes of experimentation I have been using a value of one hundred metres, but such a distance is academic, since, as you see, nothing I try to transmit travels any distance at all.'

'And this value here?' I said, jabbing my finger at another line.

'The angle. I have been using compass points. It will direct in any of three hundred and sixty degrees from the apex of the energy vortex. Again, for the time being that is an entirely academic entry.'

'Do you have a setting for elevation?' I asked.

'I am not using it. Until the apparatus is fully working I am merely aiming into the clear air to the east of the laboratory. One must be careful not to cause a rematerialisation in a position already occupied by another mass! I do not care to think what might happen.'

I looked thoughtfully at the neatly inscribed mathematics. I do not know the process by which it happened, but suddenly I was struck by inspiration! I dashed out of the laboratory and stared from the doorway due east. As Tesla had said, what lay beyond was mostly clear air, because in this direction the plateau was at its narrowest and the ground began to drop away some ten metres from the path. I moved quickly over and looked downwards. Below me I could glimpse through the trees the pathway snaking down the mountainside.

When I returned to the laboratory I went straight to my portmanteau and pulled out the iron rod I had found beside the path yesterday evening. I held it up for Tesla to see.

'Your experimental object, I do believe?' I said.

'Yes it is.'

I told him where I had found it, and when. He hurried across to the apparatus where its twin was lying, discarded in favour of the unlucky cockroaches. He held the two together and Alley and I stood with him, marvelling at their identical appearance.

'These marks, Mr Angier!' Tesla breathed in awe, lightly

fingering a crisscross patch neatly etched into the metal. 'I made them so that I might prove by identification that this object had been transmitted through the aether. But—'

'It has made a facsimile of itself!' Alley said.

'Where did you say you found this, sir?' Tesla demanded.

I led the two men outside and explained, pointing down the mountain. Tesla stared in silent thought.

Then he said, 'I need to see the actual place! Show me!' To Alley he said, 'Bring the theodolite, and some measuring tape! As soon as you can!'

And with that he set off down the precipitous path, clutching me by my upper arm, imploring me to show him the exact location of the find. I assumed I would be able to lead him straight to it, but as we moved further down the track I was no longer so sure. The huge trees, the broken rocks, the scrubby forest-floor vegetation, all looked much alike. With Tesla gesticulating at me and gabbling in my ear it was almost impossible to concentrate.

I eventually came to a particular turn in the path where the grass grew long, and I paused before it. Alley, who had been trotting after us, soon caught us up and under Tesla's directions set up the theodolite. A few careful measurements were enough for Tesla to reject the place.

After about half an hour we had agreed on another likely site. It was exactly to the east of the laboratory, although of course a substantial distance beneath it. When we took into account the steepness of the mountainside, and the fact that the iron rod would have bounced and rolled on hitting the ground, it did seem that this was a likely position in which it would end up. Tesla was evidently satisfied, and he was deep in thought as we walked back up the mountain to his laboratory.

I too had been thinking, and as soon as we were inside once more I said, 'May I make a suggestion?'

'I am already greatly indebted to you, sir,' Tesla replied. 'Say what you will!'

'Since you are able to calibrate the device, rather than simply aim your experiments into the air to the east of us, could you not send them a shorter distance? Perhaps across the laboratory itself, or outside to the area surrounding the building?'

'We evidently think alike, Mr Angier!'

In all the times I had been with him I had never seen Tesla so cheerful, and he and Alley set to work immediately. Once again I became supernumerary, and went to sit silently at the rear of the laboratory. I have long since fallen into the habit of taking some food with me to the laboratory (Tesla and Alley have irregular feeding habits when engrossed by their work) and so I ate the sandwiches made for me by the staff at the hotel.

After a longer and more tedious period than I can describe here, Tesla finally said, 'Mr Angier, I believe we are ready.'

And so it was that I went to examine the apparatus, for all the world like a member of a theatre audience invited on stage to inspect a magician's cabinet, and with Tesla I went outside and established beyond doubt that his designated target area was empty of any metal rods.

When he inserted the experimental rod, and manipulated his lever, a most satisfactory bang heralded successful completion of the experiment. The three of us rushed outside, and sure enough, there on the grass, was the familiar orange-painted iron rod.

Back in the laboratory we all examined the 'original' piece. Stone-cold it was, but undoubtedly identical to the twin that had been made of it across the emptiness of space.

'Tomorrow, sir,' Tesla said to me, 'tomorrow, and with the consent of my noble assistant here, we shall endeavour to safely transport the cat from one place to another. If that can be achieved, I take it you will be satisfied?'

'Indeed, Mr Tesla,' I said warmly. 'Indeed.'

20th August 1900

And indeed it has been done. The cat has crossed the aether unscathed!

There was a small hitch, however, and Tesla has returned

to the preoccupations of his calling, and once more I am banished to my hotel, and once more I find myself fretting about the time that is slipping away.

Tesla promises me another demonstration tomorrow, and this time he has told me there will be no more problems. I sense a man who is anxious for the remainder of his fee.

Caldlow House, Derbyshire   11th October 1900

I did not expect to live to write these words. Following the accidental demise of my elder brother Henry, and because of his having left no issue, I have finally come to the title and lands of my father.

I am now permanently in residence in the family home, and have abandoned my career as a stage illusionist. My daily routine is occupied with the administration of the estate, and by needing to attend to the numerous practical problems that have been created by Henry's whims, peccadillos and sheer financial misjudgements.

I now sign myself,
Rupert, 14th Earl of Colderdale.

12th November 1900

I have just returned from a visit of a few days to my old house in London. My intention had been to clear out the place, and my former workshop, and sell both properties on the open market. The Caldlow estate is on the verge of bankruptcy and I am in a hurry to raise some cash for urgent repairs to both the house and some of the estate buildings. Naturally, I have been cursing myself for squandering practically all the accumulated wealth from my stage career on Tesla. Just about my last act on leaving Colorado, as I returned to England in haste on the news of Henry's death, was to hand over the rest of the fee. It did not occur to me then how radically my whole life was to be changed by the news.

Returning to my home in Idmiston Villas had an unanticipated effect on me, though. I found it full of memories, of course, and these were as mixed as all such memories can be, but above all I was reminded of my first days in London. Then I was hardly more than a boy, disinherited, callow in the ways of the world, incompletely educated, not trained in any skill or profession. Yet I had carved out a life and livelihood for myself against the odds, and in the end made myself moderately wealthy and more than usually renowned. I was, I suppose I still am, at the top of the magic profession. And far from resting on my laurels, I had invested most of my money in new and innovative magical apparatus, the use of which would clearly have given my career a new momentum.

I thought in such wistful fashion for two days, and finally sent round a note to Julia's address. She was on my mind, because in spite of the fact that we separated many years ago I still identify my early days in London with her. I cannot any longer distinguish my early plans and dreams from the period in which I fell in love with her.

Rather to my surprise, but to my intense pleasure, she consented to meet me, and two days ago I spent an afternoon with her and the children at the house of one of her women friends.

To see my family again in such circumstances was emotionally overwhelming, and any plans I might have made beforehand to raise practical matters were abandoned. Julia, at first cool and remote, was obviously much affected by my expressions of shock and emotion (Edward, sixteen now, is so tall and good-looking!; Lydia and Florence are so beautiful and gentle!; I could not keep my eyes off them all afternoon) and before long she was speaking kindly and warmly to me.

I then told her my news. Even when we were married and living together I had never revealed my past to her, so what I had to say to her was a triple surprise. Firstly I had to tell her that I had once renounced a family and estate of which she had never heard, secondly that I had now returned to it, and thirdly that as a consequence I had decided to abandon my stage career.

As I should have guessed in advance, Julia appeared to

take all this calmly. (Only when I told her that she should henceforward be correctly addressed as Lady Julia did her composure momentarily break.) A little later, she asked me if I was sure I should abandon my career. I said I saw no alternative. She told me that although we were separated she had continued to follow my magic career with admiration, regretting only that she were no longer a part of it.

As we spoke I felt rising in me, or more correctly sinking out of me, a despair that I had thrown away my wife, and more unforgivably my splendid children, for the sake of the American woman.

Yesterday, before leaving London, I sought out Julia a second time. This time the children were not with her.

I threw myself at her mercy, and begged her forgiveness for all the sins I had committed against her. I pleaded with her to return to me and live with me once more as my wife. I promised her anything in my power to grant, should she accept.

She said no, but promised that she would consider carefully. I deserve no better.

Later in the day I caught the overnight train to Sheffield. I thought of nothing but reconciliation with Julia.

14th November 1900

However, I am obliged to think of nothing but money, faced once more as I am with the realities of this decaying house.

It is ridiculous to be inconvenienced by shortage of money so soon after squandering that huge amount, so I have written to Tesla and demanded a refund of everything I paid him. It is nearly three months since I left Colorado Springs and I have not had a single word from him. He will have to pay, no matter what his circumstances, because at the same time I have written to the firm of attorneys in New York who aided me in a small legal matter during my last tour. I have instructed them to start proceedings against him from the first day of next month. If he refunds me immediately he receives my letter I shall call off the hounds, but he will have to take the consequences if he does not.

15th November 1900

I am about to return to London.

17th November 1900

I am back in Derbyshire, and weary of travelling on trains. I am not, however, weary of life.

Julia has put to me a proposition about a way we could possibly be together in the future. It boils down to my having to make a simple decision.

She says she will return to me, live with me once more as my wife, but only if I resume my magic career. She wishes me to leave Caldlow House and return to Idmiston Villas. She says that she and the children do not wish to move to a house in a remote and, to them, unknown part of Derbyshire. She has put the point to me in terms so simple that I know they are non-negotiable.

To try to persuade me that her proposal is also for my own good, she adds four general arguments.

First, she says the stage is in her blood as much as mine, and that although she now sees the children as her first duty she would wish to participate wholly in all my future stage endeavours. I presume by this she means I will not be allowed foreign tours without her, so there will be no risk of another Olivia Svenson coming between us.

At the beginning of this year, she next argues, I was at the peak of my profession, but that by default the wretched Borden is on the brink of taking my laurels. Apparently, he is continuing to perform his version of the switch illusion.

Julia then reminds me that the only reliable way I know of earning money is to perform magic, and that I have a duty to go on supporting her as well as running the family estate she has never seen and had never heard of until last week.

Finally, she points out that I will not lose my inheritance by continuing to work in London, and the house and everything that goes with the estate will still be waiting for me when the time comes for retirement. Urgent matters, such as repairs, can be managed from London almost as easily as from the house.

So I have returned to Derbyshire, ostensibly to attend to matters here, but in fact I do need some time alone to think.

I cannot walk away from my responsibilities here in Caldlow House. There are the tenant farmers, the household staff, the commitments my family have traditionally made to the rural council, the church, the parishioners, and so on. I find myself taking these matters seriously, so I presume they have always been flowing, unsuspected, in the blood hitherto.

But what practical use can I be in any of these functions if I am to become, as seems likely, bankrupt?

19th November 1900

What I really want is to be with Julia and my family once more, but to do so means accepting Julia's terms. Moving back to London would not be difficult, but I do feel a terrific resistance to the idea of going back on the stage.

I have been away from it for just a few weeks, but I had not realised what a burden it had all become. I remember the day, back in Colorado Springs, when the news of Henry's demise belatedly reached me. I thought nothing of Henry and his humiliating but appropriate death in Paris. What I felt was for myself, a burst of relief, genuine and uplifting relief.

I would be free at last of the mental stresses and strains associated with performing illusions. There would be an end, a thankful end, to the daily hours of practice. No more overnight stays in appalling provincial hotels or seaside lodging houses. No more tiresome train journeys. I would be free of the ceaseless attention to practical matters: making sure the props and costumes would arrive in the same places as me and at the same time, checking the backstage areas of the theatres for the best use of my props, employing and paying the staff, and a hundred other minor chores. All these had suddenly vanished from my life.

And I had also thought about Borden. There was my

unshakable foe, lurking out there in the world of magic, ready to resume his campaign of pranks against me.

If I never went back, I would miss none of it. I had not realised how the resentment had been growing inside me.

But Julia tempts me.

There is the happy laughter from the audience when I work a surprising effect, the radiance of the lights beaming down upon me, the friendship of the other artistes I meet in the daily round, the applause at the end of my performance. Inevitably also, the fame, the admiring glances in the street, the respectful regard of my contemporaries, the recognition in the highest areas of society. No honest man could say these mean nothing to him.

And the money. How I crave the money!

It is of course no longer a question of what I will decide, but how soon I can convince myself I must do it.

20th November 1900

To London once more by train.

21st November 1900

I am at Idmiston Villas, and I have found here a letter from Alley, the assistant to Nikola Tesla. I now transcribe it:

September 27, 1900
Mr Angier, Sir:

I don't expect you have heard but Nikola Tesla has left Colorado already, and is rumored to have moved his operation to the East, probably to New York or New Jersey. His laboratory here has been seized by his creditors, and it is currently looking for a purchaser. I have been left in the lurch, with more than a month's pay due to me.

You will wish to know, however, that in some matters Mr Tesla is a man of honor, and before our work here was completed your equipment was as instructed shipped to your workshop.

Once the apparatus has been correctly put together (I wrote the assembly instructions myself) you will find it is in complete working order, and operates exactly to the agreed technical specification. The device is self-calibrating and self-regulating, and should continue to work without adjustment or repair for many years. All you should do is keep it clean, brighten the electrical contact points should they become dull, and in general ensure that no physical damage goes unrepaired. (Mr Tesla enclosed a set of spares for those parts which will, in the ordinary course, require replacement. All the other parts, such as the wooden struts, may be replaced from normal sources.)

I would of course be fascinated to learn what illusions you work with this extraordinary invention, because I am as you know one of your greatest admirers. Although you were not here to see it for yourself, I can testify that Snowshoes (the name of my children's pet cat) was safely transported several times by the device, but is back once more with our family as a domestic animal.

Let me say in conclusion, Sir, that I was honored to play some part, no matter how small, in building this apparatus for you.

Yours most sincerely,

Fareham K. Alley, Dip. Eng.

P.S.: You were once kind enough to admire, and pretend bafflement by, the small tricks I had the temerity to show to you. Since you made such a point of demanding an explanation, perhaps you would like to know that my little illusion with the five playing-cards and the disappearing silver dollars was achieved by a combination of classic palming and a card force. I was most gratified by your response to this trick, and would be delighted to send on detailed instructions about each move in turn, should you require them. F.K.A.

As soon as I read this I hurried around to my workshop. I enquired of my neighbours there if a large package might recently have been delivered from the USA, but they knew nothing of it.

I showed Alley's letter to Julia this morning, quite forgetting that I had not yet told her about my most recent trip to the USA, and what I had done there. Of course her curiosity was aroused by it, and I then needed to explain.

'So this is where all your money has gone?' she said.

'Yes.'

'And Tesla has apparently absconded, and we have only this letter to show for it?'

I assured her that Alley was trustworthy, and pointed out that he had written his letter without solicitation from me. For a while we discussed what might have happened to the package while *en route* to me, where it might be, and how we might recover it.

Then Julia said, 'What is so special about the illusion?'

'Not the illusion itself,' I replied. 'It is the means by which it is achieved.'

'Is Mr Borden something to do with this?'

'You have not forgotten Mr Borden, I see.'

'My dear, it was Alfred Borden who drove the first wedge between us. I have had many years to reflect, and I trace everything that went wrong to that day when he attacked me.' Tears had started in her eyes, making them gleam with grief, but she spoke in quiet rage and without any trace of self-pity. 'Had he not hurt me I should not have lost our first child, and the aftermath, in which I felt a great divide opening between us, would not have occurred. Your restlessness began then. Even our dear children who followed could not compensate for the cruelty and stupidity of what Borden did that day, and that the feud between you continues is proof of the outrage you too must still feel.'

'I have never spoken to you about that,' I said. 'How do you know?'

'Because I am not a fool, Rupert, and I have seen occasional remarks in the magic magazines.' I had not known she continued to subscribe to those. 'You are still prime amongst my concerns,' she said. 'I wonder only why you have never spoken to me of his attacks.'

'Because I am, I suppose, a little ashamed of the feud.'

'Surely he is the aggressor?'

'I have had to defend myself,' I said.

I told her about my investigations into his past, and my attempts to discover how he worked the illusion. Then I described the hopes I had for Tesla's equipment.

'Borden relies on standard stage trickery,' I explained. 'He uses cabinets and lights and make-up, and when he transports himself across the stage he does so by concealment. He enters one apparatus and emerges from another. It is brilliantly done, but the mystery is not only concealed by his props it is also made banal by them. The beauty of the Tesla device is that the trick can be carried out in the open, and the materialisation uses no props at all! If it works as planned I shall be transporting myself instantly to any position I like: to an empty part of the stage, to the royal box, to the front of the grand circle, even to an empty seat in the centre of the stalls! Anywhere, indeed, that will produce the greatest impact on the audience.'

'You make it sound a little provisional,' Julia said. 'You say this is still being planned?'

'As Alley says in his letter, it has been despatched to me. I have yet to receive it.'

Julia was the perfect audience for my enthusiasms about Tesla's device, and for the next hour or more we discussed all the possibilities it presented to me. Julia quickly identified the instinct that had been at the heart of it. If I were to perform this illusion on any public stage it would thwart Borden forever!

Were there any remaining doubts about what I should be doing, Julia dispelled them forever. Indeed, so excited was she that we began our search for the shipment at once.

I proposed, gloomily, that it would take several weeks to tour around the many shipping agents' offices in London, trying to trace an undelivered crate. But Julia said, in her familiar way of cutting through the Gordian Knot: 'Why do we not begin our enquiries with the Post Office?'

So it was, two hours later, that we located two immense crates addressed to me, waiting safely in the dead-letter section of the Mount Pleasant Sorting Office.

15th December 1900

Most of the last three weeks have been an agony of frustration, because I have been waiting for electricity to be supplied to my workshop. I have been like a small boy with a toy I could not play with. The Tesla apparatus has been erected in my workshop ever since I picked it up from Mount Pleasant, but without a supply of current it is useless. I have read Mr Alley's lucid instructions a thousand times! However, after my increasingly frequent reminders and urgings, the London Electricity Company has at last done the necessary work.

I have been rehearsing ever since, wrapped up mentally and emotionally in the demands this extraordinary device makes on me. Here, in no particular order, is a summary of what I have learned.

It is in full working order, and has been ingeniously designed to work on all presently known versions of electrical supply. This means I may travel with my show, even to Europe, the USA and (Alley claims in his instructions) the Far East.

However, I cannot perform my show unless the theatre has electrical current supplied. In future I will have to check this before I accept any new bookings, as well as many other new matters (some of which follow).

Portability. I know Tesla has done his best, but the equipment is damnably heavy. From now on, planning the delivery, unpacking and setting up of the apparatus is a priority. It means, for instance, that the simple informality of a train-ride to one of my shows is a thing of the past, at least if I wish to perform the Tesla illusion.

Technical rehearsals. The apparatus has to be erected twice. First for private testing on the morning of the show, then, while the main curtain is down and another act is in progress, it has to be re-erected for the performance. The admirable Alley has included suggestions as to how it might be carried out speedily and silently, but even so this is going to be hard work. Much rehearsal will be necessary, and I shall require extra assistants.

Physical layout of the theatres. I or Adam Wilson will always need to reconnoitre beforehand.

Boxing the stage. This is practicably straightforward, but in many theatres it antagonises the backstage staff, who for some reason think they have an automatic right to have revealed to them what they consider to be trade secrets. In this case, allowing strangers to see what I am actually doing on stage is out of the question. Again, more preparatory work than usual will be necessary.

Post-performance sealing of the apparatus, and private disassembly, are also procedures fraught with risk. I cannot accept any bookings until these procedures have been worked out and ensuing problems resolved.

All this special preparation! However, careful planning and rehearsal are in the essence of successful stage magic, and I am no stranger to any of them.

One small step forward. All stage illusions are given names by their inventors, and it is by these that they become known in the profession. THE THREE GRACES, DECAPITATION, CASSADAGA PROPAGANDA, are examples of some of the illusions at present popular in the halls. Borden, stodgily, calls his second-rate version of the trick THE NEW TRANSPORTED MAN (a name I have never used, even when I was employing his methods).

After some thought I have decided to call the Tesla invention IN A FLASH, and by this it will become known.

I also use this entry to note that as of last Monday, 10th December, Julia and the children have returned and are living with me at Idmiston Villas. They will see Caldlow House for the first time when we spend the Christmas holiday there.

I am a happy man, given this, my second chance. I cannot bear to think of past Christmases when I was estranged from my family, nor the thought that somehow I might again lose this happiness.

I am therefore busily preparing for what must follow, all in order to avert that which might otherwise follow. I say this with deliberate obscurity, because now that I have rehearsed IN A FLASH a couple of times, and I have learned its true working, I must be circumspect about its secret, even here.

When the children are asleep, and Julia encourages me to attend to business, I have been concentrating on the affairs of the estate. I am determined to put right the neglect my brother allowed.

31st December 1900

I write these words as the nineteenth century draws to a close. In an hour from now I shall descend to our drawing room, where Julia and the children are waiting for me, and together we shall see in the New Year and the New Century. It is a night resonant with auguries for the future, also with unavoidable reminders from the past.

Because secrecy again has a hold on me, I must say that what Hutton and I did earlier this evening could not be avoided. It had to be done.

What I am about to write will be written with a hand that still trembles from the primaeval fears that were aroused in me. I have been thinking hard about what I can record of the experience, and have decided that a straightforward, even bald, description of what happened is the only way.

This evening, soon after nightfall, while the children were taking an early nap so that they could be awake later to see in the new century, I told Julia what I was about to do, and left her waiting in her sitting room.

I found Hutton, and we left the house and went together

across the East Lawn towards the family vault. We transported the prestige materials on a handcart sometimes used by the gardeners.

Hutton and I had only storm lanterns to guide us, and unlocking the padlocked gate in near darkness took several minutes. The old lock had grown stiff with disuse.

As the wooden portal swung open, Hutton declared his unease. I felt terrific sympathy for him.

I said, 'Hutton, I don't expect you to go through with this. You may wait for me here if you like. Or you could return to the house, and I'll continue alone.'

'No, my Lord,' he replied in his honest way. 'I have agreed to this. To be frank I would not go in there alone, and neither, I dare say, would you. But apart from our imaginings there is nothing to fear.'

Leaving the cart by the entrance, we ventured inside. We held the storm lanterns raised at arm's length. The beams ahead did not reveal much, but our large shadows fell on the walls beside us. My memory of the vault was vague, because the only other time I had been inside I was still just a boy. The shallow flight of roughly cut stone steps led down into the hillside, and at the bottom, where there was a second door, the cavern widened a little.

The inner door was unlocked, but it was stiff and heavy to move aside. We grated it open, then went through into the abysmally dark space beyond. We could sense rather than see the cavern spreading before us. Our lanterns barely penetrated the gloom.

There was an acrid smell in the air, so sharp that it was almost a taste in the mouth. I lowered my lantern and adjusted the wick, hoping to tease a little more light from it. Our irruption into the place had set free a million motes of dust, swirling around us.

Hutton spoke beside me, his voice muted in the stifling acoustics of the underground chamber.

'Sir, should I collect the prestige materials?'

I could just make out his features in the lantern's glow.

'Yes, I think so. Do you need me to help you?'

'If you would wait at the bottom of the steps, sir.'

He walked quickly up the flight of steps and I knew he wanted to be done as soon as possible. As his light receded I felt more keenly alone, vulnerable to childish fears of the dark, and of the dead.

Here in this place were most of my forebears, laid out ritually on shelves and slabs, rendered down to bones or fragments of bones, lying in boxes and shrouds, wreathed in dust and flaking garments. When I cast the lantern about I could make out dim shapes on some of the nearer slabs. Somewhere, down the vault, out of the range of my lamp, I heard the scuttling of a large rodent.

I moved to the right, reaching out with my hand, and felt a stone slab at about the height of my waist and I groped across it. I felt small sharp objects, loose to the touch. The stink immediately intensified in my nose and I felt myself beginning to gag. I recoiled away, glimpsing the horrid fragments of that old life as my beam swung around.

I held the lamp high, forcing myself to look for what was there. I knew the reality could hardly be as unpleasant as my imaginings. I sensed that these long-dead ancestors were being roused by my arrival, and were shifting from their positions, raising a grisly head or a skeletal hand, croaking out their own obscure terrors that my presence was arousing in them.

One of these rocky shelves bore the casket of my own father.

I was torn by my fears. I wanted to follow Hutton up to the outside air, yet I knew I had to plunge further on into the depths of the vault. I could not move in either direction, because dread held me to where I stood. I am a rational man who seeks explanations and welcomes the scientific method, yet for those few seconds Hutton was away from me I was tormented by the easy rush of the illogical.

Then at last I heard him again on the steps, dragging the first of the large sacks containing the prestige materials. I was only too glad to turn and give him a hand, even though he seemed able to shift the weight on his own. I had to put down my lantern while we got the sack through the door, and because Hutton had left his own light with the handcart we were working in almost total darkness.

I said to him, 'I'm profoundly glad you are here to help me, Hutton.'

'I realise that, my Lord. I should not have cared to do this myself alone.'

'Then let us complete it quickly.'

This time we went back to the handcart together, and dragged down the second large sack.

My original plan had been to explore the crypt in full, looking for the best place in which to store the prestige materials, but now I was here I lost all wish to do anything of the sort. Because our lights were so inadequate at penetrating the darkness I knew that all searching would have to be done at close quarters. I dreaded having to investigate any more of those shelves and slabs that I was so readily envisaging. They were around me on both sides, and the cavern extended far beyond. It was full of death, full of the dead, redolent of finality, life abandoned to the rats.

'We'll leave the sacks here,' I said. 'As far off the floor as possible. I'll come down here again tomorrow, when it's daylight. With a better torch.'

'I fully understand, sir.'

Together we went to the left wall, and located another of the slabs. Bracing myself, I felt across it with my hand. There seemed to be nothing significant there, so with Hutton's help I lifted up the two sackfuls of prestige materials. With this done, and without saying another word between us, we returned quickly to the surface, and pushed the outer door closed behind us. I shuddered.

In the cold air of the night-time garden, Hutton and I shook hands.

'Thank you for helping me, Hutton,' I said. 'I had no idea what it was going to be like down there.'

'Nor I, my Lord. Will you be requiring anything else from me this evening?'

I considered.

'Would you and your wife care to join myself and Lady Colderdale at midnight? We plan to see in the new year.'

'Thank you, sir. We shall be honoured to do so.'

And that was how our expedition ended. Hutton dragged the handcart away towards the garden shed, and I crossed the East Lawn then walked around the periphery of the house to the main entrance. I came directly to this room, to write my account while events were still fresh.

However, a necessary delay arose before I could begin. As I entered the room I caught a sight of myself in my dressing mirror, and I stopped to look.

Thick white dust clung to my boots and ankles. Cobwebs straggled across my shoulders and chest. My hair had become matted on my head, apparently held down by a thick layer of grey dirt, and the same filth caked my face. My eyes, red-rimmed, stared out from the hollow mask my face had become, and for a few moments I stood there transfixed by the sight of myself. It seemed to me that I had been hideously transformed by my visit to the family tomb, becoming one of its denizens.

I shook off the thought with the dirty clothes, climbed into the filled bath waiting for me in my dressing room, and washed away the grime.

Now this account has been written, and it is close to midnight. It is time for me to seek out my family and household for the simple and familiar ceremony that celebrates the end of one year and, in this case, one century, then welcomes in the next.

The twentieth century is the one when my children shall mature and thrive, and I, of the old century, shall in due course leave it to them. But before I go I intend to leave my mark.

1st January 1901

I have been back to the vault, and moved the prestige materials to a better position. Hutton and I then put down some rat poison, but in future I shall have to find something more secure than canvas sacks in which to store the materials.

Hesketh Unwin reports that he has received three bookings for me. Two of them are already confirmed, while the other is conditional on my inclusion of In a Flash (which is now temptingly described in Unwin's standard proposal). I have agreed to this, and so all three bookings may be considered secure. A total of three hundred and fifty guineas!

Yesterday, the Tesla apparatus arrived back from Derbyshire, and with Adam Wilson's assistance I immediately unpacked it and erected it. According to my clock it took under fifteen minutes. We must be able to be sure of doing it within ten minutes, when working in a theatre. Mr Alley's sheet of instructions declares that when he and Tesla were testing its portability they were able to erect the whole thing in under twelve minutes.

Adam Wilson knows the secret of the illusion, as he must. Adam has been working for me for more than five years, and I believe I can trust him. To be as sure as reasonably possible I have offered him a confidentiality bonus of ten pounds, to be paid into an accumulating fund in his name after each successful performance. He and Gertrude are expecting their second child.

I have been putting in more work on my stage presentation of In a Flash, as well as rehearsing several of my other illusions. As it is several months since my last public performance I am a little rusty. I confess I approached such routine work without enthusiasm, but once I settled down to it I began to enjoy myself.

2nd February 1901

Tonight I performed at the Finsbury Park Empire, but did not include In a Flash. I accepted the commission as a way of testing the water, to experience the feeling once again of performing before a live audience.

My version of The Disappearing Piano went down exceptionally well, and I was applauded loud and long, but at the end of my act I felt myself frustrated and dissatisfied.

I hunger to perform the Tesla illusion!

I rehearsed IN A FLASH twice yesterday, and will do so twice again tomorrow. I dare not make it any more than that. I shall be performing it on Saturday evening at the Trocadero in Holloway Road, then at least once again in the week following. I believe that if I can perform it regularly enough then extra rehearsals, beyond stage movements, misdirection and patter, should not be necessary.

Tesla warned me that there would be aftereffects, and these are indeed severe. It is no trivial matter to use the apparatus. Each time I pass through it I suffer.

In the first place there is the physical pain. My body is wrenched apart, disassembled. Every tiny particle of me is thrown asunder, becoming one with the aether. In a fraction of a second, a fraction so small that it cannot be measured, my body is converted into electrical waves. It is radiated through space. It is reassembled at its designated target.

Slam! I am broken apart! Slam! I am together again!

It is a violent shock that explodes in every part of me, in every direction. Imagine a steel bar smashing into the palm of your hand. Now imagine ten or twenty more hammering down in the same place from different angles. More fall on your fingers, your wrist. A hundred more strike the back of your hand. The ends of your fingers. Every joint.

More explode *out* from inside your flesh.

Now spread the pain through your whole body, inside and out.

Slam!

A millionth of a second of total agony!

Slam again!

That is how it feels.

Yet I arrive in the selected place, and I am exactly as I was that millionth of a second earlier. I am whole in myself and identical to myself, but I am in the shock of ultimate pain.

The first time I used the Tesla apparatus, in the basement of Caldlow House, with no warning of what I was to experience, I collapsed to the floor in the belief that I had died. It did not seem possible that my heart, my brain, could survive such an explosion of pain. I had no thoughts, no emotional reactions. It felt as if I had died, and I acted as if I had died.

As I slumped to the floor, Julia, who of course was there with me for the test, ran to my side. My first lucid memory in the post-death world is of her gentle hands reaching into my shirt to feel for a sign of life. I opened my eyes, in shock and amazement, happy beyond words to find her beside me, to feel her tenderness. Quickly I was able to stand, to reassure her that I was well, to hold her and kiss her, to be myself once more.

In truth, then, physical recovery from this brutal experience is itself speedy, but the mental consequences are formidable.

On the day of that first test in Derbyshire, I forced myself to repeat the test in the afternoon, but as a result I was cast into the darkest gloom for much of the Christmas period. I had died twice. I had become one of the walking dead, a damned soul.

And the reminders of what I did then are the materials that later had to be put away. I could not even face that gruesome task until New Year's Eve, as I have described.

Yesterday, here in London, in the electrical brightness and familiarity of my workshop, with the Tesla equipment reassembled, I felt I should undergo two more rehearsals. I am a performer, a professional. I must give an appearance to what I do, give it a sheen and a glamour. I must project myself about the theatre in a flash, and at the moment of arrival I must appear to be a magician who has successfully performed the impossible.

To sink to my knees, as if poleaxed, would be out of the question. To reveal even a glimpse of the millionth-second of agony I have endured would also be unconscionable.

The point is that I have a double level of subterfuge to convey. A magician ordinarily reveals an effect that is 'impossible': a piano seems to disappear, a billiard ball magically reproduces itself, a lady is made to pass through a sheet of mirror glass. The audience of course knows that the impossible has not been made possible.

IN A FLASH, by scientific method, in fact achieves the hitherto impossible. What the audience sees is actually what has happened! But I cannot allow this ever to be known, for science has in this case replaced magic.

I must, by careful art, make my miracle less miraculous. I must emerge from the elemental transmitter as if I have *not* been slammed apart, and slammed together again.

So I have been trying to learn how to prepare for and brace myself against the pain, how to react to it without keeling over, how to step forward with my arms raised and with a flashing smile to bow and acknowledge applause. To mystify sufficiently, but not too much.

I write of what happened yesterday, because last night, when I returned home, I was in too great a despair even to think of recording what had happened. Now it is the afternoon and I am more or less myself again, but already the prospect of two more rehearsals tomorrow is daunting and depressing me.

16th February 1901

I am full of trepidation about tonight's performance at the Trocadero. I have spent the morning at the theatre, setting up the apparatus, testing it, dismantling it, then locking it away again safely in its crates.

After that, as anticipated, came the protracted negotiations with the scene-shifters, actively hostile to my intentions of boxing the stage. In the end, a straightforward cash transaction settled the matter and my wishes prevailed, but it has meant a huge dent in my income for the show. This illusion is clearly only performable if I can demand fees greatly in excess of anything I have earned before. A lot depends on the show tonight.

Now I have an hour or two of free time, before I must go back to Holloway Road. I plan to spend part of it with Julia and the children, and try to take a short nap in whatever is left. I am so keyed up, however, that sleep seems only remotely possible.

17th February 1901

Last night I safely crossed the aether from the stage of the Trocadero to the royal box. The equipment worked perfectly.

But the audience did not applaud because it did not see what was happening. When finally the applause came it was more bemused than enthusiastic.

The trick needs a stronger build-up, a greater sense of danger. And the point of arrival must be picked out with a spotlight, to draw attention to my position as I materialise. I have talked to Adam about it, and he suggests, ingeniously, that I might be able to rig up an electrical spur from the apparatus so that turning on the light is not left to a stage-hand but is commanded by me from the stage. Magic always improves.

We perform again on Tuesday at the same theatre.

I have left the best to last – I was able to disguise completely the shock of the impact on me. Both Julia, who saw the show from the auditorium, and Adam, who was watching from the rear of the stage through a small flap in the box screen, say my recovery was almost flawless. In this case it works to my advantage that the audience was not fully attentive, because only these two noticed the single weakness that occurred (I took one inadvertent step backwards).

For myself, I can say that practice with the apparatus has meant the terrible shock is not nearly as terrible as before, and that it has been getting slightly better each time I try it. I can foresee that in a month or so I will be able to bear the effect with outward indifference.

I also note that the consequent gloom I suffer is much less than after my first attempts.

In Derbyshire   23rd February 1901

My performance on Tuesday, much improved after the lessons of the weekend, gained me a laudatory review in

The Stage, an outcome more to my favour than anything else I can imagine! On the train yesterday Julia and I read and re-read the words to each other, glorying in the undoubted effect they will have on my career. By our temporary exile here in Derbyshire we will not learn of tangible results until we are back in London early next week, when we have finished here. I can wait contented. The children are with us, the weather is cold and brilliant, and the moorland scenery is ravishing us with its muted colours.

I feel I am at last approaching the peak years of my career.

In London   2nd March 1901

I have an unprecedented *thirty-five* confirmed bookings in my appointments diary, accepted for the period of the next four months. Three of these are for shows in my own stage name, and one of these is to be called *The Great Danton Entertains*; in seventeen theatres I shall top the bill; the remainder of the dates amply repay in money what they do not offer in prestige.

With this richness of choice I have been able to demand details of technical specifications of the backstage area before accepting, as well as forcing through compliance with my need to box the stage. I have made it a standard term of contract that I am supplied with an accurate plan of the auditorium, as well as being given firm undertakings about the steadiness and reliability of the electrical supply. In two cases, the theatre managements are so anxious to attract me to their houses that they have guaranteed to convert over to electricity in advance of my show.

I shall be roaming the country. Brighton, Exeter, Kidder-minster, Portsmouth, Ayr, Folkestone, Manchester, Shef-field, Aberystwyth, York, all these and many more will greet me on my first tour, as well as the capital itself, where I have several dates.

In spite of the travelling (which will be in first-class trains and carriages and paid for by others), the schedule is leisurely within reason, and as my little entourage crisscrosses the country we shall have abundant opportunity to make our necessary visits to Caldlow House.

The agent is already speaking of foreign tours, with perhaps yet another trip to the USA in the offing. There would be certain extra problems here, but none is beyond the wit of a magician in his prime.

It is all extremely satisfactory and I hope I may be forgiven for recording it in a state of unqualified self-confidence.

In Southampton   10th July 1901

I am in the middle of a week's run at the Duchess Theatre here in Southampton. Julia came down to visit me yesterday, bringing with her at my request my portmanteau of papers and files, and as I therefore have access to this diary it seems like a good moment to make one of my periodic entries.

I have been continually revising and rehearsing IN A FLASH for some months and it is now more or less a perfected skill. All my earlier hopes for it have come to fruition. I can pass through the aether without registering any reaction to the physical traumas I endure. The transition is smooth and seamless and from the point of view of the audience impossible to explain.

Nor are the mental aftereffects, which so scourged me at the outset, a problem any more. I suffer no agonies of depression, or self-doubt. To the contrary (and I confide this to no one, and record it in no other document than in this secret and lockable diary), the wrenching apart of my body has become a pleasure to which I am almost addicted. At first I was disheartened by the imaginings of death, of living in an afterlife, but now I nightly experience my transmission as a rebirth, a renewal of self. In the early days I was concerned by the many times I should have to perform the trick to keep in practice, but now as soon as I have completed one performance I begin to crave the next.

Three weeks ago, during a temporary break in my round of engagements, I erected the Tesla equipment in my workshop and put myself through the process. Not to

285

try out new performance techniques, not to perfect existing ones, but purely for the physical pleasure of the experience.

Disposal of the prestige materials produced at each show is still a problem, but after all these weeks we have developed a few routines so that the job is done with a minimum of fuss.

Most of the improvements I have made have been in the area of performance technique. My error at first was to assume that the sheer brilliance of the effect would be enough to dazzle my audiences. What I was neglecting was one of the oldest axioms of magic, that the miracle of the trick must be made clear by the presentation. Audiences are not easily misled, so the magician must provoke their interest, hold it, then confound every expectation by performing the apparently impossible.

By supplementing Tesla's apparatus with a range of magical effects and techniques (most of them familiar to professional illusionists), I make my presentation of IN A FLASH intriguing, more than a little terrifying to behold, and ultimately baffling. I do not use every effect at every performance, and deliberately vary the show to keep myself fresh and my rivals confounded, but here are some of the ways I engage and misdirect my audience.

I allow inspection of the apparatus before it is used, and, on some occasions and in some theatres, *after* it has been used.

I occasionally invite a committee of witnesses on to the stage from the audience.

I am able to produce a personal object donated by a member of the audience, and identifiable by them, after I have taken it through transmission.

I allow myself to be marked with flour or chalk or something similar, so that when I appear in my chosen place it can be seen that I am, beyond any doubt, the same man who was moments earlier fully visible on the stage.

I project myself to numerous different parts of the theatre, partly depending on the physical plan of the building, partly on the degree of effect I wish to achieve. I can travel instantly to the centre or rear of the stalls, to the dress circle, to one of the loges.

I can arrange for myself to be transmitted to other stage props or artefacts placed in view for just this purpose. Sometimes, for example, I arrive in a large net that has been dangling empty from the roof of the auditorium all through the show. Another popular effect is when I project myself to a sealed box or crate, placed on a stand fully in view of the audience and surrounded by a committee so that I might not enter through a hidden door or trap.

However, this freedom has made me reckless. One evening, almost on a whim, I projected myself into a glass tank of water placed on the stage. This was a grave mistake, because I committed the cardinal sin of the magician: I had not rehearsed the effect and I left much of it to chance. Although my sensational and aquatically explosive arrival in the water had the audience on its feet with excitement it also nearly killed me. My lungs instantly filled with water, and within a couple of seconds I was fighting to stay alive. Only quick action by Adam Wilson saved my life. It was a gruesome reminder of one of Borden's earlier attacks on me.

After this unwelcome lesson in rematerialization, if I am ever tempted to try a new effect I rehearse thoroughly first.

Of course, my act mostly consists of conventional illusions. I have a huge repertoire of tricks, and whenever I open at a new theatre I change my programme. I always present a varied show, starting with one of the familiar prestidigitations, such as Cups and Balls or Mysterious Wine Bottles. Several card tricks of different kinds come next, and then for visual flourish I perform one of a range of tricks involving silks, flags, paper flowers or handkerchiefs. I work towards the climax through two or three illusions involving tables, cabinets or mirrors, frequently using volunteers from the audience. In a Flash invariably closes my show.

I am busier than ever. I made my tour of Britain, August–October 1901. There was another trip to the USA, from November last year to February this. Until May I was in Europe, and I'm presently engaged for an extended tour of British theatres, this time concentrating on those located in seaside resorts.

Plans for the future:

I intend to take a long rest and spend much time with my family! Most of September is being kept clear for this, as is the first part of October.

While in the USA I tried to locate Nikola Tesla. I have certain questions about his apparatus and suggestions for improving its performance. I also felt sure he would be interested to know how well it has served me so far. However, Tesla has gone to ground. He is rumoured to be a bankrupt, in hiding from his creditors.

In London 3rd September 1902

A momentous revelation!

Early yesterday evening, while I was resting between shows at Daly's Theatre in Islington, a man called at the stage door to see me. When I saw his card I asked for him to be shown immediately to my dressing room. It was Mr Arthur Koenig, the young journalist from the *Evening Star* who had given me so much food for thought about Borden. I was not surprised to learn that Mr Koenig now has the position of Deputy News Editor of that paper. The years have added a touch of grey to the whiskers on his face and several inches to his girth. He entered cordially, pumped my hand up and down and slapped me around the shoulders.

'I just saw your matinée, Mr Danton!' he said. 'My hearty congratulations to you. For once the reviews do justice to a music hall act. I confess myself baffled and entertained in equal measure.'

'I'm glad to hear it,' I said, and signed for my dresser to pour Mr Koenig a small glass of whisky. When this was done

I asked the dresser to leave us alone together, and to return in fifteen minutes.

'Your good health, sir!' Koenig announced, raising his glass. 'Or should I say, my Lord?'

I stared at him in surprise.

'How the devil do you know about that?'

'Why do you think I should not? The news of your brother's death reached the press in the usual way, and was duly reported.'

'I've seen those reports,' I replied. 'None of them mentioned me.'

'I think it might be because few in Fleet Street know you by more than your stage name. It took a true admirer to connect you to Henry Angier.'

'Nothing escapes you, does it?' I said, with grudging admiration.

'Not that kind of information, sir. Don't worry, your secret is safe with me. I assume it *is* a secret?'

'I have always kept the two parts of my life separate. In that sense, it is a secret and I'd be glad if you would treat it as such.'

'You have my word, my Lord. I'm grateful you are so honest with me. I accept that secrets are your stock in trade, and I've no wish either to discover or expose them.'

'That was not always the case,' I pointed out. 'When last we met—'

'Mr Borden, yes indeed. That, I confess, is a slightly different case. I felt he was *goading* me with his secrecy.'

'I know what you mean.'

'Yes, sir, I think you do.'

'Tell me, Koenig. You have seen my show today. What do you think of my final illusion?'

'You have perfected what Mr Borden has merely shaped.'

That was music to my ears, but I asked him, 'You say you were baffled by it, but you don't feel goaded by it too, do you?'

'I do not. The sense of mystery you provoke is one I find familiar. When you watch a master illusionist at work you are curious about how the miracle is achieved, but you also realise that great disappointment would ensue if an explanation was offered.'

He smiled as he said this, then in silence sipped happily at his whisky.

'May I ask,' I said eventually, 'to what I owe the pleasure of this visit?'

'I've come to apologise in the matter of Mr Borden, your rival. I confess that all my elaborate theories about him were in error, while your theory, blunt and simple, was correct.'

'I don't follow you,' I said.

'When I came to see you before, you will recall I held some hifalutin theory of Mr Borden performing a greater magic than any that had existed before.'

'I remember,' I said. 'You wisely convinced me of it. I was grateful to you—'

'You, however, had a plainer explanation. Borden is not one man but two, you said. Twins, you said. Identical twin brothers, each taking the place of the other as required.'

'But you proved he worked alone—'

'You were correct, sir! Mr Borden's act is indeed based on the fact that he has a twin brother. Alfred Borden is a name conflated from two: Albert and Frederick, identical brothers, who perform together as one.'

'That's not true!' I said.

'But it was your own theory.'

'In lieu of any other,' I explained. 'You swiftly disabused me. You had evidence—'

'Much of which turns out to have been circumstantial, the rest of which had been falsified. I was a young reporter, not then fully practised in my profession. I have since learnt to check facts, to double-check them, then to check them once more.'

'But, look Koenig,' I said. 'I went into the matter myself. At the time, nothing was more important to me than to establish the facts. I examined the hospital records of his birth, the register of the school he attended—'

'All falsified long since, Mr Angier.' He looked at me

questioningly, as if to be sure he was addressing me correctly. I nodded, and he went on, 'The Borden brothers have built their lives around sustaining this illusion. Nothing about them can be trusted.'

'But I did investigate most carefully,' I insisted. 'I knew there were two brothers with those names, but one is two years younger than the other!'

'Both coincidentally born in May, as I recall. It does not take much skill to forge a birth record from 8th May 1856 to 18th May 1858.'

'I saw a photograph of the two brothers, taken together!'

'Yes, and one so easy to find. It must have been left as a red herring for such as you and I to stumble across. As we duly did.'

'But the two brothers were physically unalike. I saw the portrait myself!'

'And so did I. Indeed, I have a copy of it in my office. The distinction between their facial characteristics is remarkable. But surely you of all people understand the deceptive use of stage make-up, cheek-pads, and the like?'

I was thunderstruck by the news, and stared at the floor, unable to think coherently.

'Galling *and* goading, isn't it?' Koenig said. 'You must feel it too. We have both been taken in by pranksters.'

'Are you sure of this?' I demanded. 'Totally sure?' Koenig was nodding slowly. 'For instance, have you ever seen the two brothers together?'

'This is the basis of my certainty. Just once, and then only briefly, they met in my presence.'

'Were you shadowing them?'

'I was shadowing one of them,' Koenig corrected me. 'I followed Mr Borden from his house one evening in August. He walked alone into Regents Park, apparently taking a leisurely stroll. I was following at a distance of about a hundred yards. As he walked round the Inner Circle, a man approached him from the opposite direction. As they met they paused for about three seconds and spoke together. Then they walked on as before. Now, though,

Borden was carrying a small leather case. The man he had spoken to soon passed me, and as he did so I could see that he looked exactly like Borden.'

I stared at Koenig thoughtfully.

'How do you know——?' I was thinking carefully of some possibility of error. 'How do you know that the man who walked *on*, the one now carrying the case, was not the man who had spoken to Borden? Borden himself could simply have walked back the way he had come. And if that was so, wouldn't it have been him who passed you?'

'I know what I saw, my Lord. They were wearing different clothes, perhaps for reasons of subterfuge, but this fact made it possible for me to distinguish between them. They met, they spoke, they continued on their separate ways, they were identical.'

My mind was sharply focused. I was thinking rapidly about the mechanics of mounting a theatrical magic performance. If it were true that they were twins then both brothers would have to be present in the theatre at each show. This would mean that the backstage staff would inevitably be in on the secret. I already knew that Borden did not box the stage, and there are always people hanging around in the wings during a show, seeing too much for their own good. All the time I was performing the switch illusion with a double I was conscious of this. But Borden's secret, if Koenig were to be believed, had stayed intact for many years. If Borden's act was based on identical twins, then surely the secret would have leaked out years ago?

Otherwise, what was the explanation? It could only be that the secrecy was maintained before and after the show. That Borden-1, so to speak, would arrive at the theatre with his apparatus and props, with Borden-2 already concealed in one of the pieces. Borden-2 would duly make his appearance during the performance, while Borden-1 went into hiding in the props on-stage.

It was admittedly feasible, and if that was all there was to it I might be able to accept it. But many years of touring from one venue to the next, burdened with the sheer practicalities of long train journeys, the employment of assistants, the finding of lodgings, and so on, made me wonder. Borden must have a team working with him: an *ingénieur* of course, one or more assistants who appeared on stage, several carriers and shifters, an agent. If all these people were privy to his secret then their ability to keep quiet about it was remarkable.

On the other hand, and much more likely in view of human nature, if they were *not* to be trusted, Borden-1 and Borden-2 would have to engage in a comprehensive array of concealment.

Beyond this, there were the day-to-day realities of theatrical life. For example, on the days when there was a matinée performance, what would Borden-2 (the one concealed in the apparatus) do between shows? Would he remain hidden while his brother relaxed in the green room with the other artistes? Would he let himself out secretly, then skulk alone in the dressing room until it was time for the next show?

How did the two of them get into and out of the theatres without being spotted? Stage door managers are jealous guardians of the way, and in some theatres the doorman is so notoriously punctilious about checking everyone's identity and business that, it is said, even famous actors tremble at the thought of arriving late or of trying to smuggle in a paramour. There are always alternative ways into the building, notably through the scenery bay or front of house, but again this bespeaks a need for constant secrecy and preparation, and a willingness to put up with a huge amount of physical discomfort.

'I see I have given you something to ponder,' Koenig said, interrupting my train of thought. He was holding out his empty whisky glass as if to ask for a refill, but because I wanted time to think this through I rather brusquely took the glass away from him.

'Are you sure of your facts this time?' I said.

'Copper-bottomed certain, sir. Upon my very word.'

'Last time you gave me some leads so I might check your claims myself. Are you proposing something similar now?'

'No – I offer you only my word. I have personally seen the two men together, and as far as I am concerned no further proof is necessary.'

'Not to you, perhaps.' I stood up, to indicate that the interview was at an end.

Koenig picked up his hat and coat, and went to the door, which I held open for him.

I said to him, as casually as I could contrive, 'You show no curiosity about how I perform my own illusion.'

'I take it that it's magic, sir.'

'You don't then suspect me of having an identical twin?'

'I know you have not.'

'So you did investigate me,' I said. 'And what about Borden? Is he wondering how I work the effect?'

Mr Koenig gave me a broad wink.

'I'm sure he and his brother would not like you to know that they're in a lather of curiosity about you, sir.' He extended his hand, and we shook. 'Once again, my congratulations. If I may say so, it has been reassuring to see you in such good health.'

He was gone before I could respond to that, but I think I know what he meant.

In London   7th September 1902

My short season at Daly's being complete, I am able to tidy up my affairs in London for a while, and spend my long-wished-for month with Julia and the children in Derbyshire. Tomorrow I shall be heading north. Wilson has gone ahead of me to make the usual arrangements for the prestige materials.

This morning I have safely secured Tesla's apparatus in my workshop, paid off my assistants for the next few weeks, settled all my outstanding bills, and spoken at some length with Unwin about bookings for the autumn and winter. It already seems that I shall be busily engaged from the middle of October until March or April next year. My estimated income from these performances, even after all my overheads have been deducted, will make me rich beyond the wildest dreams of my youth. By the end of next year I shall, in all probability, need never work again.

Which brings me to Koenig's parting remark. Having recorded it here I feel I should also explain it.

A few months ago, when I was in the first rush of perfecting the presentation of IN A FLASH, I thought of a novel final twist to the illusion. What brought it to mind was that sensation I experienced at first, that I was somehow surviving beyond death. I have arranged, by a combination of carefully positioned lights and use of make-up, that at the end of my act, after I have passed through the aether, I look more haggard than before. I seem worn by the rigours of the undertaking. I am a man who flirts with death and who now is showing the traces.

This effect has become a routine part of my act. Throughout my show I move carefully, as if favouring my limbs so they should not hurt, I turn with stiff movements of my waist and back, I walk with my shoulders hunched. I make the best of my condition, acting as if I do not care. After I have performed IN A FLASH, and once I have been seen to have arrived miraculously intact, then I allow the lighting to do its gruesome work. As the final curtain falls I appear to most of the audience as if I am not long for this world.

Apart from the effect itself, I do have a long-term strategy in mind. Put plainly, I am planning and preparing for my own death. I am, after all, no stranger to the concept. For many years I acted the rôle of the dead man while Julia played the widow. And after so many transits through Tesla's infernal device, the idea that I could stage my own death comes easily.

Next year I wish to retire from the stage for good. I want to be free of the endless touring, of the long journeys, the overnight stays in theatrical lodgings, the endless tussles with theatre managements. I am sick of the need for secrecy about what I do, and I always fear another round of attacks from Borden.

Most of all, my children are growing up and I wish to be with them as they do so. Edward is soon to depart to university, and the girls will no doubt be wanting to marry soon.

By this time next year I shall be, as I say, financially independent, and with prudent investment the Caldlow estate should be able to provide for my family for the rest of my life and theirs. As far as the world in general is concerned the life of The Great Danton, of Rupert Angier, shall come to a cancerous end, brought on by the rigours of his career, at some point in the autumn of 1903.

Meanwhile, without publicity or announcement, the 14th Earl of Colderdale will at much the same time take up the reins of his inheritance.

Thus the explanation of Koenig's remark about my 'surprising' good health. He is a sharp-eyed and intelligent man, who knows more about me than I wish.

On this subject, I have been reflecting a great deal about his new theory that there is not one Borden but two. I remain unsure.

This is not because the premise itself is implausible – after all, my man Cutter had worked it out for himself – but because of the endless ramifications of living with the deception. I was already thinking about a few of those when Koenig was in my dressing room.

What about everyday life? No artiste is constantly in work, however successful his or her career. There are periods of rest, both voluntary and involuntary. There are necessary delays between bookings. Shows and tours can be cancelled just before they are due to start. There are holidays, illnesses, family crises.

If Borden is not one man but two, and one of the men is always in hiding so that the other might seem to be the 'only' Alfred Borden, where and how is the hiding going on? What happens in the life of the hidden man while he is hiding? How does he make contact with his brother? Do they ever meet, and if so how do they arrange not to be spotted by anyone?

How many other people know about the deception, and how can Borden be certain the secret is safe with them?

Speaking in particular of other people, what of Borden's wife? And what of his children?

If Borden is two men, they cannot both be husband to the wife, nor both be father to the children. Which of them is husband, which the father? Borden's wife is a woman of good background, and by all accounts no fool. What does she in fact know about Borden?

Is she being kept in the dark about his true identity?

Could concealment and deception extend successfully even to the marital home, the conjugal bed? Would she suspect nothing, discern no difference at all between the two men?

What about family lore, private jokes and observations, shared personal memories, matters of physical intimacy? Is it conceivable that the two men would collaborate to such an extent that even personal matters are dragged into the pre-cautions and secrecy that surround a mere stage illusion?

The contrary is if anything harder to believe, that Bor-den's wife knows the truth of the matter and is prepared for some reason to put up with it.

If that were true, the arrangement would surely have gone wrong years ago.

One of the two brothers would inevitably become seen as the lesser partner in the arrangement: one of them (let me again call him Borden-2) would not be the one who actually went through the ceremony of marriage with her. He would therefore be in her eyes less of a husband than Borden-1, and what would follow then of matters concerning conjugality?

Further to the point, Borden-2 would not be the actual father to the children. (I assume for sake of normal propriety that the Borden-2 who did not marry is the same Borden-2 who did not sire the children.) Borden-2 would therefore be uncle to the children, at a stage removed from them, emo-tionally and physically. The wife, the mother, could not help but discriminate in some way against him.

It is a situation fraught with instability.

Both of these explanations are so unlikely that I am forced to believe in a third: The Borden brothers have deliberately not told the wife the truth, and have tried to deceive her, but she has herself made the deception unimportant. In other words, she has worked out what is going on (how could she not?), but for reasons of her own has decided to acquiesce in it.

In spite of the fact that this theory contains its own mysteries I find it the most plausible explanation, but even so the whole business beggars belief.

I would go, and do go, to considerable lengths to protect my secrets, but I would not let secrecy become an obsession. Could Borden, and Borden's supposed brother, be as obsessive as Koenig makes them out to be?

I am still in two minds about this!

In the end it does not matter, for a trick is a trick and everyone who sees it knows that a deception is being performed. But Julia suffered horribly because of the feud, and my own life came damnably close its end because of it. I believe Borden *is* such a man as to make a fetish of his secrets and it was my misfortune to tangle with him.

Also my luck, as a direct consequence of the feud, to hit upon the illusion that is making my fortune.

Somewhere between Wakefield and Leeds   27th November 1902

After a long and beneficial holiday in Derbyshire with Julia and the children I am back on tour. Tomorrow I open at the King William Theatre in Leeds, where I shall be performing twice nightly until the end of next week.

Thence to Dover, where I am top of the bill at the Overcliff Theatre. Thence to Portsmouth, for the week leading up to Christmas.

I am a tired but happy man.

Sometimes people notice my appearance and comment in a well-intended way on how unwell I might be. I am brave about this.

1st January 1903

So I reach the year in which Rupert Angier is to forsake this life. I have not yet chosen an exact date for his or my demise, but it will not be until after the conclusion of my American tour.

We depart from Liverpool for New York three weeks from tomorrow, and shall be away until April. The problem of disposal of prestige materials has only partially been solved, but helping to alleviate it is the fact that I shall be performing IN A FLASH on average only once a week. If necessary I shall do what I did before, but Wilson declares that he has found a solution. Whatever the case, the show will go on.

Julia and the children will be with me during what will no doubt later become known as my farewell tour.

30th April 1903

I have told Unwin to continue accepting bookings through to the end of the year, and for the early months of 1904. However, I shall be dead by the end of September. Probably it will occur on Saturday, 19th September.

In Lowestoft   15th May 1903

After the dizzy heights of my appearing in New York, Washington DC, Baltimore, Richmond, St Louis, Chicago, Denver, San Francisco, Los Angeles . . . I am in Lowestoft, Suffolk. In the USA I might make my fortune, but in places like the Pavilion Theatre in Lowestoft I earn my living.

I open tomorrow for a week.

20th May 1903

I have cancelled both my performances tonight, tomorrow's are in jeopardy, and as I draft these words I am anxiously awaiting Julia's arrival.

I am a fool, a damned, bloody *fool*!

Last night, second performance, halfway through. I can barely bring myself to set this down in writing.

So. I must be calm.

I have recently added a new card trick to my repertoire. In this, a member of the audience is invited up to the stage. He takes a card and writes his name on the face of it. I tear off a corner of the card and give it to the volunteer to hold. The rest of the card is placed inside a paper envelope, which is ignited. When the flames have gone out I produce a large orange. I cut it in half and it is found to contain the signed card, and the torn-off corner still of course fits.

Last night my volunteer was what I thought must be a local man: he was tall and burly, had a florid complexion, and when he spoke I heard a Suffolk accent. I had spotted him earlier in the show, sitting in the centre of the front row, and as soon as I noticed his amiable, unintelligent face I had picked him out as a likely volunteer. He did in fact offer himself as soon as I called for someone to come up on stage, something which should have alerted me to likely trouble. However, while I was doing the trick he was the perfect foil, even drawing a laugh or two from the audience with his homely sense of humour and commonplace observations. ('Take a card,' said I. 'What? Do you want me to take it home, sor?' said the man, all wide-eyed and seemingly eager to please.)

How could I not have guessed it was Borden?! He even gave me a clue, because the name he wrote on the playing card was *Alf Redbone*, a transparent near-anagram, yet with my guard lowered I took it to be his real name.

With the card trick completed I shook his hand, thanked him by name, and added my applause to that of the audience as he was led by Hester, my present female assistant, towards the stalls ramp.

I did not notice that Redbone's seat was still empty until a short while later, as I moved towards the start of IN A FLASH.

In the tensions leading up to this performance, his absence registered only at the back of my mind. I knew there was something wrong, but because of the moment I could not think exactly what it might be.

As the current started to flow through the Tesla apparatus, and the long tendrils of high-voltage discharge snaked around me, and the anticipation from the audience was at its greatest, I noticed his absence at last. The significance of it came at me like a thunderbolt.

By then it was too late; the apparatus was in operation and I was committed to completing the trick.

At this point in the show nothing can be modified. Even my chosen target area is fixed. Setting the coordinates is too intricate and time-consuming to be done at any time other than before a performance. The previous night I had set the apparatus for both of yesterday's performances so that I would arrive in the highest loge at stage left, which by arrangement with the management was kept empty for both shows. The loge was at the same approximate height as the main balcony and could be seen from almost every other part of the auditorium.

I had arranged it so that I should materialise on the very rail of the box itself, picked out by the follow-spot, facing down into the stalls a long way below, apparently struggling to keep my balance, arms windmilling, body jerking wildly, and so on. Everything had gone exactly to plan during the first performance, and my magical transformation brought screams, roars of warnings and shouts of alarm from the audience, followed by thunderous applause as I swung down to the stage on the rope thrown to me by Hester.

To arrive on the rail of the loge facing down to the audience, I have to stand inside the Tesla apparatus with my back towards the loge. The audience cannot know it, of course, but the position in which I arrange my body is exactly recreated at the instant of arrival. From my place inside the apparatus I could not therefore see where I was about to arrive.

With Borden somewhere around, a terrible certainty struck me that he was about to sabotage me yet again! What if he was lurking inside the loge, and gave me a shove as I arrived on the ledge? I felt the electrical tension mounting ineluctably around me. I could not prevent myself turning anxiously around to look up at the box. I could just make it out through the deadly blue-white electrical sparks. All seemed well. There was nothing there to block my arrival, and although I couldn't see into the box itself, where the seats are placed, it did not look as if anyone was there.

Borden's intent was much more sinister, and a moment later I found out what it was. In the very instant that I turned to look up at the loge, two things happened simultaneously.

The first was that the transmission of my body actually began.

The second was that electrical power to the apparatus cut out, disconnecting the current instantly. The blue fires vanished, the electrical field died.

I remained on the stage, standing within the wooden cage of the apparatus in full view of the audience. I was staring over my shoulder at the loge.

The transmission had been interrupted! But it had begun before it was stopped, and now I could see an image of myself on the rail.

There was my ghost, my *doppelgänger*, momentarily frozen in the stance I had adopted when I turned to look, half twisted, half crouching, looking away and up.

It was a thin, insubstantial copy of myself, a partial prestige.

Even as I looked, this image of myself straightened in alarm, threw out his arms, and collapsed backwards and out of sight into the loge itself!

Appalled at what I had seen I stepped forward out of the coils of the Tesla cage. On cue, the spotlight came on, illuminating the whole loge to pick out my intended materialisation. The people in the audience looked up at the loge, already half anticipating the trick. They started to applaud, but just as quickly the noise faded away to nothing. There was nothing to see.

I stood alone on the stage. My illusion was ruined.

'Curtain!' I yelled into the wings. 'Bring down the curtain!'

It seemed to take an eternity but at last the technician heard me and the curtain came down, separating me from the audience. Hester appeared at a run. Her cue for a return to the stage was when I was taking my applause from the loge rail, and not before.

'What happened?' she cried.

'That man who came up from the audience. Where is he?'

'I don't know! I thought he went back to his seat.'

'He got backstage somehow. You are supposed to make sure these people leave the stage!'

I pushed her aside angrily and lifted up the reinforced fabric of the curtain. At a crouch I stepped beneath it and went forward to the footlights. The house lights were now on, and the audience was moving into the aisles and slowly up to the exits. The people were obviously puzzled and disgruntled, but they were paying no more attention to the stage.

I looked up at the box. The spotlight had been turned off, and in the bland house lights I could still see nothing.

A woman screamed once, then again. She was somewhere in the building behind the loges.

I walked quickly into the wings and met Wilson as he was hurrying to the stage to find me.

Breathlessly, because now I found my lungs inexplicably labouring, I instructed him to dismantle and crate up the apparatus as quickly as possible. I dashed past him and gained access to the stairs to the balcony and loges. Members of the audience were walking down, and as I started up the stairs, weaving between them, they grumbled at me for lack of manners, and apparently not because they identified me as the performer who had just so spectacularly failed before them. The anonymity of failure is sudden.

Every step I took was harder to complete. My breath was rattling in my throat, and I could feel my heart pounding as if I had just run a mile uphill. I have always kept myself fit, and physical exercise has never been much of a problem for me, but suddenly I felt as if I were lame and overweight. By the time I was at the top of only the first short flight of steps I could go no further, and the crowd walking down the stairs was forced to step past me as I leaned on the wrought-iron banisters to catch my breath. I rested for a few seconds, then launched myself up the next flight of steps.

I had taken no more than two steps when I was racked with a terrifying cough, one of such violence that it astounded me. I was at the end of my physical tether. My heart was hammering, blood was thumping rhythmically in my ears, sweat was bursting from me, and the dry, painful cough was one that seemed to evacuate and collapse my chest. It weakened me so greatly that I could barely inhale again, and when I did manage to suck in a little air I coughed again at once, wheezing and racking horribly. I was unable to stay upright, and I slumped forward across the stone steps, while the last few of the theatregoers went past, their boots only inches from my pathetic head. I neither knew nor cared what they thought of me as I lay there.

Wilson eventually found me. He raised me into his arms, and held me like a child while I struggled to regain my breath.

At long last my heart and breathing steadied, and a great chill descended on me. My chest felt like a swollen pustule of pain, and although I was able to prevent myself coughing again each breath was tentatively taken and expelled.

Finally, I managed to say, 'Did you see what happened?'

'Alfred Borden must have got backstage, sir.'

'Not that! I mean what happened when the power failed?'

'I was manning the switching board, Mr Angier. As usual.'

Wilson's place during IN A FLASH is at the back of the stage, invisible to the audience because he is concealed by the backcloth of the screening box. Although he is in contact at every moment with what I am doing he cannot actually see me for most of the illusion.

I gasped out a description of the spectral prestige of myself that I had briefly seen. Wilson seemed puzzled, but immediately offered to run up to the loge itself. He did so, while I lay helplessly and uncomfortably on the cold bare steps. When he returned a minute or two later Wilson said the seats in the top loge had been scattered across the carpeted floor, but otherwise there was nothing unusual about it. I had to accept what he said. I have learned that Wilson is a sharp and reliable assistant.

He got me back down the stairs and on to the stage again. By this time I had recovered sufficiently that I could stand unsupported. I scanned the top loge and the rest of the now empty auditorium, but there was no sign of the prestige.

I had to put the matter out of my mind. Of much more pressing concern was the fact that I had suddenly become physically incapacitated. Every movement was a strain, and the cough felt explosively coiled in my chest, ready to burst out at any moment. Dreading a return of it I deliberately cramped and confined my movements, trying to calm my breathing.

Wilson hired a cab and returned me safely to my hotel, and at once arranged for a message to be sent to Julia. A doctor was summoned, and when he belatedly arrived he carried out a perfunctory examination of me. He declared he could find nothing amiss, so I paid him off and resolved to find another doctor in the morning. I had trouble falling asleep, but I did so in the end.

I awoke this morning feeling stronger, and walked downstairs unaided. Wilson was waiting for me in the hotel foyer, with the news that Julia would be arriving at noon. Meanwhile, he declared that I looked unwell, but I insisted I had started to recover. After breakfast, though, I realised I had little strength in me.

Reluctantly, I have cancelled both of today's performances, and while Wilson has been at the theatre I have penned this account of what happened.

In London   22nd May 1903

At Julia's urging, and on Wilson's advice, I have cancelled the remainder of the Lowestoft booking. Next week's has also gone – this was to be a short season at the Court Theatre in Highgate. I am still undecided what to do about the show at the Astoria in Derby, scheduled for the first week in June.

I am trying to put as good a face as possible on the matter, but in the deepest recess of my heart I am harbouring a secret fear. In short, it is that my ill health might mean I shall never again be able to perform. After Borden's attack on me I have become a semi-invalid.

Counting the man who came to see me in the hotel in Lowestoft, and my own here in London, I have been examined by three doctors. All of them pronounce me well and showing no obvious symptoms of illness. I complain about my breathing, so they listen to my chest and prescribe fresh air. I tell them my heart races when I walk up a flight of stairs, and they listen to my heart and they tell me to be careful about what I eat, and to take things more slowly. I say that I tire easily, and they advise me to rest and to go to bed early.

My regular doctor in London took a sample of my blood, because I demanded that he should make some objective test, if only to quieten my fears. He duly reported that my blood was unusually 'thin', that such a condition was not unusual in a man of my age, and he prescribed an iron tonic.

After the doctor had left I took the simple step of weighing myself, with an astonishing result.

I appear to have lost nearly thirty pounds in weight. I have weighed more or less exactly twelve stone, one hundred and sixty-eight pounds, for most of my adult years. It is just one of those things in life that has remained constant. This morning I found that I weigh just over one hundred and thirty-nine pounds, or a fraction under ten stone.

In the mirror I look the same as ever. My face is no thinner, my eyes are not bloodshot, my cheekbones do not jut, my jaw is not angular. I look tired, indeed, and there is a sallow quality to my skin that is not customary, but I do not look like someone who cannot climb a short flight of stairs without gasping for breath halfway up. Nor do I look like someone who has just lost nearly a sixth of his normal weight.

There being no normal or logical reason for this, it must have been caused by the incomplete Tesla transmission. The first shock of it had taken place. Following this, the electrical information was only partially sent. Borden's interruption came before the second shock occurred, preventing full reassembly at either end.

Once again his intervention has taken me to the edge of death!

Later
Julia has declared herself to be on a mission to restore my strength by fattening me up, and lunch today was substantial. However, halfway through I felt tired and nauseated, and was unable to finish. I have just been taking a short nap.

On waking, I was seized by an idea, whose consequences I am still thinking through.

In the confidentiality of these pages let me disclose that whenever I have used the Tesla apparatus, whether it be in performance or rehearsal, I have always made sure to secrete two or three gold coins in my pocket. Why I should do so must be self-evident. My recent acquisition of a financial fortune is not solely attributable to performance fees.

Tesla, I should in all conscience report, warned me against such an act. He is a highly moral man, and he lectured me long on the subject of forgery. He said he also had scientific reasons, that the apparatus was calibrated for my known body-weight (with certain margins of safety), and that the presence about my person of small but massy objects, such as gold coins, could make the projection inaccurate over longer distances.

Because I trust Tesla's scientific knowledge, at first I decided to take only paper money through with me, but in doing so I created the inevitable difficulty of duplicate serial numbers. I still carry a few high denomination notes at every performance, but in most cases I have preferred to carry gold. I have never encountered any of the problems of inaccuracy of which Tesla warned, perhaps because the distances I travel are so short.

This afternoon, after my nap, I searched for the three coins I had been carrying in my pocket on Tuesday evening. As soon as I held them I felt certain they weighed less than they did before, and when I placed them on my office balance, comparing them with otherwise identical coins that had not been through the transmitter, I discovered they were in fact lighter.

I calculate that they too have lost about seventeen per cent of their mass. They look the same, they have the same dimensions as ordinary coins, they even make the same ringing sound when dropped on a stone floor, but somehow or other they have lost some of their *weight*.

29th May 1903

The week has shown no improvement. I remain debilitated. Although I am well, in that I have no fever, no apparent injuries, no pain, no sickness, in spite of all this as soon as I make any physical effort I am overtaken with fatigue. Julia continues to try to feed me back to health, but I have made only a marginal gain in weight. We both pretend I am improving, but in doing so we are denying what is obvious to us both – I shall never recover the part of me that has gone.

In this enforced physical languor my mind continues to work normally, which adds to the frustration.

Reluctantly, but on the advice of everyone close to me, I have cancelled all future bookings. To distract myself I have been running the Tesla apparatus, and passing through it a quantity of gold. I am not greedy, and I do not wish to draw unwelcome attention to myself by becoming excessively wealthy. I need only enough money to ensure the long term well-being of myself and my family. At the end of each session I weigh each coin carefully, but all is well.

Tomorrow, we return to Caldlow House.

In Derbyshire 18th July 1903

The Great Danton is dead. The demise of the illusionist Rupert Angier came as a result of injuries sustained when a trick went wrong during a performance at the Pavilion Theatre in Lowestoft. He died at his home in Highgate, London, and leaves a widow and three children.

The 14th Earl of Colderdale remains alive, if not in the rudest of health. He has had the mixed pleasure of reading his own obituary in *The Times*, a privilege not granted to many. Of course the obituary was unsigned, but I was able to deduce that it had not been written by Borden. The assessment of my career is naturally shown in a fair and positive light, but in addition I detect no jealousy, no undercurrent of subtle resentment, usually perceptible on these occasions when a rival is invited to record the passing of one of his colleagues. I am relieved that Borden was not involved in this at least.

Rupert Angier's affairs are now in the hands of a firm of lawyers. He is of course really dead, and his body was really placed inside the coffin. This I saw as Angier's last illusion: the provision of his own corpse for burial. Julia is officially his widow, and his children are orphans. They were all present at Highgate Cemetery for his funeral, a ceremony kept strictly to his immediate family. The press stayed away at the personal request of the widow, and no fans or admirers were seen on the day.

On that same day I was myself travelling back anonymously to Derbyshire with Adam Wilson and his family. He and Gertrude have agreed to remain with me as paid companions. I am able to reward them well.

Julia and the children arrived back here three days later. For the time being she is the widow Angier, but as we fade from people's recollections she will quietly become, as is her right, Lady Colderdale.

I thought I had grown familiar with surviving my own death, but this time I have done it in a way that I can never repeat. Because I can not go back to the stage, and because I am now in the rôle that my elder brother had previously denied me, I find myself wondering how I am to fill the days that lie ahead.

After the disagreeable shock of what happened to me in Lowestoft, I have settled down to what has become my new existence. I am not in decline, and my condition remains stable. I have little physical energy or strength, but I do not seem likely to drop dead suddenly. The doctor here repeats what I was told in London: there is nothing apparently the matter with me that good food, exercise and a positive outlook will not cure in time.

So I find myself taking up the life I had briefly planned after I returned from Colorado. There is much to attend to in the house and around the estate, and because nothing has been run properly for years much of it is in decay. Fortunately, for once my family has the financial wherewithal to tackle some of the most serious problems.

I have had Wilson erect the Tesla apparatus in the basement, telling him that from time to time I shall be rehearsing IN A FLASH in preparation for my return to the stage. Its real use is, of course, otherwise.

19th September 1903

Merely to record that today is the day I had originally planned for the death of Rupert Angier. It has passed like all the others, quietly and (given my continuing restlessness about my health) peacefully.

3rd November 1903

I am recovering from an attack of pneumonia. It nearly got me! I have been in Sheffield Royal Infirmary since the end of September, and I survived only by a miracle. Today is the first day at home where I have been able to sit up long enough to write. The moors look splendid through my window.

30th November 1903

Recovering.

I am almost back to the condition I was in when I returned here from London. That is to say, officially well, unofficially not too good.

15th December 1903

Adam Wilson came to my reading room at half past ten this morning, and informed me a visitor was waiting downstairs to see me. It was Arthur Koenig! I stared at his calling card in surprise, wondering what he wanted. 'Tell him I'm not available for the moment,' I said to Adam, and I went to my study to think.

Could his visit be something to do with my funeral? The faking of my own death had a deceptive side to it that I suspect could be construed as illegal, even though I can't imagine what harm might befall anyone else as a consequence. But the fact that Koenig was here at all meant he knew the funeral had been a sham. Was he going to try to blackmail me in some way? I still do not fully trust Mr Koenig, nor do I understand his motives.

I let him wait downstairs for fifteen minutes, then asked Adam to bring him up.

Koenig appeared to be in a serious mood. After we had greeted each other, I sat him down in one of the easy chairs facing my desk. The first thing he said was to assure me that his visit was unconnected with his job on the newspaper.

'I'm here as an emissary, my Lord,' he said. 'I'm acting in my private capacity for a third party who knows of my interest in the world of magic, and who has asked me to approach your wife.'

'Approach Julia?' I said, in genuine surprise. 'Why should you have anything to say to her?'

Koenig was looking distinctly uncomfortable.

'Your wife, my Lord, is the widow of Rupert Angier. It is in that guise that I have been commissioned to approach her. But I thought, bearing in mind what has happened in the past, it would be wisest to come to you first.'

'What's going on, Koenig?'

He had brought with him a small leather case, and he now picked this up and laid it on his lap.

'The . . . third party for whom I'm acting has come across a notebook, a private memoir, in which it is felt your wife would have an interest. In particular, it is hoped that Lady Colderdale, that is, Mrs Angier, might wish to purchase it. This, er, third party is not aware that you, my Lord, are still alive, and so I find myself not only betraying the person who is sending me on this task, but also the person to whom I should be speaking. But I really felt, under the circumstances—'

'Whose notebook is it?'

'It is Alfred Borden's own.'

'Do you have it with you?'

'Of course I do.'

Koenig reached down into the case, and produced a cloth-bound notebook of the sort that comes equipped with a lockable clasp. He handed it to me so that I might examine it, but because it was locked I could not see what was inside. When I looked back at Koenig he was holding the key.

'My . . . client requires five hundred pounds, sir.'

'Is it genuine?'

'Most assuredly. You would have to read only a few lines to be convinced of that.'

'But is it worth five hundred pounds?'

'I suspect you will think it worth rather more. It is written in Borden's own hand, and deals directly with the secrets of his magic. He elaborates his theory of magic, and explains how many of his tricks are done. The concealment of life as twins is alluded to. I found it a most interesting read, and I can guarantee you will too.'

I turned the book in my hand, wondering about it.

'Who is your client, Koenig? Who wants the money?' He looked uneasy, clearly not practised in this sort of thing. 'You say you have already betrayed your client. Do you suddenly have scruples?'

'There's a lot to this, my Lord. From your manner I suspect you have not already heard the main news I am bringing. Are you aware that Borden himself has recently died?' No doubt my startled expression gave him the answer he required. 'To be precise, I believe one of the two brothers is dead.'

'You sound unsure,' I said. 'Why?'

'Because there's no conclusive proof. You and I both know how obsessively the Bordens concealed their lives, so it's no surprise that the survivor would do the same when his brother dies. The trail has been hard to follow.'

'Then how do you know about it at all? Oh, I see . . . this third party who has commissioned you.'

'And there is circumstantial evidence.'

'Such as?' I prompted.

'The famous illusion is no longer included in Le Professeur's act. I have been to his shows several times in the last six weeks, and not once has he performed it.'

'There could be many reasons for that,' I observed. 'I've been to his show several times, and he does not always include that trick.'

'Indeed not. But it would most likely be because both brothers are required to perform it.'

'I think you should tell me the name of your client, Koenig.'

'My Lord, I believe you once knew an American woman by the name of Olive Wenscombe?'

I have written the name here as I now realise he said it, but in the surprise of the moment I thought he said 'Olivia Svenson'. Because of this a misunderstanding arose between us. At first I thought we were both speaking of the same person, then when he clarified the name I thought that he was talking about someone else. Finally I remembered that Olivia had taken her mother's maiden name when she approached Borden.

'For reasons you must surely appreciate,' I said when all this had been cleared up, 'I never speak of Miss Svenson.'

'Yes, yes. And I apologise for mentioning her. However, she is deeply bound up in the matter of the notebook. I understand that Miss Wenscombe, or Svenson as you knew her, was in your employ some years ago, but she defected to the Borden camp. For a while she worked as Borden's stage assistant, but not for long. You lost contact with her, I think, around this time.'

I confirmed that that was so.

'It turns out,' Koenig continued, 'that the Borden twins own a secret hideout in North London. To be precise it is a suite of rooms in a well-to-do part of Hornsey, and it was here that one of the brothers lived incognito while the other enjoyed the comforts of home in St Johns Wood. They alternated regularly. After her . . . defection, Miss Wenscombe was installed in the Hornsey flat, and has been living there ever since. And will go on doing so if the court proceedings against her fail.'

'Proceedings?'

I was having trouble taking in all this information at once.

Koenig went on, 'She has been served with notice to quit for non-payment of rent, and is due to be evicted next week. As a foreign national with no permanent abode she would then be faced with deportation. It was for these reasons that she came to me, knowing my interest in Mr Borden. She thought I might be able to help her.'

'By approaching me on her behalf for money.'

Koenig grimaced unhappily. 'Not exactly, but—'

'Continue.'

'You'll be interested to learn that Miss Wenscombe was not aware that there were two brothers, and to this day refuses to believe that she was deceived.'

'I asked her myself once,' I said, remembering the grim interview with her in the theatre in Richmond. 'She said then that Borden was just one man. She knew my suspicions. But I can hardly believe that now.'

'The Borden brother who died was taken ill while in the Hornsey flat. It sounds as if he had a heart attack. Miss Wenscombe summoned Borden's doctor, and after the body had been taken away the police came round. When she told them who the dead man was they left to make further enquiries, but never returned. She later contacted the doctor, to discover that he was not available. His assistant told her that Mr Borden had been taken ill, but had recovered quickly and had just been discharged from hospital. As Miss Wenscombe had been with him when he died, she could not believe it. She went to the police again, but to her amazement they too confirmed it.

'I heard all this from Miss Wenscombe herself. Now, from what she told me, she has no idea that Borden was maintaining a second household. He completely pulled the wool over her eyes. As far as she was concerned, Borden was with her most days and nights, and she always knew where he was at other times.' Koenig was leaning forward intently in his chair as he regaled me with his story. 'So then Borden died suddenly, and she was shocked and upset as anyone in her position would be, but she had no reason to believe there was going to be anything unusual about it. And he did most certainly die, according to her. She says she was with the body for more than an hour before the doctor arrived, and it had gone cold by then. The doctor examined the body enough to confirm death, and said that he would sign a death certificate on his return to his surgery. Yet now she is faced not only with denials from everyone involved, but also with the incontrovertible fact that Alfred Borden appears on the public stage, performing his magic, and is visibly, emphatically not dead.'

'If she thinks that Borden was only one man, how on earth does she account for that?' I interjected.

'I asked her, of course. As you know, she is no stranger to the world of illusions. She told me that after much thought she came to the sorrowful conclusion that Borden had used magical techniques to fake his death, for instance swallowing some kind of medication, and that it was all an elaborate charade to enable him to walk out on her.'

'Did you tell her that the Bordens were twins?'

'Yes. She scoffed at the idea, and assured me that if a woman lives with a man for five years she knows everything there is to know about him. She absolutely rejected the notion that there might have been two of them.'

(I had earlier raised my own questions about the Borden twins' relationship with his/their wife and children. These now take on an added level of enquiry. It seems the mistress was also deceived, but is unwilling to admit that she was, or simply never knew.)

'So this notebook has suddenly appeared, to solve all her problems,' I said.

Koenig stared at me thoughtfully, then said, 'Not all of them, but her most immediate ones. My Lord, I think that as a gesture of my good faith, I should let you examine the notebook without promise of payment.'

He passed the key across to me, and sat back in his chair while I opened the lock.

The notebook was written in a tiny hand, neatly inscribed in regular and even lines, but not at first glance legible. After I had looked at the opening pages I began to riffle through the rest as if running my fingers across the edges of a deck of cards. My magician's instinct was telling me to be on my guard against Borden's trickery. All those years of feuding had revealed the extent of his willingness to hurt or harm me. I had turned through about half the thickness of the notebook, when I halted. I stared at it, deep in thought.

This could be Borden's most elaborate attack on me yet. Koenig's story about Olivia, the death of Borden in her flat, the conveniently revealed existence of a notebook containing Borden's most valuable professional secrets, all these could be fabricated.

I had only Koenig's word to go on. What would the notebook actually contain, if it were another trick? An intricate maze of deceits which would manipulate me into some misguided response? Could there be something here that would, through the person of Olivia Svenson, threaten my one remaining area of stability, namely my miraculously restored marriage to Julia?

It seemed to me that I was putting myself in hazard, even to hold the notebook.

Koenig's voice interrupted my thoughts.

'Dare I presume, my Lord, that I can guess what is going through your mind?'

'No, you may not so presume,' I said.

'You are doubting me,' Koenig persisted. 'You think that Borden has paid me, or coerced me in some way, to bring this to you. Is that so?' I made no answer, still holding the notebook half open, my eyes staring down at it.

'There are ways you could investigate what I am telling you,' Koenig went on. 'A court action against Miss Wenscombe by the landlord of the apartment in Hornsey was heard at Hampstead Assizes a month ago. You could examine the court records for yourself. There are almoner's records at the Whittington Hospital, where an unidentified victim of a heart attack, with age and physical appearance matching that of Borden, was brought in on the day Miss Wenscombe says he died. There is also a record that that corpse was removed by a local doctor on the same day.'

'Koenig, you sent me on a trail of false evidence ten years ago,' I said.

'I did indeed. I have never ceased to regret it, and have already told you that my dedication to your cause is the result of that error. I give you my word that the notebook is genuine, that the circumstances of it coming into my possession are as I have described, and that furthermore the surviving Borden brother is desperate to regain it.'

'How has it escaped him?' I said.

'Miss Wenscombe realised its potential value, perhaps as something that might be published as a book. When her need for money became urgent, she thought it might be more valuable to you or, as she understood recent events, to your widow. Naturally, she kept the notebook hidden. Borden himself can not of course approach her for it, but it surely is not a coincidence that ten days ago her flat was forcibly entered and the place ransacked? Nothing was taken. This notebook, which she had secreted elsewhere, remained in her possession.'

I opened the notebook where my finger had come to rest, reflecting that the act of running my fingertips along the gilt-edged pages had been identical to the forcing of a playing-card by a conjuror on a subject. This thought was reinforced when I looked at a line halfway down the right-hand page, and saw my own name written there. It was as if Borden had forced the page on me.

I peered closely at the handwriting, and soon deciphered what the rest of the sentence said: '*This is the real reason Angier will never solve the whole mystery, unless I myself give him the answer.*'

'She wants five hundred pounds, you say?'

'Yes, my Lord.'

'She shall have it.'

Koenig's visit exhausted me, and soon after he left (with six hundred pounds, the surplus being partly for his trouble to date, and partly for his silence and absence henceforth) I took to my bed where I remained until the evening. I wrote up my account of it then, but the next day and the day after I was too debilitated to attempt more than a little eating and a lot of sleeping.

Yesterday I was able at last to read some of Borden's notebook. As Koenig had predicted, I found it an engrossing read.

I have been showing extracts to Julia, who finds it equally interesting. She reacts more against his self-satisfied tone than I do, and urges me not to burn up any of my precious energy by getting angry with him again.

Anger, in fact, is not being kindled in me, although the way he distorts some of the events of which I have a knowledge is both pitiable and irritating. What is most fascinating to me is that at last I have proof that 'Alfred Borden' was the product of a conspiracy between twins. Nowhere do they admit it, but the notebook is clearly the work of two hands.

They address each other in the first person singular. I found this confusing at first, as perhaps was intended, but when I pointed it out to Julia she observed that they apparently did not expect anyone else to read it.

It suggests that they call each other 'me' by habit, and this in turn implies they have done it for most of their lives. Reading between the lines of the notebook, as I must, I realise that every event or happening in their lives has been subsumed into one collective experience. It is as if they spent their lives from childhood preparing for the illusion where one would secretly take the place of the other. It fooled me, and fooled most of the audiences who saw them in performance, but surely in the end it is Borden who is the fool?

Two lives made into one means a halving of those lives. While one lives in the world, the other hides in a nether world, literally non-existent, a lurking spirit, a *doppelgänger*, a prestige.

More tomorrow, if I have the energy.

25th December 1903

The house and grounds are cut off by the heavy falls of snow that have swept through the Pennines for the last two days. We are however warm and provisioned, and not in need of going anywhere. We have taken our Christmas dinner, and now the children are playing with their new possessions, and Julia and I have been relaxing together.

I have not told her yet of a worrying ailment, newly arrived on my poor body. Several purplish sores have broken out on my chest, upper arms and thighs, and although I have spread them with antiseptic ointment they are as yet showing no sign of recession. As soon as the thaw sets in I shall have to summon the physician again.

31st December 1903

The doctor has advised me to continue with the antiseptic medication, which at last shows some indication of being effective. He observed to Julia before he left that these unpleasant and painful eruptions on the skin might be a symptom of a more serious organic or blood-related problem. Julia gently bathes the sores every night before we go to bed. I have been continuing to lose weight, although in recent days that has been slowing.

A Happy New Year!

1st January 1904

I mark the turning of the new year with the grim reflection that I doubt if I shall last to the end of it.

I have been distracting myself from my own troubles by reading the Borden notebook. I have read it through to the end, and I confess I have been absorbed by it. I find it impossible not to make notes about his methods, views, omissions, errors, self-deceptions, etc.

Much as I hate and fear Borden (and I cannot forget that

he is alive and active somewhere in the world outside), I find his views on magic provocative and stimulating.

I have mentioned this to Julia, who agrees. She does not say as much but I sense she feels, as I am beginning to, that Borden and I might have made better collaborators than adversaries.

26th March 1904

I have been seriously ill, and for at least two weeks believed myself to be on the point of death. The symptoms have been horrific: persistent nausea and vomiting, a further spread of the sores, paralysis of my right leg, a comprehensively ulcerated mouth, and an almost uncontainable pain from my lower back. Needless to say, I have been confined in a nursing home in Sheffield for much of the time.

Now, though, a minor miracle has occurred and I find myself apparently on the mend. The sores and ulcers have cleared up leaving no trace, I am getting some feeling and therefore movement in my leg, and the general sense of pain and malaise is receding. I have been at home for the last week, and although I have been bedridden my spirits have risen a little more every day.

Today I am out of bed and using a reclining chair in the conservatory. I have a view of the grounds, with trees in the distance; beyond those rises the rocky crag of Curbar Edge, where patches of snow still linger. I am in the best of spirits, and I am re-reading Borden's notebook. These last two facts are not unconnected.

6th April 1904

I have read Borden's notes a total of three times, and have annotated and cross-referenced them in detail. Julia is about to prepare a fair copy of my amended and greatly expanded text.

Although the remission from my ailments continues, I must face up to the fact that overall my health is declining. I therefore confess that in these terminal months of my life I am intending to take a last revenge on my enemy. He it was who caused this condition, he it is who must pay. Acquisition of his notebook has given me a way. I am planning to arrange for it to be published.

The literature of magic is not widely available. Many books are written and published, but with the exception of simple books for children, and a few volumes on legerdemain or sleight of hand, these books are not produced by general publishers. They are rarely if ever found in ordinary bookshops. Instead, they are printed by a number of specialist publishers, for distribution only within the magic community. They often appear in editions as short as four or five dozen copies, and are commensurately expensive. Acquiring a collection of such books is difficult and costly, and many magicians can only obtain copies when one of their colleagues dies and his collection is sold off by his family. Over the years I have amassed a small library of my own, and I have referred to these books constantly so that I might use or adapt existing illusions. In this I am no different from other magicians. The readership of such books is small, but it is one of the most concentrated and informed audiences imaginable.

While I was reading Borden's notebook it frequently occurred to me that it deserved to be published for the benefit of his fellow magicians. It contains much sensible comment on the art and technique of magic. Whatever his intentions might once have been (he declares unconvincingly that his words are intended only for his immediate family, and a 'posterity' he fondly imagines for himself) he cannot ever publish the notebook himself. How careless of him to have mislaid it!

I see it as my last act to arrange publication on his behalf, and when I have completed my annotated edition I shall see to it.

If he survives me, which is likely, he will discover that my revenge is subtle and many-layered.

For a start Borden will be appalled to discover, as he soon will, that what he sees as his greatest professional secrets have been published without his permission. His chagrin will be the deeper when he realises that I was responsible. He will be further confounded when he works out that somehow I was able to do this from beyond the grave. (He believes me already dead, a fact I elicited from the notebook itself.) Finally, should he read the annotated text he will discover the true subtlety of my final revenge.

In short, I have improved his text by making it less obscure, by expanding on many of the interesting general topics which he merely adumbrates, by illustrating his absorbing theory of acquiescence with numerous examples, by describing the methods of many of the great illusionists. I have added detailed descriptions of every trick I know him to have invented, as well as those others I know him to be capable of performing, and in each case have seemed to explain each one without actually revealing the central secret.

Above all, I have heightened the mystery surrounding the illusion he calls THE NEW TRANSPORTED MAN, but have given nothing away. The fact that the Bordens were identical twins is not even hinted at. The secret that obsessed these two men's lives remains a secret.

The surviving Borden will therefore realise that I had the last word, that the feud is over and that I triumphed. While invading his privacy I showed I could respect it. From this I hope he will learn that the enmity he fostered between us was futile and destructive, that while we sniped at each other we were squandering the talents in us both. We should have been friends.

I will leave him this so that he may reflect on it for the remainder of his life.

And there is one extra revenge, by omission. He will never discover the secret of Tesla's apparatus.

25th April 1904

Work on the Borden text goes well.

Last week I wrote to three specialist magic publishers, two in London, one in Worcester. Describing myself as an *amateur* of magic, and suggesting in an unspecified sort of

322

way that over the years I had used my position and wealth to support or sponsor various stage magicians, I explained that I was editing the memoirs of one of our leading illusionists (no name mentioned, at this stage). I asked if, in principle, they would be interested in publishing the book.

Two of them have so far replied. Both letters are non-committal, but encourage me to submit the material. These replies also remind me that I shouldn't have admitted to personal wealth, no matter how elliptically. Each letter implies that the book would be more likely to find favour should I be able to contribute to the publisher's production expenses.

Naturally, this does not these days present me with a problem, but even so Julia and I are awaiting the third response before making any decisions.

18th May 1904

With the work complete, we have submitted the manuscript to the publisher of first choice.

2nd July 1904

I have agreed a publishing deal with Messrs Goodwin & Andrewson, of Old Bailey, London EC.

They will publish Borden's book before the end of this year, in an initial edition of seventy-five copies, at a price of three guineas each. They promise abundant illustration, and intensive advertisement by personal letter to their regular clientele. I have acceded to the defrayment of one hundred pounds towards printing costs. Now that Mr Goodwin has read the manuscript he has put forward several novel ideas for presentation.

4th July 1904

Over the last four weeks my remission has ended, and the earlier illness has returned in force. First came the purplish weals, then a day or two later the ulceration of mouth and throat. Three weeks ago I became blind in one eye; the other followed a day or two later. For the last week I have been unable to keep down solid food, but Julia brings me a mild broth three times a day and that is keeping me alive. I am in such pain that I cannot raise my head from the pillow. The doctor calls twice daily, but says that I am too weak to be transferred to hospital. My symptoms are so distressing that I am unable to describe them in detail, but the doctor explains that for some reason all my body's natural immunity to infection has been damaged. He has confided in Julia (and she subsequently in me) that if my chest becomes infected again I will not have the strength to resist.

5th July 1904

I had an uncomfortable night, and as dawn broke this morning I believed that I had reached my last day on this earth. It is, however, now approaching midnight and I am clinging on.

I started to cough early this evening, and the doctor came directly to see me. He suggested bathing with cool towels, and they have helped make me more comfortable. I am unable to move any part of my body.

6th July 1904

At a quarter to three this morning my life was brought to its end by a sudden seizure of the heart, following a spasm of coughing and consequent internal bleeding.

My dying was protracted, painful, messy and profoundly distressing to Julia and my children, as well as to myself. We were all shocked by the wretchedness of dying, and have been greatly subdued by the event.

Death uniquely surrounds my life!

Once, in harmless deception, I pretended to die so that Julia might live without scandal as a widow. Every use of the Tesla apparatus later brought death to my experience, several times a week. When Rupert Angier was laid falsely to rest I was alive to bear witness to it.

I have cheated death many times. Death has therefore acquired a sense of unreality for me. It has come to be a commonplace event that by some paradox, it seems, I can always survive.

Now I have seen myself on my deathbed, dying of multiple cancers, and afterwards, after that vile and painful death, I am here to report it in my diary. Wednesday, 6th July 1904: the day I died.

No man should be so wretched as to have to see what I have beheld.

Later
I have borrowed a technique from Borden, so that I am I as well as myself.

I who write this am not the same as the I who died.

We became two entities that night in Lowestoft, when Borden caused the malfunctioning of the Tesla apparatus. Two lives, two Rupert Angiers. We went our separate ways. We have been together again since I returned to Caldlow House at the end of March, just as my temporary remission from the cancers began.

While I yet lived, I maintained the illusion that I was one. One of me lay dying, while the other of me recorded my final concerns. All entries in this journal since 26th March have been written by me.

We are each the prestige of the other.

My dead prestige lies downstairs in his open casket, and will be placed in the family vault in two days' time. I, his living prestige, continue onward.

I am the Right Honourable Rupert David Angier, 14th Earl of Colderdale, husband to Julia, father to Edward, Lydia and Florence, Lord of Caldlow House in the County of Derbyshire, England.

I shall narrate my story tomorrow. The events of the day have left me, like everyone else in the household, too forlorn for anything but sadness.

7th July 1904
The remainder of my life begins on this day. What hopes can be entertained by one such as I? The following is my story.

I

I came into being on the evening of 19th May 1903, in an unoccupied loge that overlooked the stalls of the Pavilion Theatre in Lowestoft. My life began as I balanced precariously on the wooden rail, from which I immediately fell backwards. I crashed to the floor of the loge, scattering the chairs.

My preoccupation was the terrified thought which had sprung into my mind an instant before: that Borden had somehow found his way up to the loge and was waiting for me. Clearly not! As I floundered between the loge chairs, trying to orientate myself physically, I realised that although Borden had sabotaged the apparatus in some way, it had worked sufficiently for the transportation to have been completed. Borden was not here.

Bright light flooded into the loge, as the spot was turned on it. No more than two or three seconds had elapsed. I thought: there is still a chance to save the illusion! I can crawl back to the rail, make something of it!

I rolled over, got to my hands and knees, and was about to clamber up to the rail when to my amazement I heard a voice on the stage calling for the curtain to be rung down. I moved forward, keeping my head down, and peered down at the stage. The tabs were already dropping, but before they blocked my view I briefly saw myself, my prestige!, immobile on the stage.

Built into the base of the Tesla apparatus is a compartment into which the prestige automatically falls as the transformation takes place. My old body, the prestige, is therefore concealed from the audience so as to give maximum impact to the illusion.

This time, Borden's intervention must have prevented the compartment from functioning, leaving the prestige in full view!

I thought quickly. Adam Wilson and Hester were both

backstage, and would have to deal with the emergency there behind the curtain. I was alive, strong and in full possession of my senses. I realised it was my responsibility to get to the backstage area, and confront Borden once and for all.

I let myself out of the loge, hurried along the corridor, then took the stairs at a run.

I passed one of the female attendants. I skidded to a halt in front of her, and said as urgently as I could, 'Have you seen anyone trying to leave the theatre?'

My voice came out as a harsh whisper!

The woman, staring straight at me, screamed in horror. I stood there helplessly for a moment, deafened by the terrible yell she was emitting. She drew breath, her eyes popping and rolling, then she screamed again. I realised I was wasting time, so I laid my hand on her arm to push her gently to one side. My hand sank into the flesh of her arm!

She had collapsed on the steps, shuddering and moaning, as I reached the bottom of the stairs and found the door to the backstage area. I shoved it open, recoiling as once again I felt my hands and arms pushing *into* the wood. I was preoccupied with the urgent need to find Borden, and had no time to pay much attention.

Without noticing me, Adam Wilson ran past from his position at the back of the set. I called after him but he heard me no more than he had seen me. I paused for a moment, trying to think clearly about where Borden was most likely to have been. He had somehow interrupted the supply of electricity to the apparatus, and this could only mean that he had gained access to the sub-stage mezzanine. Wilson and I had connected everything up to the terminal the management had newly installed in the basement.

I found the stairs leading down, but as I went on to the top step I heard the sound of feet running heavily towards me. In a moment Borden himself appeared. He was still wearing his ridiculous country-bumpkin clothes and greasepaint. He took the steps two at a time. I froze. When he was no more than five feet away from me he looked up to see where he was going. He saw me instead! Once again, I witnessed the look of terror that had distorted the features of the female attendant. Borden's momentum carried him towards me, but his face was contorted with shock and he stretched out his arms defensively in front of him. Almost at once we collided.

We sprawled together and fell heavily on the stone floor of the corridor. He was briefly on top of me, but I was able to slide out. I reached towards him.

'Stay away from me!' he cried, and crouching forward, stumbling and tripping, he scrambled away.

I dived at him, got my hand around his ankle, but he slipped it from my grasp. He was bellowing wordlessly with fear.

I shouted at him, 'Borden, we must stop this dangerous feud!', but once again my voice came out hoarsely and inaudibly, more breath than tone.

'I didn't mean it!' he cried.

He was on his feet now and getting away from me, still looking back at me with an expression of dread. I gave up the struggle, and let him flee.

2

After that night I returned to London, where I lived for the next ten months, by my own choice and decision, in a half-world.

The accident in the Tesla apparatus had fundamentally affected my body and soul by placing them in opposition to each other. Physically, I had been rendered into a ghost of my former self. I lived, breathed, ate, passed bodily waste, heard and saw, felt warm and cold, but I was physically a wraith. In a bright light, if you did not look too closely at me, I appeared more or less normal, if somewhat wan of aspect. When the weather was overcast, or I was in an artificially lit room after nightfall, I took on the appearance of a spectre. I

328

could be seen but also *seen through*. My outline remained, and if people looked hard enough at me they could make out my face, my clothes, and so on, but I was to most people a hideous vision of the ghostly underworld. The female attendant and Borden had both reacted as if they had seen a ghost, and indeed they had. I quickly learned that if I let myself be noticed in these circumstances, I not only terrorised most of the people whom I encountered, but I put myself in some danger too. People react unpredictably when frightened. Once or twice strangers hurled objects at me, as if to ward me off. One of these missiles was a lighted oil-lamp, and it nearly caught me. As a rule I therefore stayed out of sight when I could.

But against this my mind suddenly felt liberated from the constraints of the body. I was always alert, fast-thinking, positive, in ways I had only ever glimpsed in myself before. One of the paradoxes this produced was that I usually felt strong and capable, whereas the reality was that I was unable to tackle most physical tasks. I had to learn to hold objects like pens and utensils, for example, because a careless grip on something would usually make it slip away from me.

It was a frustrating and morbid situation in which to find myself, and for much of the time my new mental energy was directed as pure loathing and fear at whichever of the two Bordens had attacked me. He continued to sap my mental energy, just as his action had sapped my physical being. I had become to all intents and purposes invisible to the world, as good as dead.

3

It did not take me long to discover that I could be visible or invisible as I chose.

If I moved after dusk, and I wore the stage clothes I had been in during the performance, I could go almost anywhere unseen. If I wanted to move normally then I wore other clothes and used greasepaint to give my features some solidity. It was not a perfect simulation; my eyes had a disconcertingly hollow look, and once a man in a dimly lit omnibus loudly drew attention to the gap that had inexplicably appeared between my sleeve and my glove, and I had to make a quick departure.

Money, food, accommodation presented no problems to me. Either I took what I wanted when in the invisible state, or I paid for what I needed. Such concerns were trivial.

My real consideration was the well-being of my prestige.

I learned from a newspaper report that my fleeting glimpse of the stage had completely misled me. The report stated that The Great Danton had suffered injuries during a performance in Lowestoft, that he had been forced to cancel future engagements, but was resting at home and expected to return to the stage in due course.

I was relieved to hear it but greatly surprised! What I had glimpsed as the curtains came down was what I assumed was my own prestige, frozen in the half-dead, half-live condition I called 'prestigious'. The prestige is the source body in the transportation, left behind in the Tesla apparatus, as if dead. Concealing and disposing of these prestigious bodies was the single greatest problem I had had to solve before I could present the illusion to the public. Every new performance created yet another prestige.

With this news about ill-health and cancelled engagements I realised something different had happened that night. The transportation had been only partial, and I was the sorry result. Most of me had remained behind.

Both I and my prestige were much reduced by Borden's intervention. We each had problems to cope with. I was in a wraithlike condition, my prestige was in debilitated health. While he had corporeality and freedom of movement in the world, from the moment of the accident he was doomed to die; meanwhile, I had been condemned to a life in the shadows, but my health was intact.

In July, two months after Lowestoft, and while I was still

coming to terms with the disaster, my prestige apparently decided of his own accord to bring forward the death of Rupert Angier. It was exactly what I would have done in his position. This was the moment when I realised that he *was* me. It was the first time we had reached an identical decision separately, and my first intimation that although we existed separately we were emotionally but one person.

Soon after, my prestige returned to Caldlow House to take up the inheritance. Again, that is what I would have done.

I, though, remained in London for the time being. I had macabre business to attend to, and I wanted to conduct it in secret with no risk of my actions being attached to the Colderdale name.

In short, I had decided that Borden, finally, must be dealt with. I planned to murder him, or, more exactly, to murder one of the two.

Borden's secret double life made murder a feasible revenge. He had interfered with the official records that revealed the existence of twins, and had lived his life with one half of himself concealed. As only one Borden had legal existence, what would stop me from killing the other? It would finally put an end to their deception, and would for my purposes be as satisfying and effective as killing them both. I also reasoned that in my wraithlike state, and with my only known identity publicly buried and mourned, I, Rupert Angier, could never be caught or even suspected of the crime.

In London, I set my plans in progress. I was able to use my virtual invisibility to follow Borden as he went about his life and affairs. I saw him in his family home, I saw him preparing and rehearsing his stage show in his workshop, I stood unseen in the wings of a theatre as he performed his illusions, I tracked him to the secret lair he shared in north London with Olivia Svenson . . . and once, even, I glimpsed Borden with his twin brother, briefly, furtively meeting in a darkened street, a hurried exchange of information, some desperate business that had to be concluded at once and in person.

It was when I saw him with Olivia that I decided, finally, he must die. Enough feelings remained about that old betrayal to add hurt to the outrage.

Making a decision to commit premeditated murder is the hardest part of the terrible deed, I can reliably say. Often provoked, I believe myself even so to be a mild and reticent man. Although I never want to hurt others, all through my adult life I have frequently found myself swearing I would 'kill' or 'do in' Borden. These oaths, uttered in private, and often in silence, are the common impotent ravings of the wronged victim, the position Borden had so often forced me into.

In those days I had never seriously intended to kill him, but the Lowestoft attack had changed everything. I was reduced to wraithdom, and my other self was wasting away. Borden had in a real way killed us both that night, and I burned for revenge.

The mere thought of killing gave me such satisfaction and excitement that my personality changed. I, who was beyond death, lived to kill.

Once I had taken the decision, commission of the crime could not be made to wait. I saw the death of one of the Borden twins as the key to my own freedom.

But I had no experience of violence, and before I could do anything I had to decide how best to go about it. I wanted a *modus operandi* that would be immediate and personal, one in which Borden, as he helplessly died, would realise who was killing him and why. By a simple process of elimination I decided I would have to stab him. Again, imagining the prospect of such a terrible act raised a heady thrill of anticipation in me.

I justified stabbing thus: poison was too slow and dangerous to administer, and it was anyway impersonal, a shooting was noisy, and again it lacked close personal contact. I was more or less incapable of acts of physical strength, so anything that involved this, such as clubbing or strangling, was not possible. I found, by experiment, that if I held a long-bladed knife in both hands, firmly but not

332

tightly, then I could slide it with sufficient force to penetrate flesh.

4

Two days after I had completed my preparations I followed Borden to the Queen's Theatre in Balham, where he was top of the week's variety bill. The day was a Wednesday, when there was a matinée performance as well as one in the evening. I knew it was Borden's habit to retire to his dressing-room between shows for a nap on his couch.

I watched his performance from the darkened wings, then afterwards followed him along the gloomy backstage corridors and staircases to his dressing-room. When he was inside with the door closed, and the general backstage turmoil had quietened a little, I went to where I had secreted my murder weapon. I returned cautiously to the corridor outside Borden's room, moving from one darkened corner to the next only when I was certain no one was about.

I was wearing the stage clothes from Lowestoft, my habitual apparel when I wished to move unobserved, but the knife was a normal one. If I had been seen by anyone it would have looked as if the knife were floating along unsupported in the air.

Outside Borden's room, I made myself stand quietly in a shadowy alcove opposite, calming my breathing, trying to control the racing of my heart. I counted slowly to two hundred.

After another check that no one was approaching I went to the door and leaned against it, pressing my face gently but firmly into the wood. In a few seconds the front part of my head had passed through, and I was able to see into the room. Only one lamp was alight, casting a dim glow through the small, untidy room. Borden was lying on his couch, his eyes closed, his hands clasped together on his chest.

I withdrew my face.

Clasping the knife I opened the door and went inside. Borden stirred, and looked towards me. I closed the door, and pushed home the bolt.

'Who's that?' Borden said, narrowing his eyes.

I was not there to bandy words with him. I took two steps across the narrow floor, then leaped up on to the couch and crawled on top of him. I squatted on his stomach, and raised the knife in both hands.

Borden saw the knife, then focused on me. In the dim light I was just visible. I could see my arms outlined as I sat over him, the blade trembling above his chest. I must have been a wild and dreadful sight. I had been unable to shave or cut my hair for more than two months, and my face was gaunt. I was terrified and desperate. I was sitting on his abdomen. I was holding a knife, preparing for the deadly thrust.

'What are you?' Borden gasped. He had taken hold of my spectral wrists, trying to hold me back, but it was a simple matter to work myself free of him. 'Who—?'

'Prepare to die, Borden!' I shouted, knowing that what he would hear was the hoarse and horrifying whisper that was all I could produce.

'Angier? Please! I had no idea what I was doing! I meant no harm!'

'Was it you who did it? Or was it the other?'

'What do you mean?'

'Was it you or your twin brother?'

'I have no brother!'

'You are about to die! Tell me the truth! This is your last chance!'

'I am alone!'

'Too late!' I shouted, and I deliberately set my hands in the grip I had learned would give me the strongest grasp on the knife. I would lose the hold if I stabbed too savagely, so I brought the blade down to a place above his heart and began the steady pressure I knew would take the blade through to its target. I felt the fabric of his shirt slit open, and the knife point pressed down into his flesh.

Then I saw the expression on Borden's face. He was transfixed with fear of me. His hands were somewhere above my head, trying to get a grip on me. His jaw had fallen open, his tongue was jutting forward, saliva was running out of each corner of his mouth and down his jowls. His chest was convulsing with his frantic breathing.

No words came out of his mouth, but he was trying to speak. I heard the hiss and splutter of a man drowning in his own terror.

I realised that he was not a strong man any more. His hair was streaked with grey. The skin around his eyes was wrinkled with fatigue. His neck was lined. He lay beneath me, fighting for his life against an insubstantial daemon who had come to squat on his body with a knife ready to slay him.

The thought repulsed me. I could not take murder through to its conclusion. I could not kill like this.

All the fear, anger and tension poured away from me.

I threw the knife aside, and rolled adroitly off. I backed away from him, now defenceless and in my turn petrified of what he might do.

He remained on the couch, where he continued to rasp his breath painfully, shuddering with horror and relief. I stood there submissively, mortified by the effect I had had on the man.

Finally, he steadied.

'Who are you?' he said, his frightened voice uneven, breaking into falsetto on the last word.

'I am Rupert Angier,' I replied hoarsely.

'But you are dead!'

'Yes.'

'Then how——?'

I said, 'We should never have started this, Borden. But killing you is not the way to end it.'

I was humbled by the awfulness of what I had been trying to do, and the basic sense of decency that had ruled my life until this point was returning in force. How could I ever have imagined that I could kill a man in cold blood? I turned away from Borden sorrowfully, and forced myself against the wooden door. As I passed through slowly I heard him make his yelping rasp of horror once again.

5

I was thrown into a fit of despair and self-disgust by my attempt on Borden's life. I knew I had betrayed myself, betrayed my prestige (who was aware of none of my actions), betrayed Julia, my children, my father's name, every friend I had known. If ever I needed proof that my feud with Borden was an appalling mistake, at last I had it. Nothing we had done to each other in the past could justify such a descent into brutality.

In a state of wretchedness and apathy I returned to the room I had rented, thinking there was no more I could do with my life. I had nothing more for which to live.

6

I planned to waste away and die, but there is a spirit of life, even in one such as myself, that stands in the way of such decisions. I thought that if I did not eat and drink then death would simply follow, but in practice I found that thirst becomes such a frantic obsession that it takes a greater resolve than mine to resist it. Every time I took a few drops to slake it, I postponed my demise a little more. The same was true with food. Hunger is a monster.

After a while I came to an accommodation with this and stayed alive, a pathetic denizen of a half-world that was as much of my own making as it had been of Borden's, or so I came to believe.

I went through the winter in this miserable state, a failure even at self-destruction.

During February I felt something profound growing in me. At first I thought it was an intensification of the loss I had felt since Lowestoft, the fact that I was never able to see Julia or the children. I had denied myself this, believing that on balance my need to be with them was outweighed by the horrific effect my appearance would have. As the months slipped by, this sadness had become a horrible ache in me, but I could detect nothing around me that made it suddenly grow in the way it had.

It was when I thought of the life of my other self, the prestige left behind me after Lowestoft, that I felt a sense of sharp focus. I knew at once he was in trouble.

There had been an accident to him of some kind, or he was being threatened (perhaps by one of the Bordens?), or even that his health had deteriorated more quickly than I had expected. He was ill, dying even. I had to be with him, help him in whatever way I could.

By this time I was myself no great figure of physical strength. In addition to the attenuated body the accident had given me, my poor diet and lack of exercise had made me into a virtual skeleton. I rarely moved from my sordid room, and did so only at night when no one could see me. I knew that I had become hideous to behold, a veritable ghoul in every sense. The prospect of the long journey to Derbyshire seemed fraught with dangerous possibilities.

I therefore embarked on a conscious effort to improve my appearance. I began to take food and drink in reasonable quantities, I hacked at my long and dishevelled hair and stole a new set of clothes. Several weeks of care would be necessary to restore me even to my appearance after Lowestoft, but I did start feeling better almost at once, and my spirits rose.

Against this was the knowledge that the pain being suffered by my prestige was almost unendurable.

Everything was heading ineluctably towards my return to the family home, and in the last week of March I bought a ticket for the overnight train to Sheffield.

337

7

I knew only one thing about the impact of my return home. My sudden appearance would not surprise the part of me that I called my prestige.

I arrived at Caldlow House in mid-morning, a bright Spring day, and in the unwavering sunlight my physical appearance was at its most substantial. Even so, I knew I cut a surprising figure, because during my short daytime journey from Sheffield station by cab, omnibus and then cab again I had drawn many an inquisitive look from passers-by. I had grown used to this in London, but Londoners are themselves accustomed to seeing the city's stranger denizens. Here in the provinces a skeletal man in dark clothes and large hat, with unnatural complexion, raggedly cut hair and weirdly hollow eyes, was an object of curiosity and alarm.

At the house I went and hammered on the door. I could have let myself in, but I had no idea what I should expect to find. I felt it best to take my unheralded return one step at a time.

Hutton opened the door.

I removed my hat, and stood plainly before him. He had begun to speak before he looked properly at me but he was silenced as he saw me. He stared wordlessly, his face impassive. I knew him well enough to realise that his silence revealed his consternation.

When I had given him time to accept who I might be, I said, 'Hutton, I'm pleased to see you again.'

He opened his mouth to speak, but nothing came.

'You must know what occurred in Lowestoft, Hutton,' I said. 'I am the unfortunate consequence of that.'

'Yes, sir,' he said at last.

'May I come in?'

'Should I advise Lady Colderdale you are here, sir?'

'I should like to speak to you quietly before I see her, Hutton. I know my arrival here is likely to cause alarm.'

He took me to his sitting room beside the kitchen, and he gave me a cup of tea from a pot he had just been making. I sipped it while I stood before him, not knowing how to explain. Hutton, a man I had always admired for his presence of mind, soon took control of the situation.

'I think it best, sir,' he said, 'if you would wait here while I take it upon myself to announce your arrival to her ladyship. She will then, I believe, come to see you. You may best decide how to proceed together.'

'Hutton, tell me. How is my—? I mean, how is the health of—?'

'His lordship has been gravely ill, sir. However, the prognosis is excellent and he has returned this week from hospital. He is convalescing in the garden room, where we have moved his bed. I believe her ladyship is with him at this moment.'

'This is an impossible situation, Hutton,' I ventured.

'It is, sir.'

'For you in particular, I mean.'

'For me and for you, and for everyone, sir. I understand what happened in that theatre in Lowestoft. His lordship, that is, you, sir, took me into his confidence. You will remember, no doubt, that I have been much involved with the disposal of the prestige materials. There are of course no secrets in this house, my Lord, as you directed.'

'Is Adam Wilson here?'

'Yes, he is.'

'I'm glad to know that.'

A few moments later, Hutton left and after a delay of about five minutes returned with Julia. She looked tired, and her hair was drawn back into a bun. She came straight to me and we embraced warmly enough, but we were both so nervous. I could feel her tensing as we held each other.

Hutton excused himself, and when we were alone together Julia and I assured each other I was not some kind of gruesome impostor. Even I had sometimes doubted my own identity during those long winter months. There is a kind of madness where delusion replaces reality, and many times such a malaise

339

seemed to explain everything; that I had once been Rupert Angier but I was now dispossessed of my own life and only memories remained, or alternatively that I was some other soul who in madness had come to believe he was Angier.

When I got a chance I explained to Julia the limits of my bodily existence. I told her how I would fade from sight without bright light, how I could slip inadvertently through solid objects.

Then she told me of the cancers from which I, my prestige, had been suffering, and how by some miracle they had seemed to recede on their own, allowing me, him, to return home.

'Will he recover completely?' I asked anxiously.

'The surgeon said that recovery sometimes occurs spontaneously, but in most cases a remission is only for a short while. He believes in this case, you, he –' She looked ready to cry, so I took her hand in mine. She steadied herself and spoke sombrely. 'He believes that this is just a temporary reprieve. The cancers are malignant, widespread and multifarious.'

Then she told me the matters that most surprised me. It was from her that I learned Borden, or more accurately one of the Borden twins, had died, and that his notebook had come into my, our, possession.

I was astounded to hear these things. For instance, I learned that Borden had died only three days after my failed attempt on his life.

The two events seemed to me inviolably connected. Julia said it was thought he had suffered a heart attack. I wondered if it could have been brought on by the fear I instilled in him? I remembered his terrible noises of anguish, his laboured breathing, and his general appearance of fatigue and ill-health. I knew that heart seizures could be caused by stress, but until this moment I had supposed that after my departure Borden regained his senses and would eventually have returned to normal.

I confessed my story to Julia but she seemed to think the two events were unconnected.

Even more of interest was the news about Borden's note-book. Julia told me she had read some of it, and that most of Borden's magic was described within its pages. I asked her if I, my prestige, had any plans about what to do with it, but she said that the illness had interrupted everything. She mentioned that she shared some of the contrition I felt towards Borden, and that my prestige was of much the same mind.

I said, 'Where is he? We must be together.'

'He will be waking soon,' Julia replied.

8

My reunion with myself must be one of the most unusual in history! He and I were perfect complements to each other. Everything I lacked was in him; everything I had he had lost. Of course we were the same, closer to each other than identical twins.

When either of us spoke, the other could easily finish the sentence. We moved in the same way, had the same gestures and mannerisms, came to the same thought in the same moment. I knew everything about him, and he knew the same of me. All we lacked between ourselves was our separate experiences of the last few months, but once we had described these to each other even that difference was eliminated. He trembled at my description of my attempt on Borden's life, and I suffered at second hand some of the pain and wretchedness of his disease.

Once we were together there was nothing that would separate us again. I asked Hutton to make up a second bed in the garden room, so that the two halves of myself could be together the whole time.

None of this could be kept from the rest of the household and soon I was reunited with my children, with Adam and Gertrude Wilson, as well as Mrs Hutton, the housekeeper.

Everyone exclaimed about the uncanny double effect we created. I dread to think what impact this revelation of their father will have on my children in the future, but both parts of me, and Julia, agreed that the truth was better than yet another lie.

It was not long before the chilling fact of the cancers lent an urgency to the time we spent together, and we realised that if there was anything remaining to be done, now was the time.

9

From the beginning of April until the middle of May we worked together on the revision of Borden's notebook, preparing it for the publisher. My twin brother (for so it became convenient to think of my prestige) was soon ill again, and although he had done much of the initial work on the book it was I who completed the work, and negotiated with the publisher.

And I, using his identity, maintained the journal entries for him until his demise.

So it happened, yesterday, that our double life was brought to an end by his death, and with it comes the end of my own short life story.

Now there is only me, and once more I live beyond death.

8th July 1904

This morning I went with Wilson down to the cellar, where we inspected the Tesla apparatus. It was in full working order, but because it was a long time since I had used it I went through Mr Alley's notes to check that everything was in place. I had always enjoyed the sense of collaborating with the far distant Mr Alley. His meticulous notes were a pleasure to work with.

Wilson asked me if we should dismantle the device.

I thought briefly, then said, 'Let's leave it until after the funeral.'

The ceremony is planned for tomorrow at midday.

After Wilson had left, and I had locked the access door to the cellar, I powered up the device and used it to transmit more gold coins. I was thinking of the future, of my son the 15th Earl, of my wife the dowager lady. All these were responsibilities I could not fully address. Once again I felt the crushing weight of my own ineffectuality holding back not only me but my innocent family.

I had not counted the wealth we had created with the device, but my prestige had shown me the hoard he had made, kept in a closed and locked compartment in the darkest recess of the cellar. I removed what I estimated to be two thousand pounds' worth, for Julia's immediate requirements, then I added my few new coins to what was left, thinking that no matter how much we forged there would never be enough.

However, I would see to it that the Tesla device remained intact. Alley's instructions would be kept with it. One day, Edward will find this journal and realise what the duplicating apparatus can best be used for.

Later

There are only a few hours remaining before the funeral, and I cannot spend too much of that time writing in these pages. Therefore let me note the following.

It is eight in the evening and I am in the garden room I shared with my prestige before he died. A beautiful sunset is making gold the heights of Curbar Edge, and although this room faces away from the setting sun I can see amber tendrils of cloud overhead. A few minutes ago I walked softly around the grounds of the house, breathing the summer scents, listening to the quiet sounds of this moorland country I loved so much when I was a child.

It is a fine warm evening in which to plan the end, the very end.

I am a vestige of myself. Life has become literally not

worth living. All that I love is forbidden to me by the state I am in. My family accepts me. They know who I am and what I am, and that my circumstances are not of my own making. Even so, the man they loved is dead, and I cannot replace him. Better for them that I depart, so that they might at last start to grieve fully and freely for the man who died. In the expression of grief lies recovery from grief itself.

Nor have I any legal existence: Rupert Angier the magician is dead and buried, the 14th Earl of Colderdale will be interred tomorrow.

I have no practical being. I cannot live except in squalid half life. I cannot travel safely without either assuming an unconvincing disguise, or scaring people half to death and putting myself in peril. My only expectation of life is as a ghost of myself, forever hovering on the fringes of my family's real lives, forever haunting my own past and their future.

So now it must end, and I shall die.

But the curse of life also clings to me! I have already found how fierce the spirit of life burns in me, and that not only is murder ethically beyond me but suicide too is an impossibility. When once before I wished myself dead, the wish was not strong enough. I can make myself die only by convincing myself that there is also a hope I shall not succeed.

As soon as I have completed these notes I will conceal this journal, and the earlier volumes of it, somewhere amongst the prestiges which lie in the vault. Then I will unlock the compartment in the cellar, leaving the gold for my son, or for his son, eventually to find. This journal must not be discovered while the gold is yet to be spent, for it amounts to a confession of the forgery I have committed.

With all this completed I will charge up the Tesla device again and use it for the last time.

Alone, in secret, I plan to transmit myself across the aether for the most sensational manifestation of my career.

I have spent the last hour measuring and checking the coordinates to the tiniest fraction of accuracy I can manage.

I am preparing myself, rehearsing as if an audience of thousands will be watching. But this act of magic must uniquely take place while I am alone, with no one at all to witness it.

I plan to project myself into the deceased body of my prestige, and there my end will come!

I shall arrive there. Of this there is no doubt, because the Tesla apparatus has never faltered yet in its accuracy. But what will be the result of this morbid union?

If it is a failure, I shall materialise inside my prestige's poor, cancer-ridden body, dead for two days, stiff with *rigor mortis*. I too will instantly be dead and will know nothing about it. Tomorrow, as they lay the body to rest they will lay me with it.

But I believe there is a chance of another outcome, one that acknowledges my desperation to live. This material-ization might not succeed in killing me!

I am certain, almost certain, that my arrival in the body of my prestige will return life to it. It will be a reunion, a final joining.

What remains of me will fuse with what remains of him, and we will become whole once more.

I have the spirit that he never had. I will reanimate his body with my spirit. I have the will to live that was taken from him, so I will restore it to him. I have the vital spark that now he lacks. I will heal his lesions and sores and tumours with my purity of health, will pump blood once more through his arteries and veins, will soften the rigid muscles and joints, give bloom to his pale skin, and he and I will join once again to make wholeness of my own body.

Is it madness to think such a thing might be possible?

If madness it be, then I am content to be mad because I shall live.

I am mad enough, while I yet plan, to believe there is hope. That hope allows me to press ahead.

The mad reanimated body of my prestige will rise from its open casket, and be quickly gone from this house. Every-thing that has become forbidden to me will be left behind. I have loved this life, and have loved others while in it, but because my only remaining hope of life is an act that every sane person would find reprehensible, I must become an outcast, leave behind all those I have loved, go out into the world, make what I can of what I find.

Now I shall do it!

I will go alone to the end.

PART FIVE
The Prestiges

I

My brother's voice was speaking ceaselessly to me: I am here, don't leave, stay with me, all your life, not far from you, come.

I was trying to sleep, turning to and fro in the large, cold and much too soft bed, cursing myself for not having left the house before the snowstorm set in, when even now I would have been in my own bed in my parents' house. But every time I thought of this the voice insisted: stay here, don't go, come at last to me.

I had to get out of bed. I pulled my suit jacket across my shoulders and went for a pee in the bathroom across the galleried landing. The house was dark, silent and cold. My breath fumed white as I stood shivering over the bowl. After I had flushed the toilet I had to cross the landing again, naked but for the jacket, and when I looked down the large stairwell I noticed a gleam of light from the floor below. One door had a crack of light showing beneath it.

I returned to the miserable bedroom, but could not bring myself to get back into the chilly bed. I remembered the easy chair beside the log fire in the dining-room, so I put on my clothes quickly, grabbed my stuff and went downstairs. I looked at my watch. It was after 2.00 a.m.

My brother said: all right, now.

Kate was still in the dining room, sitting awake in her chair next to the fire. She was listening to a portable radio balanced on the fire surround beside her. She seemed unsurprised to see me.

'I was cold,' I said. 'I couldn't get to sleep. Anyway, I've got to go and find him.'

'It's much colder out there.' She indicated the blackness beyond the windows. 'You'll need all this.'

On the chair opposite her she had placed several items of

warm clothing, including a chunky wool sweater, a thick overcoat, scarf, gloves, a pair of rubber boots. And two large torches.

My brother spoke again. I could not ignore him.

I said to Kate, 'You knew I was going to do this.'

'Yes. I've been thinking.'

'Do you know what's happening to me?'

'I believe so. You'll have to go and find him.'

'Will you come with me?'

She shook her head vehemently. 'No way on earth.'

'So you know where he is?'

'I think I've known all my life, but it's always been easier to put it out of my mind. The hardest thing about meeting you has been that knowledge. What traumatised me when I was a child is still down there.'

2

It had stopped snowing, but the wind was an insistent rush of freezing air, penetrating everything. The snow had piled deep around the edges of the large garden, but in the centre it was shallow enough to allow me to walk through, stumbling on the uneven ground. I slipped several times, without falling.

Kate had switched on the intruder alarm, which flooded the area with brilliant light. It helped me see my way, but when I looked back I could see nothing but the glare.

My brother said: I'm cold, waiting.

I kept going. On the far side of what I supposed must be a lawn, where the ground rose up suddenly and dark trees blocked the view ahead, the light from the torch picked out the brick-built archway where Kate had said it would be. Snow was piled up against the base of it.

The door was not locked and it moved easily when I pulled at the handle. The door opened outwards, against the drifted snow, but it was made of solid oak and once I got a good hold on it I was able to push the snow far enough out of the way for me to squeeze through.

Kate had given me the two torches, saying I would need as much light as possible. ('Come back to the house for more, if you need them,' she had said. 'Why won't you come with me and hold one of the torches?' I had asked her. But she shook her head emphatically.) When I had the door open, I peered inside, letting the beam of the bigger of the two torches play ahead of me. There was nothing much to see: a rocky roof slanting down, some rough-hewn steps, and at the bottom a second door.

The word Yes formed, inside my head.

The second door had no lock or hasp, and opened smoothly at my touch. The beams of my torches swung around; one in my hand searched all about, the other tucked under my arm followed my direction of sight.

Then my foot collided with something hard that jutted up from the floor and I stumbled. The torch under my arm broke as I banged against the rocky wall. Crouching on the ground, resting on a knee, I used one torch to examine the other.

There's a light, said my brother.

I swung the single torch beam around again, and this time, close to the inner door, I noticed an insulated electricity cable, neatly tacked to the wooden frame. At shoulder height was an ordinary light switch. I flicked it on. At first nothing happened.

Then, further down in the cavern, deep inside the hill, I heard the sound of an engine. As the generator picked up speed, lights came on for the full length of the cavern. They were only low-power light bulbs, roughly attached to the rocky ceiling, and protected by wire visors, but there was now enough light to see without the torch.

3

The cavern appeared to be a natural fissure in the rock, with extra tunnelling and hollowing carried out latterly. There were several natural shelves created by jutting rock strata, and many of them had been deepened and lengthened by cavities hollowed out later from the softer layers around them. There had also been an attempt to smooth the floor, as it was laid with numerous small chips and chunks of rock. Close to the inner doorway a spring trickled water down the wall, leaving a yellow calciferous deposit in its course. Where the water reached the floor, a crude but effective drain had been put together with modern pipes, which conducted the water into a rubble-filled soakaway.

The air was surprisingly sweet, and significantly warmer than the chill gale outside.

I went several paces down the cavern, balancing myself with my hands against the rocky walls on each side. The floor was uneven and broken, and the light bulbs were weak and widely spaced, so in places it was difficult to find a safe foothold. After a distance of about fifty yards, the floor dropped steeply and turned to the right, while to the left of the main tunnel I noticed a large cavity which to judge by the roundness of the entrance had been hollowed out artificially. The ceiling was about seven feet high, giving plenty of headroom. The opening was not electrically lit, so I shone my remaining torch inside.

I immediately wished I had not. It was full of ancient coffins. Most were stacked horizontally in heaps, although about a dozen were leaning upright against the walls. They were of all sizes but the greater number of them, depressingly, were small ones obviously designed for children. All the coffins were in various degrees of decay. The horizontal ones were the most decrepit: the wood dark, curled and fractured with age. In many cases the lids had fallen in on the contents, and several of the ones placed on the tops of the piles had sides which had fallen away.

At the base of most of the heaps were piles of brown, broken fragments, presumably of bone. The lids of the vertically stacked coffins were all loose, and standing propped against the box.

I stepped back quickly into the main tunnel and glanced up towards the door by which I had entered. There had been a slight curve, and my escape was now out of sight. Somewhere deep inside the cavern, the generator continued to run.

I was trembling. I could not help but think: that distant engine, this torch, only these lay between me and a sudden plunge into darkness.

I could not go back. My brother was here.

Determined to resolve this quickly, I followed the path down and to the right, curving away more steeply from the exit. Another flight of steps followed, and here the lights had been placed closer together because the steps were uneven in height and tilting to the side. Supporting myself with my hand on the wall I went down them. The tunnel immediately opened out into a wider cavern.

It was full of modern metal racks, brown-painted, held together with chromium-plated nuts and bolts. Each rack had three broad shelves, one on top of the other, like bunks. A narrow gangway ran next to each rack, and a central aisle ran the whole length of the hall. A light was positioned above every gangway between the shelves, illuminating what they held.

4

Human bodies lay uncovered on every shelf of the racks. Each one was male, and fully clothed. They all wore evening dress: a close fitting jacket with tails, a white shirt with black bow tie, a modestly patterned waistcoat, narrow trousers with a satin strip along the seams, white socks and patent-leather shoes. The hands wore white cotton gloves.

Each body was identical to all the others. The man had a pale face, an aquiline nose and a thin moustache. His lips were pale. He had a narrow brow and receding hair which was brilliantined back. Some of the faces were staring up at the rack above them, or at the rocky ceiling. Others had their necks turned, so they faced to one side or the other.

All the corpses had their eyes open.

Most of them were smiling, showing their teeth. The left upper molar in each mouth had a chip missing from the corner.

The corpses all lay in different positions. Some were straight, others were twisted or bent over. None of the bodies was arranged as if lying down; most of them had one foot placed in front of the other, so that in being laid on the rack this leg was now raised above the other.

Every corpse had one foot in the air.

The arms too were in varying positions. Some were raised above the head, some were stretched forward like those of a sleepwalker, others lay straight beside the body. Several of the bodies wore gloves which had been soaked in red ink.

There was no sign of decay in any of the corpses. It was as if each one had been frozen in life, made inert without being made dead.

There was no dust on them, no smell from them.

5

A piece of white card had been attached to the front edge of each shelf. It was handwritten, and mounted in a plastic holder that was clipped ingeniously to the underside of the shelf. The first one I looked at said this:

Dominion Theatre, Kidderminster
14/4/01
3.15 p.m. [M]
2359/23
25g

On the shelf above it, the card was almost identical:

Dominion Theatre, Kidderminster
14/4/01
8.30 p.m. [E]
2360/23
25g

Above that, the third corpse was labelled:

Dominion Theatre, Kidderminster
15/4/01
3.15 p.m. [M]
2361/23
25g

On the next rack there were three more corpses, all labelled and dated similarly. They were laid out in date order. By the following week, there was a change of theatre: the Fortune, in Northampton. Six performances there. Then there was a break of about two weeks, followed by a series of single appearances, about three days apart, in a number of provincial theatres. Twelve corpses were thus labelled, in sequence. A season at the Palace Pier Theatre, Brighton, occupied half of May (six racks, eighteen corpses).

I moved on, squeezing down the narrow central aisle to the far end of the cavern. Here, on the top shelf of the final rack, I came across the body of a small boy.

6

He had died in a frenzy of struggling. His head was tilted back and turned to the right. His mouth was open, with the corners of his lips turned down. His eyes were wide open and looking up. His hair was flying. All his limbs were tensed, as if he had been fighting to be free. He was wearing a maroon sweatshirt with characters from *The Magic Round-about*, a small pair of jeans with the bottoms turned up, and blue canvas shoes.

His label was also handwritten, and it said:

Caldlow House
17/12/70
7.45 p.m.
0000/23
og

On the top was the boy's name: Nicholas Julius Borden.

I took the label and shoved it into my pocket, then reached forward and pulled him towards me. I scooped him up and held him in my arms. At the moment I touched him, the constant background presence of my brother faded away and died.

I was aware of his *absence* for the first time ever.

Looking down at him in my arms, I tried to shape him into a more comfortable position for carrying. His limbs, neck and torso were stiffly pliant, as if made of strong rubber. I could change their position, but the moment I released them they swung back into the shape in which I had found him.

When I tried to smooth his hair, that too moved intransigently back to its former position.

I held him tightly against me. He was neither cold nor warm. One of his outstretched hands, clenched in fear, was touching the side of my face. The relief of finding him at last overwhelmed everything – everything except the fear of this place. I wanted to turn around so that I could head back towards the exit, but to do so involved moving backwards out of the gangway. I held my past life in my arms, but I no longer knew what might be standing behind me.

There was something there, though.

7

I eased myself backwards, not looking. As I reached the main aisle and turned slowly around, Nicky's head brushed against the raised foot of the nearest corpse. A patent-leather shoe swung slowly to and fro. I ducked away from it, horrified.

I saw that at this end of the hall there was another chamber, just five or six feet away from where I was standing. It was from here that the sound of the generator's engine was emerging. I went towards it. The entrance to the cavity was slanting and low, and there had been no effort made to widen it or to make access to it easier.

The sound of the generator was now loud, and I could smell the petrol fumes being emitted from it. There were several more lights within the chamber, beyond the entrance. Their radiance spilled across the uneven floor of the main hall. I could not go through the gap without putting down Nicky's body, so I bent over to try to see what might be within.

I stared across the short stretch of the rocky floor I could see, then I straightened.

I wished to see no more. A chill ran through me.

I had seen nothing. Any sounds there might have been were drowned by the mechanical clattering of the generator. Nothing moved within.

I took a step back, then another, as quietly as possible.

There had been someone standing inside that chamber, silently, motionlessly, just beyond my line of sight, waiting for me either to enter or retreat.

I continued to step back down the shadowy narrow aisle between the racks, easing my body to and fro so as not to scrape Nicky's head or feet against the bodies on the shelves. Terror was draining strength from my body. My knees were juddering and my arm muscles, already strained by Nicky's weight, were aching and twitching.

A man's voice said, from within the chamber, reverberating around the hall, 'You're a Borden, aren't you?'

I said nothing, paralysed by fear.

'I thought you'd come for him.' There was a harsh intake of breath, a rattling of phlegm. The voice was thin, tired, not much more than a whisper, but the cavern gave it an echoing resonance. 'He is you, Borden, and these are all me. Are you going to leave with him? Or are you going to stay?'

I saw a vestige of a shadow moving beyond that rough-hewn entrance, and then to my horror the sound of the generator faded quickly away.

The light bulbs died down: yellow, amber, dull red, black.

I was in impenetrable darkness. The torch was in my pocket. I shifted the weight of the little boy, and managed to get a grip on the torch.

With my hand shaking, I switched it on. The beam angled crazily as I tried to get a good grip on the torch and keep Nicky's body held tightly in my arms. I twisted around.

Shadows of raised legs whirled about me on the cavern walls.

With the crook of my arm clumsily shielding Nicky's exposed head I shoved my way along the rest of the aisle through the racks, my shoulders and arms colliding with the shelves, and dislodging several of the plastic labels.

I dared not look behind me. The man was following! My legs had no strength, I knew I could fall at any moment.

As I mounted the crooked steps out of the hall, my head collided with a spar of rock in the roof, and it hurt so much I almost dropped Nicky's body. I kept going, staggering and hunching, not even trying to keep the torch beam steady. It was all uphill, now, and Nicky's deadweight seemed heavier with every step. I turned my foot, fell against the tunnel wall, recovered, kept lurching on. Fear drove me.

The inner door appeared before me at last. Barely pausing, I pulled it open with my booted foot and forced my way through.

Behind me, on the stone-laid floor of the tunnel, I could hear the footsteps following, pacing steadily over the loose stones.

I ran up the stairs to the surface, but snow had blown in and was covering the top four or five steps. I slipped, fell forward, and the little boy rolled out of my arms! I lunged forward, pushed the door open with all my weight.

I saw: snow-covered ground, the black shape of the house, two windows lighted, an open doorway with a light beyond, snow hurtling from the sky!

My brother yelled in my mind!

I turned back, found him sprawled across the steps, and picked him up. I stumbled out into the snow.

I floundered and staggered through the thick snow, aiming for the doorway, turning my head constantly to look back over my shoulder at the black rectangle of the open vault, dreading to see the emergence of whatever it was that had been following me.

Suddenly, the intruder light mounted on the side of the house came on, half-blinding me. The blizzard thickened in the glare. Kate appeared at the open doorway, dressed in a quilted coat.

I tried to shout a warning to her but I could not find the breath. I continued on, sliding and staggering in the snow, Nicky's body held before me. At last I reached the yard in front of the door, slithered on the snow-covered concrete and pushed past her into the brightly lit hallway beyond.

She stared wordlessly at the body of the little boy in my arms. Gasping for breath, I turned around and went back to the doorway, leant against the post, looked back across the snow-covered garden at the indistinct shape of the vault entrance. Kate was beside me.

'Watch the vault!' I said. It was the only sentence I could get out. 'Watch!'

Nothing was moving, over there on the other side of the snow. I took a step back, put down Nicky's body on the stone-flagged floor.

I fumbled in my pocket and found the label that had been on Nicky's rack. I shoved it at Kate. I was still struggling for breath, and I felt as if I would never again breathe normally.

I gasped, 'Look at this! The handwriting! Is it the same?'

She took it from me, held it up in the light, and gazed intently at it. She looked straight back at me. Her eyes were wide with fear.

'It is, isn't it?' I shouted.

She put her hands around the upper part of my arm, and held herself against me. I could feel her trembling.

The intruder light timed itself out.

'Get it on again!' I shouted.

Kate reached behind her, found the switch. Then she held my arm again.

The snow whirled in the blaze of light. Through it, vaguely, we could see the entrance to the vault. We both saw the slight figure of a man emerging from the door of the vault. He was dressed in dark clothes, and was covered up against the weather. Long black hair straggled out from under the hood of his jacket. He raised a hand to protect his eyes from the glaring light. He showed no curiosity about us, or fear of us, even though he must have known we were there, watching him. Without looking at us, or anywhere in the direction of the house, he stepped out on to the flat ground, hunching his shoulders in the blizzard, then moved to the right, between the trees, down the hill, and out of our sight.